World Cup Wishes

Eshkol Nevo

Translated from the Hebrew
by Sondra Silverston

Chatto & Windus
LONDON

Published by Chatto & Windus 2010

First published in Israel, as *Mishala Achat Yamina*, in 2007 by Kinneret,
Zmora Bitan, Dvir Publishing House Ltd

2 4 6 8 10 9 7 5 3 1

Copyright © Eshkol Nevo 2007
Published by arrangement with The Institute for the Translation of
Hebrew Literature

Eshkol Nevo has asserted his right under the Copyright, Designs
and Patents Act 1988 to be identified as the author of this work

First published in Great Britain in 2010 by
Chatto & Windus
Random House, 20 Vauxhall Bridge Road,
London SW1V 2SA
www.rbooks.co.uk

Addresses for companies within The Random House Group Limited can be
found at: www.randomhouse.co.uk/offices.htm

The Random House Group Limited Reg. No. 954009

A CIP catalogue record for this book
is available from the British Library

ISBN 9780701184421

The Random House Group Limited supports The Forest Stewardship
Council (FSC), the leading international forest certification organisation.
All our titles that are printed on Greenpeace approved FSC certified paper
carry the FSC logo. Our paper procurement policy can be found at
www.rbooks.co.uk/environment

22nd June 2002

To Whom it May Concern

1. On 1 June 2002, I was asked by the family of Mr Yuval
   Freed to collect his belongings from the police station on
   Dizengoff Street in Tel Aviv. Among the things that
   were given to me by Ms Esther Loel, who is in charge of
   the property room, was a plastic bag containing a large
   bundle of papers. Since Mr Freed never informed me or
   his other friends that he was trying his hand at writing,
   my first assumption regarding the abovementioned bundle
   of papers was that it must be one of the translations he
   did for liberal arts students at the university to earn some
   money. However, there was no name or telephone number
   written on the plastic bag, and the title of the article in
   English did not appear at the top of the page, as is
   customary. I mention all of this to explain why I thought
   it justified to spend several hours skimming the bundle of
   papers. I did so not out of voyeurism, but out of a genuine
   desire to determine the identity of its intended recipient
   and what I should do with it.
2. The brief reading I allowed myself made it clear that,
   in fact, this was not a translated article but a text written
   by Mr Freed himself. A more thorough reading revealed
   that it was the manuscript for a book entitled *World Cup
   Wishes*, which Mr Freed had been working on over the

last year, and that its protagonists are Mr Freed himself and three of his friends. A telephone conversation with Mr Freed's father confirmed that his son had indeed intended to publish the manuscript as a book, and that he had already reached an agreement on the matter with the Efroni Publishing House in Haifa, owned by their family. According to the father, the only thing left to be done before publication was copy-editing and, to the best of his knowledge, his son had intended to assign that job to me, the undersigned.

3. To avoid any doubt, I should say that I am not at all sure that the father was correct in thinking that Mr Freed wanted me to edit the book. The more I read of the manuscript, the more puzzled I grew: why did Mr Freed decide to ask one of the protagonists in his book, a character portrayed in the most negative light, to do the editing for him? Nevertheless, since Mr Freed himself was naturally unable to confirm or deny any of this, and since, as a friend, I considered it extremely important to complete the book by his deadline I reluctantly took it upon myself to do the job.

4. The temptation to make changes in the manuscript was very great. The undersigned, as previously mentioned, is ridiculed in the text. Embarrassing and harsh things that I never said are attributed to me and, worst of all, the book is filled with factual inaccuracies which, in any other situation, would, based on my legal experience, be sufficient grounds for a libel suit. Nevertheless, in the end, I decided to act with a modicum of restraint and minimise my corrections and changes as much as possible, for two reasons. First, despite the many inaccuracies, and despite the generous 'poetic licence' Mr Freed granted himself, there is a sense of truth about the entire text, and I was afraid that any change I might make was liable to damage that sense. Second, 'fixing' the text without Mr Freed being able to respond or agree to the changes

seemed to me to be a betrayal of him and his trust, and since I had already committed one such betrayal during our friendship, I did not wish to add insult to injury.

5. Despite all the abovementioned, I could not avoid making some changes in my capacity as copy-editor, a role that has been imposed on me. Most of them were cosmetic changes: replacing a comma with a full stop, replacing a full stop with a colon, changing awkward sentence structure, and so on. In only one place in the text did I allow myself to make a factual correction: on page 4 of the original manuscript it is stated that in the 1994 football World Cup final, Germany played against Brazil, while in fact, it was Italy against Brazil. Based on the many years of my friendship with Mr Freed, I have no doubt that it was a slip of the pen that he would not have wanted to remain in the text.

6. With the exception of that correction, three minor comments and a short epilogue I thought it necessary to add, everything in this book was written by Mr Yuval Freed, my beloved friend, and he bears sole responsibility for it.

Yoav Alimi (Churchill), Attorney-at-Law

1

It was Amichai's idea. He always had ideas like that, even though the official ideas man in the group was Ofir, but Ofir wasted all his creativity in ad agencies writing copy for biscuits and banks, so he took advantage of the gang's get-togethers to be boring and was quiet a lot and talked only a little, using simple Haifa words, and sometimes, when he drank a bit too much, he'd hug us all and say: how lucky we are to have each other, you have no idea how lucky. Amichai, on the other hand, sold Telemed subscriptions to people with heart disease, and even though he sometimes managed to pick up a great story from the sales conversations he had, usually with Holocaust survivors, you couldn't say that he got much satisfaction or excitement from the job. Every few months, he'd announce that he was leaving Telemed and taking a course in Shiatsu, but something always came up that made him put it off. Once they offered him a bonus. Once they offered him a car. And then there was his marriage to Ilana the Weeper. And then the twins. So all the joy of life bubbling inside him that he couldn't express in his meetings in the old people's homes or in bed with Ilana came gushing out with us, his three best friends, in the form of all sorts of brilliant ideas, like taking a trip to Lake Kinneret to celebrate the tenth anniversary of our outing to the Luna Gal Water Park there, or signing up for a karaoke competition and really working on an a cappella rendition of a Beatles song. Why the Beatles? Churchill asked, and you could guess from his tone how that new idea would end up. Why not? There are four of them and four of us, Amichai said, trying to be persuasive, but from his tone you could tell he realised that this idea, like all the others before it, didn't stand a chance. Without Churchill's backing, it was hard for us to get anything off the ground. And when Churchill squashed someone, he did it so offhandedly and so precisely that it made you feel sorry for the defence lawyers who had to go up against him in court. It was Churchill who founded our gang in high school. He didn't really found it, it's more accurate to say that we flocked around him, like lost sheep. Every feature of his broad face, each untied lace of his trainers, even the way he walked – it all projected the sense that he knew what was good. That he had some kind of internal compass that guided him. All of us, of course, faked self-confidence in those years, but Churchill really had it. The girls twisted a curl around their fingers when he walked past, even though he wasn't good-looking in the movie-star sense, and we picked him with a communistic majority of votes to be captain of the class football team, even though there were better players than he. It was there, on the team, that he got his nickname. Before the semi-finals against a class of seniors, he got us together and gave a rousing pep talk saying that all we had to offer against the seniors was blood, sweat and tears. We were almost in tears when he finished, and then on the field, we just gave it our all, including a constant fight for the ball and painful slides on the asphalt, which didn't keep us from losing three-nil because of three bad mistakes Churchill himself made: once he passed the ball to the opponent's striker, once he lost a fateful ball in midfield, and to top it all off, he scored a breathtaking own goal when he tried to clear a corner and, instead, sent the ball straight into the goal where I was standing.

No one was angry with him after the game. How could

you be angry with someone who, a second after the final whistle, gets everyone together in the centre of the field and, with lowered lashes, takes all the blame on himself? How can you be angry with someone who, to make up for it, takes the whole team to a Maccabi Haifa match when everyone knows he's taking the money out of his own pocket because his parents don't have any? How can you be angry with someone who puts his heart and soul into writing birthday greetings, who listens so well, who travels all the way to the Negev to visit you in basic training, who lets you stay in his apartment for three months till you get settled in Tel Aviv and insists that you sleep in his bed while he sleeps on the sofa?

Even after what happened with Ya'ara, I couldn't be angry with him. Everyone was sure I'd be furious. That I'd explode with rage. Amichai called me the minute he heard – Churchill really fucked up, but I have an idea: let's all go to a paintball game and the three of us can shoot him with paint pellets. We'll really let him have it! I talked to him and he says OK. Are you up for it?

Ofir walked out of a campaign meeting for three-layered toilet paper just to say: Bro, I'm with you. You have every reason. But I'm begging you, don't do anything you'll regret. You have no idea how lucky we are to have each other, you have no idea.

The truth is, they didn't need to beg. I couldn't work up the anger anyway. One night I even went to his place hoping that the drama of doing that would light a fire under me, and on the way I kept saying out loud to myself, bastard, what a bastard, but when I got to his building, I didn't feel like going up any more. Perhaps if I'd seen a faint silhouette moving in his flat, that would have clenched my fist, but I just sat in the car and sprayed water on the windscreen and turned on the wipers, sprayed and wiped, till finally, when the first long ray of light touched the solar water tanks on the roof, I left. I couldn't picture myself hitting him. Even though he had it coming. Even though, when we wrote wishes during the last World Cup, all three of mine had to do with Ya'ara.

*

It was Amichai's idea, those wishes.

After Emmanuel Petit scored the third goal and it was already clear that France would take the Cup, and there was a faint sense of disappointment in the air because we were all rooting for Brazil; after we'd finished off the tear-flavoured *burekas* Ilana had baked and the last nut had been cracked and only one piece of the watermelon and feta cheese was left, the piece no one felt comfortable taking – after all that, Ofir said, you know, something just hit me. This is the fifth World Cup we've watched together. And Churchill said, how do you get to five? Four, max.

And we started going over them.

Mexico '86 we saw in Ofir's father's house in Tivon. And when poor, naïve Denmark lost five-one to Spain, Ofir cried his heart out and his father said that's what happens when a boy is raised by his mother. The '90 World Cup final we each saw in a different city in the territories, but there was one day when we all went home and met at Amichai's place to watch the semi-final. No one remembers who played because his little sister was walking around the house in a red baby-doll nightie and we were soldiers and couldn't keep our eyes on the screen. In '94, we were students. Tel Avivians. Churchill was the first to move there, and we all trailed after him to the big city because we wanted to stay together and because Churchill said that it was the only place where we could be what we wanted to be.

But we actually saw the '94 games in Rambam hospital in Haifa, Ofir remembered. Ri-i-ght, I said.

In the middle of supper at my parents' place, I had the worst wheezing asthma attack of my life. There were moments in the panicky ride to the hospital when I was seriously considering dying. After they stabilised me with injections and pills and an oxygen mask, the doctors said I had to stay in the hospital for the next few days. For observation.

The final was the next day. Italy against Brazil. Without telling me, Churchill got the guys together and put them all into his beaten-up Beetle, and on the way, they stopped at the Pancake House in Kfar Vitkin to buy me peach-flavoured iced tea, because that's my particular passion, and a couple of bottles of vodka because, in those days, we pretended to be into vodka, and ten minutes before the match started, they burst loudly into my hospital room (they bribed the guard with a bottle of Keglevich when he tried to stop them because visiting hours were over). I almost had another attack when I saw them. But then I calmed down and breathed deeply, from the diaphragm, and together we watched the tiny TV hanging above my bed and saw Brazil take the cup after 120 minutes. Plus penalty kicks.

And . . . so we came to '98, Churchill summed up. Four World Cups altogether.

It's a lucky thing we didn't bet, Ofir said.

It's a lucky thing there's a World Cup, I said. That way, time doesn't turn into one big, solid block, and we can stop every four years and see what's changed.

Awesome, Churchill said. He was always the first one to understand when I came up with a remark like that. Sometimes the only one.

You know what's lucky? It's lucky that we have each other, Ofir said. You have n-o-o i-ide-ea how lucky we are, we all completed the familiar remark.

Bro, I don't understand how you manage with all those ad men, you're such a pussy, Churchill said, and Ofir laughed, OK, that's what happens when you grow up with your mother, and Amichai said, I have an idea.

Wait, let's just watch them hoist the cup, Churchill said,

hoping that by the time they were finished hoisting the cup, he'd forget his idea.

But Amichai didn't forget.

Did he know that the idea he was about to suggest would turn out to be a true prophecy that would disappoint us time after time over the next four years and, amazingly enough, would preserve its prophetic power?

Probably not. Concealed under his agreeable exterior was the stubborn determination that enabled him to listen to Telemed customers for hours, to put together jigsaw puzzles with thousands of pieces on his balcony and run ten kilometres every day. In all kinds of weather. I think it was that determination, more than anything else, that caused him to speak again after Didier Deschamps hoisted the Cup and the crowd waved.

What I was thinking, he said, is that each of us should write down on a piece of paper where he dreams of being in another four years. Personally, professionally. In every sense. And at the next World Cup, we'll open the papers and see what happened in the meantime.

What a great idea! Ilana the Weeper yelled from the den.

We all turned to look. For all the years we'd known her, we'd never heard her get excited about anything. Her droopy face always had the same gloomy expression (even at their wedding. That's why there's a lot of Amichai on the video tape doing his standard dance move – tapping lightly on his stomach – and very little of her), and most of the times we were all at Amichai's she would drift away after a few minutes and bury herself in a book. It was almost always a book on her field of research in psychology, something about the connection between depression and anxiety. We were already used to her non-present presence in the living room and her coolness towards Amichai, and suddenly – such enthusiasm?

She came hesitantly out of the den and walked over to

us. I was just reading an article here, she said, by an American psychologist who claims that correctly defining an objective is half of achieving it. The next World Cup is in four years, right? That means you'll all be thirty-two. Those are exactly the . . . plaster years.

Plaster years?

It's a concept he uses, this psychologist. It means the years when personality hardens and takes shape, like plaster.

She waited a few seconds, expecting to observe the effect of her words, and then, disappointed, turned around and went back to the den.

Amichai gave us a look.

We couldn't let him down. Not when she'd finally got excited about something. When he'd finally broken through in his efforts to make her happy.

OK, bring paper, I said.

But let's be organised, Churchill said. Everyone writes three things. Three short sentences. Otherwise, there'll be no end to it.

Amichai passed out thick psychology books so we'd have something to rest the paper on. And pens.

*

I had no problem with the first wish. It had formed itself in my mind the minute Amichai tossed out the idea.

1. At the next World Cup, I still want to be with Ya'ara, I wrote.

Then I got stuck. I tried to think of other things I wanted to wish for myself. I tried to expand the scope of my desires, but my thoughts kept going back to her, to her silky, caramel-coloured hair, her soft, slender shoulders, those green eyes of hers encircled by glasses, the moment she takes them off and I know we're about to . . .

*

We'd met two months earlier in the cafeteria in the Naftali building on campus. At the beginning of the break, she came in with two guys, carrying a large tray with a small bottle of grapefruit juice on it. She walked with her back straight, a brisk walk that made her caramel-coloured ponytail bounce, as if she were in a hurry to go somewhere else, and they lurched heavily along behind her to the table. She had trouble opening the bottle of juice, but didn't ask for help. They were talking about a play they'd seen the night before. That is, she was talking, very quickly, and they were looking at her. She said that they could've done a lot more with that play if the director had only had a little inspiration. For instance the scenery, she said and sipped her juice, why do the stage sets in this country always look the same? Can't they think of something a little more original than a table, coat hooks and an armchair from the flea market? She kept talking – about the music and how the director could have got more from the actors if he'd done his job out of a real love for the profession. She stretched out the 'o' in 'love', pronouncing the word with all her heart, and as she said it, placed her open hand on her shirt. That is so-o-o true, the guy sitting across from her said without taking his eyes off her shirt. You're absolutely right, Ya'ara, the other one said. Then both guys got up and went to their class, leaving her sitting alone at the table, and suddenly, for a fraction of a second, she looked small and lost. She took some papers out of her bag, pushed her glasses more firmly onto her nose with her little finger, crossed her legs and became engrossed in reading. Every time she turned a page, she touched a finger lightly to her tongue, and I watched her, thinking how incredible it was that such a gesture, a librarian's gesture, could be sexy on the right girl. And I also thought that it would be interesting to know what that serious face looked like when she burst out laughing. And if she had dimples. And I thought that I'd never know, because I'd never have the guts to talk to her.

Hey, she said, looking up from her reading, do you have any idea what the English word 'revelation' means?

Every impairment has its moment of glory. That's how it was with my colour blindness. Apart from the embarrassment it caused me all my life (children, do you see the bright-coloured anemones? Who said 'no'?!), it saved me at the right moment from the corps assignment officer's plan to make me a lookout.

And that's how it was that instant, when Ya'ara asked me a question. Years of a spartan Anglo-Saxon education, a ridiculous quantity of tea with milk, chronic emotional constipation and a basic sense of alienation instilled in me because my parents never stopped feeling like outsiders here, in the Levant, and kept speaking Anglicised Hebrew to each other for thirty years after arriving in Haifa from Brighton –

All this, for one moment, worked to my benefit.

I explained to her authoritatively in Hebrew that revelation meant exposure or disclosure, and when I saw that she was satisfied with my answer and was about to go back to her reading, I quickly added that it could also mean 'epiphany'. Depending on the context.

She read me the whole sentence. Then another sentence she had trouble with. So I gave her my phone number, in case she needed more help, and amazingly enough, she called that same night and we talked about other things, too, and the conversation flowed like wine, and then we went out, and kissed, and made love, and she put her head on my stomach when we were lying on the grass near the Music Academy and tapped on my thigh to a piano melody that was coming from one of the rehearsal rooms, and bought me a turquoise shirt because 'enough of all that black', and I kept looking for the catch the whole time, how could it be that a girl who disproves Churchill's three-quarters theory – 'There are no girls who are pretty and smart and horny and also available. One of these elements is always missing' – how could it be that a girl like that would pick me, of all people? True, a few months before she met me, she split up with a guitarist who had made her miserable with five years of cheating on her and then begging her to take him back, but there were enough guys wandering around campus who were taller than me and would have been happy to be a corrective experience for her. And anyway, that whole story with the cheating guitarist didn't make sense. Who would want to cheat on someone like her? Who would ever want anything but more and more of her?

*

Amichai pushed me to finish. Everyone but me had already given back the pens.

I looked at the first sentence I'd written and added impulsively:

2. *At the next World Cup, I want to be married to Ya'ara.*

3. *At the next World Cup, I want to have a child with Ya'ara. Preferably a girl.*

Now you give me the slips of paper, Amichai said. And I keep them closed in a box till the next World Cup.

Why you? Ofir objected.

Because I'm the most stable guy here.

What does that mean? Ofir said, getting angry.

He's right, Churchill said, trying to soften it. He has a wife, a flat, twins. We'll probably go through ten flats before the next World Cup, and slips of paper like these are just the kind of thing that gets lost in packing.

OK, Ofir said. But let's read them out loud first.

Are you kidding?! Amichai shouted. That kills the whole surprise.

Fuck the surprise, Ofir said angrily. I want to know what you all wrote. Otherwise, I won't give you mine.

Delayed gratification isn't exactly your thing, is it? Amichai said sarcastically, then added casually, well, this is what happens when a kid is raised by his mother.

You know the story about the man who delayed

gratification? Ofir shot back. There's this guy who delays gratification. Delays, delays, delays – then he dies.

I have an idea, Churchill interrupted before Ofir and Amichai got carried away into one of their verbal clashes – sudden, meaningless rows that brought out a nastiness it was hard to believe they were capable of. How about if everyone reads only one of the three things he wrote? Churchill said. That way we can keep the element of surprise and we'll still have the teasing. That is what you advertising people call it, yeah?

Teaser, Ofir corrected, and a shadow crossed his eyes, the way it did every time someone mentioned his work.

OK, I'll go first, Amichai said, unfolding his slip of paper.

By the next World Cup, I'll have opened an alternative therapy clinic.

A-a-men, Churchill prayed, putting into words what all of us felt. If it came true, we hoped, perhaps Amichai would stop talking about it so much.

Ofir unfolded his slip of paper.

By the next World Cup, I will have kissed the advertising world goodbye and published a book of short stories.

Short stories? I said, surprised. Didn't you say you'd make a movie about us?

Yes, Ofir said, but the whole movie was based on the idea that one of us . . . dies in the army. And you promised that if no one did, then . . .

If it's still an option, I'm ready to die any time, I offered (and as I did, a too-pleasant shiver ran through me, as it always did when I thought about the possibility).

Don't worry, Ofir said. It's not necessary. Lately, I'm more into the short story thing. My head is full of ideas, but when I get home from the office at eleven at night, I don't even have the energy to turn on the computer.

So *yallah*, I urged him, get a move on. You have time till the next World Cup. In any case, you already have an English translator.

Thanks, man, he said and patted me on the shoulder, his eyes glistening. You have no idea how lucky . . .

Churchill quickly unfolded his slip of paper before Ofir could start weeping.

By the next World Cup, he said in a very serious tone, *I plan to have slept with at least 208 girls.*

Exactly 208? Amichai said with a laugh. Why not 222? Or a round 300?

Do the numbers, Churchill explained. Four years, 52 weeks a year. One girl a week – a total of 208. Just kidding. Do you really think I'd waste a wish on something that's going to happen anyway?

So what, then, you were just playing us? Amichai asked, his voice dropping. For a person doomed to one Ilana the Weeper, the thought of a wish that included 208 different women must have lit up his imagination.

Obviously, Churchill said with a laugh and read from his list:

By the next World Cup, I want to have an important case. In an important area. I want to be involved in something that will lead to social change.

Ofir and Amichai nodded in admiration and I thought to myself that it was a bit embarrassing to read one of my wishes out loud after what Churchill had just read.

OK, your turn now, Amichai said to me. I looked at the slip of paper and took comfort in the fact that at least I didn't have to read all three.

At the next World Cup, I still want to be with Ya'ara, I read in a fading voice.

And, as expected, everyone attacked me.

Yallah, yallah, this Ya'ara doesn't even exist, Ofir said.

Till we see her, that wish isn't valid, Churchill added a legal opinion.

I think she's probably ugly, I think he's keeping her under wraps because she's ugly, Ofir said and looked at me to see if I was annoyed.

Cross-eyed blind, Amichai said.

With an arse the size of a helicopter pad.

Tits down to her knees.

Football-player shoulders.

She's probably a man who's had a sex change. Before that, they called her Ya'ar.

Oka-a-a-y, I said, I give up. You're all invited over to mine on Tuesday to meet her.

But on that Monday, I put off the meeting for a week with the excuse that I was ill, and then I cancelled the postponed meeting too, saying that we had to be at her parents' house in Rehovot for dinner, and finally, the one who put an end to all those postponements was Ya'ara herself, who told me, one-third as a joke and two-thirds seriously, I'm starting to think you're ashamed of me. Don't be silly, I said. Then why don't you introduce me to your friends? she asked. No reason, I replied, it just hasn't happened yet. And she said, I'm dying to meet them. You talk about them so much. And I said, I never noticed. You mention them in practically every sentence, she said. And your living room is full of pictures of them. Out-of-focus pictures, but still. And every five minutes, one of them calls you, and then you get into long, deep conversations with them. Not the kind of practical conversations men have, but real conversations. It just seems to me that you all have a very strong connection, don't you think?

I don't know, I said. Sometimes I think we do. That it's for our whole lives. Like a year ago, we went back to our school for the Memorial Day ceremony and I noticed that all the other groups of friends from our year had broken up, and we were the only ones standing there together, close, during the siren. And the truth is that I have no idea why. Whether it's inertia or whether even now, after eight years in Tel Aviv, we still only feel like we belong when we're together. But there are other times when I don't understand what we're doing together, like there's no reason for it. But maybe that's how it is, and that endless dance of getting close and growing apart is just the basic movement among friends. What do you think?

A fa-a-a-scinating analysis, Ya'ara said, but don't change the subject. Next Tuesday we're cooking them dinner, she said firmly, and took off her glasses. And I said OK because it's hard to say no to green eyes and because I couldn't find a good reason to object, except for the vague feeling I had that it would end in tears, a feeling I attributed to my chronic pessimism.

But the dinner was actually a great success. They devoured the stuffed vegetables we made, and Ya'ara easily found a common language with each of the guys. She laughed with Ofir about the whole world of advertising (it turns out that she once worked as an assistant producer on a laundry detergent ad). She argued with Churchill about the leniency the prosecutor's office showed towards public figures. She told Amichai about the acupuncture treatment that cured her – to the amazement of her conventional doctors – of mononucleosis. And she kept touching me the whole time, rubbed the back of my neck, put her hand on mine, her head on my shoulder, and twice she even kissed me lightly on the neck, as if she suddenly sensed what I had been trying to hide from her through all the months we'd been together: that I was afraid of losing her. That I'd never had anything like us before.

So? I asked when they'd gone. We could still hear their footsteps on the landing.

They're terrific, your friends, Ya'ara said and hugged me.

Explain, I said, and went to wash the dishes. Two or three stuffed vegetable corpses were still stuck to the plates.

That Ofir is so sensitive, I heard her voice behind me. How many years has he been in advertising? Six? It's not easy to stay who you are in that cynical world. And Amichai, that guy has so much patience. I think he really could be a great alternative therapist. And all of them, she said and

17

hugged me from behind, seem to love you very much. So we all have at least one thing in common.

And Churchill? I asked, and I could feel her loosen her grip, then drop her hands.

Seems like a smart guy, she said in a hesitant voice.

But . . . ? I turned around to face her. My hands were still wet with dishwater.

No buts, she said, moving away a little.

It had the sound of a but, I insisted.

Forget it, it's not fair to judge after one meeting.

I knew she was right. And that it was much easier to label a person than to stay open to the possibility that there's more than one side to him. But I couldn't help it.

Come on, say it, I pressed. I've known him for so many years that I can't tell any more what kind of first impression he makes.

The truth is that there's something conceited about him. As if he's looking down at the three of you. From the VIP box. I don't like that. And I don't like the way he talks about women either. Did you notice that whenever he talked about male politicians, he called them 'Minister' or 'Mayor', and when he talked about women politicians, it was 'the airhead ' and 'the bottle blonde'?

Could be, I said coldly. And even though I'd asked for it, I felt the anger rise up in me at how insufferably easy it was for her to criticise my friend. You should know that he's an amazing person, I shot the words at her. When he graduated from law school, he had offers from private firms that would have paid him a lot of money, but he went to the prosecutor's office because he thought it was more important, and a few weeks ago, at the World Cup final, we each wrote down on a slip of paper where we dream of being at the next World Cup, in four years. We all wrote totally egotistical things, and he was the only one who wanted to do something significant that would affect Israeli society, so maybe . . . maybe you should wait a little before you decide what he's like.

What did you write? Ya'ara asked. Her eyes were seductive above her glasses. This was the first time since we got together that I'd let myself be angry with her, and strangely enough, she seemed to like it.

It's a secret, I said, trying to keep a certain meanness in my tone. If you want to know, you'll have to stay with me till the next World Cup. That's when we read the slips of paper.

No problem, Ya'ara said, pressing up against me and putting her hands into the back pockets of my jeans – you can't scare a romantic girl with love.

Two weeks later, she was with him.

There are a few contradictory versions of how that happened.

Churchill claims that she bumped into him on the street, during his lunch break, and told him she thought they'd had a communications failure during dinner, and if he was up for it, she'd like to buy him a cup of coffee so they could start again. He agreed, because he felt it was important to her. So they sat in a café and talked and didn't notice the time passing. And in the end, when they stood up to go, she said that there were a lot of things they'd talked about that were left open and perhaps they should meet again the next day to close them.

Ya'ara claims that he was the one who called her, three days after the dinner, and said that ever since he met her, he hadn't been able to stop thinking about her and couldn't fall asleep at night. She told him she didn't know what to say, and he said he wanted to see her. She said, what are you talking about, they couldn't do something like that behind my back. But he pleaded with her and said that a lot of criminals, rapists and murderers, were walking out of court free men because he hadn't been able to function since he met her. She laughed and agreed to see him, just for a few minutes, just for coffee, just because of the rapists. After coffee, when they got up to go, he said that there were a lot of things they'd talked about that were still left open, and perhaps they should meet again the next day to close them.

I imagine that she was probably telling the truth.

I'd like to believe that he was telling the truth.

Either way, the outcome was the same: they continued to see each other secretly for a week, and in the end, she came to my flat and said she was confused. And needed time to think. And she kept her graceful neck bent the whole time she was speaking. And touched me a lot. But she didn't take off her glasses even once.

He called that evening and was, as usual, clear and focused. Told me what happened. Said he was sorry. Said he knew that his apologies weren't worth a damn. Said he'd understand if I wanted to stay away from him for a while. And that he hoped it wouldn't be for long, because I'm his best friend. And that just made what he did even more despicable (he used the word despicable – that's how clear and articulate he was).

I slammed the phone down on him, of course. But even that didn't manage to make me shake with rage. Even that couldn't change the fact that what I was feeling was mainly relief.

My life had been sailing smoothly along (some might say it was scraping the bottom of an empty pool) before Ya'ara shook it up. I was making a living from the translations I was doing for liberal arts students. The money paid for my everyday expenses, nothing else, but it had never been my ambition to save, not to mention get rich. To tell the truth, I had no ambitions at all. At twenty-eight, I had no idea what I wanted to be at thirty. Even the smallest olive tree seedling knows what it's meant to be and grows naturally, without hesitation, into an olive tree. But I had no idea in which direction to grow. And in the meantime, moving at the pace of a traffic jam on the Ayalon Freeway, I wrote my philosophy dissertation entitled 'Metamorphoses: Great

Minds who Changed their Minds', and every summer I bought all the university catalogues so I could pick up a new, more practical field of study from them.

In a moment of weakness, I went to one of those institutes that give advice about choosing a profession. The counsellor, with baby cheeks and lots of good will, looked at my tests and said that, based on the results, all possibilities were open, I could choose anything I wanted. I said that was just the problem. That I don't want. Then she said: that's why I'm here, to help you clarify what you want. And I said, you don't understand, I don't want anything. I'm devoid of motivation. I'm a horse standing in his stall who would rather watch the other horses compete than gallop himself.

She survived in my presence for another two meetings, then recommended warmly that I try therapy. I gave her a small nod, but I didn't go to a therapist. What for? After all, going into therapy – or Alcoholics Anonymous or a self-awareness workshop in the desert – means you first have to believe that people are capable of change. Besides, I already knew what the therapist would say: the restraint that characterises my family relationships has become transformed in me into an overall indifference. The fact that I wasn't hugged enough when I was a child restrained my desire to act. (Funny, the tutor in the creative writing workshop I'm doing now talks about restraint as 'one of the greatest powers a writer has'. He says the hotter the content of a story, the colder the narrator should be. But, he claims, you also have to be careful not to fall in love with restraint. And you have to know when to put cracks in it.)

My restraint, in any case, was deeply cracked the minute I met Ya'ara. During the months we were together, my horse burst out of the stall with me on its back, my legs dangling on either side of the saddle. I raced with her to the school she'd gone to and she showed me the small yard – she remembered it as being larger – where the girls in her class decided to ostracise to her; I raced with her to plays she went to see mainly so she could be disappointed and explain to me later, her cheeks red with passion, how she would have done it differently, more intensely; I raced with her to a party in Jerusalem that went on all night, and when she danced, her hair whipped my face, and it hurt and felt good, felt good and hurt; I raced with her to my parents' house in Haifa and watched her win them over in five minutes; I raced with her to wherever she took me, throwing off my calculated caution, and that way, feeling light, I could keep going to distant regions in my soul and hers. Every night, in bed, she told me things: how the affront she'd felt when her girlfriends decided to ostracise her in her first year in high school still stung, making her keep a safe distance from women, and how that guitarist threatened to hurt himself if she left him, and three weeks later, he left her, and for the first time in my life, I didn't make do with listening and told her that before her, there'd been nothing, and I'd already reconciled myself to a life without love, except the love I had with imaginary women I created for myself every night, and then during the day, I scoured the streets, the shops, the campus lawns for girls who looked like them. With the appropriate self-mockery, I told her about my collection of imaginary women, trying to create the impression that they were all in the past, while at the same time, the suspicion was growing in me that she herself was imaginary, and when we'd finished racing around together, there would be a very non-imaginary fall. I even felt a slight yearning for that fall. For those first seconds after you fall, when everything is suddenly silent. And when it finally came –

I didn't bang my head against the wall. I didn't empty a bottle of sleeping pills. I didn't stroll around on the window ledge. I took on more and more translation work so I wouldn't have time to think, and I told Amichai not to ask me over to watch the football for a while because I wouldn't.

But that's not fair, he protested, it's not fair that Churchill did what he did and you're the one who's out in the cold. I'm not out in the cold, I choose not to be with all of you, I said, almost yelling at him, as if raising my voice would make my decision logical, and when Ilana the Weeper called on the pretext of needing help with translating some article, confessing a second later that she actually wanted to tell me that they all missed me a lot, and she didn't understand why I was denying myself their support when I needed it most – I told her that I just couldn't. And she said I could see just her, if I wanted, and her voice was gentle and empathetic, very different from the sharp voice she used with Amichai when we were around, but I still said, thanks, Ilana, really, thank you, but no.

*

To tell the truth, it wasn't easy. Without my Haifa friends, Tel Aviv went back to being the ugly, inhospitable city it had been when I moved there, half-heartedly, after the army, only because of the impulsive promise I made to Churchill on the last Independence Day before we were drafted.

We were sitting in the playing field stands and Churchill announced that this time we were going to Tel Aviv, and Ofir said he'd read in the papers that there was a party in Malkei Israel Square, and Amichai said it was probably expensive because everything in Tel Aviv is expensive, and Ofir said, you dimwit, it's in Malkei Israel Square, how can they take money in an open place, and Amichai said, you're the dimwit, what's the problem with fencing it off, and Churchill said, enough, if it costs money, we'll pay, it's our last Independence Day before the army, and when he finished the sentence, they all looked at me because I was the only one who had not only a driving licence, but also his parents' car, and I said yes, but on one condition, that we leave early because I don't like driving when I'm tired, and Churchill patted me on the shoulder and said, whatever you say, Freed, but when I came to pick him up, he was far from being ready, and Ofir, who was always next on the route to be picked up, had fallen asleep watching a Fellini film and we had to pull him off the couch by his curly hair and make him two cups of instant coffee, and Amichai decided he'd stay at home to help his brother study for an exam and wouldn't change his mind until Churchill explained that not going out on Independence Day is like thumbing your nose at your country, but even after he gave in, we had to wait for him to have a shower and find an outfit he thought would cover the blotch on the bottom of his neck that had first appeared after his father was killed by a road bomb in Lebanon. From some angles, that blotch looked like a map of Israel, which turned Amichai, against his will, into an attraction in civics class and left him with a permanent complex about his appearance. That night, he tried three different shirts and three pairs of matching trousers till he found a combination he was happy with, and that's why we didn't start driving south until one in the morning. Churchill said we had nothing to worry about, things in Tel Aviv started late anyway, and when we reached the Glilot junction and got stuck in a horrible traffic jam, he said, everyone's probably going to that party in the Square, I think it's going to be the party of our lives, but the traffic didn't move, and the radio said there'd been an accident on Namir Road and 'traffic in the area was heavy', and Ofir said, isn't this Namir Road? And Amichai said, what are you talking about, this is Haifa Road and Ofir said, you cretin, Namir Road and Haifa Road are the same thing, and Amichai said, you're the cretin, why would they give the same road two different names? And Churchill leaned over to me and whispered under their voices, take a right here, and when I did, he signalled me to park on the pavement and said, *yallah*, let's walk, how far can it be, got out of the car, slammed the door hard and started walking towards the distant lights of the big, unfamiliar city,

24

and we all hurried after him without knowing exactly where we were going.

We walked through a neighbourhood of tall buildings with marble lobbies and underground parking, and through neighbourhoods of low buildings without marble lobbies or underground parking, and we barely saw another human being the whole way, just a few scared girls wearing miniskirts who Churchill called babes, it's unbelievable how many babes there are in this city, and Ofir said, like someone in the know, you ain't seen nuthin' yet, Bro, when we get to the Square you'll have to put on your shades so your eyes don't get burned, but when we reached the Square, sweaty and wrinkled after an hour and a half of walking, it was totally empty, there was no one there except a lone demonstrator holding a 'Stop the Occupation' sign. That was before the army, and we didn't even know what or where the occupation was, so we just asked the demonstrator if there'd been a party there, and he said no, there hadn't been any party because you need a reason to party. No party? How can that be? Ofir asked us, ignoring the demonstrator, I swear that I read in the papers that . . . Maybe you read it in 'Teen Dreams', Amichai jeered, and Ofir defended himself, no, I swear, it was in the weekend *Yediot Aharonot*, in the Seven Days section, and Amichai said, only you, Ofir, only you, Seven Days has interviews with retired generals and football players, parties are listed in the Seven Nights section, and I looked at my watch, thought about the long drive home waiting for me and said, it's four in the morning already, maybe we should start back? But Churchill shot a withering look at me and said, are you crazy? Go back? It's Independence Day! We have to find a party! We have to!

Ah . . . guys . . . I'm dying of thirst . . . Amichai started mumbling, then added, I have an idea! Can't we stop somewhere and buy something to drink? But Churchill said no and started walking again, and we followed him because we always followed him, not only because we were in awe of him, but also because of his enormous lust for life that had something contagious and beautiful and joy-inspiring about it, and really, after a short walk on Frishman Street – which Amichai insisted was named after the Hapoel Tel Aviv basketball player, Amos Frishman, and Ofir said that didn't make sense, because Amos Frishman was alive and they don't name streets after living people – we heard dance music coming from a flat and Churchill said, come on, we're going up there, and Amichai said, what do you mean? We don't know anyone there, that's just the point, Churchill explained, we don't know anyone in this city, so we can be whoever we feel like being, and Ofir said that if they ask, we'll say we're friends of Daniel, because Daniel is both a guy's name and a girl's name, and it's an international name too, and I looked at my watch again and remembered the straight, monotonous section of the road after Hadera where you could easily fall asleep while driving, and I thought there was something embarrassing, not to mention humiliating, about crashing a party, but still, I trailed up the steps behind them to the third floor, holding my nose so the stench of urine coming from the walls and the steps and the windows wouldn't make me vomit, and I thought, I wonder what a party in this city is like, it's probably different, the people here must dance differently, but after Churchill pressed the buzzer and we heard a mechanical bird cheep and the front door opened, it turned out that there was no big party going on behind it, there was just one girl with wild hair and a wild neckline who gave us a look that was both dead and hungry for love, a look I know very well today, after ten years in this city, but then, it still amazed me with the inner contradiction it reflected.

Did you want something? she asked, pulling back her hair into a wobbly ponytail. Her tone was surprisingly matter-of-fact, as if she were used to people ringing her bell at four-thirty in the morning. As if she were a waitress

26

in a café and we were her customers. We're friends of Daniel . . . Ofir began, but Churchill interrupted him and said, the truth is that we heard music on the street and just . . . thought there was a party going on here. A party? the girl said, giving Churchill a head-to-toe look that lingered a bit on his broad chest. There actually is a party going on here, she went on, but it's a . . . private party. Very private, Churchill said and smiled at her, pointing to the empty space behind her. Yes, she smiled back at him, very private is a good way to put it. And . . . is there any way we can join this 'very private' party? Churchill asked as he leaned against her doorframe. She let down her hair, then pulled it back into a ponytail again and said, I don't know. I don't really know any of you. Ah, that's not a problem, Churchill said. I'm Yoav. And these are my friends from the pilots training course, Ofir, Amichai and Yuval. Pilots training course? the girl said, surprised but not very enthusiastic, as if she'd already heard every possible lie. Yes, Churchill said, we have a forty-eight-hour pass, and we've been looking all night for a place to dance, but without any luck. Till we came here. To you.

I have no idea how you did it, Yoav, but you've managed to get my sympathy, the girl said and moved back a little so we could walk in. As I passed her, my elbow rubbed lightly against her waist and I got a whiff of her perfume, which was very different from the ones used by the Haifa girls we went out with, and I had the urge to turn around and bury my head between her breasts for a few seconds and inhale that bitter smell, but two songs later, she was pulling Churchill into the bedroom, and the three of us were left behind, in the living room. We kept on trying to convince ourselves we were dancing, facing each other, but then we realised how ridiculous that was, so we turned the music down and sat on the black leather sofa in the middle of the living room, and Amichai shot a quick glance at the bedroom door and said, that's something else, isn't it? And

Ofir said, right out of the movies, and I said, maybe you really should put it in your film, Ofir, because years ago, before he wrote down his World Cup wish to write a book, Ofir had said that after the army, he wanted to make a film about the four of us, something like *Late Summer Blues*, which had been such a big hit, and every once in a while he'd bring a video camera when we went to the beach and tape us playing volleyball, or puffing out our chests on the waves, and he'd say he was 'gathering material', and we were all sure that he really would make a film in the end because he was obviously bursting with talent and there wasn't a single Purim play at school or in the Scouts he didn't write, and in our junior year, he won second place in the national screenplay writing contest, when the first place winner was a kid from the Talma Yellin performing arts high school, whose surname was suspiciously the same as one of the judges'.

It's not a bad idea to put a scene like this into the film, Freed, he said, patting me on the shoulder. Not bad at all. Even though . . . none of this will be worth a damn if one of us doesn't die in the army. Someone has to die in the army, he sighed, otherwise I don't have a film. But why? Amichai said angrily, perhaps because his father really did die in the army, and Ofir again raised his argument that every successful movie or book in Israel since the state came into being has a dead soldier in it, and the part about the dead soldier is always the most moving part of the movie or book. Zvilich in *Late Summer Blues*? Ori in *He Walked in the Fields*? Yehoram Gaon in *Operation Thunderbolt*? Ofir raised a finger for each example, then kept piling on details of cases that clearly proved his argument, till Amichai fell asleep, and he wasn't satisfied till I promised him that if none of us died spontaneously in the army, I was ready to take on the job. His head dropped onto the wide shoulders of his eternal adversary and I was left alone in that girl's living room. I didn't know her name,

28

but I could already tell you what kind of sounds she made when she had an orgasm. Or faked it.

I got up and walked around her flat, which didn't look like any I'd ever seen, and not like any I'd ever dreamed of either. It had huge paintings on the walls, all in intensely bright colours. Not posters of paintings you buy for fifty shekels, but original works. I had the feeling she painted them herself, even though I had no evidence of that. There were some very ugly papier mâché sculptures on her book-shelves and I guessed she made them, too. I didn't see one familiar book, except for *The Little Prince*, and that made me feel like a philistine. There were lots of art books and poetry books, and very few novels. I took a small book from the poetry section. It was titled *Poems of Love and Sex* by David Avidan, and I remembered our literature teacher mentioning his name once or twice, but we never studied any of his poems. I read the first one standing up, and then I couldn't sit down. 'A woman so beautiful and a man so ugly/And she's married to him. A crime' – were the first lines to hit me. 'Two Sex Toys' was the name of the poem on the next page. I didn't know if I liked these poems, but I couldn't stop rolling the new phrases around on my tongue: 'Lolita Splendita', 'A reliable little sex animal', 'A strong moment of weakness', 'We rose, ready to go'. I even copied a few of them down on a piece of paper I found in the kitchen so I could show them to Churchill later, on the drive home, and hear what he thought of them.

He thought it was 'a scandal that they don't teach that' and 'literature teachers would rather teach dead poets because they have lesson plans on them all prepared'. And he also said that it would be just like Atalya – that, it turns out, was the name of the girl from Tel Aviv – to have a book like that in her house. Why? I asked, because I knew from the tone of his voice that he wanted me to ask, and he opened the car window, leaned his elbow out with that post-coital euphoria and said that Atalya had been having an affair with a married man for a few years, and a couple of hours before we arrived, he told her he couldn't sneak out to see her that night even though he'd promised he would, and she was so upset that she had to dance out all her anger, otherwise she would have exploded, or even worse, jumped out of the window, and that's when we knocked on the door looking so pure and innocent in our jeans and T-shirts that she just had to touch the smooth innocence she was losing as her affair with this man was becoming tangled in a web of lies, but she couldn't end it, she couldn't leave him because if she did, she'd be alone, completely alone.

Churchill went on describing in minute detail everything they said and everything that happened in the bedroom, and I didn't stop him because it excited me and helped me get through the section of the road after Hadera without falling asleep, and when we started up Freud Road and the sun was painting the Carmel Mountains in sleepy gold, he said, look, Freed, there's nobody on the road but us, this city is dead. Dead. We have to get out of here the minute after we're discharged. If we stay, in a few years, we'll get homogenia.

Homogenia?

We'll be like everyone else, Churchill said. We'll go to work, come home from work. Grow a pot belly and a mort-gage. We can't let that happen. We can't!

OK, Churchill, I said. O-o-OK. But that wasn't enough for him, and after we dropped off Ofir and Amichai, he made me swear that after the army, I'd move to Tel Aviv with him because without me, 'I'll never have the guts to do it'.

I was surprised that the great Churchill needed me so much and I felt a little weird swearing to do something that would happen in another four years. Not only that, but just two hours earlier, I'd promised Ofir to die in the army for his movie, but Churchill said he'd get out of the car if

I didn't promise, and I was tired, very tired from that whole Independence Day, so I swore to him, and with us, subjects of the British Empire, teatime is teatime and giving your word obligates you, so three months after we got out of the army, I went to his apartment to go through the 'Flatmates Wanted' listings he'd taken from the Student Union for me, and in the years that have gone by since then, I've never felt at home in a single one of the six Tel Aviv flats I lived in, but on the other hand, with time, I stopped feeling like a temporary visitor and even started to have an affection for certain places where the four of us spent a lot of time together – like the far bank of the Yarkon, or the boisterous square in front of the Cinematheque, or the American Colony on the way to Jaffa – but even those modest affections faded, faded very much, when that business with Ya'ara happened.

Without my Haifa friends, the streets of the big city seemed like dead-ends to me again. The shoreline looked like a hotel lobby again. And the people walking on the promenade looked hopelessly different from me again. Their joy of life seemed superficial to me. Materialistic. Pathetic. I ridiculed them and envied them at the same time. I felt purer than they were. Deeper. And at the same time, I felt that they had a kind of wonderful lightness I would never have, only because in my heart, I was still a Haifa boy.

I was anxious to know whether any of my Haifa friends missed me at the annual spring barbecue. Or at the screening of *Late Summer Blues* every Memorial Day. I found out how boring and sad it was to watch football alone, especially Israeli football. I found out how hard it was to make new friends at our age. I tried to get chummy with a few of my clients, and I even went out with some of them to an Irish pub near the beach. But it didn't work. Too many things had to be explained because they didn't understand immediately what I meant. It all smacked of benefits to be gained. And overcrowded schedules (apparently it's no accident that most friendships are born in high school or on trips. You need a generous stretch of time to get close).

Mostly, all those Irish outings made me miss my old friends. And Churchill more than any of them.

After getting our BAs, we'd taken off, just the two of us, on a long trip to South America. Ofir had just started working in an ad agency and was afraid they'd fire him if he took a too-long holiday, and Ilana the Weeper was already pregnant with the twins, so Amichai dropped out too, and it was just the two of us, Churchill and me. Me and Churchill. Nights. Days. In piss-smelling rooms. In Indian markets bustling with colour. In central bus stations that had no information desks. In long waits that went on for hours. In long rides that went on for days.

On a trip like that, you're exposed to the true nature of the person you're travelling with, and he's exposed to yours. At home, you can somehow hide it, smooth it out, play nice. But on a trip like that, everything comes out. Floats to the top. And is laid open.

I never imagined, for example, how much Churchill was addicted to attention. I always thought there was something about him that projected: I have my own way and I make it on my own. It wasn't till that trip that I realised, for the first time, that it all depended on feedback. If we didn't meet any new people for a few days, he withered. His shoulders drooped. Even his speech became hesitant.

He never imagined what a neatness freak I was. I tried desperately to turn every miserable little room we rented into a home. And when he threw his clothes on the floor, I told him to pick them up as if I were his mother, and that provoked him so much that at some point in the trip, we decided that, for the good of our friendship, we should sleep in separate rooms even though it cost more. And it also drove him crazy that I couldn't communicate until I had my morning tea-with-milk. And his constant complaints against the locals drove me up the wall. Look at all the natural resources they have, he'd say, pointing out of the bus window at cascading waterfalls, it's incredible that they don't do a thing with them. Let me enjoy the scenery, I'd think, and move slightly away from him, but he wouldn't let it go: of course they're poor, they're lazy, like they can't help themselves. They have no desire to change their situation.

For the first few weeks, I argued with him (perhaps it's a different way of life? Perhaps they choose to be like that?) and then I just kept quiet. I listened to him complain (look at this terrible road. Why is it such a big deal to get it fixed? This is not a way of life, it's just plain laziness) and prayed he'd shut up. Or bother someone else on the bus.

But despite everything, we didn't separate for more than a day on that whole trip. And despite everything, we were closer when we came home. Perhaps because, as Aristotle claims, 'Men cannot know each other until they have eaten salt together', and perhaps because the trip gave each of us at least one chance to learn that he really could depend on the other.

When Churchill came back, he told everyone how I saved his life when he drank the San Pedro. I thought he was exaggerating a little, all I did was go to see how he was eight hours after he'd left the ranch with a bag full of green cactus juice the Indians used when they wanted to talk to the gods. Any friend would've done that. Before he left our shack, he said he was going to drink that juice, but I had nothing to worry about because there was no way it would have any effect on him. I believed him. After all, he was Churchill. And when I went out to look for him, I was sure I'd find him swimming naked with two Israeli girls in one of the natural water pools scattered around the ranch.

He really was naked when I found him. But alone. Covered in his own vomit and in the throes of a very serious attack of paranoia. It seemed that the gods had spoken to him and told him to undress. It seemed that he thought the hill we were standing on was full of tigers that had horses' heads. It seemed that he thought everything he said was coming out enormously loud and could be heard all around the globe. And he was afraid his parents would hear it back home. In fact, his parents had come to visit him here, now, after he vomited. And he finally told his father what he thought of him and his women. But now he was scared. No, not of his father. Of the Indians' gods. They were angry with him and he couldn't understand why. And he was thirsty, as thirsty as if he'd walked through the desert for forty years, but he couldn't put a drop of water in his mouth, so maybe I could drink for him, instead of him, he meant.

I opened my bottle of water and shoved it in his mouth. Then I helped him get dressed and dragged him back towards the ranch. I kept a close watch on him, waiting for the effects of the drug to start fading, meanwhile making sure that he drank and ate enough. At night, after I thought he'd recovered, he suddenly had a horrible attack of anxiety that if he fell asleep, he wouldn't be able to tell the difference between reality and dreams when he woke up. I promised him I'd be his sign of reality, that every time he wasn't sure, he could call me. He called me a dozen times that night. And every time, I got up, went over to his bed and stroked his head till he fell asleep.

I want you to know, amigo, that I'll remember you my whole life, he told me two days later, inside a van that was taking us back to the city. We were leaning on our rucksacks and a pleasant sun was dancing on our naked chests.

It's nothing, I said.

It definitely isn't nothing, he insisted. If you hadn't come looking for me, I would've dehydrated. At best. At worst, *bandidos* would have passed through, shaved off my *pauchos* and for dessert, shot me through the heart, I mean *corazonos*.

Don't exaggerate, I said.

I'm not, he insisted.

Anyway, I owed you for Cusco, I said.

OK, now that really was nothing, he said.

*

It wasn't nothing. I didn't think so and neither did the local doctor (who was also the local pharmacist and also the local travel agent and also the only person in town who spoke English). He examined me in a storeroom full of empty cardboard boxes, behind the pharmacy, after my temperature went up to 39.4 centigrade, and I had chills all through my body. You have 'gringo fever', he said, and explained that it was a fever that mostly tourists got. There is no medicine for it, and it could last from a week to a month. The only treatment is rest, lying in bed and waiting patiently for it to pass. And you, Big Guy, he said to Churchill, stay close to your friend. Make sure he drinks and check his temperature every few hours to see that it doesn't go past forty. If that happens, let me know right away because that means the disease has entered its second stage.

Churchill followed the doctor's orders meticulously.

At the end of the first week, he met a girl in Posada named Keren, who'd been at university with him. She'd had a boyfriend then, but not now. They started having breakfast together and went out at night after I was asleep.

Churchill spoke passionately to her. To be accurate, I'd never heard him talk to a girl like that. That Keren has something, he said. She has a secret.

A few days later, she suddenly vanished from his stories. I asked about her, and he said she'd gone. Continuing her trip.

So why didn't you go with her? I asked.

I asked her to wait a little, till you got well, and then we'd go. She said that 'Whatever is supposed to happen will happen', and that 'If we're meant to meet, we'll meet'.

Too bad you didn't go with her, I said. She had a secret.

That's crap, Churchill said angrily, she pretended she had a secret to drive me crazy.

I didn't say anything. The way Churchill spat out that 'crap' was proof that giving up Keren wasn't easy for him at all.

My thermometer beeped and he took it out of my mouth. We're getting better, he said. Thirty-eight point six. And after a short break, he added, as if to himself: girls come and go. Friends stay.

*

I reminded him of that remark when he called to confess about Ya'ara.

He was silent. Didn't deny that he'd said it. Didn't claim that I was quoting him out of context.

I kept on reminding him of that remark even in the internal dialogues I had with him later on. What happened? I'd ask him. What changed in the three years that passed since then? Did your priorities change or did you just turn into a shitty person?

He never answered me. That's how it is with internal dialogues, you can sling as much mud as you want and there's no one to answer back. And so, in my mind, I wished he would lose all his cases from now on, not just lose, but lose for the most humiliating reasons. Because he didn't prepare witnesses properly. Because he misplaced the plastic bag with one of the main pieces of evidence inside. Or because the defence attorney surprised him with a legal precedent that every lowly clerk should know, and he'd have to explain that to the district attorney. And lower his eyes as he spoke.

I wished him all that – and I missed him. His inner fire that had something inspiring about it. The way he focused totally on every conversation with a friend, no matter how busy he was. Or troubled. Or tired. That quick, smiling glance he'd give me when I spoke a private thought out loud, signalling to me that he knew *exactly* what I was talking about: that he'd seen the movie, read the book or, like me, he'd picked up on the absurdity of a situation everyone mistakenly thought was serious.

It had been with that kind of look that our friendship came into being. It was the week of our junior year when we went out for pre-army training. All the junior classes were moved to an army camp in the south, and for five days, we played soldier. They dressed us in uniforms. Split us up into companies. Ran us ragged. Hassled our arses. And we gave ourselves up to the new order. That is, most of us did. Only a few stood at the window wondering why the hell we had to cross that bridge before we got to it. That is, if we were doomed to be shackled, we'd be shackled. But why start it in high school?

Hey, you think they'll let us out for the weekend? I asked during one of the short canteen breaks they gave us, and no one thought it was funny. Except Churchill. I think it's a definite – perhaps! he said, imitating the decisive voice of our buzz-cut unit commander, smiled at me with his eyes and when the break was over, asked me, only me, if I'd like to skip the next parade with him. When that made me hesitate (it's one thing to laugh at the accepted routine, and another to deviate from it), he said he'd checked it out and they had no legal authority over us. In fact, he promised, they can't do a thing to us if we don't show up for parade. Not a thing.

I was persuaded and stayed in the canteen with him. And it had the taste of rebellion. We ate chocolate bars and talked about how Rona Raviv looked good even in uniform, and how the movie *Dune* wasn't nearly as good as the book, and why it was better to learn how to drive on a manual than on an automatic. Churchill held forth and I mostly listened, but he was curious about the few things I did say, and that encouraged me to talk more than I usually did. I found myself telling him that I played chess once a week in an old men's club. And he didn't make fun of that, instead he asked me to play against him on Saturday. *If* they let us out for the weekend, I reminded him. And he laughed again. I thought it was generous of him to laugh at the same not-very-funny joke twice. After our game on Saturday, he talked me into going out to the Little Haifa pub because an aircraft carrier from the Sixth Fleet was anchored in the port then, and there would probably be a lot of American sailors in white there, getting drunk and singing with wet throats, 'Bye bye Miss American pie'. That is a sight you really have to see, he said. After that Saturday, we became friends. I'd had friends before him, but they were all my type: short, gloomy, the ones stuck to the walls at parties, and during breaks at school they read science-fiction magazines. They were the ones who knew the Maccabi Haifa line-up by heart, including subs, but never went to matches, who made fun of everything in beautifully constructed sentences, but started stammering the minute a girl said something to them.

Churchill wasn't afraid of girls. He wasn't afraid of life at all and approached it with a bare chest, sweeping hand movements and untied shoelaces, and although I knew in my heart that I would never be completely like him, I believed, or wanted to believe, that gradually, just from the many hours we spent together, some of his lust for life would rub off on me and also, I would stop treating girls as if they were marble goddesses. I too would step away from the wall and join the party.

*

After what happened with Ya'ara, I felt that again, as if ten years hadn't passed, I was stuck to the wall and had withdrawn into my comfortable old gloominess.

It's embarrassing to admit, but I even went to the phone a few times to call Churchill. And once I actually started dialling his number. I knew that he was the only one who could understand, without my having to explain, why I could no longer look at those ads featuring beautiful women wearing glasses, why every time the word 'revelation' appeared in an article I was translating, I pushed the bundle of papers aside, and why, after Ya'ara, every girl I went out with felt like a compromise.

But I also knew there was a chance she'd be the one to answer the phone in his flat.

So I didn't call.

And one day, driving to give a translation to a client, I saw them. It was on Nahalat Benyamin Street, near the fabric shops, and they were in the car in front of mine waiting for the lights to change. At first, I wasn't sure it was them, so I took my foot off the brake and let the car slide forward, like a piece of cloth slipping off a chair, till it almost touched theirs, and I still wasn't one hundred per cent sure – after all, I hadn't seen either of them for months. But then, with that gesture of hers, she took off her glasses, and he leaned over and they kissed. And kissed. The lights turned green and they were still kissing. I could have honked my horn, I should have honked my horn, but I stayed still and saw how she ran her fingers through his hair and how his hand held the back of her neck and how her eyes closed and how his eyes closed and how her shoulder gleamed and how the ends of her caramel-coloured hair rested in the hollow between her gleaming shoulder and her throat and how his finger played with the ends of that hair. The green light had already turned into a flashing yellow light, and I still didn't honk. And he kept kissing her, and her head tilted slowly back, and I could picture her small breasts in the V of her shirt, and then they weren't kissing any more, they were just wrapped in a tight, hot embrace that continued until the yellow had turned to red. Her body was enveloped in his arms and his head rested on her breast, and her shoulder was gleaming again and he raised his head slightly and kissed her naked skin, bit it gently, and she stroked his head as if urging him on, to bite her harder, deeper, and he raised his head for a moment and saw that the lights had turned green again –

And they laughed. I could almost hear their laughter

bursting out of the windows. They were laughing about their recklessness, or perhaps because Churchill had impressed her with his famous imitation of the airborne traffic reporter, and through the propeller noise he made with his lips, he told his listeners about a couple kissing in their car and blocking traffic on Nahalat Benyamin Street.

Or perhaps he was telling her about the wish I'd written on my piece of paper. And that was what amused them so much, a second before they started driving.

I waited a little longer, ignoring the loud honking behind me, so I could make sure they were moving away. As far as possible. Only then did I start driving. My heart frozen. Frozen stiff.

*

I stayed away from my friends for almost six months.

I resisted all Amichai's pleading and temptations (the championship league game! on a 40-inch screen!! Ilana the Weeper's tear-flavoured *burekas*!!!).

I held out even when he switched to threats (if you don't come here, we'll come to you. If you don't open the door, we'll break it down –).

But when he called to tell me that Ofir had had a breakdown at work, all my determination buckled like a pile of pears in the supermarket, and I left straight for the hospital.

From: 'Metamorphoses: Great Minds who Changed their Mind', an unfinished philosophy thesis by Yuval Freed

What caused Wittgenstein, who asserted that words have value only if they represent reality, suddenly to say years later: I made a mistake, concrete reality is not at all relevant, the meaning of words derives entirely from the 'game of a specific language' in which they take part, and therefore, contrary to my earlier claim, it is not important to ask to what extent words fit the world, but: what do people do with words?

Was it, as is customarily believed, a slow, gradual metamorphosis that led to this sharp shift in Wittgenstein's thought? Or was there a particular moment in which he clutched his forehead and said: *Grösser Gutt!*? Did this change of mind occur while he was building his sister's house in Vienna, or did it happen during one of the lessons he gave as a not-very-popular school teacher in an Austrian village? Or perhaps the insight came to him while he was watching one of the ballgames he so loved to use as metaphors in elucidating his ideas? I picture him sitting in the Centre Court at Wimbledon in 1934, watching that year's championship game between Fred Perry and Jack Crawford. The spectators' heads move from side to side, following the white ball from side to side, from side to side. When suddenly one head stops moving: Wittgenstein realises that he has made a mistake.

And I am curious to know: was the word 'mistake' projected onto the screen of his mind before he broke into a sweat of panic, or did he first break into a sweat of panic and only then did the word 'mistake' appear?

And how much courage does it take for a person to deny his own ideas? (Especially those that have become public. And have admirers. And earned Wittgenstein the respect of scholarly philosophers all across the continent.)

How much courage, or despair, or honesty with oneself that is brutal to the point of despair, does it take for a person to toss away all of that? And start from the beginning?

2

In the first picture on the right on my living room wall, Ofir and I are standing back to back, holding petrol hoses as if they were rifles. As if, in another minute, we'd take ten paces, turn around suddenly and start to duel. We're both wearing petrol company uniforms and, in my case at least, it looks like a costume. The Carmel Mountains are in the background, but that's not unusual: almost anywhere you take a picture in Haifa, the Carmel or the sea will be in the background.

A week after being discharged from the army, I started working with Ofir at his father's petrol station. Ofir said it was considered 'essential work', and if we stuck with it for six months, we'd get a grant from the army. Besides – he tossed another reason at me – loads of women in red cars came to the station, and sometimes, if they liked the way you looked in your attendant's uniform, they asked you to check other things besides oil and water. That's how his father met his second wife. And the third. And, in fact, that's how he met Ofir's mother – when she came in to put air in her tyres.

After two weeks, we were fired in disgrace. Ofir's father said we worked too slowly and talked too much. And work like that was for real men, not for the kind raised by their mother.

To tell the truth, I was relieved. The petrol fumes didn't

do my asthma any good. And the only woman with a red car who came into the station during those two weeks got pissed off with me for not cleaning her windscreen.

But Ofir took it hard. He said that what bothered him most was the army grant. He'd been counting on using it for his trip to Thailand, but I knew that the whole story of working in the petrol station was just an attempt, another attempt, to get closer to his father.

He never gave up on that. A year after the petrol station fiasco, he took all the money he'd saved for Thailand and invited his father on a man's tour of eastern Turkey. He laid out the plan for me the night before they left: we'll sleep in tents, cook in the field. Finally we'll have the chance to really get to know each other!

The first worrying signs appeared at the airport. His father thought it wasn't appropriate to board a plane wearing jeans torn at the knees. Ofir said he didn't get it, why people feel the need to dress up for a flight. You know what, do what you want, his father grumbled, but I want you to know that your trousers are a personal insult to me. Ofir went into the bathroom and changed, consoling himself with the thought that all beginnings are hard. But later on, when they started their trip through the mountains, things just got worse. Ofir's father didn't understand why they needed such long breaks that disrupted their walking, and Ofir thought that those moments, when you take off your rucksack and you sit back and enjoy the scenery while the wind cools the sweat on your back, were the best moments of the trip. You know what, his father said, we'll take turns deciding when the break is over. Great, Ofir said, thinking that at long last it was starting to happen. But later, when they went down to the city to buy supplies, the problems began again. His father didn't understand how you could walk around a new city without a map. Ofir thought that all the magic was in walking around a new city without a map, without knowing where you're going, just walking around and absorbing the sounds, the smells, the colours. You know what, if I'm getting in the way of your 'absorbing', then carry on without me, his father grumbled, and after a week of petty arguments, Ofir's nerves were frayed, so he said, you know what, Dad, that's exactly what I'm going to do, and they spent the last day of their trip, in Istanbul, apart.

They didn't go to the airport together either, because Ofir wanted to take a taxi and his father said that his mother always spoiled him, and that a taxi was a waste of money, and Ofir said it was his money and he'd decide what to do with it. And it continued like that on the plane – insult, silence, insult, silence – till Ofir's father got up and moved to another seat.

But even the failure of the trip, however much it hurt, didn't break Ofir. After a short recovery period, he tried again, armed with a new insight: the mistake on the trip was – he explained to me – that I tried to force my father to do things with me that I like to do. Tomorrow I'm buying a model aeroplane and on Saturday morning, I'll join him down below, you know, on Freud Street.

Every Saturday morning, in an open field at the entrance to the city (where today, a retail park has blossomed), fathers and sons would get together to fly model aeroplanes. When Ofir was a boy, and his father was still married to his mother, his father asked him to go there with him a few times. But Ofir would always want to stay at home with his mother and play Scrabble, and later too, when the third wife had already given birth to two girls, Ofir's father continued to go down to the open field, alone, to fly his model plane, alone, and heard the cries of excitement coming from children who were not his.

That would be an amazing way to close the circle, Ofir told me. I'm not even planning to tell him I'm coming, so it'll be a complete surprise. It's a great idea, don't you think?

Definitely, I said supportively. I wondered why he was always the one to make the attempts to get closer, but his enthusiasm was so innocent, so touching, that I was carried away by it. And I hoped for him.

You should have seen my father's face when he saw me walking over with the model plane, Ofir said emotionally when he called me on Saturday night.

He was surprised?

Shocked.

And how was it later?

Later?

With the planes?

Good . . . it . . . there was a small collision between my plane and his, which is worth ten thousand shekels. And they both crashed onto the road. Then he said that perhaps I'd better leave. He didn't need me to help him pick up the pieces. But I'm telling you, the expression on his face . . . when he saw me coming . . . he said he appreciated it. He said he appreciated it very much. And this morning I had a great idea. A fantastic idea. You know, they opened a new petrol station across the street from his, and they're stealing his customers. That's a classic problem that advertising can solve. I talked with the art department in our office and they volunteered to do everything, free of charge. I'm telling you, in another month, I'll be in his office with a campaign that'll bring back his old customers and get him a lot of new ones too!

Ofir mustered all the creative talent he had and worked for a month and a half preparing that winning campaign for his father's petrol station, including stickers, posters, flyers and banners, but a day before the formal presentation –

His father had terrible pain in his lower jaw, asked his secretary to make a dentist's appointment for him, and an hour later, collapsed on his office carpet and died.

A heart attack.

If he'd had a subscription to Telemed, we might have been able to save him, Amichai whispered to me at the funeral.

46

And Ofir was left to glide like a model aeroplane over the chasm that had always existed between him and his father, doomed to wonder whether the great campaign might have succeeded where all other efforts had failed, and why did he need a campaign, dammit, why didn't his father just love him?

*

When I reached the ward where Ofir was, the others were already there.

Churchill. And Amichai, holding a huge tape recorder, and Ilana the Weeper, and someone from the ad agency, talking on his mobile.

There was a pungent smell of chicken soup in the air. And on the TV, someone wearing a white apron was explaining how to make steak fillets in teriyaki sauce. My legs wouldn't budge. Couldn't move forward. Couldn't move back. I was flooded with warm happiness at the sight of my friends, but along with it, the affront that had been growing in me over six months rose in my throat, as well as a feeling of cold, uncontrollable aversion towards Churchill.

Amichai took the initiative and came over to me with the huge tape recorder. Churchill, behind him, kept a safe distance.

His mother's inside, Amichai explained. When she comes out, they'll let us go in.

How is he? I asked, careful to look only at Amichai.

Looks like he'll live, he replied.

But what . . . how . . . what does it mean, he had a breakdown?

Two months ago, they offered him a promotion at work. A managerial position. He didn't want it. He told us a few times that he didn't want to be a manager. That after working in eight different agencies in seven years, he finally came to the conclusion that all advertising does is manipulate people into buying things they don't need, and if he

47

doesn't believe that what he does is important, then how can he persuade other people that it is?

OK, I said, swallowing my frustration at not having been a part of that whole process of trying to decide. So how did we get from that to . . .

That's just it, Amichai said playing with the tape recorder buttons, it was a bit weird. Two weeks after non-stop talking about that whole manipulation business, he calls Churchill one day and says, hey man, congratulate me.

So I said, congratulations, Bro, Churchill continued – speaking to me for the first time, but not looking me in the eye – but it would be nice if you told me what for. And then he said to me, like he was really proud of himself, you're speaking to the new creative director of Sheratzki-Shidlatzki.

That's Ofir for you, I said.

Churchill and Amichai nodded in agreement.

Wait a minute, I said, so when did he have a breakdown? And what is a breakdown anyway? What does it mean?

In professional jargon, they call it 'a psychotic episode', Ilana the Weeper said. Almost five per cent of men in the United States experience breakdown at least once in their lives. And you have to remember that we're talking about men here, so there are an awful lot more who don't report it.

That's actually your field, isn't it? I said, turning to her.

Her eyes lit up. A flush spread across her cheeks. I thought that even her breasts rose slightly.

Look, she said with quiet authority, there's been a lot of pressure on Ofir recently. And when you add that to an unstable emotional make-up that stems from his childhood, it's only logical that this would happen to him.

Of course, we all agreed. Except I saw that Churchill was actually taking a breath to object, and I knew exactly what he was going to say, that 'every petty criminal blames childhood abuse for his actions, and that's how determinism has become the last refuge of every bad guy, and if you take Australia, for example, which was settled by prisoners and the children of prisoners, then contrary to what you would expect based on the deterministic theory, crime rates are actually lower than the average –'

But he held back on his usual rant and let her keep talking.

The good news, she said, is that the kind of breakdown Ofir had is over in most cases after only a few days of rest. There's no reason it should be any different with him.

Ofir's mother came out of his room, straight over to me, to me, of all people. A year ago, after years of working as a medical secretary, she decided to take a course in facilitation. The man she was living with tried to put her down, he laughed at her, claimed there was no point in starting something new at her age, and there were no jobs to be had in that field anyway. But she didn't give up. Not even when she found out that the only course opening then was all the way in Tel Aviv. At Ofir's request, I helped her make her way through the bureaucratic labyrinth of academia, and ever since, she has been particularly fond of me.

It was nice of you all to come, she said.

We're worried about him, I said (how quickly you're back to saying 'we', the thought flashed through my mind).

You can go in, she said. He's waiting for you.

*

Ofir was lying in his bed, as white as the penalty spot in the eighteen-yard box. His feet, as flat and long as fins, were sticking out from the under the blanket. Those light-brown curls of his, which always made girls think he was a *moshavnik* who was going to inherit his parents' farm, were drooping. There was a new sadness in his cheeks.

I bent down to hug him. The last time his bones had stabbed me like that was at his father's funeral.

I'm a mess, he said when I let him go.

A little bit, I said and smiled.

Something in me is fucked up. Something basic in me is fucked up.

That's crap, Amichai said.

Don't be an arsehole, Churchill joined in.

We're all a bit fucked up, aren't we? I said. Just because we're human beings.

I missed those remarks of yours, Ofir said and gave me a tired smile.

I missed you too, I said.

You know, he said quietly to me, you went a little too far. It's OK to be angry with us, but six months?

I nodded in surrender.

It's a shame you don't really appreciate what you have, he continued rebuking me, and he seemed to be talking about himself too. It's a real shame, because you have no idea . . . he said, and then, a second before he could finish that trademark sentence of his, he fell asleep.

There's nothing new about people falling asleep while listening to other people talk. Once I myself fell asleep in the middle of lecture in the army on 'Working in Parallel', and because of that little doze, I was automatically kicked out of the officer training course, putting an end to the brilliant army career my father, and only my father, had predicted for me. But I never saw anyone fall asleep while his mouth was still forming words.

The nurse, a tall woman, skinny as a test tube, explained that he was exhausted. And that more than anything, he needed rest now.

Amichai put the tape recorder on the bedside table and asked her if it was OK for him to play something for Ofir.

I don't think that's a good idea, the nurse said, giving the tape recorder a hostile look.

Maybe just this once, Amichai pleaded. It's something we put together especially for him. To cheer him up.

No, I'm sorry, the nurse stuck to her guns, it's against hospital policy.

Amichai took the tape recorder off the table, looking very embittered. Perhaps that's where the seed was planted for what, in less than two years, would turn him into a familiar face in every Israeli home. It's hard to know.

But Ilana the Weeper and Churchill looked enormously relieved.

Only later, in the café in the hospital basement, did they explain what the nurse had saved us from. In a box he kept stored away in the house, Amichai had found an old tape recording of songs from our high school graduation play, and he had the idea that we'd all stand next to Ofir's bed in the hospital and sing the ballad he'd written to the chemistry teacher to the tune of that year's hit song, 'Big in Japan' (Oh, Shimon my man, tonight, Shimon my man, all right, Shimon my man, give me oxygen?).

We'll do it after he's discharged, I said (only because Ilana the Weeper was there and I didn't feel comfortable laughing at the idea).

Two weeks later, Amichai called me. Ofir was home. The four of us would get together on Thursday to watch the Maccabi game. Oh, and he was sending me an email with the words to 'Shimon My Man', in case I didn't remember them. And I should practise it once or twice alone. So there won't be any slip-ups.

There were no slip-ups.

Because, in the end, we didn't sing to Ofir on Thursday.

On Tuesday, he handed in his resignation, took out all the money he'd saved over the seven years he'd been working in advertising, bought a plane ticket, borrowed a big rucksack from Churchill and called to reserve a place in a hostel for the first night.

In the airport terminal in Lod, he checked out the adverts to see if they were effective.

In the Amman terminal, he did it less.

And in the Delhi terminal, almost not at all.

He told us all that excitedly, on the phone. But on the other hand, he said, India is full of Israelis high on weed. And it reeks of cow shit. And fried food. And the noise. You can't believe how much noise there is here. Listen, he said, and held the receiver out towards the street. The rumble of motor scooters reached us from across the ocean. Hear that? It's nothing. You should hear the cows. And there are children here that they raise inside urns, can you believe it? They raise children here in urns so their pelvises get twisted and they can earn more begging. Isn't that horrible?

Horrible.

For the life of me, I can't see anything spiritual in that, or in diarrhoea, he said, and that if it keeps on like that, he'll go to the Thai islands. Or come home. He had no idea. But it was very important for him to keep in touch with us in the meantime. Because actually, we were the closest thing to family he had. So he promised to call every first Thursday of the month as soon as the Maccabi game was over. And it would really mean a lot to him if all three of us were there.

Churchill and I were sure he wouldn't call. You can't stick to a strict schedule of obligations when you're travelling. Especially in India. But Amichai insisted that we give the guy a chance. So on the first Thursday in question, we watched the game together, and ten minutes after it was over, the phone rang.

And that's how the ritual that lasted almost a year was established. Every first Thursday of the month, we got together to watch the Maccabi game. Amichai would buy peach-flavoured ice tea for me, Churchill would stop on the way and buy too many nuts, and I would bring one of my bottles of booze (a student who worked in the family alcohol-importing business paid for my translations in kind). We didn't have weed because that was traditionally Ofir's job, and now that he wasn't here, no one had the energy to bother. Anyway, Amichai was tired of arguing with Ilana the Weeper about the nauseating smell, as she put it, that lingered in the house afterwards. I didn't like the fact that rolling joints had turned from an underground act into a social obligation. And Churchill, even though he wouldn't admit it, breathed a sigh of relief. Whenever we'd pass around a joint, he'd be torn between his strong desire to get high and his constant fear that the police might break in and catch him in the criminal act of smoking weed, thereby putting an end to his promising legal career.

During the game, we were divided into three camps: Amichai rooted for Maccabi because 'they represent our country in Europe', Churchill rooted against Maccabi because 'they're a monopoly and a complaint should be filed against them with the Anti-Trust Commission', and I was indifferent. Basketball, unlike football, always seemed to me like a too-planned, too-polite, too-much-like-me game, and I could never get excited by it. So I drank my ice tea quietly, poured everyone a drink and waited for the broadcast to end. And for Ofir to call. Amichai had gone out and bought a phone with a speaker, partly so the three of us could talk to him together, but mainly so we could listen. Ofir had a tremendous need to share, to tell us everything, otherwise he 'wouldn't be sure that it happened', and he didn't care if the call cost him a fortune because 'why did he work in advertising for seven years if not so he could enjoy the money'.

And so, conversation after conversation, month after month, we heard him change.

Funny. When a friend's with you and you see him every day, the changes taking place in him are so small that you don't even notice him changing. But from a distance –

It started with the rhythm of his speech, which became slower. More drawn out. As if every word had a profound meaning worth lingering over (along with the natural delay of a trans-oceanic call, it sometimes had a confusing effect: he would pause between every word. We were sure he'd finished his sentence, and stick in one of ours, which would reach him after a delay and get jumbled together with the continuation of his sentence, which reached us after a delay).

Then he started talking a lot about nature. Told us he'd spent two days sitting next to a lake in the Parvati Valley looking at a single lotus. Only when you're close to nature, he said, can you grasp the true frequency of the world and connect to it. In Haifa, he added, at least we had the Carmel, the sea. Since we moved to Tel Aviv, we have no connection to the earth. The air. The trees. And moving away from nature, that's against our nature. There's something sick about big cities, he claimed. A kind of background noise that doesn't let you hear your inner voice.

Oh come on, really, Ofir, Churchill said, unable to control himself, cities serve the human need to gather together. Besides, if cities were such a bad idea, they wouldn't be such a success.

Even though I agreed with Churchill, we all went hiking on the Carmel that Saturday, with no apparent connection to that conversation. We walked down the Kelah riverbed to the stone bridge, then back up to Little Switzerland, something we hadn't done in years. The soles of our shoes filled with pine-needle mud, we made up legends about how the strawberry tree got its name, we breathed in pine and oak air, and were amazed to find that autumn isn't just a word, but a real season.

*

After another long season of wandering, Ofir settled in one place and decided to take part in a series of workshops entitled 'Touch Meditation'. The idea behind touch meditation, he explained, is that the best way to attain the greatest inner clarity is actually to devote yourself completely to giving to someone else, through the body.

We weren't too excited.

We were sure that in one of our next conversations, he'd tell us that he'd left those workshops for totally different ones. Even back in high school, he was the one who talked us into leaving good parties for other, seemingly better ones by saying that his flat feet hurt him and it was hard for him to stand in one place for too long. And in the army, he routinely submitted transfer forms from his first day in a new unit, and that's how, in three years, he managed to be a tank driver, an aerial photograph interpreter, an army meteorologist, a command-post gardener, an NCO in charge of religious soldiers and also an NCO in charge of women soldiers. He would never buy return bus or train tickets, despite the discount, because he thought that was too big a commitment. And he always did the same dance with women: two or three weeks of blazing passion, then annoying, nagging questions about whether there might be someone better past the shoulder of the girl he was dancing with. Over time, we developed an almost scientific method of predicting the changes in Ofir's life: the minute he started talking enthusiastically about something or someone fantastic, we knew that he was about to leave it. Or her. We knew that the gushing words of praise were his final attempt to keep his flat feet on the ground before they sent him elsewhere.

*

My touch meditation teacher says I have natural talent! he told us proudly. Even the other people in the workshop say there's electricity in my hands, that I just touch them – and they already feel better!!

Terrific, we told him. But we had our doubts. Of the four of us, Ofir was the least anchored. His hugs were always the most evasive, his handshakes the limpest. And if you reached out to pat him on the shoulder and came too close to his face, his whole body would instinctively draw back, as if you were about to slap him. Or as if someone had already slapped him in the past.

Ofir? An alternative therapist? Amichai protested. But that's *my* dream! That's *my* World Cup wish!

Forget it, don't get worked up, he'll drop it in a day or two, Churchill pronounced. And reminded us of his '360-degree theory', according to which anyone who changes too drastically usually makes a full circle and comes back to himself. And you know something else? he added, I don't buy into all that talk about the urban man who 'doesn't connect with his body' either. What is that bullshit?

I agreed with him. But still, as if it had nothing to do with that, I went for a run on the beach promenade on Saturday morning after years of not running there. Just before Frishman Street, I saw a familiar, broad face running towards me. Run with me, Churchill said, running on the spot as he spoke. I was running on the spot too, panting pretty hard, and it frustrated me that he wasn't. Even that came easily to him. Come on, he said, looking me straight in the eye, run with me.

We'd met quite a few times over the past few months, but our eyes never had. I thought of staring back at him till he lowered his glance. I thought, those are the eyes that blinked me the right answers on the university entrance exam (one blink, question one; two blinks, answer number two). I thought, those are the eyes that enticed Ya'ara into sitting in that café with him.

Are you coming? he asked. And his tone was ingratiating and arrogant at the same time.

No, we're not going in the same direction, I said. And continued on towards Jaffa.

*

After a few weeks of touch meditation, the name Maria started popping up in Ofir's conversations with us.

They met in one of the workshops, he told us. He was treating her and she started to cry in the middle. That scared him and he apologised. Thought he'd hurt her.

56

She said, of course not, those were tears of joy. He was surprised: how can you cry with joy? She was surprised that he was surprised. What? He'd never felt so happy that he couldn't stand it any more? No, he admitted. So let's swap places, she said. He spread his long legs on the mattress and she started treating him. After a few of her touches, he felt his spirit soar. As if something that had been dammed up inside him for too long was finally breaking free. The problem was that it wasn't only his spirit that was soaring. And he was wearing a *sharwal*. A thin one. So he asked her to stop. And she was hurt. Wasn't she good enough? No, it's not that, he said, and explained to her quietly, in a whisper, what had happened. She looked in the direction of his groin and burst out laughing, and at that moment, because of her wild, free, unapologetic laughter, he fell in love with her.

It's incredible, he tried to explain to us. There's something . . . clean about her. Maybe because she's from Denmark. Maybe because it's her. I don't know. But she has this ability to be happy that I've never seen in any Israeli girl. And she's an amazing mother too. You should see her with her daughter.

Her daughter?!

Seven years old. A little genius. She calls me Ofi.

Ofi?

You know, a kind of pet name.

Ah, a pet name. What's her daughter doing there?

They're travelling together. Like two girlfriends. The father left when Maria was pregnant, and it's been just the two of them ever since.

Touching.

Very. OK, *ya'allah*, I have to hang up now. I promised the girl I'd buy her some *burfi*.

Burfi?

It's a kind of cake, made of biscuits and caramel and banana.

Yuck.

Why yuck? How do you know it's yuck?

*

OK, so it's a classic case of holiday romance, Churchill said after we'd hung up.

I have to agree with my learned colleague, Amichai said. Knowing 'Ofi' the way I do, at some point, he'll see what kind of *burfi* he's got himself into.

You got that right, Churchill said with a snigger. In our next conversation, he'll be with someone else.

That poor little girl, I said. Never mind Maria, but that little girl . . .

And I think you're wrong, all of you, Ya'ara said. You always make the same mistake.

Please, dear, tell us how we've erred, Churchill said and put his hands together in a gesture of fake pleading.

Your problem is that you all refuse to recognise the possibility that Ofir might have really changed and that something good is happening to him on this trip. You're so fixed in your ideas of him that it's funny. You know what you remind me of? A bunch of old labour party guys who meet in a café in Ahuzat Hacarmel in Haifa on Fridays, talk down to the Russian waiter and act as if they're still running the city.

There's no such place as Ahuzat Hacarmel, there's Ahuza or Central Carmel, Churchill corrected.

O-o-kay, Ya'ara said, and threw a pillow at him. Which hit me.

*

The first time Ya'ara joined our conference calls with Ofir was by accident.

Usually, whenever Churchill watched basketball with us, she would go to see her only girlfriend and he would pick her up at the end of the evening. But once, her girlfriend went out, she just forgot that Ya'ara was supposed to come, and Ya'ara called up from downstairs to say she'd been walking around the streets for two and a half hours already and asked Churchill to ask me if she could come upstairs to pee. I said OK, for humanitarian reasons. And when she came in, I acted as if I wasn't the one who'd vetoed her for the last year. I went over to her, kissed her on both cheeks, asked her to join us in the living room and pretended that her presence filled me happiness. Not pain.

Wait a minute. Why am I lying?

My creative writing tutor says that honesty is one of the most important things for a writer. Especially if the text is written in the first person. 'Take a light and illuminate the inside, the dark places. Expose the ugly things. The un-presentable ones. There's nothing more off-putting than an "I" who tries to put a nice face on things,' he warned us. And here I am, doing exactly that. Acting like a true product of the Anglo-Saxon home I grew up in, hiding the pathetic, embarrassing truth: I didn't have to pretend I was glad to see Ya'ara. Because, really, I was happy to see her, to kiss her on the cheek, to smell her hair, to hear her unwavering opinions on every issue, to listen to her shoot clever ripostes in all directions, maching-gunning words in that rapid-fire, confident speech of hers, and to know that all those niceties concealed a huge vulnerability, and that when she comes, sob-like sounds emerge from deep in her throat, as if her orgasm makes her sad, and afterwards, something completely unravels inside her and she loves to curl up next to you like a little girl, fold her legs against your stomach, rest her head on your chest –

To know all that and to speak to her quietly, while the others are focused on the game, to ask her how she is, to hear again that she 'just needs to get ninety-one thousand dollars together' and then she'll 'finally go to London to study theatre direction'. To wonder again why ninety-one thousand and not ninety. And why she has to be in London. Not to say anything to her about that, of course. And not to say that I noticed the new burn on her thumb and

I know that means she's gone back to holding lit matches a second too long. But to say that I was sure she'd be a great director. To see her raise suspicious eyes above her glasses: you do? Really? You really think so?! To say yes, I think so. To tell her how my delightful father is, to lie about how I am, to see her forehead listening, to see her soft, left earlobe shining through her hair, to feel some- thing, to feel something real after all the dull dates I've had since she left –

But that isn't the whole truth either. I still have to do some peeling. With a knife. And talk about the humili- ation. And the pleasure in humiliation. About the moments that followed it, when Ya'ara's presence at our get-togethers became permanent. And Churchill, assuming that it didn't bother me any more, allowed himself to touch her. And my eyes would follow his hand as it stroked her knee. Or her thigh. And I'd be filled with a sweet, fucked-up feeling.

You know you don't have to take it, Ilana once said to me quietly, at the door, and touched my arm suddenly. I was surprised at her concern and played dumb, take what? And she said, I'm sure that if you ask Churchill, he'll control himself. And I bit my lip and kept quiet because how could I explain to her that it was like watching a sick, exploitive reality show on TV, and even though you know that it's sick and exploitive, you can't help watching.

And I can still keep peeling.

Digging to get to the core.

And in the core, I nurtured a shameful hope. That the whole Ya'ara and Churchill thing was temporary. That the small cracks I saw at those evenings – like her tendency to bicker with him about everything, or his tendency to blatantly check out every woman who appeared on the screen – would widen, they had to widen, into the Afro- Syrian fault, and one day she'd knock on my door, wearing the blue skirt she knows I like, or her light-coloured jeans (I had a few scenarios like that in my head and I'd reconstruct them and fix them up and add details), and I'd open the door and she'd bury her small, cold nose in my neck and say: I made a mistake. I picked the wrong friend. Can I still change my mind?

Ofir, in any case, didn't change his mind.

Contrary to our predictions, he was still talking about Maria in our next conversation, and in the one after that, and when we demanded it, he put her on the phone and her voice sounded pure and happy, just as we could have expected from his descriptions, but we explained to him that a charming voice isn't enough and he should bring her here so we could give our final approval. He laughed and said that he wanted to, he wanted to very much, but it was a problem because of the girl, and he was thinking now that he'd go back to Copenhagen with them. And try living with them there.

What? Churchill blurted out. You're sure that's a good idea? Two months ago, you didn't even know each other.

And I asked: tell me, 'Ofi', when we wrote down our World Cup wishes, didn't you have a dream about writing a book of short stories? What language will you publish it in there? Ancient Danish?

That's just the problem with the Western way of life, Ofir explained in a calm voice. We set goals for ourselves and then we become slaves to those goals. And we try so hard to achieve them that we don't notice that, in the meantime, they've changed.

Nice, Ya'ara said.

The Indians, he went on, have an expression they use all the time: *sab kuch milega*, which means 'everything is possible'. At first, it drove me crazy. Then I realised that that's life here. You get up in the morning and there's a terrible monsoon, and all of a sudden the monsoon stops and in seconds, the sky is blue without a single cloud. You get on a bus in the yellowest desert ever, and six hours later, you're in the greenest valley ever. Not to mention that the bus never leaves on time. And when you ask someone at the station when it's supposed to come, he'll answer, 'After some time', and he isn't lying. Because the whole thing about time works completely differently here.

Differently? How?

Isn't it true that in Israel it's really hard to catch flies? So here, the flies move so slowly that there's no problem catching them. And if there's a small accident here between two cars, or between a car and a rickshaw, no one gets road rage. They just keep driving. And there are always these weird meetings that you feel a second before they happen. Let's say, yesterday morning I suddenly remembered the secretary who was with my father the day he had the attack, and I thought, I wonder what's happening with her, and half an hour later, her daughter shows up in the guest house where I'm staying. And when stuff like that happens, you realise that instead of trying to force yourself on reality, it's better to accept what life dishes out and be open to its natural flow. Because, anyway . . . *sab kuch milega*.

Nice, Ya'ara said again.

What's so nice?! Churchill said, getting angry. Leaving your friends like this is nice? A year ago you said we were like family to you, and now you tell us in that flow of yours that you're leaving Israel?

I'm not leaving Israel. But I have to admit that I don't really miss Israel. Or Israelis.

And I have to remind you that we're Israelis, Churchill said.

Well, I miss you.

So what's your problem? I don't understand.

Forget it, it's complicated. It's not for the phone.

But the phone is all we have right now.

It's just . . . I've had a lot of time this year . . . a lot of time to think. And I've come to the conclusion that nothing happens by chance. You know why I had that breakdown that day in the office? Because I looked down into the abyss.

What abyss?

Every creative person walks on a very narrow bridge over a river of fear – fear that one day, it won't come any more.

What won't come?

The ideas, the inventions – one day, all your creative juices will dry up. And the only thing left will be a cold stone that has no copper or gold under it. And the thing of it is that you can't let yourself think about that day. You can't look into the abyss.

So why did you?

Because . . . Wow, just thinking about it depresses me. I can't believe I'm standing here across from the Himalayas talking about this –

Come on, spit it out.

That day in the office, I was supposed to fire one of my team – an unattractive woman – because one of our big clients told the boss that he didn't like having to look at her every time he came to the office. And a minute after she walked out of my office in tears, I was arguing with the production manager and yelling at him like an animal to lower his price, or else I'd make it my personal mission to see that he never worked in the business again. And then I was supposed to go into a meeting and come up with a brilliant idea for a campaign for our biggest client. And all of a sudden, I couldn't. I was terrified that this was it. It was all over. My well was dry. So I locked myself in the toilet to think quietly, to concentrate, perhaps an idea might still come to me, but I heard my heart pounding in my temples and I heard my heart pounding in my temples and my forehead and I heard my heart pounding in my temples and my forehead and my eyes and my neck and I heard them paging me, again and again and again, till at some point . . . at some point, I stopped hearing.

You never told us that.

I didn't tell you because I . . . I didn't understand the big picture.

And what . . . what's the big picture?

I fell apart because I'd reached the end of my tether. And I reached the end of my tether because they sucked everything out of me. And they sucked everything out of me because I was part of an aggressive system that uses words only to sell. And that system . . . it doesn't work alone, you see? It's part of a whole society . . . that's pure aggression. It starts from the occupation, from the fact that we rule another people, and it goes on to . . . the smallest things, like how we drive. Or how we queue.

And there are no things like that in Copenhagen? Or other annoying things?

Pata-nahi.

Pata-what?

Pata-nahi. Maybe yes and maybe no. How can I know what's in Copenhagen if I've never been there?

*

I'm telling you guys, it's that Maria, Churchill said after we'd hung up. 'Aggressive system'? 'It all starts with the occupation'? Since when does 'Ofi' talk like that? She's brainwashed him. She's probably one of those bleeding-heart Europeans who switched from being anti-Semitic to being anti-Israel.

But what he said is pretty accurate, Ya'ara said. Quietly.

Of course it is, Churchill said angrily. But the solution is not to run away. It's to stay here with his friends and fight. To be involved. To influence, to do things that have meaning.

That's your solution, Ya'ara continued to put herself in danger of getting a pillow in her face. You can't impose your solution on other people.

We fell silent. The commentator on the field was interviewing a Maccabi player who was trying to find a reason why the team lost. Ilana's fingers were still typing her doctoral dissertation in the den. One of the twins began crying in his sleep. Amichai got up to settle him and I thought, there's always been something about Ofir that projected: I'm here temporarily, I'm a freelancer. And there was that propensity of his for small, totally unnecessary exaggerations. Like when he told us that the salary he was getting at the ad agency was net, when it was actually gross. And when he didn't feel like going out, he'd say he had a high fever and ask us to come over to his. And once, we saw a really gorgeous girl walk across the square in front of the cinema, and he claimed he'd gone out with her, and later, Amichai met her when he went to sell her father a subscription to Telemed and it turned out that she'd never heard of Ofir. And after years of more and more of that needless, ridiculous shtick, I felt I couldn't completely trust him (or, as Churchill put it once: there are people you trust enough to shoot odds and evens with over the phone. Ofir Zlotochinski wasn't one of them).

But I did admit to myself that life without Ofir Zlotochinski would definitely be a lot more boring: without that regular Saturday night phone call when we tried to guess the headlines in the Sunday sports section. Without those phone calls that burst into the middle of our days, hey Bro, turn on the radio, there's a new song by . . . Without those group outings to see bands whose names – 'Circus Video Art', or 'Sunrise Jam at the Heriya Garbage Dump' – were enough for us to know they'd be rubbish. Without those weird moments like the time he talked me into going with him to sketch nude models even though neither of us knew how to draw, or the time he asked me to sit at a table next to him and his date in a café and pretend I was reading a newspaper, then tell him later what I thought, because that was already their fifth date and he couldn't make up his mind.

It won't be the same without Ofir, I thought. But on the other hand, we'd been without him for almost a year. And there's always something in us that adjusts.

*

I have an idea, Amichai said when he came back from the twins' room. Let's take out a personal ad titled, 'Friend Wanted'. Under that, it'll say: 'Three childhood friends seeking a replacement for the fourth guy who went to live abroad.'

'A Haifa past – essential. Love of football – an advantage', Churchill said with a laugh.

Terrific! Ya'ara said enthusiastically. I'll help you audition the candidates.

We'll ask them to sing 'Shimon My Man', Amichai suggested. First a solo, then together with us.

We'll check his family background, I said, faking enthusiasm. The more sisters, the better.

Ya'ara gave me a long look. I thought perhaps she was disappointed to see that there were women besides her I might be interested in.

What you guys really need, she said, is a friend with technical skills. You all have two left hands. You know what Mr Churchill, our senior attorney here, does when the sink drain is blocked?

What?

He calls me.

A mechanic, Churchill said, agreeing. We need a friend who's a mechanic. That would really set us up.

'A Haifa past – essential. Love of football – an advantage. Preference to mechanics', Amichai summed up and said that in his opinion, a small ad shouldn't cost a lot, and if we split it, it'd come to less than a hundred shekels each. And if it turned out to cost more, we could always advertise on the web, that's free.

Go for it, we told him. And perhaps we really would have taken out an ad, just because laughing about it made us feel better, if a week later, Ya'ara and Churchill hadn't made the surprise announcement that they were getting married, and two weeks before the wedding, Ofir hadn't made the equally surprising announcement that he, Maria and the girl were coming for the event.

3

There's this dreadful custom of giving close friends pictures taken during the wedding and writing something warm and personal on the back. Ya'ara and Churchill were considerate enough not to do that in my case. So the only picture I have of that occasion was taken secretly by Maria's daughter, and Ofir gave it to me, in a sealed envelope, two weeks later. I look fine in it, that's what's so weird. I have eyes and a nose and ears and skin and a shirt and buttons. And you could never guess what was going on inside. I've looked at that picture dozens of times, trying to find a sign. Lowered eyelashes. A double chin. The slightest paleness. And nothing. I'm standing with a tall cocktail glass in my hand, smiling broadly at the camera. Wishing them well.

*

The 'alternative area' at the wedding included two treatment beds, and was located in an excellent spot: between the buffet table and the artificial lake. Ofir, wearing loose white clothes, stood at one of the beds. Maria stood at the other, a big woman with a big smile and a big necklace of big beads on her chest. Her daughter stood at the entrance pouring strong, hot *chai* from a clay pitcher for everyone in the queue.

I queued like everyone else. I could have signalled to Ofir to let me go ahead of the others, but that's not how I was brought up.

When it was my turn, Ofir pointed to his bed (I breathed a sigh of relief. I kept picturing what happened the first time Maria treated him. And I was afraid that if she treated me, the same thing would happen).

Lie on your stomach, Yuval-ji, he said. And take d-e-e-p, l-o-o-ng breaths.

You do remember that I have asthma? I asked, alarmed. This treatment is OK for people with asthma?

It's not a treatment, he said, laying both hands gently on my back. It's just a light massage to release tension. Looks to me like you could do with some tension release, am I right?

Yes.

*

That wedding hit me like a supersonic boom on a clear day. Usually, such things follow a certain order of events: you get to know each other. You go to parents' houses for Friday night dinner. You spend a weekend in a cabin in the Galilee. You move in together. Raise a dog. Or a calico cat. You think seriously about splitting up. You drive the whole world mad with feigned indecision. And only then do you start making the rounds of wedding venues and caterers and fighting about the guest list.

And here – it all happened too fast. The Maccabi game ended, Ofir called, and at the beginning of the conversation, Churchill mentioned that he had something important to say, and that he was really glad Ofir had called because now he could hear the news at the same time, or at least with a delay of a second and a half, and –

So?!! we all groaned in expectation. We were sure he was going to tell us that he'd been appointed district attorney. Or that he'd shot straight up to supreme court judge.

Then he took Ya'ara's hand. And entwined his thick fingers with her delicate ones.

And even before he spoke, an air pocket had already formed in my chest.

*

After they left, I questioned Amichai and he swore by the twins that he hadn't known anything, and, from where she was sitting in the den, Ilana the Weeper said that they don't even sound happy about the announcement, and that Churchill was too childish to get married, and it could only be that she's pregnant and doesn't want an abortion, and if that's the story, then it's very stupid of her, though not surprising, considering her personality construct, which contains an element of self-destruction.

It wasn't until the stag night, which took place a couple of nights before the wedding, that we found out what had really happened.

Churchill didn't want us to organise a proper party. He said it wouldn't be the same without Ofir. Anyway, he reminded us, the last stag night we had did not end well.

That party had been for Amichai, and was in a dimly lit club in a dimly lit industrial area. From the outset, we weren't too happy about the idea, but Amichai said that his friends at work had been there and had enjoyed it. We sat at the table reserved for us near the stage, just the four of us. We were surrounded by table after table of serried ranks, clapping enthusiastically. An ultra-Orthodox guy was standing at the back of the hall, masturbating, swaying back and forth like a *lulav* in the wind. We'd ordered a lot of alcohol and were trying hard to be happy for Amichai, but the music was terrible and there was something depressing about the whole thing. Especially the dancers. Their eyes were empty, their movements predictable, and the most embarrassing moment of all was when they sat on our laps and started listing their prices in business-like voices: fifty shekels to stroke their arse. One hundred for touching their breasts. Two hundred for going into the back room. We didn't touch and we didn't pay, so they went off to another, more profitable table. And after a quick exchange of glances, we asked for the bill, paid and got up to leave. To escape. But two bouncers blocking the exit asked us where we were going. Churchill, speaking for all of us, said it had been a great evening, thanks, but we were leaving. They said we didn't give any money to the dancers. Churchill said we didn't give anything because we didn't want anything. And that's our right. They moved a little closer to him and said that no one goes out of the club without leaving money for the dancers. They didn't seem angry, and that's what made the situation ominous. I remember my fists clenching in my jacket pockets and I was horrified to realise that, even though I wanted to get out of there in one piece, I wanted a fight with those guys just as much. I hadn't felt that little thug since the Intifada, when I first discovered he was hiding inside me (and perhaps inside every man?), but I don't want to talk about what happened then, during the Intifada. This time, Churchill conducted negotiations that led to a quiet agreement: we'd leave three hundred shekels with the bouncers and they'd let us out of there. It was either that, or a brawl, he explained afterwards in the street. And it's not that I'm scared, but when fists start flying, you can never know how it's going to end. The police could come and charge us all, and if they charge me, that's the end of my job in the prosecutor's office.

Right, we all nodded in agreement. And swore never to have any more stag dos, and we wouldn't have had one for Churchill if Ofir hadn't called to say he was coming home. Maria insists, he said. She says it's my best friend's wedding and that's something I shouldn't miss. Anyway, she's dying to get to know all of you. And Israel. She says that even if we decide to live in Denmark, she wants to see up close where I was born. Where I grew up and what the conditions are in the Palestinian refugee camps.

Terrific! we said happily. And Amichai said they could

71

stay at his place while they were in the country. He assumed they'd understand that he was just being polite, but a couple of weeks before the wedding, they just knocked at his door.

Ilana the Weeper hid her shock as she looked at the three people standing at the door, hoping to stall for time till Amichai came out of the bathroom and she'd have to ask them in. She managed to see that they had too few suitcases, that the girl looked like the little angels in church paintings, and that Ofir, taller and more handsome than ever, his light-coloured eyes smiling out of the tangle of his curls, was leaning gently on the child's mother as if he were having a hard time standing.

A rickshaw drove over my foot, he explained before Ilana asked. On our last day in Delhi, three hours before the flight.

How terrible, Ilana said, still holding the door, blocking the way in.

Sab kuch milega, he said, embarrassed. And she didn't understand why he was speaking Hungarian to her.

Bro-o-o-o!!! Amichai came running out of the bathroom and threw his arms around Ofir in an enormous bear hug. You're here! I don't believe it! It's so great that you're here!

When the hugging and back-slapping and teasing and rejoicing were over, Ofir walked into the house and spread his arms to hug Ilana too. She hugged him and his girl-friend, who for some reason also insisted on hugging her, and after she helped them unpack, she pushed Amichai into the twins' room, closed the door behind them and said: one night, that's all. And that's only because it's not nice to throw a limping person out on the street. I've put up with your friends and their nonsense for ten years, but this time you really went too far.

One night, Amichai agreed submissively.

In the end, they stayed for two weeks.

*

The first evening, when Ilana the Weeper sat far away from everyone – a hardback English book entitled *Depression as a Predictor of Anxious Thoughts* separating her from us – we ignored it because we were used to it. But Maria thought it was a bit strange that someone who was sitting in the living room with us was never included in our conversation, so she went over and sat down beside her, tried to get her to talk a bit about the book, then told her that as a teenager, she had suffered from permanent winter depression because in the winter months there are very few hours of daylight in Denmark. She was strongly affected by it, especially as a teenager, and in fact, why was she saying 'as a teenager'? Until she went to India, those symptoms would recur with varying degrees of intensity every year. Every winter, she would seriously consider suicide, she said with a light-filled smile, and Ilana the Weeper put her hand on Maria's arm and said with glistening eyes, that must have been so hard, and Maria didn't move her hand away as she said, yes, when you're teenager, you can bear those thoughts, everyone around you is flirting with death, but as a mother, it's more complicated. You have responsibilities. Yes, Ilana the Weeper nodded, I know exactly what you're talking about. And at that moment, while we were arguing about what songs the DJ should play at the wedding, the spark that turns people into friends was suddenly ignited between them.

Maria's daughter also turned out to be a treasure. It seemed that, for years, she had longed for a younger brother or sister. And now the rare opportunity to have two brothers at the same time had come her way. She and the twins became a threesome. They both fell in love with her, of course, and vied for her attention with the eagerness of six-year-olds, and she was always kind to them, first to one, then to the other, making sure each was left with a bit of hope, so he could keep idolising her.

The mothers, finding themselves suddenly free of the need to occupy their children, spent the time excitedly discovering each other. Maria taught Ilana the Weeper

73

the secrets of vegetarian cooking, and they spent hours in the kitchen concocting wonderful dishes based on tofu and red lentils. Ilana the Weeper took Maria on a personal tour of the university and introduced her to the most up-to-date research methods in her field. Maria persuaded Ilana the Weeper to come to the beach with the children (Amichai couldn't believe it was happening. He'd been begging her for years and she'd absolutely refused, arguing that the sea was too polluted), and they came back happy and covered in tar. Ilana persuaded Maria to come to the meeting of a support group of teenagers suffering from depression and to tell them about her own personal experience. Then she took her to a Women Go All the Way event. And then to a meeting of Women Against the Occupation.

Don't you feel a bit superfluous? Ofir asked Amichai during one of their joint dinners around the extended dining table, after Ilana the Weeper had tossed Maria another complicated English sentence full of professional jargon they apparently both understood. We've been feeling a bit superfluous here lately, Amichai said to his wife, his lips set in complaint.

That's because you really are superfluous! Ilana the Weeper said and roared with rolling laughter. Maria's laughter.

Amichai looked at her in amazement and thought, really, laughing suits her. And he also thought: incredible. I've been trying for years to make her happy, with no success, and this Maria suddenly lands in our house, and without the slightest effort, brings out this joy in her.

Maybe you should do something with yourselves, Ilana the Weeper said, a hint of a smile still hanging on the corners of her mouth. Your friend is getting married in two days. Perhaps you should take him out to celebrate? Just the boys, I mean.

Great idea, Amichai said. And the two of them called

me, and we went together to pick up Churchill, who said he'd come only on the condition that there'd be no strippers or dancers, and that we didn't let him drink too much because he's getting married the day after tomorrow and doesn't want to get in trouble. We promised to take care of him, even though it was clear to us, even as we promised, that if he wanted to drink, it would be very hard to stop him. He has a strong will that's very easy to bend to, and in fact, when Ofir tried to say something after the third drink, Churchill gave him a look that drained us all of the desire to argue with him. And he went on to the fourth drink. And the fifth.

With the sixth drink, his secret came out.

It seems that even after he and Ya'ara became lovers, he'd secretly continued to see Sharona, the law clerk he'd occasionally slept with over the last few years. I don't even know why, he said and looked deeply into our eyes, one by one, as if we were a jury and he wanted to convince us to acquit him. It's not because of the sex. Absolutely not. The sex with Sharona is a total nothing compared to what I have with Ya'ara. I don't know, maybe I got scared. You all understand, he said, his eyes lingering on me, that sometimes, when I'm with Ya'ara, I can't believe there's someone like her in the world. And that I'm the one she chose. So maybe I wanted to leave myself an escape hatch, in case she changed her mind. Or maybe I'm just fucked up, like my father.

We didn't know what to say. In all the years we'd been friends, we'd never seen Churchill confused.

In any case, he went on, Ya'ara found out. She was sitting in a café eavesdropping on a conversation two girls were having at the table next to her. It was just my luck that those girls were Sharona and her best friend. And that was the day Sharona had decided she couldn't hold back any more and had to tell someone about our Sunday Culture Club, as she and I called it.

Oy, Amichai blurted out.

It's a small country, Churchill said with a nod. When I got home from work, there was a message from Ya'ara: come over, we have to talk about Sharona. She didn't sound upset on the answering machine. Just the opposite. She sounded like she'd already come to a decision. I went over to hers, and on the way, I decided to go for a plea bargain. I confessed to all the charges against me and asked for leniency. I told her it was a vestige of the old Churchill. That since I met her, I'm a different person. A better person. And Sharona – Sharona is just a vestige I've been dragging along with me. She said she couldn't care less, vestige or no vestige, after the guitarist who'd played with her heart for five years, she'd sworn that she'd never let another man treat her like that. No matter how much she loved him. So she was asking me to go.

That's when you proposed? Ofir asked and scratched his forehead. The whole story seemed to astound him. As if in his new world of purified energy there was no room for that kind of deception.

No, of course not, Churchill said. You should have seen her when she opened the door. There was absolutely nothing to say. And when I showed up at her flat the next day without calling first, with a ring, and got down on my knees, she said, are you kidding? and turned her back on me.

Very good, I blurted out.

Amichai gave me an angry look.

If she had said yes right away, it would have been less interesting, I tried to explain. I felt as if I were sticking my foot deeper into my mouth.

Wait a minute, so how did you finally convince her? Ofir asked quickly, to get me out of the sticky situation.

You'll be surprised, Churchill said, pouring himself another drink. It has to do with you.

Me? Ofir said, drawing back. The story was astounding him more and more.

Yes, Churchill said. She argued that if it was my nature to cheat, a wedding wouldn't change me. So I said, people can change completely. Just look at Ofir. Who would've thought a year ago that he'd be wearing loose, white clothes and that he'd be so calm.

Amichai and I looked at each other. As far as I remembered, of all of us, Churchill was the most sceptical about the changes in Ofir.

Are you telling me that's what convinced her? Amichai said doubtfully.

No, Churchill said. But that was when I saw that look in her eyes for the first time, the look that says a person is ready to be convinced. Then came a week of crying and begging. And small gifts. Till she finally agreed, on two conditions: the first, that we have a reform ceremony performed by a woman rabbi. And second, that I don't say a single word to my friends about the circumstances that led to the wedding. I want them to think you're so in love with me that you just couldn't wait. That's what she said. And I kissed her on the lips and said that was the truth.

So why are you telling us? Why are you breaking your promise?

It's your fault, Churchill accused us. I didn't want a stag do. I knew this would happen if I drank. But you insisted.

We were silent. Amichai and Ofir looked down. I didn't.

So that's it, now I'm in your hands, he said and looked at me. His eyes already had that alcohol glaze. If you want, you'll keep this conversation to yourselves. If you want, you'll tell me – I mean her.

Why should we tell? Amichai quickly reassured him. We're your friends.

It would be stupid to tell her, Ofir said. It's against the direction of love.

I didn't say anything. I thought about the raven in Ovid's *Metamorphoses*, which was given its black colour after it informed on one of the gods.

The three of them looked at me expectantly. As if the bill had already come and they'd all put cash on the table and I still had to add my share before we could give the little plate with the money to the waiter.

Do you love her at all? I asked.

Of course, Churchill said, taken aback. What do you mean? What kind of question is that?

Because the way you tell the story, I persisted, it sounds like you're talking about one of your cases. It sounds like the whole point here was to win.

Churchill looked at me sadly. It's because I talk like that, he said. Everything with me always sounds calculated. But you're my friends, you all should know that . . . I mean . . . you especially . . . his eyes on me.

He poured himself another beer. His hand shook and a few drops fell onto the table.

I'm lost without her, he said, and a tear glistened in the corner of his eye. I'm completely lost without her.

Amichai and Ofir looked at him in alarm, unable to accept the new Churchill.

I couldn't tell if something had really cracked in him or whether this was just another prosecutorial trick meant to guarantee that we'd keep his secret. But still, the 'you especially' managed to touch me. So I made a zipped-up gesture across my lips and said, it's OK, Churchill, you have nothing to worry about from me.

*

On the other hand, I politely refused the offer to be one of the four people to hold up the poles of their wedding canopy. There's a limit, right? I stood at a slight distance, a bit cut off, while the woman rabbi performed the ceremony, and I thought, what a shame that Ya'ara is wearing contacts, because she looks better in glasses. But even so, she's breathtaking. Outward beauty isn't the thing with her. It's those contradictions between innocence and keen intelligence, between assertiveness and gentleness, between playfulness and seriousness. That's what makes her so Ya'ara. And I thought, I'm the only guy at the wedding, except for the groom, who's slept with the bride. And I thought, that's no consolation. It's pathetic that two years later, I'm still in love with her. It was a mistake to come. An unavoidable mistake. And I thought, that rabbi thinks she has a sense of humour, but she doesn't. And I thought that the congratulatory message from all of us that Ofir read aloud was written beautifully, and that it was a shame that those years in advertising had left him fed up with words.

I thought and moved around and thought and moved around, my face expressionless, from the table where I was sitting with the guys to the table with the 'we-don't-know-where-to-put-them-so-we-sat-them-with-other-people-we-didn't-know-where-to-put' guests, where my parents were sitting.

Churchill had also invited Amichai's mother and Ofir's mother, but my parents were the only ones who showed up because 'if you're invited – it's impolite not to go'. As usual, my mother charmed everyone with her glowing optimism, preparing the ground for my father's questions about the occupations of the others at the table – questions meant to provide him with the natural opportunity to hand out the family printing house's business card. They both tutted in perfect synchronisation about the increased security (what a sad state of affairs if we have to be afraid at weddings!), and both watched me the entire time: my mother with an expression of blind admiration, and my father with a look of disappointment bordering on despair.

It's always been like that. When I brought home my school reports, she was always thrilled with my marks in literature and history and he would resign himself to the ones I got in physics and maths. She thought it was mag-ni-fi-cent when I decided to study liberal arts in Tel Aviv, and he didn't understand why liberal arts, for crying out loud, what are you going to do with it? How will you make a living? What's going to become of you?

'What's going to become of you' was the regular question he asked me from the living room armchair as he cut a pear or an apple into small, precise slices – but at the wedding, I thought I saw a new, more burning question in his eyes: how could I have lost him Ya'ara?

From the minute she set foot, in her bouncy walk, into our house in Haifa, he was captivated by her. Two hours later, at the dining room table, the unbelievable happened, and for the first time in his life, he told a joke. She laughed at his joke. She rolled with laughter. And he blushed. I'd never before seen him turn red with anything but anger.

Then he asked her if she were cold. Perhaps she wanted him to turn on the heating? Or get her a blanket? Or perhaps one of Marilyn's sweaters?

I'm fine, it's very pleasant here, she said with a laugh, but now I know where your son got his gentlemanliness from.

Later they became engrossed in a conversation on how wonderful British theatre was and how Israeli theatre couldn't hold a candle to it (my father worked as a stage hand in the West End? Exactly when was that? How hadn't I known that till now?), and when they broke into a duet from an Andrew Lloyd Webber musical, my mother and I decided we'd had enough and stood up to take the dishes into the kitchen.

What was that supposed to be?! I asked her.

You know how your father always wanted a daughter, she said, supplying the convenient, pleasing explanation, as usual.

Yes, I know, I said, and thought: perhaps a daughter really would have freed that man of all his tightness and restraint, and I – I would have enjoyed the leftovers.

(Once, on the way home from grade school, I was caught in the Haifa rain, which falls more densely and in bigger drops than the rain in Tel Aviv. I didn't have an umbrella, and by the time I got home, my clothes were stuck to my skin like a diver's suit. It was a Tuesday, the day the whole city closes up at noon, and he was home. When I opened the door, his face broke into an oh-my-God expression, but his mouth said only, it's a bit rainy today, isn't it? Then he sat me down in front of the big kerosene heater that broke down at the beginning of every winter, peeled off my layers of clothes carefully, without hurting me, and wiped my whole body with the thick green towel he fetched from the bathroom. His movements were long and measured, and his large hands were gentle. Not a single wet spot was left on my body when he was finished, and yet, even though I was already burning from being so close to the heater, he insisted on wrapping another large towel around me, so that, God forbid, I wouldn't catch pneumonia or anything like that.

For weeks afterwards, I'd deliberately forget my umbrella on Tuesdays, in the hope that it would rain.)

*

Come here, he dug his nails into my arm during one of my stops at their table, let me introduce you to Yanke'le Richter.

A guy my age, wearing a suit and tie, shook my hand so hard that it hurt.

Yanke'le works in hi-tech industries, my father explained. He tells me they have a special programme for people who want to change career, like you.

Like me?

You know, the ones who studied lying on the grass, my father said, winking at Yanke'le Richter, and went on, I told him that you'd probably want to hear details about this programme.

What I wanted was to get away from there. Very much. Or, alternatively, to jump into the artificial lake and turn into something else, like in *Metamorphoses*: a swan, a water lily, a man with a purpose. And perhaps I would have gathered enough despair to jump into the lake if it hadn't been for Ofir's touch meditation.

There really was electricity in his hands.

All he did was put his palms on my shoulders. OK, he might have moved them a bit. And touched the back of my neck at some point. But no more than that. In any case, when I stood up from the treatment table, I felt the bitterness that had been weighing down on me all evening disintegrate, my body became light and an oceanic love of the world rose up in me.

Man, I said and hugged Ofir, you have to open a clinic. You're really good at this.

Really? he said, smiling. You have no idea how important it is to me to hear that from you. I mean, hearing it from strangers is not the same as hearing it from friends.

Your boyfriend is phenomenal! I said to Maria, to underline what I'd said.

I know he is, she said and looked at Ofir with moist eyes (perhaps it was the treatment that influenced my perception of reality, but for a minute, it seemed as if their love had a material presence, that I could actually see it floating in the air between them).

I'm happy for you, Bro, I said after a short silence.

I know, he said.

And we didn't have to say any more. Because it was clear to both of us that beneath that happiness were sad, past moments in Ofir's life that we had been through together. The nervous breakdown, his father's death. But it was actually those moments that gave the happiness its validity.

Will the two of you come to dance later? I asked.

Of course, he said.

And after a few songs, he and Maria and the girl joined us and we all danced together in a non-circular circle, winding around each other in figures of eight, touching lightly, cheering, sweating love, drinking as we moved, dripping onto our shirts, hoisting Churchill and Ya'ara onto our shoulders and letting them join together in a kiss, doing a perfect imitation of Amichai's famous, one-and-only dance move – patting his stomach with his hand – screeching with dry throats, 'Shimon My Man' and the 'Yehudim' song, 'If you go, take me with you, listen, it's me', which Ya'ara had requested, and a series of Bruce Springsteen songs that Churchill had asked for, which drew a few representatives of our parents' generation onto the floor, but they took off as fast as they could the minute the trance started. I'm not usually too crazy about that kind of music, but that night, when Ya'ara kicked off her high heels and began dancing in front of me, occasionally whipping me with her hair, I couldn't help being carried away into it, feeling the heartbeats of the music competing with my own heartbeats, closing my eyes, not to think, to forget where I was, for a few minutes to be only rhythm, rhythm, rhythm, rhythm –

When I opened my eyes, Ilana the Weeper was dancing in front of me. For a moment, I wasn't sure whether I was hallucinating or not. Most of the time when we went out dancing, she didn't come along, and if by chance she found herself at a party, she would sit self-consciously on the side till Amichai took pity on her and left us, with an apologetic look, to take her home.

At the wedding, she didn't dance at first either. She sat alone at the friends' table, picking up cheesecake crumbs with the pads of her fingers. And thought how much she hated that music. And thought she wanted to go home. To her children, to her research. And thought: why did Amichai insist on coming with one car? She sat alone at the friends' table and no one went over to her because we were all used to the way she was at parties. But Maria wasn't used to it. She went and sat down beside her, close. And asked her about the people who were sitting at the table next to them. And Ilana the Weeper told her all the relevant gossip down to the smallest detail. Her tone was still bitter as she spoke, but her posture was a bit less droopy. Then Maria said, I'm a bit shy about dancing on my own out there with the guys, will you come with me? And Ilana the Weeper said, no, I don't think so. And Maria put her hand gently on Ilana's arm and said, maybe just this once, for me?

*

It's funny how certain images remain burned in your mind.

A few months later, in Haifa, when all of Ilana's university colleagues would talk about how serious and earnest she was, and her students would talk about how she was always ready to help, even after her office hours, and her mother would say, even as a child, she was responsible, sometimes I thought she was a little too responsible –

All I would think about was that moment, at the wedding, when I opened my eyes and saw Ilana the Weeper in front of me, jumping around with charmingly clumsy movements, a smile on her freckled face, her shoulder straps fallen onto her arms, and her always perfectly straight bob swinging wildly.

From the Introduction to 'Metamorphoses: Great Minds who Changed their Mind', an unfinished philosophy thesis by Yuval Freed

If we accept the hypothesis that one of the characteristics of the world of concrete experience is its endless changeability (outside my window, the leaves are moving. The sun, which was in the middle of the sky at noon, is now nearing the horizon. A cool wind blows suddenly through the window) and if we accept – and we have no choice but to accept – the fact that our minds never rest for a moment, it too is a constant dance (as I write the Introduction to my thesis, a thought about my favourite football team's upcoming match flashes through my mind), then one way to understand the nature of existence and the universe would be to try to identify the pattern of the variability, to formulate a kind of 'movement report' of life and consciousness. Therefore –

This paper will not deal with the well-known coherent theories of several philosophers, but will focus particularly on their moments of confusion, of intellectual and emotional embarrassment. Not only because there is something human and touching about them, but also to explore the possibility that there – in the faltering, in the regret after the fact, in the lack of knowledge that led to a change – the key to understanding the true nature of thought may lie.

(And again, forgive me, a thought about my favourite team's game sneaks into my mind, this time as a metaphor: anyone who wants to understand the magic of football will not succeed by simply asking about the team's line-up. Or the results. Because the true nature is found, not in the results, but in the moments between the goals. In the movement of the ball from foot to foot to head. And especially in those moments when suddenly, for no apparent reason, the game shifts direction.)

4

There are almost no pictures of Ilana the Weeper in the album. She had some sort of complex about not being photogenic.

Still –

Sometimes I look at a picture and know, I just know, that she took it.

There's the series she took of us watching the match Israel lost to Cyprus in the '98 World Cup qualifiers. It's a series of three photographs: in the first, we're tense and expectant, in the second we're leaping up after an atrocious miss, and in the third, we're gutted after the Israeli team's deciding match ended in another loss. What's nice about that third picture is that she managed to capture perfectly, intimately, the terrible emptiness that drags a fan's body down when his team loses. Ofir is sprawled on the couch, wiped out. Hugging a cushion. Churchill is massaging his temples. Amichai is listening to the post-game commentary, trying to find consolation. I'm smiling a bitter little smile.

And based on the number of times Amichai appears in them, it was Ilana the Weeper who took the pictures at Churchill's swearing-in ceremony in Jerusalem after he passed his bar exams. Here's Amichai when Churchill's name is called. Here's Amichai handing Churchill his robe. Here's Amichai with the sunset in the background. And the

Valley of the Cross in the background. And in every picture, he's photographed at angles that don't show the blotch on his neck. And in every picture, he looks a bit better than he does in real life.

Couples are misleading. You think you know a couple well, but you have no idea what goes on between them after the guests leave. Ilana the Weeper never showed her love for Amichai when we were around. I remember the first time we met her. It was after we'd been hearing about her for a few weeks. He said he'd met the love of his life. A fantastic girl. Gorgeous. Brilliant. Exciting. Someone he'd marry tomorrow if she said yes. We were twenty-one, and weddings were something theoretical that happened to older brothers and sisters and cousins. But even so, we couldn't remain indifferent in the face of all that excitement. I remember that I even had a haircut before we went to meet her. Churchill wore his date shirt. And Ofir came on time (till he met Maria and became 'Ofi', he always arrived everywhere late).

I'd like you to meet my future wife, Amichai proudly introduced the skinny girl who came into the room, and we shook her hand, one after the other. Her handshake was limp, evasive. And she had a glum look, as if we'd already managed to disappoint her somehow. Her face wasn't ugly, but it was very pale and very freckled and surrounded by thin, stiff-looking hair. Her posture was stooped and mousey, and she was wearing beige, high-waisted, old-lady trousers.

Well, she probably has a great personality, we thought. But she answered all our interested questions with a vague mumble. And she didn't ask us anything or laugh at our jokes. She wasn't properly impressed by Ofir's cleverness and Churchill's pronouncements. And she went to the bathroom in the middle of the evening. And didn't come back for a long time. A very long time.

Isn't she incredible? Amichai asked us after she'd gone (all of a sudden, she had to go home urgently).

Churchill didn't say anything. Even a white lie is a lie,

he always says. I looked at Ofir. He opened his mouth to speak, and I was afraid he wouldn't be able to resist the temptation to blurt out one of his smart-arse remarks, something along the lines of, 'incredibly terrible'.

So I spoke first: yes, Bro, I said. She's something, that Ilana of yours. Everything you said about her is true. She's really a special girl.

We have to give her time, I thought to myself. After all, a group like ours could be threatening, with our inside jokes and mutual associations and hidden currents of understanding.

But till Maria showed up, Ilana was always reserved around us. For years, she would leave us in the living room to go into her study or take care of the twins or talk to her students on the phone, and she only came back to put her home-baked *burekas* on the table or to take pictures of us, with a kind of remoteness, as if we were subjects in one of her research studies.

Amichai, for his part, never stopped admiring her. Out loud, so she could hear, he would boast to us about her academic successes: they offered Ilana a three-year research grant! Her students gave her the best feedback of any teacher in the history of the department!! They want to give her a full teaching position!!!

Every once in a while he would go to the study to see if he could do something 'to make her happy'. And if she happened to pass through the living room, he would be very attentive to her, touch her, caress her, compliment her.

She never touched him in our presence.

But when I see a good picture of him in the album, I know she took it.

*

It all began with routine plastic surgery.

I don't understand why you need it, Amichai said. I think your nose is great. Kind of a Latin nose . . . sensual.

You must really love me if you think my nose is sensual, Ilana the Weeper said. My nose is ugly, but that isn't it.

So what is it? Amichai asked. He really and truly didn't understand.

It's that I've gone through a profound inner change these last few months, and I want it to show on the outside, too, Ilana the Weeper answered.

*

It's all because of that Maria of yours, Amichai said to Ofir the next day – one-third joking, two-thirds serious.

The four of us were lying in huge hammocks in the wooden house that Ofir, Maria and her daughter had rented on the beach in Michmoret. Maria had decorated the house tastefully. She filled the living room with light-coloured wooden furniture, and hung the walls with delicate *thangkas*, Buddhist paintings they'd bought – she once told me proudly – from the artist himself. She'd spread a large rug on the floor and put two large cushions on it that you just felt like sinking into, and on the shelves she herself had built, she'd put Ofi's magnificent, ostentatious CD collection, along with some small leather drums, giant-size wooden clogs, Indian notebooks, shampoos and soaps made by the Himalaya Company. I could go on describing more and more of that house, but I still wouldn't be able to capture the special music she managed to create in the spaces between all those objects, music that said only one thing: home.

It's . . . nice that you're working so hard at it, even though we'll be going to Denmark very soon, Ofir said cautiously one evening when he saw her taking a handful of screws out of the toolbox again.

Ofi, my love, haven't you heard? We're not going to Denmark after all, she said without putting down the screws.

We're not? Ofir said, standing stock still.

I like it here, she said. Most of the people in the streets know English, there's light twelve months a year, and God has given me Lana as a gift.

But didn't we decide to try living together in Copenhagen? Ofir said, surprised.

That's just the problem with Western thought, she said the familiar-sounding words. We make decisions, and then we become slaves to our decisions. And we try so hard to make them work that we don't notice that in the meantime, they've become irrelevant.

But wait a minute, he tried to fight for the good-life-in-Scandinavia dream, what about the occupation? And the living conditions of the Palestinians? That doesn't bother you any more?

Just the opposite, Maria said. Now that this Intifada, you know, number two, has started here, I have to stay. To keep going to those women's meetings with Lana. To make sure that, in all this war, people on both sides keep their humanity. That they don't turn into animals.

Every Tuesday, Maria and Ilana the Weeper went to a meeting of Women Against the Occupation. And every other Saturday, they'd go to stand at one of the army checkpoints on the West Bank and document the injustices taking place there. On Mondays, they'd meet to work on the article Ilana had started writing, 'Coping With Winter Depression: the Danish Case'. On Wednesdays, they'd take the children to Yarkon Park. Or to the unspoiled beach at Michmoret. And on Thursdays, they met regularly to work on marketing the new touch therapy clinic Maria and Ofir had opened at home (only a few weeks after they opened it, appointments were already hard to come by. Ilana the Weeper gave the first push when she circulated their phone number to the weary-bodied academic sector, and it spread from there. Which didn't prevent her and Maria from continuing their Thursday meeting 'to maintain the momentum').

And so, every day for weeks, Ilana the Weeper was exposed to the light Maria radiated. And it gradually began to have an effect on her.

She stopped wearing those eternal beige trousers of hers and switched to dresses that flattered her stem-like body.

She smiled occasionally.

She stopped sitting off to the side during get-togethers at her house. Instead, she would find a place next to Maria and join the conversation every once in a while (most of her comments were still critical, but at least she participated).

She began investing a lot of time preparing healthy meals. (Actually, I missed her home-baked *burekas*.)

She showed a slight interest in football and made a very charming effort to understand the difference between active offside and passive offside.

She found out that, for years, we'd been calling her Ilana the Weeper behind her back, and instead of bursting into tears, she burst out laughing – after which, it was hard to keep calling her that.

Wife, you're changing right in front of my eyes, Amichai told her one night. In the dark. In bed. A car alarm broke into sporadic shrieks, then was silent.

Don't exaggerate, Ilana said.

No, really, Amichai insisted gently. Something is happening to you.

So how do you feel about it? Ilana asked, and stroked his chest.

I'm glad . . . I mean . . . I love you . . . I mean . . . I'm glad you're happy . . . It's just that . . .

Just that . . . what? Ilana asked, trying to drag it out of him.

Amichai didn't say anything. She thought he'd fallen asleep when he suddenly said in a choked voice: it's just that I'm not the reason for it.

Ilana was glad it was dark and he didn't see her smile. What do you mean? she asked, trying to sound serious.

It's all because of Maria, Amichai said. Everything started when you met her. And I've been trying for years . . . to make you more . . . and couldn't do it.

Maybe sometimes it takes a new person, Ilana said cautiously. Someone outside the circle.

Amichai took Ilana's hand off his chest and curled up into himself.

She wound herself around him again. She didn't want him to distance himself. The car alarm began shrieking again.

But what . . . he stammered, what exactly does she do . . . What does she do that I don't?

It's not something she does, Ilana said, caressing his back. She's just my friend. For the first time in my life, I have a real friend and it's . . . it's changed the way I look at things.

And I'm not your friend? Amichai asked.

You're the man I love and she's my friend. Those are two different things.

In what way?

Ilana sighed. It seemed she would be forced to say what she would rather have kept unsaid. You're a man into happy colours, she said. That's why I fell in love with you. I remember when you walked into the Personal Affairs office on the base and talked to the officer, and I watched you fling your hands around and thought, this is the kind of man I want, a man who's happy with whatever life hands out.

But Maria's a very positive person too, Amichai persisted.

Yes, Ilana explained. But she's paid a visit to the opposite pole too. The darkness. She fell into the pit, pulled herself out of it and isn't afraid to look into the pit again every now and then. You don't ever let yourself fall into that pit.

The way you say that, it sounds like an accusation, Amichai said, and a memory flashed through his mind: a boy who always has to be happy climbs onto his mourning mother's lap, strokes her face and says, Mummy, where's your smile? Your smile got lost?

Not at all, Ilana said, and began rubbing his neck. It's what I love about you, your optimism.

Amichai hesitated, troubled by the memory. So . . . so because Maria was in the pit, that makes her . . . makes her what, actually?

I feel normal with her, Ilana said. I feel like I'm OK. That my sadness is OK. That my heaviness is OK. That my need to hide from the world every once in a while is OK. I feel understandable when I'm with Maria. Completely understandable.

And with me you don't? Amichai said, unable to control himself. With me you don't feel understandable? Ilana hugged him tighter from behind.

Yes, she said, but in a different way.

Amichai felt as if he didn't understand anything. He felt a huge sense of despair spreading through him. He felt the way he did after a two-hour sales talk that ended with nothing. And then he felt his wife's hand reach between his legs.

You're my man, she whispered to him, and her breath warmed his earlobe. You're all I want.

But Amichai didn't cooperate. Why should he? He can't be bought so cheaply. He took her hand off him again and tried to bury himself in the insult. Bury himself so deeply that he'd reach the pit Ilana was talking about. But Ilana wouldn't give up. She put her hand back and massaged him lightly on his weak spot, three fingers below his belly button, and she rubbed her thigh against his and licked the Israel-shaped blotch on his neck, from the Galilee to Eilat, slowly –

*

You sound knackered, I said to him on the phone a few days later, after we'd decided who would pick up whom on the way to Michmoret.

Ilana is sexually harassing me, he complained.

I was surprised. Of the four of us, Amichai talked about sex the least. But from the way he leaned forward whenever Churchill started talking about his conquests,

94

you could tell that he cared about the subject, and I had always assumed, without actually checking it with him, that the reason he didn't talk was that he had nothing to say.

'Sexually harassing' is terrific, I said, happy for him.

I don't know, he said doubtfully, and told me about the night-time conversation with his wife. It's all fine, he said with a sigh, it's just that . . .

Just that . . . what?

I'll tell you, but not a word to Ofir, OK? I've been having this weird feeling lately when we have sex. I feel as if Maria is there with us. As if she's fantasising about Maria when I touch her.

Sounds a little paranoid to me.

Paranoid? So how do you explain that, all of a sudden, after eight years, she discovered me? Me and my . . . dick, we were there before. It's not that she never wanted to . . . but not . . . not like this.

It's because she's feeling better now, I said, trying to reassure him. Her friendship with Maria is making her happier, and you're reaping the fruit. What's so bad about that?

I don't know, he said, refusing to be convinced. And what's the story with Michmoret? It's almost an hour and a half with traffic jams. Why did Ofir have to move there? So far away from all of us?

Stop, Amichai, I said with a laugh. It's not like you to complain like this. The guy is only trying to live by values he believes in. He thinks big cities are materialistic and corrupting, so he doesn't want to live in one. Makes sense to me.

Maybe you're right, maybe I should be easier on him, Amichai said. And he managed, with a great effort, to maintain his positive attitude for almost twenty-four hours, until Ilana told him about the cosmetic surgery she wanted to have done on her nose – and again he felt the ground open under his feet. And all the way to Michmoret, he kept on at me and Churchill:

Her nose is just fine.

What does she need it for?

All those operations . . . they challenge God. First it's her nose. Later it'll be her whole face. In another few years, people will change their entire bodies with surgery.

And what if it comes out ugly? There was that girl in our class who had an operation. Calanit Kalter. Remember?

I don't understand why Ilana needs it.

Those things were never important to her before.

Her nose is just fine, isn't it?

Just before we got to Netanya, Churchill had had enough. Shut up, will you? he snapped, and his tone was so harsh that Amichai went quiet and didn't say another word till we reached Michmoret. But he kept stewing over it, and when we were lying in the hammocks, he said to Ofir again, a quarter joking and three-quarters serious, that it was all Maria's fault.

Ofir said he should think before speaking. And Amichai got pissed off and said, don't get on your high horse, Ofir, just because your clinic's doing well now doesn't mean you have a right to talk down to your friends.

Ofir took a deep breath, as if he were struggling with the old, spoiling-for-a-fight Ofir that was threatening to burst out of his mouth. He rocked in his hammock a bit. Then got out of his hammock. And took an Indian drum off the shelf and drummed on it in a monotonous rhythm, and put the drum back on the shelf. And then he said: all Maria said to Ilana is that she thought her nose actually looks nice on her, but if she thinks it'll make her happy, she should go for it, because we can't always explain why things make us happy, and sometimes they don't have to be logical.

'Make her happy?' Amichai mocked him. Since when are those things important to Ilana? I know her, and I'm telling you that she never cared about all that crap before.

It's not crap at all, Ofir said, raising his voice slightly. People who understand say that the next millennium is going to be the millennium of the body. And besides . . . if it's such crap, Amichai-ji, why do you try so hard to hide that blotch of yours?

Amichai opened his eyes wide. We never mentioned his Israel-shaped blotch. Friends don't do things like that in our unwritten code. (Do not mention the blotch on his neck to him. Do not talk about my being short. Do not give birthday presents, but do send birthday cards. Do not tell someone the results of a match if we know he's taped it. Do express an opinion about something that's happening in a friend's life, but when you're finished, add: listen, man, it's your decision. Do not keep track of whose turn it is to call. Do not keep track of money, because in the end, it all balances out. Do not take books from me because I'm obsessive about keeping them clean. Do not take CDs from Ofir because even after he became spiritual, he remained appallingly materialistic about anything related to his music collection – about two thousand, including every genre and a few really rare ones – and God help anyone who takes a CD out of its case and doesn't put it back, and God help anyone who creases the booklet with the lyrics on it. Do not compliment one of Amichai's twins without complimenting the other. Do not get into political arguments with Churchill because he always wins. Do not trust Ofir's directions because we once ended up in Jenin because of him. Do not steal a friend's girlfriend. Unless she's Ya'ara. Do be happy about each other's successes even if, in your heart, you're jealous. Do not use the terms 'my brother', 'his brother' or any other of the other slick versions of the good old 'Bro'. Do not lie to a friend. But on the other hand, do not always tell him the whole truth. Do not gossip. Do stick together. Do not leave. And – do not bring new people into the group, not because we have anything against new people, just because it would take them years to learn all these rules.)

Do me a favour, Amichai finally said between clenched teeth, don't call me *ji*. And shut up about my blotch. I'm telling you that I know Ilana and this whole business just doesn't add up.

Maybe you don't know . . . all the different sides of her, Ofir said.

Maybe you don't know all the different sides of Maria, Amichai retorted. How long have you been together? Two weeks?

And maybe you'll both shut up, Churchill said. I've had a shit week and I came here to watch football, not to hear you two fight like morons.

I looked at him. That was the second time in an hour that he'd been nasty to us. And that was definitely unusual. Churchill's charisma was always the quiet, unforced kind. And even in the courtroom, he was cool and level-headed. And he usually let the defendant tie the rope around his own neck.

It must have been because of the new case he'd been assigned recently, I thought. A case with broad social significance, just like he'd asked for in his list of World Cup wishes. The director general of a government office was suspected of accepting a sexual bribe to promote the authorisation of land for building, and he claimed that some businessmen he had refused to make exceptions for were trying to frame him. The senior attorney appointed to the case had resigned from it because of a sudden illness, and the district attorney had decided to let Churchill, his assistant, take over. There was quite a bit of tutting about it – how did such a young guy get such an important case? – but the district attorney, who had been grooming him for bigger things from his first day in the system, told him to ignore all that talk and focus on the job at hand.

I looked at him now as he cracked sunflower seeds with characteristic resolve (one precise press of his teeth, never more). I hope he succeeds, I thought. And at the same instant, a small voice inside whispered let him fail, let him fail.

Then I too turned my eyes to the TV screen. For the first few seconds, I stared at the ball lurching from side to side and had a tough time telling the teams apart – one was playing in red shirts, the other in green, and those are exactly the colours I can't see because of my colour blindness. But soon enough, I noticed that one team had white shorts and the other black shorts, so I could follow the game, which was the kind I liked: the team playing a more defensive, uglier game scored a goal by accident during the first few minutes. And in the time that was left, the really good, more creative and skilled team tried to break through the defensive wall and right the wrong. Happily, just before the end, they managed to do it – they scored two quick goals and turned the result around.

Who said there's no justice in football? the commentator waxed lyrical.

And Amichai said, those guys from Barcelona, they don't play football, they dance.

True modern dance, Churchill agreed. And I said, when football reaches a certain aesthetic level, it becomes art. And Ofir got out of his hammock and said, who's up for *chai*? As we drank the sweet, spicy *chai* that spreads through your body, Maria and her daughter came in from a visit to Ilana. Ofi! Ofi! the girl cried, and ran straight into Ofir's arms, as if the short separation of a few hours from him had been hard for her, and only now, when she was pressed up against his chest, was her mind at ease again. He asked her how it was at Ilana's place, and she told him about all sorts of scientific experiments she and the twins had done together: they'd mixed vinegar and bicarbonate of soda and saw how a small volcano erupted. They'd poured starch into a glass of iodine and saw how the colour of the iodine changed. He listened intently, stroked her fine, blonde hair and asked small, fatherly questions. Meanwhile, Maria gave each of us one of her long hugs.

The first few times she'd hugged us, we were totally flustered. We'd look over her shoulder, trying to find out from Ofir when, for Buddha's sake, it would end. When would she let us go? Then we became addicted to it, abandoned ourselves to it, and returned the pressure, the tightness, we too rested our heads in the hollow between her shoulder and her neck and felt the heat of her body seep into us, felt her large breasts rocking us, so much so that if she skipped someone on her round of hugs, he would complain and demand his hug.

This time, Amichai was the last to get a hug from her. And despite the accusations he'd hurled at her in her absence, he didn't draw back. On the contrary. It seemed as if their hug was the longest, warmest of all, as if they poured into it all their concern and mutual love for Ilana. In any case, after that hug, the atmosphere in the wooden house in Michmoret seemed much more relaxed. Ofir gave us all more *chai*. The commentators in the studio had already begun talking about the return match in two weeks, and Churchill said, I'm going to say something now that Ofir always used to say.

It starts with 'you have no idea'? Amichai guessed.

You have no idea what mood I was in when I came here today, Churchill said without a smile. That case ... well, I can't really talk about it ... I just wanted to say that seeing you all ... It made me feel so good ... It made me put things in perspective ... Reminded me of what's important in life.

We didn't say anything.

We could have asked what exactly had happened. Tried

to help. But his tone didn't invite questions (and perhaps it was us, still trapped in our perception of him as a rock). So we were quiet. And sipped our *chai*.

Amichai looked at Ofir and said, you were right before, what you said.

Ofir stroked the little girl's hair and said, I don't remember any more what I said.

Amichai laughed, it's better that way, and that spark we all knew lit up in his eyes, the one that meant, in a little while, we'd be updated on a brilliant new idea.

And sure enough, a few days later, we all got phone calls inviting us to a farewell party for Ilana's old nose. We'll all meet at a Chameleons gig, Amichai said enthusiastically, and then we'll go for a drink and have our pictures taken with the nose, which would have a 'before' book as a memento.

The Chameleons was our group. I mean, of course each one of us had his own separate musical favourites: Amichai liked movie soundtracks and Israeli twilight time songs. Ofir liked clever rappers when he was still in advertising, and then, when he came back from India, he liked instrumental music better. Churchill, on the other hand, thought lyrics should have meaning, so Ehud Banai was his favourite in the daytime and Meir Ariel at night. I liked British groups best. The Smiths. And later, the Stone Roses. And then I went by the song, not the group. But in any case, I didn't listen to Israeli groups very much, except for the Chameleons, whose first album came out when we were in the army and pierced us with its beauty. Throughout our army service, lines from 'It's Not Black-and-White' were embedded in our conversations and starred as the opening lines in our birthday wishes to each other. I remember one of Churchill's birthday greetings that began with the quote, 'And you have to remember, always remember, that spring comes in the end'. I don't recall any more why he wrote that. Perhaps it was after we came back from our trip, when for no apparent reason, I fell into a kind of depression that bordered on panic.* Anyway, we stayed loyal to the Chameleons even when it turned out that their next albums weren't as good. And even after one of their performances we'd attended together was stopped in the middle because the two singers got into a fist fight. I believe them, Churchill said, trying to explain to Ya'ara why we were stuck on that group in particular. Their songs are getting worse, but I always believe them.

You all see your youth in the Chameleons, Ya'ara claimed. I think that's what it is. You always hear them twice: as the people you are now and also as eighteen-year-olds.

Both she and Churchill were right, apparently. But still, I told Amichai I wouldn't be at the show or afterwards at the farewell party for Ilana's nose.

But why not? he asked, disappointed.

How many times can a person see the Chameleons? I

---

* Mr Freed's normally accurate memory betrays him on this point. The quote from the Chameleons song did not appear in a birthday message I wrote him, but in a letter I sent him through Mr Amichai Tanuri, our mutual friend. At the time, Mr Freed was serving in a company of soldiers that handled day-to-day security matters in Judah and Samaria, and in that capacity was posted, along with another nine soldiers, on the roof of a building in Nablus. Further on in this book, Mr Freed describes at length the weeks he spent on that roof, and even quotes from the letter he wrote to me from there.

That letter aroused my concern, as well it should have. Mr Freed was always very restrained with regard to anything related to public expressions of distress, and most of the time used his self-deprecating humour to protect himself and those listening to him. But in the afore-mentioned letter, his distress and confusion were apparently too great to contain or turn into a joke. Reading his words, I sensed that the despair he was expressing might reach the point of no return.

Then too, like today, the thought of life – of the world – without him, seemed incomprehensible, unbearably sad, and I tried with every fibre of my being to choose the right words in my reply to cheer him up. In the end, it turns out, it was those words from the Chameleons song that left an impression on him. (Y.A.)

lied. That's it. I'm sick of them. Besides, lately their songs are all Tel Aviv. There's nothing left of their Haifa-ness.

Like you haven't been a Tel Avivian for seven years now, Amichai chided me. But forget it, if you don't feel like seeing them, no problem. Meet us afterwards.

Maybe, I said, trying to get out of it. I don't know. Why do you care so much whether I come?

What are you talking about? Amichai said, raising his voice. You're my friend. And Ilana's. I don't understand the question. Is it because the three of us are couples now and you're not?

Honestly . . . yes, I said, half truthfully. I'm happy for all of you, but I don't always feel comfortable at those couples' nights out.

OK, Amichai said, his tone measured. And after a brief silence, he added: just don't forget that everything's fluid.

What does that mean?

Listen to this story. Yesterday I had a call from Mr Bass from the Parents' Retirement Home in Rishon le Ziyon. Pardon me, but I hope you remember me, sir, he says to me. And I think: remember, of course, how can I forget. Five hours – five hours! – he kept me sitting across from him. He told me his whole life story, including the time he spent in the forest with the partisans, and in the end, he said, with no shame at all, that he'd never had any intention of buying a subscription. Why should he? Anyone who survived the camps has a heart strong enough to take anything. A year goes by, and he calls me again and asks if the offer I made at our last meeting is still on the table. Yes, I tell him. Including the special discount for people born in Austria? Yes, I tell him. What happened, Mr Bass? You've changed your mind? Circumstances have changed, he tells me, and asks for an appointment the same day because it's very urgent. And what does he tell me at our meeting? A few months earlier, a young woman named Shulamit came to live at the home and 'a great love the likes of which I have never known in my life' ignited between them. He was married to Chaya'le for fifty years, he explains to me. We had a good life together. We built a home and raised a family together. But I never felt excitement like this. And I never imagined such a thing could be possible, he says. Well, that sounds wonderful, I say, trying to share his happiness. But then I see that he's a bit pale. My heart, he says and puts a hand on the wrong side of his chest. All I have to do is say her name for it to start pounding. And she might be young, but I'm not.

This is exactly where we at Telemed come into the picture, I say, taking advantage of the opportunity to channel the conversation in the direction I want, and I spread booklets and documents in front of him and explain why a gold subscription would be better than a regular one. And as he's being convinced and has started signing, there's a knock at the door and Shulamit, the young woman, walks in.

This is the boy from Telemed I told you about, he introduces us and I shake her hand politely. A grandmother at least seventy years old, not one whose beauty you could say is still visible on her face, but she seems like a bit of a devil. You should have seen how he looked at her when she came in. How he trembled when he took her hand as she sat down. I swear. I was afraid he'd have an attack on me right then and there. But she laced her fingers with his and gave him this quiet kind of look and said to me, 'We have undergone a rejuvenation.'

Nice language, I said admiringly.

Yes, Amichai said. The funny thing is that it's catching. Even now, telling you the story, their language is suddenly coming out of my mouth.

A nice story, I admitted.

But did you get the moral? Amichai asked.

What, that if I wait till I'm ninety, I might be rejuvenated?

No, that now you're alone and we're all couples. But we

104

still have our whole lives to be friends. And everything's fluid. Everything can change.

*

I have no idea why he said that. It was much more like Ofir to philosophise like that. Perhaps, as a practised salesman, he was trying to soften my objection with a remark I would like.

I'm not a big believer in mysticism either (though I'm ready to accept the fact that, sometimes, a hidden oracle inside you knows what's going to happen before you do).

Anyway, I didn't go to the farewell party for Ilana's nose. Three weeks before, I had met a girl named Hani.

I translated an article into English for her, 'The Collapse of the Soviet Union: Revolution or Evolution?' and something about her hesitant manner attracted me. Most of my clients were totally uninhibited about their requests and saw nothing wrong with paying me to do something for them that, in principle, they were supposed to do themselves. Hani, on the other hand, stammered and blushed with shame when we met for the first time to set up the schedule. I would have done it myself, she told me, really, but my English . . . Where I grew up, they don't study English at all, and I'm trying to catch up now . . . Trying very hard . . . Do you understand?

After all the sophisticated girls I'd gone out with since Ya'ara, her naivety was refreshing. I was also curious to find out how her hair, which was always tied back in a severe ponytail, looked when it was loose. So when I brought her the translated text, I asked if she wanted to go out, and she did.

On the actual date, it turned out that 'the place where they don't teach English' was the ultra-Orthodox community of Bnei Brak, and she had given up religion a year earlier. I mean, it was a gradual process that began when she was a teenager. She had looked at her mother, how her mother lived, and knew that she wanted more. She didn't even put it into words for herself at first. Then it was only a vague feeling of hunger, hunger she couldn't satisfy. And she had no one to share that feeling with because where she grew up, you don't wash your dirty linen in public.

So, very slowly, she began to lead a double life. On the surface, she kept going to the religious girls' school, but secretly read books like *Spinoza and Other Heretics*, or, at the other extreme, *Lady Chatterley's Lover*.

Actually, she said, I'd already stopped being religious in my heart when I was eighteen. But it took another three years before I ate pizza.

Pizza?

Not kosher, I mean. It was in Givatayim. And I ate it so quickly that I burned my tongue on the bubbling cheese, and I was sure that was a punishment from God. So I put things off for another few months. Then I bought culottes, which is a kind of interim stage between a skirt and trousers. And I wore them, but only at university, of course. And a year ago, I bought my first pair of jeans, and the sky didn't fall in on me. And with the doing of the deeds, one grows to love them. Until I finally left home.

It takes a lot of courage to do what you did, I said (and thought: with my restraint, I probably would have stayed in Bnei Brak).

In the end, it wasn't courage any more, she said, I had no choice.

Maybe that's how it is in life, I said. You have to suffer, to hit bottom, before you can change.

I don't know, she said. That's a very pessimistic thing to say. Are you always so pessimistic?

*

To my great surprise, and in total contrast to the shyness she projected in her every movement, we ended the night in bed together. You have to understand, she said as she let down her ponytail and her honey hair cascaded to her shoulders, I'm five years behind the rest of the class. I still have a lot of catching up to do.

I wasn't her first. But I was the first to give her pleasure. At least, that's what she told me. And anyway, there was something infectious about her beginner's enthusiasm. Everything we did was new for her, a first: oral sex. The Ein Kerem Inn. The lone bench on the cliff overlooking the sea at Beit Yanai. All those 'magical' places were magical for her, without the quotation marks. She had never seen a midnight showing of *The Rocky Horror Show*. Didn't know that the singers Ehud Banai and Meir Banai weren't the same person. And she wanted to go dancing at the Coliseum on New Year's Eve. I explained to her that the Coliseum had been closed for a long time, and she said she knew, but for years, she'd read about that party in the Coliseum in the newspapers her mother didn't allow her read, and a fantasy gradually took shape in her mind of a New Year's Eve party where she'd dance till she dropped to the music of the DJ Ilan Ben-Shahar (he and no other) and bid her final farewell to the religious world.

Ah . . . Look . . . We can find out if Ilan Ben-Shahar is appearing at a different club on New Year's Eve, I suggested. But, uncharacteristically, she shook her head and said, we could, but it wouldn't be the same.

So on the eve of the millennium, we put on party clothes and took our battery-operated Discman and two speakers, along with a collection of hits of the '80s chosen by Ilan Ben-Shahar, and went to where the Coliseum used to be. We walked up the steps to Atarim Square, which was as dirty and deserted as usual, but Hani didn't care about that, she had a fantasy in her mind and she was determined to live it down to the smallest detail.

At eleven-twenty, we went through a broken window into the dark space of the dead club.

At eleven-twenty-five, we connected the Discman to the

speakers and she flung her hair from side to side to the music of Duran Duran's 'Girls on Film'.

At eleven-fifty-five, we switched to the radio to hear the countdown to the new millennium.

At exactly midnight, we had a long, long, long kiss, surrounded by electric wires, broken windows, pieces of plaster, torn posters of Grace Jones, and beer bottles that didn't even smell of beer any more.

And at twelve-thirty – as we started walking away from the Square – her mother called.

It was a ritual. Every night, her mother called to swear at her, and this time, as if her maternal antennae had sensed from a distance how much her daughter was enjoying herself, her tone was louder than ever: you're a whore, Chana, you know that? No? Really? So tell me, what's the difference between you and a whore?

But Mum . . . Hani protested feebly.

No, really, Chana. Explain it to me. You have relations with a man, you sleep with him in his house. You know what? You're worse than a whore because a whore at least gets money for what she does. With you, it's free.

Enough, Mum, enough, Hani pleaded.

Don't tell me it's enough, her mother continued lashing out at her. I hear that music in the background there. Have you no shame, Chana? To celebrate a Christian holiday? You know what, maybe you should just convert. Your man isn't a Jew anyway, is he?

Hani didn't answer. She didn't even have the strength to utter that pleading 'enough'. So she just breathed deeply into the mouthpiece and let her mother become more and more offensive. Until she said her usual, 'I don't want to hear from you. Don't expect me to call you any more' that closed their night-time conversations every time.

I don't get it, why don't you tell her I'm Jewish? I asked after a silence.

We were walking slowly along quick streets. A Robbie Williams song came from a building we passed.

I don't know, Hani said, chastised.

And I don't understand why you let her talk to you like that. Why do you even answer the phone?

Because . . . that's her way . . . of keeping in touch with me. It's our way of communicating now, Hani said.

The Robbie Williams song came out of the next building too. Rhythmic, happy, great.

Hani clung tightly to me, not trembling, not crying. Sorry I ruined tonight, she said.

You didn't ruin anything, I said, tightening my arm around her shoulders, and I felt a slight warming in my chest. The kind you feel after a shot of vodka. I wasn't sure what to call that warming – sadness? pity? love? – and I had no idea how long it would last. But I was afraid of risking everything by seeing Ya'ara. Even if we were both surrounded by people who'd be talking about Ilana's nose. Even if we didn't say a word to each other all evening.

The nagging thoughts about Ya'ara hadn't stopped when I started going out with Hani. They actually intensified. I thought about Ya'ara when I was kissing Hani at the Coliseum. I thought about Ya'ara when I was having sex with Hani. I thought about Ya'ara when I was with Hani in the Ein Kerem Inn. I remembered that I'd planned to take her there, but I never got the chance. I thought about how I would feel if she were sitting across from me now with those green eyes of hers. And if she were to take off her glasses.

I was ashamed of those thoughts. And that I occasionally took out of the closet the single sock Ya'ara had left behind, a red sock with a yellow stripe at the top. There was nothing special about that sock, except for the fact that it was hers, but it alone was enough to make me feel a pang of yearning every time I touched the thin, feminine fabric and crushed it between my fingers (and that was just the half-normal perversion, the one I'm willing to admit without the protection of parentheses. There was also a video tape of the wedding, and I knew exactly which frames Ya'ara appeared in alone. And there were the chairs she'd sat in when the group met up and when she got up, I would sit on them quickly to feel the outline of her buttocks still left on the fabric. And there were others).

*

Sorry, man, it looks like you'll have to manage without me this time, I told Amichai.

OK, he said without hiding his disappointment.

And tell your wife I wish her luck.

What are you talking about, he said. It's just cosmetic surgery. She goes in at nine in the morning, and she'll be home by five in the afternoon.

5

The four of us are buried in sand, only our heads are sticking out. Ofir's curly, unkempt head. Churchill's wide, crew-cut head. Amichai's round head. And my small, economy-size head. We worked for three hours on South Beach in the blazing July heat digging graves, and then it took the woman filming us another hour and a half to put the sand back and pat it down around our bodies so it'd look as if we couldn't get out. I don't remember what product it was that Ofir had to produce an ad for in his copywriting course. Life insurance? Nose drops? In any case, the four of us played people about to die (in the final edit, Ofir managed to include a shot of circling vultures he'd taken from some Western), and each of us had a short script, a sentence or two expressing regret for something he'd never managed to do during his life. I don't remember my sentence. I just remember that Amichai had to say, 'One woman. To have slept with only one woman since the age of twenty-two. What a waste, what a waste', and that he couldn't say it with the inner conviction Ofir was expecting, so they had to shoot that take over and over again, and my nose itched madly, and I had nothing to scratch it with because my hands were buried in sand, and the woman with the camera, someone from Ofir's course, poured mineral water into our open mouths over and over again so we wouldn't dehydrate.

When I started to feel an unpleasant coldness spreading from my feet to my hips and waist, I thought, perhaps this is the coldness of death, perhaps this is what you feel when you die, and what would happen if I died now, in the middle of this day of shooting, and I was depressed to discover that I didn't really care, I mean, I didn't want to die, but at the moment, when my life wasn't going anywhere, or more accurately, when it was going nowhere, I didn't really care.

My thoughts must have been visible on my face because a week later, when Ofir ran the edited film in class, his teacher remarked that none of the men buried in the sand looked like they were about to die, except for the one on the left, the one with the small head, who was probably a professional actor.

*

Ofir was the one who told me.

Something terrible happened, he said on the phone. His voice was so salty that I didn't recognise it at first.

But how? Churchill mumbled. It can't . . . it can't be.

There was some rare complication . . . with the anaesthesia . . . a blood clot . . . I explained to him what Ofir had explained to me.

The funeral's tomorrow at one. We're meeting at the gate to the Haifa cemetery, Ofir told us two hours later.

Can we call Amichai? I asked. Is he answering the phone now?

He's not speaking. Not just to us, not to anyone, I explained to Churchill. Ilana's brother has taken charge of making all the arrangements and he's keeping Ofir up to date.

I'll wait outside for you tomorrow at twelve, Ofir told me. I might come alone. Maria isn't . . . Maria fell apart completely when she heard. I don't know if she'll be able to pull herself together by tomorrow.

*

We just passed Hadera, where are you? Churchill and Ya'ara called from their car the next day.

We just left Michmoret, I said. We'll probably get there a little after you.

So maybe we should stop at the entrance to Haifa and buy something. What do you bring to a funeral? Churchill asked.

Ofir was sitting in my back seat, very close to Maria, who in the end had decided to come and whose body hadn't stopped heaving with wracking sobs from the minute she got into the car.

Tell them to buy flowers, he leaned forward and said to me, one of those big round bouquets. And after a long silence, he added, tell me, do you also have the feeling that all the cars on the road are on their way to Ilana's funeral?

*

Amichai didn't speak at the funeral. We surrounded him on all sides, except the front, facing the grave. Ofir put his hand on his right shoulder, Churchill on his left, and I supported him from the rear. There were a lot of people at the cypress-studded cemetery near the sea. I only knew a few of them. The weather was strange. Hot and humid. Like in South America. To the left of Ilana's open grave was one with a headstone in the shape of a guitar, and I thought to myself, that's good, because Amichai won't have a problem finding the grave even twenty years from now. My grandfather is buried in the huge cemetery in Holon, and every year when we visit his grave on the anniversary of his death, it takes us hours to find the plot, and last year, my grandmother fainted while we were searching, and the ceremony was cancelled. I'd like to cry now, I thought as the cantor rent the clouds with the *El Malei Rachamim* prayer, and remembered that Amichai once told me that Ilana had said to him that of all his friends, she liked me best. I never understood why. What I did to make her like me. We'd never had a conversation that lasted longer than five minutes. Perhaps it was that diary I wrote for her five years ago. She was doing research on 'Depressive Thinking in Everyday Life' and asked all of us to keep a diary for a week, documenting our most secret thoughts. I don't have enough men for the sample, she said when she came into the living room carrying instruction sheets. Out of politeness, we each took a sheet, but I was the only one who really wrote in the end. I hadn't kept a diary since I was ten – that one was written in English and Hebrew by turns to impress the potential reader with my bilingualism – but from the minute I put pen to paper, the words flowed with surprising ease. It was a few months after I came back from my big trip to South America with Churchill and I was still jet-lagged. I still hadn't wrapped myself in those layers of impassiveness that allow you to reconcile yourself to life's small compromises. So I wrote about it. And about the oppressive loneliness I always felt even during the warmest moments with the guys. And about the Friday night dinners with my family, when no personal remarks were made even though the atmosphere was very pleasant. And about the fact that – this was before Ya'ara – I had still never really loved a girl. And what was going to become of me?

I also wrote down my smaller thoughts. The stupid ones. Like: how come TV presenters never sneeze on air? Or: how come there's more water under the sand on the shoreline? And also: does everyone have masturbation fantasies as detailed as mine, or do they make do with general plot lines?

I didn't hide anything. Not my name either. It didn't bother me that Ilana would read everything. Perhaps part of me even wanted that.

'There was something about you that made people want to open up to you,' one of Ilana's students eulogised her. She read from a prepared speech, slowly, words carefully chosen, but after that sentence, she suddenly broke apart, like a cloud. She started to cry and couldn't go on.

Ilana's older brother spoke after her. He spoke directly to Ilana as if she were still alive, told her that even though he was the older brother, she had always been the one to watch over him, and he begged her to keep watching over him from up above.

Her mother stood up to speak, too. But her resemblance to Ilana was so unnerving – the slim figure, the bob, the nose – that I couldn't concentrate on what she was saying. Only isolated, broken words reached my ears: mummy's little girl . . . you were born out of love . . . and to love you will return . . . how . . . when you were small . . . why didn't I say . . . your soul . . .

Then there was silence. Some people glanced at Amichai, expecting him to speak as well, but he didn't open his mouth. Not then and not through the seven days of mourning at Ilana's parents' house in Haifa. He sat the whole time on a black plastic chair and stared straight ahead. If someone spoke to him, he didn't answer. Sometimes he nodded. Usually, he ignored it.

There was something terrifying about his silence. Especially because this was Amichai, the guy gushing with brilliant ideas, the positive thinker. The weirdest dancer in the world, and it didn't bother him in the slightest. The guy that thirty-year-old men who were healthy as horses bought Telemed subscriptions from just because he inspired their trust.

He's in shock, Churchill said. His reaction reminds me of the way people on trial react when they're sentenced to life.

He blames himself, Ofir hypothesised. He was against that operation, remember? Besides, his father died when he was a boy. And he never really had the chance to mourn him. So maybe now . . .

You don't understand, Maria interrupted. You never really got along with Lana . . . So maybe that's why it's hard for you to understand . . . But he loved her. Theirs was a huge, beautiful love. I have never . . . never in my life seen a man love his wife like that.

Ofir put a hand on Maria's shoulder. She didn't move his hand away but she didn't abandon herself to his touch either.

We hardly saw her during the week of the shiva. Without being asked, she took on the job of taking care of the twins. She talked to them. Explained, as much as it was possible to explain, what had happened. She stroked and hugged and massaged. She dressed and undressed and fed them. She cancelled all her appointments at the clinic and got up every morning at six at Michmoret so she could be in Haifa at seven-fifteen to get the twins organised and take them out for a while, to the beach or the playground or the shopping centre. Because it isn't healthy for small children to be around black plastic chairs all day.

At first, Ilana's family didn't know what to make of all that giving of hers. But Amichai explained to them, his glance piercing, that he thought this was a good solution. And that he wasn't open to discussion on the subject. So they had no choice but to accept it and explain to curious guests that the large, blonde woman was 'a good friend of Ilana's whom the children are very attached to'.

But Ofir wasn't completely happy with the situation. You don't have to do it, he told her over and over again. Until one morning, when he tried to persuade her not to take the trip to Haifa that day, to rest a little, see to things at the clinic – she blew up at him. You don't understand anything, she yelled. You don't understand anything.

What? What don't I understand? he asked, alarmed. She had never raised her voice to him.

I want to die, she said in a strange, cold voice. I want to die, Ofi. And the only reason I don't is the children. They need me, and I'll stay alive till their father is himself again. After that, I don't know, do you understand? I don't know if I want to live.

*

Only twice during the shiva did Amichai come out of his deep, brooding sorrow.

The first time was when Shahar Cohen showed up out of the blue. Shahar Cohen had been one of our group till the army. When he was sent to a military prison for leaving his gun at a hitchhiker's station, we went to see him, but later he was given a psychiatric discharge and moved to London to study law. At least that's what his sister, who stayed in Haifa, told us. He himself cut off all contact with us. No letters, no phone calls, no emails. Later, Ofir's mother told us that she saw him, his hair grown long, playing the harmonica in the Paris metro. But when she talked to him, he acted as if he didn't know her. Then there were two objective sources that claimed he was a DJ at a party they'd danced at in Amsterdam. On the other hand, there were reports from people who'd been in Budapest and saw him, or someone who looked exactly like him, walk through the gates of the school of veterinary medicine there. On a ship in the Galapagos Islands, Churchill and I met a gorgeous German lesbian. The minute she heard we were from Haifa, she asked if we knew Shahar Cohen. We mumbled that we did, and she told us that he was one of the dominant figures in the Berlin gay and lesbian community, played bass in an Abba covers band, produced cultural events, designed subversive posters. We explained to her that Shahar Cohen is a common name in Israel and the Shahar Cohen we know can't be gay, because that's ridiculous . . . if he was . . . then we definitely would have sensed something . . . he was just the opposite . . . always talking about fucking . . . fucking girls, we mean. The German girl gave us a supercilious smile of forgiveness that made us shun her for the rest of the journey. But when we came back to Israel, it turned out that Amichai had met someone from high school who knew someone who claimed that Shahar Cohen had been in the country the previous summer and was seen walking hand in hand with an Aryan-looking guy. Just as we were getting used to the sensational news and remembered that, really, we never did understand why there were four different posters of Freddie Mercury hanging in his room, we heard a new story that shook our confidence once again. A former Haifaite, a woman who used to work at the prosecutor's office with Churchill, went off to the Ramon Crater to be alone and took her dog with her so she wouldn't feel too alone. After a few hours in the desert sun, the delicate city dog started to convulse and vomit, so she drove in a total panic to Mitzpe Ramon. There she was referred to Dr Luis, the local vet. But the person who opened the door to the clinic was none other than Shahar Cohen, who claimed he didn't have the slightest idea who Shahar Cohen was, and as proof, pointed to his diploma from the veterinary college in Turin, where the name Ricardo Luis was written in large Latin letters. He treated the dog with outstanding professionalism and revived it. Then he invited both of them to spend the night in his apartment and touched the lawyer's arm, as if accidentally, when he took her credit card, and mentioned casually the collection of aromatherapy massage oils he kept in his bathroom, and in other words tried to come on to her in a totally heterosexual way.

Excited by the possibility that the mystery of Shahar Cohen was close to being solved, we decided to take action and drove down to Mitzpe Ramon. When we reached the town, after having to stop five times because the engine of Churchill's Beetle kept overheating, it turned out that the girl from the prosecutor's office hadn't misled us: yes, there really was a vet in Mitzpe Ramon, and yes, even though there was no trace of an accent in his speech, he called himself Ricardo Luis. But a few days earlier, he'd closed up his clinic – and vanished.

This is Mitzpe, the locals explained placidly. Things like that happen here all the time. But we'd had enough. After that miserable trip to Mitzpe Ramon, we decided once and for all to declare Shahar Cohen a myth. A symbol. An ideal. We stopped trying to find him and started using his name in our conversations the way you use a joker in a card game.

Why didn't you come on Friday?

I went out for a drink with Shahar Cohen.

Where are you? The match starts in two minutes.

Sorry, Shahar Cohen held me up.

How many were injured in the terrorist attack?

Shahar Cohen and five others.

With time, and with the use of the name Shahar Cohen in even more contexts, the Shahar Cohen label moved so far from referring to the real person who inspired it that we almost forgot there'd been such a person, and that he'd once been our friend. That's why, when he suddenly walked into the living room during the shiva, even Amichai couldn't hide his shock. He didn't say a word, but his eyebrows rose in astonishment.

Bro, I heard what happened and came right away, Shahar Cohen said, leaning over and crushing Amichai in a hug. Then he went from one member of Ilana's family to the other and hugged them too, the way you hug people you love very much, mumbling, what a tragedy, what a terrible tragedy, and he even shed a tear.

Then he sat down, straightened his light-coloured tie, smoothed his dark suit and asked a few questions about Ilana. At first, he directed them to Amichai, but when he realised that he'd get no answers from him, he turned to the others. He wanted to know exactly what had happened. What was the chain of events that led to her death. And he wanted to know what kind of person she was. The people in the room answered quite willingly. In great detail. They laid out their complaints to him too, as if he represented the government or the law, and had the power to right the terrible wrong. Or at least give it meaning.

We followed the exchange of words. And tried to reconcile all the stories we'd heard about Shahar Cohen over the years with this new person wearing good clothes and speaking in such a moderate, measured way.

So how are you? Churchill asked, the first to break (if he hadn't asked, I would have. The suspense was unbearable).

I . . . I'm good, Shahar Cohen said in an ingratiating stammer, as if he were uncomfortable talking about himself.

And where . . . I mean what . . . what are you doing these days? I asked.

Business, he said offhandedly.

What kind of business? I persisted.

International, he said, and looked with embarrassment at the people in the room again, as if he wanted them to see that he was being forced into speaking against his will.

I didn't want to let him off the hook. I had no intention of missing the opportunity to find out what had really happened to him. But then a huge delegation of relatives from Kibbutz Givat HaMacam burst into the living room, and for a long time, the room buzzed with 'I'm so sorry for your loss' and the noisy moving of chairs in order to provide all the heavyset kibbutzniks with places to sit.

When the tumult died down a bit, Shahar Cohen leaned over to Amichai and said, I brought you something, but it's downstairs in the car. Can you come out with me for a minute?

We waited expectantly for Amichai's response. Since the beginning of the shiva, he hadn't moved from his permanent place on the black plastic chair closest to the kitchen. At night he slept on the living room carpet and even vetoed suggestions to put a mattress under him. But to our great surprise, he didn't turn down Shahar Cohen's suggestion. He got up and went out with him.

We followed right behind them, curious but worried. From the way Amichai was walking, it looked as if his legs couldn't carry the weight of his loss and he might collapse at any moment.

Shahar Cohen led us to his car, and contrary to what we might have expected from an international businessman, it was just a Subaru station wagon. He opened the boot, revealing an impressive sight: dozens of small, red inhalers were arranged in small, white cardboard boxes. They reminded me of Ventolin inhalers. So what do you do, import medical equipment? I asked.

You could say that, Shahar Cohen said with a phoney smile. There's laughing gas in those inhalers. It's a big hit now at parties in Europe. It's just starting to come into Israel.

He took one of the inhalers out of its box and said, I buy one like this for two dollars in Lubliana and sell it for fifty shekels in Tel Aviv.

And what . . . what does it do? What kind of an effect does it have? I asked.

Try it, he said. And handed me an inhaler.

Thanks, I apologised, but I have asthma.

I'm more into natural substances now, Ofir hurried to say.

I'd love to, Churchill said sadly, but I work for the prosecutor's office now and . . . we're here in the middle of the street . . . and . . . this business of yours, it's not completely legal, is it?

Amichai reached out and took the inhaler.

Take three short drags, Shahar Cohen explained. Wait a little while. Then take a long one the fourth time, deep into your lungs.

Amichai did what he said. We waited with bated breath for the results, but even after a long minute, we couldn't see any change in the mourning wrinkles of his face.

Shahar Cohen didn't miss a beat. How do you feel, a little dizzy? he asked and Amichai nodded. That can happen the first time, it takes the brain a while to get used to the substance. Take another few of these and try again in two hours. It'll definitely work in the end. That stuff never fails.

Amichai accepted another few inhalers from him and nodded in thanks.

Shahar Cohen took out a business card with gold edges and drew a circle around one of the phone numbers written on it. That's my private number, he told Amichai, and surprised us by getting into his car. Call if there's a problem. And you guys, he said to all of us through the window, don't be pricks, keep in touch.

A few days later, we called him to complain that Amichai still wasn't laughing.

A metallic voice message informed us that the number had been disconnected.

A few months later, there was a picture in the papers of someone who looked exactly like him, and the caption said that a vet named Ricardo Luis had been convicted of dealing in illegal medical equipment and was sentenced to two years in prison.

But then, six months later, Amichai received a postcard from Sydney, Australia. Shahar Cohen had written to him in the crooked handwriting we remembered from high school, saying that he was thinking about him a lot and hoped he was good. He ended the card with, tell the guys I miss them. See you soon.

The second time Amichai got up from his black plastic chair was when Sadat came in.

There had been a terrorist attack that day. The third that week. And the visitors who streamed into his house brought not only their condolences, but also updates on how many were injured and how the hunt for the terrorist was going.

That's why, when Sadat arrived – shoulders stooped, cheeks sunken, eyes frightened – the instinctive reaction of the people in the room was to straighten up like a military squad on alert.

The fears grew when Sadat – without shaking hands with Amichai or any of the other family members, as is customary – sat down on one of the chairs, stared at his shoes and didn't say a word.

Excuse me, who . . . who are you, sir, if I may ask? Ya'ara dared to be the first to speak. Her voice shook slightly.

I . . . I'm sorry . . . I . . . This is the shiva for Ilana, isn't it? I . . . at the checkpoint . . . I heard from her friends what happened . . . And I said . . . I have to go . . . to talk . . . so they gave me the address . . .

What's your name? Churchill asked. His tone was aggressive, as if he were questioning a witness.

I'm sorry . . . I didn't say . . . My name is Sadat . . .

And your surname?

What? Ah . . . Sadat Khuria.

And . . . what's your connection to Ilana, Sadat? Ya'ara asked quickly, before Churchill could continue with that tone of his (and she put a restraining hand on his thigh as she spoke).

I . . . I have no connection – Sadat said, shifting his eyes from Churchill to her in relief – I mean . . . there is a connection . . . we are not friends or anything . . . no . . . just once . . . Ilana, she helped me, she helped me very much.

Everyone in the room moved their black chairs closer to hear better. The ones working in the kitchen left their work for a minute and came into the living room. Even Amichai leaned forward.

I should have . . . Sadat began to speak and stopped, choosing his words again. I . . . I have cancer. And I need to go for medical treatment . . . to a hospital in Israel. They have the medicines only in Israel. And the army lets me out for a month, two months. And then one day comes the checkpoint, and a soldier doesn't let me out. Why? My cousin from Gaza was mixed up in hostile actions. That is what they call them. And the soldier says because of that I have no permit to go out. I go to the officer. The officer says no too. And it was like that for three weeks, every day I go there and they don't let me out. Sometimes I sleep at night in a workers' van. Sometimes I sleep on the ground, near the checkpoint. To be the first in line. But they don't let me out. And, meanwhile, cancer. Till Ilana . . . Ilana is standing there. She sees me . . . gives me a bottle of water . . . to drink . . . asks what happened . . . I tell her . . . and she says, I will take care of it . . . and she does.

How? Churchill asked. How did she take care of it? And his tone was already less interrogating and more interested.

I don't know . . . One day I come to the checkpoint and they tell me it is all arranged. And that she takes me to the hospital now.

What she? Ilana took you to the hospital?

Yes . . . she . . . what she tells me . . . that she checked in court and they are not allowed to do that . . . and besides . . . she tells them . . . she is responsible to take me and bring me back to the checkpoint the same day.

Did you know about this, Amichai? Churchill asked. Amichai didn't answer.

Sadat looked at Amichai with interest. You are Ami . . . I remember she talked on the phone to you . . . when we were driving . . . you . . . *ya'ani* . . . you are her husband?

Amichai lowered his head in confirmation.

You . . . you had a very special wife . . . because of her I don't go to the hospital today . . . I come here . . . so you will know . . . that she was for me . . . not just for me . . . for many . . . like an angel.

Amichai didn't speak. His eyes glistened with tears about to fall.

Then he stood up from his chair, walked towards Sadat

and threw his arms around him. He let out a huge, chilling sob, and he continued to tremble in his arms, soundlessly, for a long minute.

The entire time I had the feeling that it wasn't real, Ya'ara said later. That Arab . . . the way he suddenly showed up. It was like a scene from a movie.

There's something about a shiva that's . . . I said. And I couldn't find the word.

Yes, she said.

*

I gave her a lift back to Tel Aviv. She'd come to Haifa with Churchill, but half an hour later, he was called back to the office because one of the prosecution's main witnesses had decided to retract his testimony.

She'd asked me, in front of everyone, if she could go back with me, and I felt uncomfortable refusing in front of everyone. So at five in the afternoon, we left the mourners' house and she stopped for a minute at the entrance to the building to change her normal glasses for her prescription sunglasses, and I stopped with her, well practised in that change, and she smiled at me, and we both knew why. The muscles of my mouth stayed tensed till we reached the car, and I opened the door for her with the key, like a gentleman, even though I could have just pressed the remote. Then, inside, I said excuse me when I leaned over to release the security lock, and even though she moved her leg, my hand brushed against her thigh. So I said excuse me again.

As we drove slowly down Freud, I looked at the sea. From the Carmel, the sea looks so enormous that it reminds you that land accounts for only one-quarter of the planet. The sun hadn't set yet, but it was close. There wasn't a cloud on the horizon. I thought about the fact that actually, I hadn't been alone in the same space with Ya'ara for two years, and that even though she'd changed her perfume, under it her smell was the same. A clean smell.

We didn't speak until the palm trees at Atlit.

Then she talked about the Arab. And how terrible it was, what was happening. And how, for years, there'd been a feeling that there was hope for change, and now we were back in the same vicious circle. And worst of all, no one cared any more.

For a quick second, I thought of that horrible 1990 World Cup, in the territories, and I said, it's not that no one cares, it's just that we don't know how to deal with it, so we'd rather forget about it.

And she said, it seeps inside you. We ignore it, but it seeps inside and comes out in other things.

And I thought about an article I was translating then that dealt with the years-long denial by Soviet scientists of the existence of chromosomes. The writer of the article claimed that Soviet scientists had disregarded chromosomes for decades because research into heredity didn't fit the Stalinist line, which maintained that environment, not heredity, is solely responsible for human change. I thought about mentioning that article then, but I wasn't sure exactly how to connect it to the conversation.

So I kept quiet.

And Ya'ara said, sometimes I don't understand why we insist on staying in this damned place. Why we don't move to a more normal country.

Because . . . our friends are here, the response came out automatically.

Yes . . . But when I hear about cases like Sadat's . . . I ask myself . . . if friends are a good enough reason.

I don't know, I said. Because I didn't.

And Ya'ara said, it's a good thing that there are people like Ilana who save our honour. And she also said, I feel like I missed her completely, that I didn't know her at all. I don't know, I always had the feeling she couldn't stand me.

She really couldn't stand you, I said.

And we laughed.

126

And we were silent.

And I felt that thing begin to swell up in my chest.

After the Zichron junction, she said, I forgot how much fun it is to drive with you. You're so calm behind the wheel. When I drive with your friend, all my muscles cramp from the tension. He has this thing where . . .

He always has to brake at the last second, I said, finishing the sentence.

At the last hundredth of a second, she said with a smile.

He's insanely busy now, isn't he? I asked in an attempt to continue the complaining-about-Churchill line.

Yes, she said, shifting in her seat. It's completely taken him over, that case.

Well, it really is an important case, isn't it? A corrupt land deal and sexual bribery. Each of those is heavy enough in its own right.

Yes, but . . . I don't know.

What? I asked, giving her a long, sideways glance.

Keep you eyes on the road, she said.

Then stop being so pretty, I almost blurted out the familiar next line of the regular dialogue we'd had when we were together.

Sometimes I think . . . she said, you know, those slips of paper, the wishes you wrote during the World Cup . . . He told me what his first wish was.

So?

It'll sound stupid to you, but sometimes I think he's obsessed with making it come true by the next World Cup. And he's even said it to me a few times: I'll be very dis-appointed if I don't keep my promise to myself.

But that's how you succeed in life, right? You set a goal and work towards it.

Yes, she said, turning her head to the window, but there's also something obsessive about it.

We passed Hadera. I slowed down slightly. So our drive together wouldn't end so quickly.

She was silent, looking out at the dark landscape.

Obsession is the name of a perfume, I said.

What?! she said and turned her head.

There was once a book called *Obsession is the Name of a Perfume*.

You read it?

No, I just remember the name.

She turned her head back to the window. What a fool I am, I flogged myself. I thought she'd remember. We'd once played a game when we went down to the Sinai desert together. One of us said the name of a book and the other had to answer with the name of a book that began with the last letter of the first one. *East of Eden*, she could have said. Or *Emma*. There are plenty of books that begin with the letter 'e'. But she didn't remember the game at all.

You're such Haifa boys, she said suddenly (the car had just crossed that point – a bit after Hadera – after which Tel Aviv is closer than Haifa).

Why? What do you mean? I said defensively.

That whole idea ... of the wishes ... during the World Cup ... and how you all are now ... with Amichai ... it's so Haifa.

Be more specific, I said. What does that 'Haifa' mean?

I don't know, Ya'ara said and stopped speaking. It wasn't till Netanya – when I already thought she'd forgotten – that she said: you all care.

What?

You wanted me to define that Haifa quality you have. So here's the definition: you all care about each other. And there's something sort of old-fashioned about it, you know. These days, no one really cares about anything. Except money.

Now that's a huge generalisation. There are also a few people in Jerusalem who care.

No, it's just the Haifaites. And you know what? Actually,

it's only the four of you. The world around you has become more and more cynical and violent, and you four hold on to that closed group of yours, where people care about each other.

But that's exactly the definition of friends, isn't it? An oasis that lets you forget the desert . . . or . . . a raft whose logs are glued to each other. Or . . . a small country surrounded by enemies. Don't you think?

I have no idea, Ya'ara said. You know I never had any friends.

I didn't say anything, and changed the radio station. I knew very well where that I-have-no-friends complaint was leading and I didn't want to have that conversation again where I lie to her that it's bad luck or a sorry coincidence that she has no friends except for her boyfriend, when it was clear to both of us that she just wasn't ready for the commitment that friendship with someone not in love with her demanded.

Tell me, she said, turning her whole body towards me after a brief silence (the strong fragrance of citrus trees filled the car, even though the windows were closed), what did you write?

Where? I asked, feigning ignorance.

On those World Cup slips of paper. What was your wish? Churchill didn't tell you?

I couldn't get him to tell me.

So you won't be able to get me to tell you either, I said and stepped on the accelerator.

It's OK, she said with an old, familiar gentleness. If you don't want to, don't tell me. I was just curious . . . You talk so little about yourself. So I thought . . . you know what . . . Just tell me this. The wish you made, are you close to fulfilling it? Do you think you'll fulfil it?

No way. Every day that passes just takes me further away from it, I said.

That's sad . . . It makes me sad to hear that, she said. And then she touched me softly on the shoulder and smiled: but it's a long time till the next World Cup, right?

Yes, almost two years.

So who knows.

Who knows, I repeated her words and kept driving. The shoulder she touched was burning. And continued burning, the way your body feels after you get sunburned at the beach, till we were in Tel Aviv. At their flat.

You've never actually been in our place, she asked-said.

No, it's just never happened, I said and thought that, even without having to be physically present inside it, I knew exactly what their flat looked like: hanging on the living room wall was that red cloth he'd brought from Bolivia and had moved with him to all of his previous flats. In the corner was her small dressing table that impossibly bore the enormous weight of all the objects lying on it. Above it was her collection of old posters of London theatre productions. In another corner were, of course, a few wretched plants (he always put plants in his flats and then didn't have the energy to look after them). In their fridge was Diet Coke, Diet Sprite and low-fat cheese slices because he was afraid of getting as fat as his father had become lately. And in their medicine cabinet was a packet of sleeping pills because she was afraid she wouldn't fall asleep at night. They had one small TV because he thinks that having a large TV is corrupt. And above the TV was a large picture of London because she'd been there with her parents when she was a child and was planning to go back to study when she had ninety-one thousand dollars. There was a huge bed in the bedroom, the kind she liked. And under the bed, next to his wide, bursting shoes stood her small, delicate ones. And the smell of her had collected between the tight, light-coloured sheets, the smell of her skin and hair and sweat and juices –

You want to come up for a drink? she interrupted my thoughts. Her tone was mainly polite.

Yes, I thought. I want to come up. Of course I want to come up. And on the steps, I want to grab you hard around the waist. And give you a small, fluttery kiss on the back of your neck. Where your spine ends. And then, inside the apartment, I want to bury my nose in your hair and smell your scent, smell you until the smell turns into taste, and then, still from behind, I want to unbutton your white blouse. The first two slowly, and the others, I'll rip open. Because I just can't any more. Because I can't any more can't any more can't any more –

No, thanks, I said. I think I'll go home.

*

(Once, on a school trip, I wrote to a girl on her back. My fingers meandered over her thin blouse and, letter after letter, I wrote her name. I didn't have the courage to write the real thing.)

*

I called Hani while I was still on the road, and as I was punching in the numbers, I already knew I was making a mistake. That this wasn't a good time. But still I asked her to come over. And she said yes, as usual. And she knocked on the door, as usual, two tentative knocks, even though I'd told her a thousand times that she could come in without knocking. I opened the door for her. And she stood there in the doorway with her beautiful hair loose because I liked it that way. And her deep, secular neckline. And waited for me to hug her. So I hugged her. Tightly. Especially because I wasn't feeling anything, I hugged her very tightly. And she said, wow, it was worth stepping out of the fold for that hug alone. And suddenly, that 'stepping out of the fold' annoyed me. Why can't she say 'I stopped being religious' and leave it at that? Suddenly everything about her annoyed me. The beautiful Hebrew, the naivety. The transparent dreams of homesickness about her mother that she dreamed at night, then asked me to interpret in the morning. And the two charming little stories about her day that she dredged up for me – the taxi driver who listened to meditation chants, the guy who fell asleep in the library with his head on *Maseket Baba Metzia* from the Talmud – those two stories annoyed me too. And I didn't know what to do with this irritation, not a familiar feeling for me, and she didn't deserve it. So I touched her and started to undress her, perhaps the contact would make me forget it. But it was all so bland and ended quickly. Even though I was horny, I came in a minute. And she was fine about it, really nice, which just annoyed me even more. And suddenly I wanted her to go. To get up and go and take all those things of hers that had messed up my neat flat: her shampoo. Her soap. Her shirt. Her hairbrush. Those childish loose-leaf binders with the hearts on the covers. I wanted her to put them all into large rubbish bags and go and let me be quietly alone with Ya'ara's sock.

And she felt it. She felt that something was going on inside me. And tried to ferret out what it might be: how was it in Haifa? How's Amichai?

The same, I grumbled.

It's nice of you to go there every day, she said. And I said, almost shouting, what does nice have to do with it? He's my friend. That scared her, of course, and she said, that's what I meant. After a short silence, she added, is everything all right? You're a bit distant today. And I looked her straight in the eye and confessed bravely that I was still in love with another woman. And it left no room in my heart for someone new.

I'm putting a nice face on things again.

I didn't confess anything to her. I said I was tired, that's all. And we'd talk tomorrow. But the next day, I didn't answer her calls and didn't reply to her messages. And the day after that too.

I took the cowardly way. With velvet cruelty.

And on the morning of the third day, she reached me.

You're on the way to Haifa, she said.

Yes, I admitted.

Today's the last day of the shiva, right?

Right.

Would you like me to go with you?

No, I don't think so.

She was silent on the other end of the line and I thought that if this conversation gets any longer, I'd leave too late and get stuck in traffic.

I wanted to ask . . . she hesitated.

Yes? I urged her.

My girlfriends tell me that you're trying to break up with me. That this is how it works with you secular people. You know I have no experience in such things.

I felt a warm affection for her rising inside me despite myself. And perhaps that was why, wanting to suppress that warm, mutinous affection, I gave her a particularly nasty answer.

Perhaps your girlfriends are right, I said. (It would have been bad enough to say, 'Your girlfriends are right.' But by prefacing it with 'perhaps', I planted a slight doubt, something to hold on to, the way you hold on to a drifting plank of wood in the middle of the ocean until you freeze to death.)

*

That day, the road north looked more beautiful than ever. The wind blowing through the window was just cool enough to keep me from having to turn on the air conditioning. I felt as if I'd done the right thing. I'd said no to concessions. No to compromise. No to cold love.

Although around Hadera, perhaps because of the electric power station, my feelings got completely turned around and for a few minutes I felt I'd missed an opportunity with Hani. That there'd been a moment there, on New Year's Eve, when my heart almost opened to her. And that it's easier to fantasise about old loves than to truly embrace new love. But when the song on the radio ended and the ads started, that temporary feeling was replaced by the previous one. The more comfortable one.

I pondered this reversal of feelings until Atlit. And how hard it is to know something for sure. And how almost everyone close to me finds it hard to know what he really feels, and fools himself endlessly, and perhaps that's only a generational thing, perhaps the number of distractions and options our generation has confuses us so much that we lose our inner path, unlike our parents, who knew what they wanted because they didn't have many choices, although who knows whether there wasn't a great sadness concealed behind all that, or at least a vague sense of missed opportunity we couldn't make out because we were children and unable to see what they were really like (or we could see and preferred, for our own good, not to?).

From Atlit, all those theoretical musings were replaced by a much more practical question: would Ya'ara be there on the last day of the shiva?

6

In Ya'ara's room in her parents' house, there was a huge picture of her as a child. And when I say huge, I mean an actual poster that hung above her bed in a red frame. I remember that the first time we slept together in that room, I could feel Ya'ara the child watching us, which added a certain element of perversion to everything that happened between us that night. The Ya'ara in the poster was a beautiful girl with caramel-coloured hair and a ribbon in it, mischievous, not entirely innocent eyes, and light-skinned calves that emerged from her short, dark jeans. But not even all that beauty explained the enormous size of the poster and the fact that it continued to hang in her room long after her childhood had ended.

Don't look for explanations, Yuval. I left that picture on the wall just because it makes me feel good, that's all, she answered when I asked.

Those visits to her parents' home in Rehovot also made her feel good. She didn't understand why my trips to Haifa were steeped in a sense of disappointment even before I set out. And why every time we left to go back to Tel Aviv, I would heave a sigh of relief. OK, they really did treat her like a princess in her house. She had three older brothers who were a bit in love with her, and were thrilled to see her whenever she made her entrance. So tell me, brother, can you still see your feet? she'd tease the eldest brother as she rubbed his architect's swelling pot belly. Then she would sniff her second brother's cheeks and say that his aftershave made her dizzy, simply made her dizzy. And finally, she and the third brother would give each other the special 'swan's hug' they'd invented when they were kids, where one of them thrust their neck into the hollow of the other's neck.

The three brothers competed to see who could compliment her more, make her laugh more and pamper her more. But none of them had a chance against her father, who was both her strict boss at work and her chief admirer at home. And something in all that inspired Ya'ara with confidence in her femininity, and gave her some very practical knowledge about how men worked. Yet there was something about it that diminished her. That trapped her in the geisha role and drew her to it with silk threads again and again, even when something inside her wanted very much to escape.

At home, they called her little Ya'ara. She took gender courses and talked about independence and feminism and self-realisation, and she had a clearly defined opinion on almost every subject, but they continued to call her little Ya'ara and treat her with admiration that bordered on patronising.

She didn't feel that. She loved it when they called her little Ya'ara and loved going there for Friday night dinners, and I loved her and wasn't sure that my entire diagnosis of her family wasn't just a cover for the jealousy I felt because she had such a happy family and I didn't. And in any case, I knew that she'd soon put together her ninety-one thousand dollars, stand on the moving walkway at the airport waving goodbye to her father and all her brothers and take off for London to fulfil her dreams. And at some point, I would join her in the white, warm apartment she'd have in Golders Green because it's always good to have someone with you who speaks English fluently. And because we'd still be a couple, of course.

*

I have only five or six pictures of the grown-up Ya'ara. And just one of us together, taken on the outing in Haifa that I planned for us.

It was a few weeks after we'd started going out and I wanted to show her that Haifa wasn't what she thought, so I convinced her to take a day off and we drove north, and at Atlit we turned right so that our first entrance into the city would be on the winding, forested Beit Oren road, and she said, wow, this is like being in another country, and I said, wait, you ain't seen nothin' yet, and I stopped for a few minutes at that spot, at the crest of the mountain where you can see both sides of the sea, and then we drove down along the route of my childhood, the Moriah road, to the Bahai Temple, whose opening hours I'd checked in advance, and we parked there, in the large observation garden, and caught our breaths at the sight of the glittering white marble steps that had been carved with such mathematical precision, and at the beautifully tended, brightly coloured gardens that surrounded us with their symmetrical forms, and then we surreptitiously joined a group of tourists to hear the Bahai guide explain that 'the beauty of the gardens is meant to act on their beholder like background music and create an unconscious harmony that will enable him to listen to himself'. I wonder what they're hiding under these gardens, Ya'ara whispered, and when the group had moved away a bit, she put her head on my shoulder and said, but you know, that whole business about unconscious harmony really works, ever since we came here, I'm a lot calmer, and I said, shame there's no Bahai branch in Tel Aviv, and she kissed me on the mouth and said, thanks, thanks for showing me all this beauty, and later, when we left, she smiled and said, maybe you'll become a Bahai? You're organised too, an aesthetics freak, and I said, not a bad idea, there's just one small problem, I think the Bahais are only allowed to be with other Bahais, and she laughed, for you I'm ready to be a Bahai too, and then we walked hand in hand to the panoramic promenade I'd already strolled along with other girls, promising myself that one day I'd come back here with one that I truly loved, and here I was, and here was Ya'ara. Look down, I told her, that's the port, I said, and on the other side, you can see the old city of Acre, and there in the distance are the Galilee mountains, and even further away is Syria.

It's getting a bit chilly – I remember her saying – and I gave her my jacket even though I was cold too, and she put it on and hugged me from behind with her slender arms, and we leaned on the railings and watched together as evening fell on the bay and small lights were turned on in the houses, and rivers of light began to flow on the roads, and she said, what a perfect day you planned for us. And I thought how amazing it was that nothing had gone wrong so far, that usually, when I over-plan and have high expectations, something happens to ruin everything, but this time – this time, no. From the minute we left the house, everything had gone smoothly, and the weather was good, contrary to the forecast for rain, and we didn't even meet people who knew me from high school, the thing I was most afraid of, for some reason. Later though, on the way to the car park, a car passed and someone inside wearing a white T-shirt yelled: hey, you two don't go together! But that was so bizarre, so out of the blue that we decided we must have heard wrong and he had actually shouted, 'Hey, how's the weather?' or 'Hey, Green Monkeys for ever!' which is the nickname for Maccabi Haifa's most ardent fans. And in any case, there's no sign of that strange shout in the picture, or of the fact that two weeks later she would leave me.

In the picture, we look like a pair of European tourists on their honeymoon in Haifa: Ya'ara has that half-mischievous half-serious look in her eyes, the one that makes everyone want her, and I look taller than in reality, and in the bottom corner of the frame, the photographer – a security guard in the Panorama Shopping Centre who Ya'ara enticed into leaving his post – managed to capture a large white ship that was making its way back into the port, or perhaps sailing out of it. At that point, it was hard to tell the difference.

*

Ya'ara didn't come to the last day of the shiva. On the whole, there were fewer people. And most of the black chairs remained black. There were mostly family members at Amichai's side, and perhaps it was the absence of witnesses that allowed the money issue to come to the surface.

It had popped up a few times even before then.

One day, a tall man had asked in a low voice whether they intended to file suit.

Someone from Givat HaMacam talked about a woman from their kibbutz who was left with an ugly scar on her knee after undergoing hair removal by laser, and she was awarded one hundred thousand shekels compensation. But that was before privatisation, so she was screwed because it was actually the kibbutz that got the money. She looked over at Amichai when she finished the story, but Amichai kept silent on that subject too, just as he'd kept silent on other subjects. As the days passed, his silence had turned from being a threatening and deeply meaningful one that sucked all the air out of the room, into the kind that everyone there had grown used to: they still had a certain respect for it, but allowed themselves, more and more, to ignore it.

Till the last day –

Speaking into the space of the room, Ilana's aunt said that she had consulted with the attorney for the company where she worked and he told her that they could expect at least one million in compensation. At least!

And a distant cousin of Amichai's – she too addressing no one in particular – said that a lot depended on the attorney. And that they should invest in a good one because, in the end, it would pay off.

And a widowered accountant, who every day of the shiva had described in detail – whether it was appropriate or not – the difficult time he'd had after his wife's death, took a fountain pen out of his shirt pocket, unscrewed the cap and said that they should also take into account the deceased's life insurance, so the final amount could grow to two million shekels and even more.

And Ilana's brother mumbled, a million, two million, what does it matter. Nothing will bring her back.

And Ilana's mother said, at least the children will be taken care of.

And Amichai's mother sighed – a sigh of both sadness and surprise – two million is money. Maybe you'll finally be able to move into a more spacious house.

And Ilana's brother, no longer mumbling, said what do you mean, a house? What do they need a new house for now? They'd be better off putting the money into a savings account.

Then the widower removed the cap from his fountain pen again and said, excuse me for butting in, but a house is an investment that can pay an excellent dividend. Especially the way the market is now, with such low prices because of this new Intifada.

And Ilana's mother raised her voice, I don't understand all this talk! Aren't you ashamed? Obviously the money should go straight into a trust fund!!

And Amichai's mother – who had been trying to hide her reservations about Ilana's mother throughout the entire shiva, and it was that exaggerated attempt that gave her away over and over again – said: it's obvious to you.

And Ilana's mother narrowed her eyes and said, what does that mean?

And Amichai's mother said, exactly what you think it means.

And Amichai rose from his chair, slowly, and for the first time that week, opened his mouth and said: enough.

Since I'd had nothing to contribute to the financial conversation, I'd been watching his facial expressions while it was taking place.

At first, his eyes were sunken, dark. His chin drooped. Defeated. The words seemed not to be reaching his ears. Then – perhaps he caught a snatch of something, a sliver of a word – his eyebrows were stirred into action and began to follow the exchange. Then his lower lip started to tremble and he tried to bite it, control it. But the trembling spread to his upper lip.

Then he stood up.

I looked into his eyes. I was sure I'd see a terrible fury in them, but no. To my surprise, the old, familiar spark was there, the one that always heralded a brilliant idea.

Enough, he said. I don't want to hear this kind of talk. I earn enough money at Telemed to take care of my children's future. And if there's any compensation money . . . or insurance . . . I plan to use it for something else . . . something Ilana would have wanted . . .

What, for instance? Ilana's brother asked, a touch of puzzlement in his voice.

I don't know yet, Amichai replied, a bit embarrassed. Maybe I'll establish some kind of non-profit organisation. An NPO. Maybe something else. I don't know.

An NPO? For what? her brother persisted.

I just told you, I don't know, Amichai replied reluctantly. And sat down. And wrapped himself in silence once again.

*

Yeah, right, Churchill said sceptically when I called to tell him what Amichai had said at the shiva.

He's confused now, Ofir said. I've treated people in

his condition and you shouldn't take anything they say seriously.

*

But a month after Ilana's death, the three of us received calls from Amichai. We'll meet at my place, he told us. I want to ask your advice about the organisation.

I don't know, Churchill said to me dubiously. It sounds like another one of those Amichai Tanuri far-fetched ideas. He doesn't even know what this charitable organisation of his will be for. Mark my words: it'll end with him wanting us to sing 'Shimon My Man' together.

He's counting on the fact that I was a copywriter, Ofir complained to me, but I'm all rusty now when it comes to that whole business of . . . you know, words.

What does it matter, I said, trying to persuade them. Your friend wants help, so you help him. Then ask questions.

*

A few hours before we were supposed to meet, Amichai called to cancel. There was a tape of children's songs playing too loudly in the background.

We had a rough night, he told me. I think they're only just starting to comprehend it now. Noam called out to her in his sleep. And Nimrod got up this morning and said he wasn't going to school till Mummy came back.

What did you tell him?

That it was OK not to go to school today. And then Noam decided that he didn't want to go either.

Of course.

To cut a long story short, I promised them both I'd take them to the amusement park. And I don't know when we'll get home. And in what . . . condition. So I think we'll postpone the meeting for a week. Will you let everyone know?

*

Maybe it's better this way, Ofir said when I told him. So he doesn't waste his . . . chi.

You see, I told you nothing ever comes of Amichai's

142

ideas, Churchill asserted, and didn't show up at the first, historical meeting of the NPO, which took place – despite all our scepticism – a week later.

*

Where's Churchill? Amichai asked when Ofir and I sat down. Maria and her daughter went to the twins' room and Ofir watched them worriedly. Her big smile had shrunk during that time. She stopped hugging us. And she almost completely stopped working in the clinic. One night, Ofir got up to go to the toilet and saw her sitting and crying in the living room, so he sat down next to her and captured her tears with his tongue as they ran down her cheeks, and when she calmed down a bit, he suggested that they go to Denmark, maybe that would make her feel better, but that only made her angry and she started crying again and said that he doesn't understand, he doesn't understand anything, there are only seven hours of light in Denmark now, and darkness is dangerous for her, she's afraid that the darkness will creep inside her and fill her from within, and besides, there are the twins, she can't just get up and leave them.

She went to Amichai's three times a week to be with them, and they were very happy to see her. Perhaps because they felt, with the sensitivity of children who'd just lost their mother, that while all the other grown-ups only pitied them, she also needed them. Or perhaps because her daughter, the object of their great love, came with her, and now that they were motherless, their love for her had become desperate.

*

Where's Churchill? Amichai asked again.

He . . . he wanted to come, I said evasively. But he's busy with that case of his, you know.

A look of bitter hurt flared in Amichai's eyes. Too bad, he said, I especially wanted to hear what he had to say.

We were silent. We let his disappointment fade. Across

143

from us, on the living room wall, hung a picture of Ilana. The serious expression. The pale freckles. The decisive nose. The vague sense of disappointment (with life? with herself?) around the lips. Of all the pictures of her, this was the one Amichai had chosen to enlarge – a picture that didn't flatter her at all, but captured her as she truly was. I suddenly missed her, missed the good, simple, close conversations we could have had and never would. I missed her home-baked *burekas*. Her astute, psychological analyses. Her quiet, inexplicable liking for me.

It's like this, Amichai said, bending towards us. It turns out that the compensation money from the insurance company isn't as much as I thought. The clinic admits that they hid from her the fact that the operation could have complications, but they found some clause in the agreement form she signed that protects it. To cut a long story short, in the end, together with the insurance, we're talking about a few hundred thousand shekels. But that has no bearing on our plan. I want to establish an NPO in Ilana's name that will represent the patient's side.

The patient? we asked. What do you mean?

You know, he said, looking at us both. When you go to the hospital . . . when the ambulance . . . with Ilana inside . . . reached the hospital . . . the paramedics ran into A & E with the trolley . . . and I ran in after them . . . I ran as fast as I could . . . but the guard stopped me. He wanted identification. I yelled that my wife was there, inside. So he said, 'Please don't shout, sir', and checked me slowly . . . on purpose . . . that's why I got inside about a minute after them. And no one could tell me where Ilana was. The nurses sent me to admissions. At admissions, they sent me back to the nurses. No one knew where she was. Finally, some patient who was sitting in the corridor – a patient, get it? – said that maybe they didn't have time to admit her and I should check intensive care. I ran to intensive care and it turned out that she really was there. I asked to go inside . . . to see her . . . they said I couldn't. I wasn't allowed. I asked . . . so what am I supposed to do now? They told me to sit on the bench and wait for them to come to me. So I sat and waited for hours. I don't know if it was hours, but it felt like hours. Let's say that I sat there like a dog for at least an hour and no one came to talk to me. Then all of a sudden, some doctor yelled from inside, 'Where's Tanuri? Is Ta-nuri here?' and the way he said my name . . . I can't explain it . . . as if he thought it was funny . . . that already gave me a bad feeling about him . . . then he came over to me, and without introducing himself, he started asking me about Ilana . . . what illnesses she'd had . . . allergies to drugs . . . hereditary diseases . . . I answered him, and all the time, I was waiting for him to tell me what was happening . . . and he didn't . . . so I finally asked him . . . what's happening with her? And he didn't answer . . . he didn't give me an evasive answer, you understand . . . or a partial answer . . . it's like . . . like I'm not there . . . and he turns around to go . . . so I saw red and I grabbed his shirt from behind and said, I want you to answer me, doctor, and he shoved my hand away . . . hard, you know . . . and said, don't you raise your hand to me, Mr Tanuri . . . and I said . . . I didn't raise my hand to you . . . I just asked . . . and he interrupted me and said it wasn't his fault that we went to a private clinic instead of doing the cosmetic surgery in the hospital . . . was it?! That really made me mad . . . I didn't understand what he was getting at . . . so I asked him straight out what his credentials were and if he was even qualified to treat cases like this . . . and again he didn't answer me . . . so I said that I demanded a second opinion . . . and he shut up for a minute, then gave me a kind of crooked, disgusting smile and said, you want a second opinion? So take your wife and go to another hospital.

That's what he said to you?! Ofir and I said.

Yes.

Unbelievable.

After he went, a nurse came over to me and said that Dr Gabrinsky is an excellent doctor. Don't worry, you're in good hands, she told me. And that . . . that just pissed me off even more, because the last thing I felt was that I was in good hands. So I sat in the corridor and thought I was going mad . . . that I was dying. There was no one to talk to. No one came over to me. Till morning. And all the time there was this strong smell of drugs and cottage cheese. Once every few minutes, there'd be a wave of the drug smell. And then a wave of the cottage cheese smell. I haven't been able to eat cottage cheese since. I just hear the words cottage cheese and I remember that corridor. I sat there like some kind of homeless guy, like a soldier they forgot to relieve from guard duty, and at five in the morning, a different doctor, not Gabrinsky, came over to me. And from his face, I already knew it was over . . .

Amichai was choked up. The picture he was seeing in his mind must have been painfully sharp.

We poured him a glass of water. But he didn't touch it.

He coughed and went on, the second doctor was actually OK. But that Gabrinsky. Where had he disappeared to at five in the morning? He didn't have the guts to come and talk to me even . . . no . . . the fact that he didn't even bother to come out to me . . . that's what . . .

Maybe he had emergency surgery, Ofir tried to come up with a reason.

There's nothing . . . nothing that should have kept him from coming out to talk to me . . . he couldn't find someone to take over for him for a minute?

We didn't say anything. A cold wind came in from the open balcony door, but no one got up to close it. The wind chimes that Maria had made for Ilana for her last birthday tinkled lightly.

But you know what? That's how it is, Amichai said after

146

a long moment, and his tone was more measured now. That's how it is with public health. The patient is a nuisance. And the people who come with him are a disaster. You should have seen it. There was an Ethiopian family sitting in the corridor with me. They didn't know Hebrew, so even when someone finally came to talk to them, they didn't understand. How can it be that not even one person in the entire hospital speaks Amharic? Isn't that outrageous?

We nodded. We didn't dare take the chance of giving any other response.

You know, he went on, his eyes blazing, everything depends on the doctors' good will. And it's not that doctors are necessarily bad people. But the conditions they work under, the long shifts, the fatigue. A doctor goes to school for twelve years to get his licence, and in all those years, he doesn't get any training in how to deal with patients on an emotional level. So for some, it comes naturally, and for others, it doesn't. That's how it is. Instead of being, well, a basic principle, it becomes a game of roulette. Which doctor just happens to be on duty when you come in, and whether he had a good night's sleep.

Wait a minute, I don't understand, I said, trying to clarify things. This is an NPO that will be against the medical establishment or for it? And what does it have to do with cosmetic surgery? It's a whole different story, isn't it?

You're right, Amichai said, but his voice had lost none of its confidence. The whole thing isn't fully formed yet. But you're my friends, and I wanted to hear your opinion. I mean, how does it sound to you, you know, as a preliminary idea?

I didn't say anything. On the one hand, I remembered all my severe asthma attacks and the helplessness I felt when I had to explain my condition (in as few words as possible – every word wasted valuable air) to impatient doctors. And once, they gave me the gown with the opening in the back and didn't bother to tell me about it and I walked with it like that, open, to the nurses' station. And there was the time when they asked me to take my medical file from one department to another, and I looked inside and saw that a doctor who had no authority to make that kind of diagnosis had written that I had 'a slight tendency to melancholy'.

On the other hand, none of the doctors who treated me had abused me. Condescending, yes. But not abusive.

Then on still another hand, there was Amichai.

But an NPO? What do I know about such things?

I think it's a great idea, Ofir said. It's just what alternative medicine says, you have to treat a person holistically, not like just a collection of symptoms.

They both looked at me, waiting to hear my opinion. Even Ilana stared at me from the wall.

I think she would really like it, I said, pointing at her (and thought to myself that maybe she would be happier about an organisation to help the Palestinians at the checkpoints, but I knew there was no use bringing that up, because there was no way that Amichai, whose father had been killed by Palestinians in Lebanon, would be willing to establish that kind of organisation).

Yes, I also think she'd be for it, Amichai said and glanced quickly at Ilana's picture, as if he was afraid that if he looked at for too long he might sink into it. And drown.

So what's next? Ofir asked.

We meet here again in two weeks, Amichai said. Meanwhile, I'll start a round of meetings to find out what forming an NPO entails. After all, we don't have the slightest idea.

What about us, what's our job?

Don't let me give up, Amichai said. That's all for now.

*

You think anything will come of all this? Ofir asked me when all four of us – Maria, her daughter, he and I – were on the street.

Honestly? No, I said. But what difference does it make? The main thing is that it'll keep Amichai busy. So he won't have time to think.

It's a good thing he has the twins, Ofir said. It keeps his head above water. For the time being. If he didn't have to get up in the morning for them – I don't know what would happen to him.

Those children . . . Maria sighed, they're . . . I don't know.

How are they? I asked.

Nimrod's OK, she said. He cries. He says he misses Lana. The way he should. The one who worries me is Noam. He's too quiet. He leaves everything inside. That's very bad for a child.

It's very bad for an adult, too, Ofir said. Did you see how thin Amichai is? Did you notice that he didn't touch any of the refreshments for the three hours we were there? And the blotch on his neck, did you see that the whole Galilee is suddenly gone? How can that be? And the balcony, did you notice that he opened the balcony? Only two years ago, they spent forty thousand shekels to close it off! Not to mention the puzzle, did you see the puzzle he has there? Two thousand pieces of the *Titanic*. The *Titanic*, get it? They're all warning signs, I'm telling you. I've been there, in that state. He's going through the motions, but we have to watch him all the time. Because if, God forbid, he does something to himself, we'll never forgive ourselves.

From: 'Metamorphoses: Great Minds who Changed their Mind', an unfinished philosophy thesis by Yuval Freed

In April 1901, the philosopher Bertrand Russell and his spouse are staying with their friends, the Whiteheads, in their mansion in Oxford. In the evening, the Russells go out and when they return, they find, to their horror, that Mrs Whitehead is lying on the sofa in the throes of an attack of severe pain. She is curled up like a foetus, moaning. Then, she writhes for several seconds and curls up again. Russell wants to go to her, to help her. But Mr Whitehead stops him. Nothing can be done, he explains. It's Evelyn's heart disease. We have to wait for it to pass.

As he stands there watching the woman moaning on the sofa, Russell experiences a dramatic internal change (he himself uses the religious term 'conversion' when he describes the event in his autobiography). In sharp contrast to other devel- opments his thinking had undergone over time, the conversion that occurred that night was not preceded by tightly reasoned logic; nor was it supported by precise formulas. The ground, as he himself writes, is simply pulled out from under his feet during those five minutes he stands watching Mrs Whitehead's suffering, and suddenly — according to his own testimony — he understands everything: he understands that the human soul is infinitely alone in its pain. And that that loneliness is unbearable. He understands that the only way to penetrate and touch that private loneliness is through unconditional love of the sort clerics preach, and that any act that is not derived from such love is harmful and pointless. This leads him to the conclusion (it is amusing to see that Russell's apparently mystic flow of thought here actually evolves logically, almost like a mathematical proof) that war is evil, that public school education is disgraceful, that all use of force is to be condemned, and that in interpersonal relations, a person must penetrate the core of another's loneliness and speak to it.

For several months after that event, Russell felt that he had had an epiphany and that he was able to read the innermost thoughts of anyone he met on the street. Those mystic feelings faded with time, but he never forgot that moment in the Whitehead home, and he claimed that it lay at the root of his shift from imperialism to pacifism. The same Russell who grew up in a family of political conservatives and, from earliest childhood, absorbed the belief in the supreme importance of preserving the great British Empire, that same Russell who, only two years earlier, in 1899, had wholeheartedly wished for Britain's victory in the cruel war to suppress the Boers in South Africa, became in five minutes, so he claimed, a pacifist who championed conscientious objectors, and later, preached against Britain's participation in the First World War . . .

7

Apart from that picture with Amichai, on the roof, I don't have any photos from the Intifada. I don't think I felt that what we were doing in Nablus, in Jabalya or Raffiah would ever merit nostalgia. Perhaps that's why I don't have any good friends from the army. Ofir's father, for instance, would get together with his mates from the Armoured Corps three times a year, and he'd start getting excited about their meetings a month beforehand. Churchill's father has three friends from the Paratroopers, and one of them paid for another's operation abroad not too long ago. I think that for them, and for many of their generation, the army was the breeding ground for friendship. And with me – just the opposite. My friends are from before the army. And when I happen to see someone who served with me in the territories, we say as little as possible to each other, and I think we both flinch inside. True, it might be that I'm the only one who flinches, and perhaps it's all because of my tendency to always be in the opposition – Amichai, for example, still has friends from the army, and if you ask him, he'll tell you a completely different story about the Intifada, a story of the brotherhood of fighters, of thwarting terrorist attacks and kill-them-before-they-kill-you, and he'd say that the army gave him Ilana and saved him from his gloomy family and the role he was forced to play in it, and those three years were the first time he felt he was able to live since his father died –

But I'm the narrator here, and I want to say that there are too many moments in my army years that I'm not proud of, and the lowest ebb was during the 1990 World Cup, in an unplastered, raw concrete building on the outskirts of Nablus.

Not even my friends know about that moment. And I didn't want to mention it here either – I've been so taken with the spotless image of myself my words have created – but this confession has been knocking on the door of this book for quite a few pages already, and it's blasting out of me now like a bullet.

We were supposed to stay on the roof of that building in Nablus for three days, but in the end, we stayed three weeks. They were supposed to bring us food once a week, and they brought field rations. We were so tired and hungry there that at some point, I started looking at the other nine soldiers who were with me and wondering which of them would be tastiest if we cooked him. And I had no doubt that if it came to that, I would be the one to cook him. The nine guys with me on the roof had done all their training together, and I was sent to join the company a week before we went down to Nablus, after I'd been kicked out of the officers training course. All of them – I wasn't sure how – knew I'd been kicked off the course because I fell asleep during a lecture by the training base commander, and they enjoyed yelling 'Good morning, Freed!' into my ear every time they thought I was drifting off. Also, they gave me the hardest shifts and deliberately came late to relieve me, they shared the few special treats they received among themselves and never offered me any, and they made fun of me for writing too many letters to my girlfriend.

I didn't have a girlfriend. But when they asked me who I was writing to, I couldn't admit that it was to Churchill and Ofir, so I made up a girlfriend named Adva, who was stationed at an intelligence base on the Egyptian border and missed me so much that I had to write to her every day to calm her down. I hated the fact that I was lying to them. I hated those long observations in a futile attempt to identify hostile children. I hated detaining the night-time arrests in strange houses. Scared shitless. I hated the vulgar jokes. And the racist jokes. And the fact that, at one point, I was the main teller of those jokes.

But more than anything, I hated myself after the game between England and Cameroon.

It was Doron's idea. He was the one who said, you see that house with the TV set? How about we go in there, do a small search, and while we're at it, watch England–Cameroon?

I remember that I smiled. I thought he was kidding. But then Commander Harel himself asked, England–Cameroon? When does it start? The broadcast starts now, Doron answered, the game in half an hour. Commander Harel said, that should be one hell of a game. Then without another word, he began cleaning his gun in preparation to move out. And that's how, in unspoken complicity, all of us except the guy on guard duty, took our weapons and combat vests and headed out in two columns to the parallel street and the small house that had a blue light flickering in its windows.

*

As I begin marching now, beside that Yuval, the soldier, I immediately sense that smell of the territories, which most closely resembles the smell of a sweatshirt on the morning after an all-night camp-fire. I see a Palestinian flag waving from the power lines above us again, even though we made them take it down the day before. I see the black slogans written on the walls and torn fragments of burned tyres. And I feel the sewage flowing between my feet, muddy and reeking and sticking to the soles of my shoes. And, as if more than ten years hadn't passed, that fear begins to pound inside me, the fear that someone would drop a breeze block on us from the roofs, or a fridge.

The few people who were out in the street began walking faster then and looked at us: children two or three years old were still looking at us with open curiosity, but the fear was already visible in the eyes of the four- or five-year-olds. I glanced away from them and looked down at the shoes of the soldier marching in front of me, trying to convince myself that what we were going to do now wasn't necessarily terrible, and perhaps something good would come out of it and we'd find ourselves sitting and watching the game with the family that lived in that house we were marching towards, and for ninety minutes, the barriers would fall and we would no longer be occupier and occupied, stoner and stoned, Jew and Arab, but just people. Watching the World Cup together.

*

But from the minute we pushed the door open, everything went south.

The family into whose lives we had burst was watching a quiz show on TV and didn't understand why Commander Harel was demanding so insistently that they change the channel, what did that have to do with searching the house? My brother's son, he's from Jordan, the father tried to explain, he . . . *ya'ani* . . . he's on this quiz show . . . that's why it's so important for us to watch it . . . it's over in a few minutes . . . please, sit down. The father's explanation sounded reasonable, and his tone was straightforward. But the commander thought otherwise, and for no reason, slapped him hard. His two sons, who, till then, hadn't said or done anything, stood up and went to stand at either side of him, and then Doron pointed to one of them and shouted, hey, that's the bastard who dropped that breeze block on us yesterday!

Within seconds, a God-awful commotion began that ended with all the objects in the living room, except the TV – vases, pictures, bowls, lamps – shattered. The boy who had dropped the breeze block on us (or perhaps it wasn't him?) was standing handcuffed in a corner of the room, his right arm twisted. Doron had twisted it, exactly as the krav maga instructor had taught us in a lesson a week before. I remembered their panting as they struggled, and the muttered incantations and curses of one of the old Arab women that came later. I remember that we pushed her and the rest of the family with our rifle butts and our hands into a small side room.

Then we fiddled with the dial till we found the game.

*

When I say we, that includes me.

There were extenuating circumstances. Of course. I was a kid – what's nineteen? A boy! And I was just following orders, naturally, what can a soldier do except follow orders? Even Rabin himself said, 'Break their bones', the Rabin of the Rabin assassination! So what could a boy from Haifa do? Anyway, I didn't raise a hand to anyone. I swear! When Doron was beating up that boy, I even pushed (too hard? too eagerly?) the old woman and the children into the side room so he wouldn't beat them too. And another time, in Jenin, a Palestinian who was hit with a rubber bullet was lying in the middle of the street and my commander told me to leave the bastard there, let him die, but I screamed that I was a medic and had to treat him, and I kneeled next to him and managed to stop the blood that was spurting out of him so rapidly. I was able to stop the bleeding and save him, and I didn't care that, afterwards, the whole unit called me Yuval-bleeding-heart and Yuval-the-leftie, and I didn't care that I was confined to the base for insubordination.

*

But I too sat in the living room of that family from Nablus and watched England–Cameroon. And stretched my legs to rest them on an armchair that wasn't mine. And I was glad when England evened the score to two-all (I think I was so excited that I even stood up). I too ate the pitta and hummus we took out of the family's fridge. And agreed that those Arabs really knew how to make hummus. I too heard the sobs of pain coming from the handcuffed boy. And the pleading of the women to be let out so they could go to the toilet. I too saw Commander Harel walk over and turn up the volume so all that noise wouldn't bother us.

I too wanted to stay a while longer, when the game was over, to see the replays of the goals. And a little longer than that, to hear the post-game interviews.

*

Only later, when we went back to the roof, did I have an attack of nausea when I thought about what I and the guys from the company had done and about that damned World Cup, and I tried to tell myself that it had been a one-off moral lapse, but I knew it wasn't, I knew that, over the last few weeks, I'd become as brutalised as everyone else there. I kept twisting and turning in my sleeping bag that night, unable to find a position in which my conscience could fall asleep. Suddenly, it seemed to me that there was no way out. No future. It was as clear as the dark night to me that no one would ever come to relieve us. That I was going to stay on that roof, with those people, my whole life. And that the curse that the old Arab woman had muttered before we pushed her into the room would haunt me my whole life.

I pulled myself out of the sleeping bag and went to a far corner of the roof where no one could see me. I took small, Charlie Chaplin steps until I was standing right on the edge. I looked down to the street and thought, what would happen if I jumped now and ended it all?

Ofir can make his movie, was the bitter-sweet answer that surfaced from the depths of my memory. After all, I had promised him that if none of us died in the army, then I would.

I looked down again. This building isn't tall enough, I said to myself. With my luck, I might stay alive. Paralysed.

*

Dear Bro in intelligence, I wrote to Churchill that night, holding a torch in one hand and a pen in the other.

I don't understand what I'm doing here. I don't understand who's fighting who. I don't understand any more what's behind the word 'I'. I don't understand what the difference is between me and an animal. I don't understand how I got to this. I don't understand why I insisted on hiding my asthma so they'd take me into a combat unit. I don't understand why I'm tired now and can't fall asleep. I don't understand why I want to shout and no sound comes out of me. I don't understand what there is to understand here. I don't understand why they don't come to relieve us. I don't understand why I don't care whether they come to relieve us. I don't understand anything.

You're in intelligence. You probably know. Maybe you can explain it to me?

*

Three weeks after the weapons carrier dropped us off under the roof, they came to relieve us. It was twilight. I was the one on duty then. And when I saw someone who looked like Amichai get out of the weapons carrier, I thought I was hallucinating. Amichai? No way. He isn't even in this division. I must be very far into the twilight zone if I'm seeing my friends in the middle of Nablus.

But it was Amichai. With his MAG slung over his shoulder, and those broad shoulders and that happy walk. For a few seconds, I heard his familiar steps echoing on the stairs, and then, all at once, as the sun setting behind him illuminated his hair in golden, nearly messianic light, he burst onto the roof.

I knew it! he shouted, running happily towards me. I knew I'd see you here! I told the guys, you're about to meet my best friend! He crushed me in a huge hug, then introduced me to the soldiers who'd come with him to relieve us. They shook my hand and I could feel in their handshakes that being Amichai's friend won me a lot of points with them.

This is amazing! he went on happily. For us to meet here! Churchill and Ofir won't believe it when they hear it! Come on, let's take a picture so we have proof.

Move your arse, Freed, we're waiting for you down here, the soldiers who'd been on the roof with me called from down on the street. But suddenly, I didn't care about them. Suddenly, because Amichai was there, I felt like a human being again.

*

In the picture, we look like one of those 'before and after' ads. Except that with us, the 'after' looked horrible. Unshaven. Tired. With a blue ink stain near his shirt pocket. And murky eyes. And the 'before', who was Amichai, actually looked great. Fresh uniform. Shiny equipment. A bold, direct stare into the camera.

I don't know a lot about photography, but of all the pictures in the album, I think that's the only one with a chance of making it to a gallery exhibition. Because of the soft, minute-after-sunset light. And because of the sharp contrast between me and Amichai, which neither of us was aware of. And also because in the background, the camera had unintentionally caught a Palestinian boy of about five or six on one of the other roofs watching the whole scene.

After our picture was taken, Amichai gave me the letter Churchill had asked him to pass on to me. And he hugged me again. You came just in time, Bro, I whispered in his ear. You came a minute before I was going to throw in the towel. And it's good that of all the guys, you're the one who came. Because there's no one like you to remind me that there's also good in the world (and perhaps I didn't tell him all that, and now, as I write, I'm taking advantage of the opportunity to say it).

Then I climbed down from the roof and joined the unit

waiting for me on the street. The sun had already set and a frightening trip in the dark back to the battalion base was awaiting us.

Where does he know you from, that MAG guy? someone asked me after the weapons carrier had started moving.

Amichai? I replied. He's my friend, in civilian life.

*

I think that was the first time I called him my friend and really meant it.

Our friendship didn't ignite with a single spark, the way my friendship with Churchill and Ofir did, but grew over the years. Patiently. From event to event. That meeting in Nablus, for instance. Or the first time he asked me to his family's home in Haifa, in Ramat Hadar.

The first friend I ever had, Oren Ashkenazi, had also lived in Ramat Hadar, and as a child, I was jealous of that and begged my parents to move us to the empty flat above his family.

Why should we move to Ramat Hadar? my mother asked with a grown-ups-who-know smile, and I said excitedly: there's this giant yard where the kids go to play football and frisbee, and there's a lift in every entrance that makes this scary whistling sound when it goes up, and there are twelve floors in every building and the twelfth floor is really high and sometimes you can look at the clouds when you're on it, I mean, really see them from up there!

I wasn't a child any more when I went to see Amichai in Ramat Hadar. Oren Ashkenazi and his family had already gone to live in America, and the neighbourhood looked different to me: intimidating buildings. Too wide. Too grey, almost like the buildings in Kieślowski films.

I stood on the ugly bridge that connected the car park to the building entrance, looked at the play area that had once seemed so wonderful to me, and noticed that it was bordered on all sides by high concrete walls. There was no way out of it. No landscape. Like a prison yard.

There were no children in that now. Not even one. Just a bearded man in rags standing in the centre of it talking out loud to himself, but not loudly enough for me to hear him. Had he already been talking to himself then, when we played there? Had he grabbed the ball once in the middle of a game and refused to give it back? Or was my memory deceiving me?

I stood on the bridge for another few minutes, then took out the slip of paper on which I'd written the number of the entrance where the Tanuri family lived.

*

Hanging on the living room wall was a huge picture of the father in uniform, and he didn't resemble Amichai in the slightest. He had light hair and dark self-confidence. And shrewd, crafty eyes. I remember that there were no other pictures in the living room, just plaques of recognition the father had received from the various units he'd served in. *In appreciation for. In acknowledgment of. Wishing you success in your new post. From your friends in the company, the battalion, the division.* I remember that it wasn't his mother who served the food at the table, but Amichai, and that her plate was empty throughout the entire meal. She looked like someone who hadn't eaten for a long time, and when a strong wind came through the window, I was afraid for a minute that it would blow her out of her chair and swirl her around the room. Every once in a while she took a quick glance at the blank screen of the TV that stood in the middle of the living room, and I was sure she had asked for it to be turned off because of me, so I wouldn't get the impression that the Tanuris needed a TV to keep them together. She tried very hard to have a conversation with me. She asked me about school and my father's printing house and my plans for the future, and I felt how much effort every question, every word cost her.

I wanted to console her. That woman with the large brown eyes and the freckles that gave her a slightly childlike look.

I wanted to shake her. To save her (me? twenty years younger than her? I was the one who would save her?).

But I just kept answering her questions.

At a certain stage, two of Amichai's brothers started fighting (perhaps to rescue her from having to continue asking the guest questions?). Amichai let them push each other for a few seconds, then said in a quiet voice, 'Guy and Shai, that's enough.' And they stopped immediately and sat up in their chairs obediently.

I looked at him, amazed. I couldn't make the connection between the insecure, inarticulate guy who hung out with us, and the mature, authoritative person I was suddenly seeing.

*

Later, during the first few years in Tel Aviv, our friendship was constructed slowly with brick after brick of small deeds. Every time I asked him to help me move, for instance, he was right there. Not three hours late, like Ofir. Not trying to convince me, like Churchill, that hiring a removal company would be cheaper in the end.

Whenever he needed an emergency babysitter – usually when Ilana was in one of her moods and he felt he 'had to take her out for some air' – I would go there and read the twins stories and change their nappies and feel pangs of longing for children of my own, which would turn into sharp stabs of impatience the minute one of them started to cry, then back into pangs of longing again when they fell asleep.

Once a week, between meetings with one Telemed client and another, Amichai would come to visit me. Always with delicious cookies Ilana had baked. Always insisting on making the coffee himself. Always collapsing on my sofa with the same old Yiddish cry of pleasure, *a-machayeh*.

The conversations that came after the coffee were excruciatingly predictable: he would tell me about the new treatment he was trying to remove the blotch on his neck, and I would say that no one noticed it but him and that if he weren't with Ilana, a lot of women would want him. And then I would tell him about another awful date I'd been on, and he would agree with me too quickly that the girl wasn't worth it anyway. And interspersed were updates on Ilana's latest successes in academia and the twins' latest antics, complaints about work at Telemed, empty words about the possibility of leaving everything and signing up to study shiatsu that same year and circular debates about the new line-ups of Maccabi Haifa or the Israeli national team.

Quite a few times, I stole a glance at the clock while he was there.

But even so, I was filled with light when I saw him through the peephole of my door a week later.

There they were, the broad shoulders. There they were, the earth-coloured eyes. There it was, that feeling that everything would be OK.

*

After Ilana died, he kept coming once a week. But he didn't talk any more. Not about the blotch, not about Maccabi Haifa, not about the Israeli national team. He would hug me limply at the door, then go into the living room, sit down on the sofa and remain silent.

At first, I tried to get him to say something.

Do you want to talk? I asked.

Yeah, but . . . he slowly dragged the words out of his mouth . . . it hurts.

Want something to drink?

No.

Eat?

No, Bro, thanks.

So what . . . what can I do for you?

Nothing. Sit . . . Sit here with me.

*

So I sat with him. Once a week, on the sofa. And we were silent together. On the wall across from us hung framed pictures of the guys. In front of us, on the table, the cookies he bought at the grocery shop. Sometimes, as I stared into space, I'd start thinking about a word I'd come up against in a translation, or about clients' cheques I had to cash, or I'd try to concentrate and read his thoughts, or I'd try to wordlessly pass a thought of my own to him, let's say a thought like, Bro, stop feeling guilty, you did what you could to prevent the surgery, and anyway, who could have known that such simple surgery could suddenly go so wrong? Or a thought like, you're so strong, Amichai, so much sorrow would have turned anyone else, including me, into a well a long time ago, like it did to Egeria in *Metamorphoses*.

*

But it didn't matter what thoughts I tried to pass on to him. After half an hour, he would get up and walk to the door.

Usually, he would give me a quick hug and leave without saying a word. Only once did he linger a bit at the door and say, this stays between us, OK, Yuval?

Of course, I promised. Even though I didn't understand what was supposed to stay between us.

And he would lean on the wall of the staircase, smile mournfully and say, you're . . . you're a friend.

8

When Amichai opened the door to us two weeks later, we were shocked to see that his blotch had almost completely disappeared. Ilana's death had succeeded where all the salves and cosmetic treatments had failed, and now not only had the Galilee been erased from his neck, but also the Negev and Jerusalem and the Judea Plains and, in fact, except for a small spot left where the greater Tel Aviv area had been, there was nothing left of that Israel-on-the-neck that had screwed up his self-confidence for years.

He was also very thin. His shirt was hanging on him, his chin had sharpened, his cheekbones protruded, adding a tragic, Jacques Brel dimension to everything he said.

I have bad news and bad news, he announced at the beginning of our meeting.

At least you have no problem about what to start with, I said. But that didn't make him smile.

The bad news, he said, is that we don't have enough money at the moment to set up a serious NPO, and we need donations from foundations. The worse news is that we can't get donations if we don't establish an NPO that looks like it's active.

Ilana watched us from the wall with bitter disappointment. Predictable, her expression said. It was so predictable that in the end you guys wouldn't do anything.

Unless, I said, we manage to reach people personally.

But how? Ofir wondered. None of us is Teddy Kollek.

Through Ya'ara, I said. Her parents lived in Miami for twelve years and they have close ties to all the rich Jews there.

But what exactly will we say to those rich Jews when we meet them? Amichai asked.

That's easy, Ofir asserted. You tell them your own personal story. That always works. And then there'll be a presentation that I'll write . . .

And I'll translate, I said, finishing the sentence.

But what'll the presentation say? Amichai persisted. I mean, what'll it be about?

We scratched our heads in puzzlement. More accurately, each of us scratched the place he scratched when he was stumped: I scratched my cheek. Amichai his upper neck. Ofir his curls.

Where is Churchill when you need him? the question ricocheted from one mind to the other. He would know how to turn our muddled, general ideas into a coherent, reasoned plan.

*

Churchill was busy. Very preoccupied with 'one the most important trials in Israel's public history', as described by Michaela Raz, the legal correspondent for TV's major channel. Every once in a while, his face would flicker in one of her reports, and black-and-white drawings of him, with an unflattering emphasis on his wide nose, appeared in the financial papers,

It was very hard to get him on the phone. And when he did answer, he was always in the middle of something. Or a minute before something. And always in a hurry to end the conversation. So I decided to take action, to go to his office and grab him by his starched collar and issue him an injunction: habeas your corpus down here, your friends need you.

When I arrived at the prosecutor's office – it took me an hour to find the entrance, which was squeezed in between dark buildings as if someone were ashamed of it or wanted to appear unassuming – I was told he was not in his office. I learned from a more thorough enquiry that at that very moment he was making a court appearance in his big case. That didn't stop me, and I walked quickly to the court, a few pedestrian crossings from there, determined to ambush him when the session was over and let him know just what I thought of the way he was treating Amichai.

I had never been in the temple of justice before, and in the first few seconds after I went into the entrance hall with its very high ceiling, I felt guilty. Very guilty. I wasn't sure what my crime was – perhaps the '90 World Cup in Nablus? – but as I stood there, I had the strong feeling that in another minute a lawyer would come and ask me politely but firmly to accompany him to my hearing.

No one came up to me. Dozens of people crossed the hall from all sides, diagonally or in a zigzag. Walking. Walking rapidly. Running. Some of them were moving so fast that I was afraid they'd trample me. Others limped. In fact, many limped. One leaned on a cane. One clutched his waist. A third dragged a recalcitrant leg. I had never noticed before how few people walk straight. Some were dragging small suitcases on trolleys – only later, when I went into the courtroom itself, did I realise that that was how legal documents were transported – but the suitcases didn't lend the place an air of foreign travel. Just the opposite. There was something very local, very Israeli about that entrance hall. The expression on the lawyers' faces was one of urgency. And on the faces of the ordinary people, the workers, the ones who weren't lawyers, there was an expression of restrained Israeli concern. A few metres from me, near one of the large columns in the centre of the hall, was a sculpture of hands spread open to the sky. I moved closer and saw that the name of the sculpture was 'Senna Bush'. I never thought of a bush as something that could feel pain. Someone standing near the bush was yelling into his mobile:

'I can't trust him any more!' And then he yelled, 'He'll pay for this.' The thought passed through my mind again that 'he' was me. And that I would pay for my original sin. A woman passing behind me, her high heels clacking rapidly, said, 'It would be much easier for them to turn over from their stomachs to their backs than from their backs to their stomachs.' As far as I could tell, she was talking to herself. I looked to the right and to the left. I didn't know which way to go. Where was my hearing? Or where could I find Churchill here? So I did what he would have done and went up to the prettiest woman in the place, a young, lawyerly-looking attorney whose white blouse perfectly suited her chocolate skin. She knew immediately what I was talking about and said that Churchill's trial was being held in Judge Dovev's court. District court.

District court? Where's that? I said in alarm. 'District' sounded like a grey building near the Tzrifin army base.

It's here, third floor, on the right, she said reassuringly, and pointed me to the lift.

*

Churchill didn't notice me entering the courtroom.

I sat down quietly in the last row, next to the wall.

He was speaking. His normally broad back looked broader under the robe, and his arms were spread to the sides like large, eagle-like wings. I tried to follow the discussion, something about a certain document that Churchill claimed was admissible by virtue of its existence, but not as evidence. Or the opposite. After a few minutes, I gave up trying to understand the big picture and started trying to grasp the small details: the way Churchill responded and lowered his voice to add authority to his words, or repeated the same word over and over and over again, or suddenly asked rhetorically: what are we talking about? The way he touched his finger to his tongue before he turned a page, a gesture he had copied, simply copied, from Ya'ara, and how phrases like *actus reus* and 'derivative liability' and 'a priori' were suddenly interspersed into his speech. Though I had never heard him use them when we watched football together, he didn't sound phoney or as if he were trying too hard because under all those beautiful words and gestures you could feel the quiet, inner conviction I knew so well from arguments in our group, an inner conviction that left the listener with no alternative but to submit, or at least to doubt, for one fateful moment, the rightness of his own view.

The defence attorney at his right rubbed his chin in confusion, as if he were wondering how to deal with the cascade of words Churchill had thrown at him, and with the slightly amused, slightly condescending tone in which they were spoken, and perhaps he was already regretting his choice of profession, and he was probably regretting having underestimated this young attorney, thought by everyone to be too young for such a case. That's what the court reporter, who was sitting at the foot of the judge's raised table, must have thought, and perhaps that's why her eyes were focused on Churchill, especially on the way his neck muscles expanded when he spoke, and she lost concentration for a few seconds and didn't notice that she had to insert more paper, and the judge reprimanded her and asked Churchill to wait for her to insert the paper, and Churchill said, yes, Your Honour, of course, Your Honour. Then he looked away and his eyes caught mine for a moment. A fraction of a moment. Then went right back to his papers. He didn't smile at me. Didn't say hello. Of course not. He wouldn't let anything get in the way of achieving his goal. He'd known he wanted to be a lawyer from the time he was in high school. And after a year in the army, he'd wrangled a transfer to the intelligence base at Gelilot so he could have time to polish his Hebrew by writing intelligence reports and also take some night courses in law at the Open University. Yes, while we were eating stones in Nablus, he was accumulating credits for his bachelor's degree and sleeping with half the girls on the course and, naturally, with the woman lecturer too. Then he was accepted into the Tel Aviv University Law School, like he wanted. And he graduated on the Dean's List, like he wanted. And arranged to intern at the prosecutor's office, like he wanted, and perhaps – the thought passed through my mind – it was because of that sense of mission that drove him, and not only because of Ya'ara, that I was secretly jealous of him and wished, as I watched him, that he would flounder in the middle of his speech, that he would stumble, that he would fall.

The defence attorney stood up to address the court. But even as he spoke, Churchill continued to work. Every time he argued something Churchill didn't accept, he waved his hand dismissively. And when the defence attorney used three foreign words in a single sentence, Churchill wondered aloud, 'Why don't you speak Hebrew? We're in an Israeli courtroom. The defendant is Israeli. Why all those foreign words?'

After several minutes of calculated restraint, during which he read through his binders and straightened his robe on his shoulders, letting the poor defence attorney believe he was allowing him to develop his argument quietly, Churchill suddenly said, 'What the defence is trying to argue here is diametrically opposed to the ruling in the State of Israel versus Aharoni, in which the court was asked to hand down a verdict on a similar matter.' Aharoni? the defence attorney repeated, trying to gain time, perhaps recall the case. But Churchill's words were flowing again, demonstrating and proving, jesting and serious, all of it in that elegant Hebrew, 'erroneously accused', 'quite the contrary', 'in my humble opinion'.

Far from me, on the other side of the courtroom, sat an old man with a plaster on his bald head. He didn't look as if he were connected to the case. Perhaps he came just to enjoy the Hebrew that people used to speak once, in his youth, and that now lived only in books and inside court-room walls?

For a moment, I thought that the silver-spectacled judge was also enjoying Churchill's Hebrew, because he leaned forward a bit, a thin smile on his lips – perhaps Churchill reminded him of himself when he was young? – but a few minutes later, as Churchill's speech grew longer and longer, the soft smile of pleasure was replaced by a small, jerky twitch in his cheeks and a quick drumming of his finger on the table till he finally interrupted him and said, Mr Alimi, you have made your point quite sufficiently. I think I am prepared to make my ruling.

Ah . . . Your Honour . . . if you will permit me . . . The defence lawyer tried to address the court. But the judge cut him off too and dictated his decision to the court reporter, who was sitting on his right. The judge spoke so quietly that it was difficult to hear him, but from the way Churchill clasped his hands on the back of his neck, I under-stood that the verdict was going his way, because when Churchill is pleased, for instance when Maccabi Haifa wins, he clasps his hands on the back of his neck in exactly the same way.

He wasn't in a hurry to come over to me after the judge sent the sides out for a recess, as if it embarrassed him to show signs of friendship in the courtroom, and he just signalled to me with his eyes that he'd see me outside. Tightly pressed clusters of lawyers and clients spoke together and lowered their voices when I walked past. I looked for a quiet corner without lies or secrets, and found one next to the vending machine. Churchill came out of the courtroom and walked straight to me as if he knew I'd be waiting for him there, as if ten years of friendship had enabled him to guess exactly where I'd choose to wait for him, and suddenly he hugged me, something he hadn't done in two years. Ever since Ya'ara, the most we did was nod hello, and on several occasions, when he approached me with that pre-hugging look in his eyes, I drew back. But he must have thought that here, on his home turf, I wouldn't feel comfortable pushing him away. And the truth is that I hugged him back, though not as tightly as he hugged me, and also, my right hand got tangled in his robe, making it hard for me to give him a full hug.

Did you see? he asked me when we'd disentangled and moved away from each other. Did you see me pull the Israel versus Aharoni case on him? He didn't know what hit him.

I saw, I confirmed. And reluctantly mumbled: way to go.

Churchill put his hands on the back of his neck and said, yes, but what you saw is only one battle in a long war. And my defendant, he's no sucker. He's a powerful man. Rich. Connected. That's why it's so important to nail him. Because if he falls, it'll make a real change. People will think twice before they take sexual bribes. They'll say to themselves: if a big shark like him could fall, then perhaps we should be careful.

And then you'll have exactly what you wanted, right?

What do you mean?

That was one of your World Cup wishes, to be responsible for the ruling on a big case, for something that would bring about social change.

Yes, that's true, Churchill said in a tone that feigned deep thought, pretending he'd forgotten those World Cup wishes, never imagining that Ya'ara had told me that he hadn't forgotten them for a minute.

Tell me, he suddenly wondered, why did you actually come here?

We're getting together this Thursday at Amichai's place to talk about his NPO.

So?

So, do the right thing, come round, even for half an hour. It's really important to him.

I don't have half an hour, if you can believe it? I don't even have a quarter of an hour.

A sudden sunbeam that emerged from between the clouds sliced through the large window and hit him directly in the eyes, and he shaded them so he wouldn't be blinded.

You don't have a quarter of an hour for your friend? I persisted.

He lowered his hands from his eyes and put them on his waist. Then dropped them to his sides. Then put them back on his waist.

I'll tell you the truth, Freed. Doctors in hospitals may not be saints, but they do sacred work. And who are we to trip them up? Anyway, I'm not too keen on that whole NPO thing. I think . . . there's something fucked up about it. The things you're talking about, they're things that, in a properly run country, the public institutions should be handling. So why should a private organisation take on the responsibility? It just perpetuates the existing distortions.

Properly run, improperly run, what does it matter?! I wanted to shout. Your friend needs you!! Aren't you the one who, right before we were drafted, got us to sign forms – funny ones, written in a mishmash of legal jargon and football-fan language – that we promised to stay friends in the army and do whatever it took to see each other. To talk. And to write as often as we could. So what happened? When did you change your mind?

Before I could ask, Churchill said he had to go back to the courtroom now. And we'd talk in the evening.

*

I waited for his call that night the way you wait for a call from a girl. I put the phone close to me so that, God forbid, I wouldn't miss it. I took the phone with me to the shower. And the toilet. And my bed.

But the call – never came.

*

So we met without Churchill. First, once every two weeks, and then, when things started getting on track, once a week, in Amichai's living room. Across from the large picture of Ilana.

Every now and then, Amichai's attention would wander and he'd stare at her picture for a long time. We would keep on talking and wait for him to rejoin the conversation when he was ready.

Every once in a while, Ofir and I would also look up at the picture for Ilana's approval of one decision or another that we'd taken.

As a start, we gave the organisation a name: Our Right (Ofir suggested more provocative names like Antidoctor or It's My Body, but we decided, with Ilana's silent support, to go with a positive approach).

Then we wrote a brief description: the non-profit organisation to advance human rights in the health system.

And after several surprise visits to hospitals and research on similar bodies abroad, we outlined the future structure of the organisation:

Mediating Arm – that will have a representative of the organisation present in accident and emergency departments throughout the country.

Educational Division – that will act to instil human rights principles among doctors and patients.

Legal Division – that will provide initial assistance to those whose rights have been infringed.

Amichai suggested adding a Doctors' Rights Division to those three. All the problems stem from the fact that doctors work inhuman shifts, he claimed. You can't expect a person who slept one hour at night to preserve the patient's human rights.

Ofir objected strongly to the new division. It blurs our message, he said. People don't have the ability to absorb more than one message in a campaign. And if we try to convey more, no one will understand what we actually want.

Why do you call it a campaign, it's not a campaign at

all, Amichai said angrily. Drop the ad-man shtick. We're not trying to sell Coke here.

It doesn't matter, Ofir insisted. You can't, you just can't cover all the issues in the world. Why don't we set up a special division for women's rights and a special division for controlling prices in hospital cafeterias?

*

They kept that argument going for a whole week and, because of it, cancelled their weekly squash game for the first time ever.

Every Tuesday night at ten, they would sweat rivers on the number two court of the university's sports centre, smashing the small black ball against the wall, against the glass, hurrying, their soles squealing, to get at it before it bounced twice, bumping into each other accidentally, or deliberately.

Then they would sit in the upholstered stands that looked down on the courts, drink water (Ofir) and chocolate milk from the vending machine (Amichai), watch the female students coming back from their aerobics class, and argue about which one looked hot.

Argue about whether it was better to rent on property or buy one.

Argue about whether jogging on tarmac damaged their feet or not.

Argue about whether the name of the boy who was abducted once by the ultra-Orthodox was Yoss'ele Shumacher or Yoss'ele Tzurbacher.

Amichai and Ofir never agreed on anything, ever. And even if at a certain moment in a conversation, there was, God forbid, the chance they might agree, one of them would immediately harden his position so there would be tension. When I first met them, I thought it was a matter of time before those endless arguments destroyed their friendship, but as the years passed, I began to understand that those arguments were exactly what held them

175

together, and when Ilana died, Amichai asked his brother to call Ofir first, and that says a lot, because the decision about who to call first after a very happy or terribly sad event comes from your gut, not your mind. You call the person you feel closest to, your best friend, and that was what Amichai must have felt towards Ofir, perhaps because they had those weekly squash games of theirs, which allowed them to be as nasty as they wanted to each other, no explanations needed, to channel all the tension that had built up between them into scoring points, into winning, into the satisfaction you get from beating a person who has something basic that lights a fire under you.

Over the years, those Tuesday squash games managed to survive everything – even the time when Ofir, back from India, announced that he wouldn't play for points any more because competitiveness is the mother of all sin, and also the time when Amichai lost on purpose as another way of punishing himself after Ilana's death.

And now it was that petty argument about the Doctors' Rights Division that suspended the institution we had all been sure would last for ever.

Without the squash, there was no place where they could vent their anger at each other. And from one meeting about the organisation to the next, their tone grew sharper, closer to the one they had used with each other before Ofir had donned his *sharwals*.

In the end, they deteriorated to the lowest point of any argument: historical generalisations.

That's always been your problem, Amichai said. Everything with you has to be black or white.

No, that was always *your* problem, Ofir countered. You always have to insert something way out in your ideas so they can't be put into action.

I listened to them sorrowfully. I knew that if it continued that way, our NPO would fall apart even before it was

176

established. And then there would be nothing to keep Amichai from falling apart.

I didn't know what to do. Usually, Churchill would get them out of those skirmishes: he'd quieten them down, sometimes reprimand them, and they would retreat to their corners of the ring till the next round. But Churchill was busy and there was no one to stop their mad dash down the slippery slope of anger and resentment.

I have an idea, I said after another bitter argument about the Doctors' Rights Division ended with Amichai going out to the open balcony to work on the *Titanic* puzzle and Ofir putting his papers into his briefcase and threatening to leave.

They both looked at me unenthusiastically.

What do you sa-a-a-y . . . – I tried to stretch out the time in the hope I'd get an idea – What do you say about instead of having a Doctors' Rights *Division*, we have a Doctors' Rights *Unit*.

What do you mean? they asked together. My suggestion was so vague that there was no way to explain it except by repeating it with nicer phrasing.

I mean . . . that alongside the three main arms, there'll be a smaller, secondary unit to handle doctors' problems.

Ofir put his briefcase on the floor. Amichai came back from the balcony into the living room, but remained standing.

I think I can live with that for the time being, Ofir said without looking up from his briefcase.

Look, it's not ideal . . . Amichai said tentatively.

Think of it as just a declaration of intention, I encouraged them. Things will still change when the organisation is actually established.

OK, if it's just a declaration of intention, he said.

*

After that huge hurdle had been removed from the agenda, the way to finishing the presentation was open. At the same time, we gave Ya'ara the green light to arrange meetings with potential donors.

At her suggestion, we limited our search at the start to people who might have a personal connection to the subject: someone with a relative who recently died of a disease or, even better, someone who personally suffered from an infringement of his rights or from medical negligence. It wasn't easy to find people among the wealthy of Miami who fitted that description. Most of them had private doctors who had extended their lives and those of their relatives time and time again. Another difficulty we faced was Amichai's restriction: a potential donor had to be someone who occasionally visited Israel, because as much as he might like to, he couldn't go abroad with the presentation and leave his children here, without their father.

In the end, with massive help from her father, Ya'ara succeeded in arranging a month of appointments for us around Passover time.

On the phone, she dictated to me the names of the hotels and the exact dates, and when she finished, she said, don't get your hopes up too high. Those people didn't become millionaires because they spread their money around, you know.

Still, I said, you did a great job organising this.

I think that what you're all doing to help Amichai is very . . . moving. The way you're helping him to keep busy.

Honestly, I admitted, it's fun. Since our high school graduation play, we haven't done anything together but watch football. And there's something . . . bonding about it. You should see Ofir. The way he enjoys sitting with us, thinking, creating. You can see how much he misses it. It's just a shame that Churchill . . .

Yes, I think it's a shame too, she agreed.

How much longer will that trial of his go on? I asked. Isn't it supposed to be over already?

Are you joking? she said. Only on TV do trials start and

end in the same episode. It's not like that in real life. Even so, she added, I don't think it's right that he's not helping you. I told him I don't buy all that crap about 'a well-run country'.

And what did he say?

I'm not sure he was even listening. He's so preoccupied with that trial. He works every day till midnight, and there are nights when he sleeps in his office so he doesn't have to waste time going back and forth.

So how do you manage to fall asleep? I asked. I remembered that she hated sleeping alone. A week after we started dating, she was already sleeping at my place regularly because there were 'noises' in her apartment.

I don't, she said. I get up ten times a night to check whether there's a burglar. I keep a canister of pepper spray under my pillow, but that just stresses me out even more. Sometimes I fall asleep for half an hour or an hour. And then I have nightmares that . . . .

Someone is chasing you down the street with a huge kitchen knife and your shoes aren't right for running. You try to take them off while you run, but you can't, so you try to turn yourself into a rabbit so you can move faster, but you can't, and then, when he catches up to you . . .

I wake up. I can't believe you remember that.

(I haven't forgotten anything, I thought. Not your nightmares and not that, under your expensive skirts, you wear plain knickers you buy in the open-air market, and not how horny you are the day before your period, and not that you turn off the alarm clock three times before you get up, and not that you think that your bum is a bit too big, but there's no way you'll diet because you don't have the self-control it takes, and not that you're jealous of your older brother who, for some reason, you think is cleverer than you, and not that you feel a bit agitated when you don't manage to come, and not the way your eyebrows contract when you're listening hard, and not the special way you say the word l-o-o-ve, and not that the only time a producer, your brother's friend, made you a concrete offer to be the director's assistant on a play, you declined, saying that the play didn't interest you, and not that, hidden under your self-confidence is a lack of self-confidence, and hidden under that lack of self-confidence is a hard core of conceit. I haven't forgotten anything, Ya'ara, as hard as I've tried.)

It's hard to forget, I said, when someone wakes you up in the middle of the night twice a week to tell you the same story every time.

Incredible. I've been stuck with that dream since I was twelve. So many things have happened to me since then, and only that stays constant.

Like a loyal friend.

Exactly. You know, you're one of the only people in the world who knows that I'm afraid to sleep alone.

Why, are you ashamed of it?

Yes. Anyway, people don't believe me. It doesn't fit with the image I project. Admit that you were surprised the first time I told you about it.

Yes, but there's something so appealing about that contradiction . . . between the way you are during the day . . . and at night . . . All the contradictions about you are appealing . . .

It's nice of you to think that.

Nice is a word you can use on your sister.

I don't have a sister.

Shame. She could come to sleep with you.

Bastard.

*

The last, arrogant words of that dialogue were never spoken. I have a tendency to make myself sound overly clever when I recreate conversations with Ya'ara. But in fact, we all rewrite our lives when we tell them to ourselves, don't we? Besides, those lines that I made up aren't very far from the truth. Ya'ara and I really did talk a lot during that period. Amichai and Ofir appointed me liaison with her. I protested mildly, but they insisted, claiming that she had a weakness for me. Perhaps guilty feelings. In any case, it was worth exploiting for the good of the organisation.

There was always a legitimate excuse for her night-time phone calls: an update on the changed time of an appointment. Inside information on a donor that we should keep in mind when preparing the presentation for him (this guy's a right-winger, that one's a left-winger. This one has a weakness for the Russian immigration, and that one is interested in the Ethiopians. This one has a heavy Texas accent that's very hard to understand, and that one, who insists on meeting in Jerusalem, is used to having people agree with everything he says and show enthusiasm for every idea he has, so it isn't enough to say 'of course' after his every remark, say 'absolutely!').

Great, that's important to know, good work, I would say to Ya'ara, and write down all those tips in the organisation notebook – and then we'd slip into talking about other things.

Like in the past, I'd tell her about interesting articles I was translating (for example, an article claiming that four times more women suffer from depression than men because they have a different brain structure from men). And, like she used to, she would offer subversive interpretations of the research data (different brain structures? Bullshit. Men just aren't willing to admit that they're depressed. Not to themselves and definitely not to the researchers).

Like in the past, she would tell me about especially grotesque moments that occurred during business meetings she attended as her father's constantly reprimanded assistant. ('And then the marketing vice-president, who'd said five minutes before that he strongly objected to that strategy, began to explain why it was inevitable', or 'You wouldn't believe it, we've been sitting for three days with the management consultant to create a vision for our company. What's the deal? Everyone knows that the only vision is for my father to make more money.')

As in the past, I believed her with all my heart when she said that working for her father was only temporary, till she gathered the courage and ninety-one thousand dollars and did what she truly wanted to do: go to London.

Unlike in the past, I didn't stop the conversation every five minutes to tell her how much I loved her. And how magical she was. The fact that everything was taking place on the phone, and the fact that she was married to my friend, enabled me to keep a proper distance between us, the kind that would let me tease her. Mock her. Even be slightly disappointed by her.

I hated those conversations with her. And so looked forward to them.

And I took out her sock over and over again from where it was hidden in the closet.

*

The first presentation of the Our Right non-profit organisation was in the Hilton Hotel. A small surprise was waiting for us at the entrance. The security guard who checked our briefcases was none other than Yoram Mendelsohn, the school genius. In the ninth grade, they promoted him to the tenth. And in the middle of junior year, he disappeared and they said that he had moved to Jerusalem with his family and joined a secret national programme to train the country's future scientists. We all knew that one day, he'd win a Nobel –

And now he was standing in front of us at the entrance to the Hilton with a wispy moustache, asking if we had any weapons.

Mendelsohn! Yoram Mendelsohn!!! we said happily, but he kept his expression blank and scanned us with his wand.

What are you doing here, Mendelsohn? Ofir asked.

Working, he answered curtly.

But . . . aren't you supposed to be at . . . the Weizmann Institute or something like that?

I quit. They wouldn't let me keep working on my research.

They wouldn't let you? Why not?

They said it wasn't practical, he said with contempt. It was so predictable that they'd say something like that.

Predictible?

If I prove what I set out to prove, it would undermine everything they believe in. All their axioms. People are very attached to their axioms, you know.

What exactly are you trying to prove?

It's complicated. I've been working on it for three years already. That's why I took the job here, because it's mindless and doesn't interfere with my thinking.

About what? What do you have to think about?

Sorry, I'm keeping that to myself, for the moment.

OK, we won't press you. Even though . . . we'd very much like to hear.

I'm really sorry, Yoram Mendelsohn said with a shrug, and we took our briefcases from him and were about to walk into the hotel, but as we took the first step, he suddenly began to speak.

OK . . . if you're so interested . . . I'm trying to build a physical, mathematical model that will explain reincarnation.

Reincarnation?

Look – he ran a finger across his moustache as if he were wiping milk off it – the separation between the world of life and the world of death is an axiom that the Western world accepts. But think about how much death is an inseparable part of life in this country, for example. So why can't life also be a part of death? Not to mention that reincarnation is an accepted concept in many places in the world. And here too, if you go to the Druze village of Dalit-al-Carmel, they'll tell you stories . . . that will make your neurons jump.

And in India . . . Ofir began to say.

Not only in India, Yoram Mendelsohn interrupted him, everywhere in the world people report on reincarnation, and to this day, no scientist has ever tried to deal with that scientifically and thoroughly. Don't you think that's suspicious?

It's more than suspicious, it's a conspiracy, I said, looking at my watch to signal that we were in a hurry.

So you're still friends, Yoram Mendelsohn said, looking slowly at the three of us (whenever we met people we went to high school with, they always had the same surprised-envious expression when they saw that we had remained friends after so many years), good for you. I don't have friends. I had some at the Institute, but the minute I started talking about reincarnation, they kept their distance from me as if I were a leper.

Well, that's how it is with work friends, Ofir said.

Don't worry, Amichai said, putting his hand on Yoram Mendelsohn's shoulder, you'll have other friends.

And if you don't have friends now, then maybe in your next life, I said.

Yoram Mendelsohn was quiet for a moment, as if he were going to feel hurt, but then he let out the wild, uncontrollable, hiccupping laugh of a seventeen-year-old.

We said goodbye to him with a promise to 'get together sometime' and went into the lobby.

A young man in an old man's tie came over to us and told us in English to wait a few minutes till Mr Eisenman called us up to his conference room.

Eisenman?! There must be . . . a mistake . . . I said. We're supposed to meet with Mr Goldman (likes young girls. Likes nightclubs. Is looking for passion in the eyes of the person proposing a social project, so it's a good idea to use the words passion or passionate or passionately in every sentence during the presentation).

Sorry, but there's no mistake, sir, the guy in the tie said in a forgiving tone, Mr Eisenman will meet with you to hear your proposal, and only then will he recommend to Mr Goldman whether to consider it.

OK, sir. Of course, sir. Absolutely.

*

We sat down in the armchairs that overlooked the sea. Soft carpets throbbed under our feet. A Japanese waitress asked us in Hebrew what we'd like to drink. A mix of foreign languages surrounded us on all sides. English, French, German, Russian.

Don't you think that what people say in a foreign language sounds more intelligent? Ofir asked.

I smiled, but Amichai didn't. He was looking out of the window at a flock of birds approaching us. Perhaps he was thinking about the possibility that Ilana's soul had re-incarnated into one of those birds, and now she was flying towards us to wish us good luck. And perhaps he wanted to join the flock and fly as far away as he could from his own life.

It's unbelievable that of all the places in the world, people decide of their own free will to spend their holidays in this ugly city, Ofir said, and neither of us had the strength to answer him any more. Amichai kept watching the birds, and I was picturing the luxurious chandeliers over our heads falling from the ceiling and crushing us. I was almost sinking into my why-not-end-it-all mood again when the guy in the tie suddenly appeared and said that Mr Eisenman was waiting for us.

*

You can call me Ron, he said when the meeting began.

None of us dared to call him Ron then, not during the rest of the meeting either, but even so, everything went beautifully. First, Amichai spoke a few words. Then Ofir continued with the PowerPoint presentation, elegantly interspersing illuminating examples from his personal experience and from the newspapers. I watched him from the side. His curls were bristling, his eyes were shining with an inventor's glow and the suit he was wearing, I had to admit, looked a lot better on him than the traditional *sharwal*.

When he finished, I took over for the last stage of the presentation: Mr Eisenman asked questions, expressed a few reservations, and I replied. I could see that he was very impressed with my English. In general, I had a strong feeling that he was taken with our idea.

Look, he said when we'd finished, I think your idea is important. And I'm impressed by the fact that you're so committed to it. It warms my heart to see that there are young people with a vision in Israel, and I have no doubt that it's important to support this kind of project.

*

Two hours later, he called Ya'ara and told her that he'd decided not to recommend us to his boss.

But how can that be? we cried. He was so . . .

American, Ya'ara said knowingly. They have a completely different way of communicating. With them, yes is no and no is perhaps. And even that isn't a rule you can always rely on.

So what now? we asked.

The next meeting is the day after tomorrow. Do what you can to improve the presentation. And pray that it works.

We did what she said. We added a biblical verse to the top of every page to show that our idea was firmly grounded in Judaism and its values. We took a home-video camera to the shopping centre next to the hospital and interviewed people about the treatment they'd received. We put two of those testimonies into the presentation and decided to use them if needed. We added the words 'empowerment' or 'sustainability' at least once to every slide, the way we'd seen it on the home pages of other human rights organisations in the US.

We also came to the conclusion that the division of labour among us at the first presentation was too stiff, and we practised a different division that would look more spontaneous.

And again we went to the Hilton. And again met Yoram Mendelsohn at the entrance (who told us that he'd had a huge breakthrough in his research, we'd all be hearing about it soon, and we'd be proud to know him).

And again the presentation went off without a hitch.

And two hours later, the donor told Ya'ara that he wasn't interested.

Bastard, we hissed.

Who needs his money.

Did you see the way he looks? Like the Jews in those Nazi caricatures.

I hope the neo-Nazis take power in America. I'd like to see him then, looking for refuge here.

Hey guys, Ya'ara said, trying to cheer us up, you have a few more meetings. Don't give up now.

We didn't give up. Why should we give up? We kept wandering from hotel to hotel, from Tel Aviv to Jerusalem, hearing 'no' over and over again. Like mice in a maze that get slapped down time after time, at some point we even stopped trying to understand why we were failing. And we continued to go to meetings at Amichai's place simply because we were afraid to leave him alone.

What's he like? we asked Ya'ara tiredly before the last meeting.

Who?

The one we're supposed to meet the day after tomorrow.

He's . . . Ya'ara stammered, he's . . . not easy. He hasn't contributed a single cent to anyone for thirty years. Since his wife died last year, he's been liquidating his businesses one by one. He only agreed to see you as a personal favour to my father. But Dad made it pretty clear that we shouldn't count on him. That's why I scheduled him last.

*

The day before the final presentation, Amichai called me. It's Noam, he panted into the phone, I can't find him. He didn't come home from school . . . he told Nimrod he was staying in the library to do his homework, but the librarian says he wasn't there at all.

Have you called the police?

They say not enough time has passed for them to start looking. But meanwhile . . . I have no idea where he is . . . and he's only a kid . . . a little boy . . .

I'll be there in five minutes, I said, alarmed. And called Ofir.

*

On the way to Amichai's, I tried to think about where, where could a little boy be? When I was his age, I always wanted to run away from home. My mother had a miscarriage then, I think. To this day, I'm not sure. But for a few months, they talked to me about the new little sister I was going to have, who'd be 'like a friend to me' – and then, all of a sudden, my mother was taken to the hospital because of a 'throat infection', and when she came back, the little sister wasn't mentioned any more.

My mother then became engrossed in arranging the collection of photos of the royal family she'd inherited from her mother and kept adding to it in Israel, with the help of subscriptions to magazines like *Royal Romances* or *Monarchy at Work*.

My father vanished into his proofs.

As for me, I was a child and didn't understand anything. I just felt that there was no oxygen at home, especially when my parents were both there together. And that even Queen Elizabeth, whose picture hung on the living room wall, looked as if she wanted to step out of it and escape back to England.

I wanted to run away too. I even picked a place to run to: the playground on Einstein Street. And I made up an imaginary friend named Ofir (that was his name, as if I were prophesising) so I wouldn't be all alone when I ran away. But at first, Ofir wouldn't come with me, and by the time I persuaded him, the courage to pack a bag, go out of the front door and hide in the space under the round-about as I'd planned had trickled away – so instead, I had my first asthma attack.

*

Is there a playground around here? I asked Amichai when I got there.

A playground? In the middle of Tel Aviv? There's only one, on Carmiya Street, but that's far from here. And Noam has never been there.

So let's start searching the area near his school, I suggested.

I've already done that, Amichai said impatiently. His hands were shaking. His hair was in a panic.

Let's do it again, I insisted. Now there are two of us. And Ofir will be here. It's completely different when you search in a group.

During the long minute we waited for Ofir, Amichai laced his fingers on his stomach and fell into a tense silence. I remembered that one night, when Ilana was still alive, I babysat the twins and Noam woke up. I was sitting in the living room watching a replay of the league championship game when all of a sudden a little person in pyjamas was suddenly walking towards me in small steps. Hi, Noamon, why'd you wake up? There's a lion in our room, Uncle Yuval, he said in a pretty calm voice. You dreamed there's a lion in your room? I said, trying to dilute his fear. No, I didn't dream it, he insisted, there really is a lion in our room. Come and see. OK, I said, and went into the chil-dren's room. I took a quick glance inside, then turned and said, I think it's already gone, the lion that was here. No, it's not gone, Noam said, shaking his head. You just can't see it because it's black. Black? Yes, that's the special camouflage colour it has so nobody can see it in the dark. Then maybe we'll turn on the light and it'll leave? I suggested. No, Noam said, scolding me. We can't do that, Uncle Yuval. We'll wake up Nimrod. Every little thing wakes him up. So what do you suggest we do? I asked, stroking his head. I have an idea! he said – with the same intonation his father had – maybe I can watch some football with you? No problem, I said, and made room for him on the sofa. He climbed up and sat down next to me, and after a few minutes of watching the game, his head dropped onto my right thigh, and a few minutes after that, I carried him back to his bed. How light he was in my arms, I remembered as Ofir got out of his car and walked worriedly towards us. How soft his pyjamas were.

*

An hour later, the university called. It seems that Noam took a bus to Ramat Aviv, got off at the right stop, passed the security check, went into the psychology building, walked up to the third floor and knocked on the door to what used to be Ilana's office.

It seems that somehow he still harboured the suspicion that his mother was at work. That she just hadn't come home from the office.

It seems that this is a common phenomenon. Think about how much we adults refuse to recognise death, explained the psychologist who put him back in our arms. It's totally normal for each of the twins to react differently to loss, she said. Each one has probably developed his own way of coping as a reaction to the other's.

She offered these analyses to me and Ofir. Amichai was too agitated to listen to her. He was hugging and stroking Noam as if checking to see that all his limbs were in place, and he kept repeating the same words over and over again.

My little boy. My little boy. My little boy.

On the way back to the city, Amichai asked me to drive. He sat in the back kissing Noam on the cheek and the forehead, on the cheek and the forehead, saying, you and your brother are all I have left, all I have left are you and your brother, we're all that's left.

*

I tried not to listen. The longer he kept talking, the less air I had in my lungs. And I thought, it's a good thing this is a relatively short journey, otherwise I'd have an attack.

When we reached their place, he said he was sorry, but he didn't think he'd come to the presentation tomorrow. It was too much for him.

Ofir said that if he didn't come, there was no point in having the meeting. Even if you just sit there without saying a word, Ofir tried to convince him gently, it would be OK. And I added that tomorrow was that American's last day in the country. And that if we cancelled the meeting, we'd blow our last chance to get funding.

I don't know, Amichai said. I don't know if I can.

But I insisted, amazed at myself for doing so – where does all that determination come from? Ofir I could understand. That NPO had come along just in time for him, a minute before his flat feet started bothering him there, in Michmoret. But me? Since when had I become emotionally involved in the project?

You remember what you asked us at the beginning, I heard myself say. That we shouldn't let you give up?

Yes, Ofir joined in. This is not the time to retreat, Amichai. It goes against the flow.

9

They're standing on either side of her, barely reaching her shoulders. She's looking at the camera with that piercing stare of hers (the girl's too smart, Maria once told us. If we don't watch her, she'll grow up to be bad), and they're looking at her. Not exactly at her. It would be more accurate to say they were looking in her direction (and perhaps they were just giving each other sideways glances? Trying to see who was closer to her?).

I'm almost positive that the one on the right is Noam and Nimrod is on the left. But perhaps I'm wrong. Noam's forehead is broader, but you can only see it when he has a certain kind of haircut. And on each small head, there's a concealing, festive crown of leaves.

Amichai took that picture on their last birthday, when Ilana was still alive. They pursued Maria's daughter subtly then. Shyly. But as soon as their mother died, it was as if some inner restraint was released, and the war for the heart of their beloved became totally uninhibited. And we, who at first had watched that threesome with smiles of amusement (ah, the sweet love of children), now had an expression of concern on our faces (what, can the sweet love of children be that intense?).

When Noam was brought home after his flight to the university, Nimrod was not happy. You're such a baby, you did that just to get attention, he said. And it was clear whose attention he was talking about.

When Nimrod competed in the district judo championship, Noam sat next to her in the stands and tried to dampen
her enthusiasm. He's the biggest boy in his age group, he
whispered in her ear, that's why he beats everyone.

They competed in front of her in all sorts of weird
contests: who could remember a nine-digit number by
heart? A ten-digit number? Who could hold his breath
longer? Who could eat the most strawberries without
throwing up?

She was the judge in those contests. And she decided
who the winner was. But she kept delaying the biggest,
most crucial decision.

You're being mean, Maria rebuked her in the end at
home (Ofir told us about this conversation like a father
talking about his daughter).

But why, *Mor*? the girl asked her mother, looking up at
her, and in a characteristic gesture, tucked some unruly
hairs back into the yellow bun on the top of her head.

Because you enjoy the two of them showering attention
on you, and you don't care that you're hurting them, her
mother said firmly.

But *Mor*, I really love them both, the girl protested.
Really!

Perhaps she's right. Who says that we have to love only
one person? Ofir ended the story on a contemplative note,
and Ya'ara flashed me a look (or was I only imagining that
she flashed me a look?).

*

In the end, Amichai showed up for the meeting with the
donor.

Unshaven. Wearing once-white trainers.

Before we went inside, he asked us to handle the presentation because he was still recovering from yesterday. But
the minute Ofir showed the first slide, he interrupted him.

Stop, he said. I can't bear those slides any more.

Listen, he said to the shocked millionaire, and began to

tell him about Ilana. Ofir and I exchanged looks that screamed 'help!'. We hoped that he would at least explain the connection between Ilana and our plans to set up the NPO, but no. He simply told the man about Ilana. How he went into the army office and it was full of girls laughing together and one girl sitting on the side with a mangy cat on her lap. How his heart went out to her at that moment, but it took three months for him to work up the courage to talk to her, to ask her for some form. And later on, for another form. And later on, he asked her if she wanted to go to the canteen with him for a cup of coffee and a chocolate bar. Then it turned out that she had wanted him secretly for three months. That she was yearning for him too. And that was exactly what he always loved about her, that under her cold, despairing surface, hidden springs of warmth flowed, and only he knew about them. He and the abandoned cats. And then he and her weakest students. And then he and the Palestinians at the checkpoints. The rest of the world – his family and friends – thought she was just another depressive girl. His mother even warned him before the wedding that 'he should think hard about what he's doing. That if she's like that now, who knows what the hormones will do to her after she gives birth.' But he didn't care. And he didn't care that he was the first of his friends to get married. And have children. And he didn't care that she really was a bit depressive. Which meant that he was fated to bear sole responsibility for the joy of life in their relationship. And doomed to live in constant fear that one day he'd come home and find that she'd given up.

You know what it's like to come home every day afraid that you'll find your wife hanging from a rope or lying next to a bottle of pills? Amichai asked the millionaire.

I watched him as he spoke and thought about all the times over the last few months that he'd sat on my sofa never saying a word about those things.

The millionaire didn't answer. From the look on his face

it was hard to tell whether he was shocked, curious, or just waiting impatiently for Amichai to stop babbling.

Amichai, for his part, kept talking. It wasn't till our twins were born, he said, that I could relax a little because she was so involved with them that I was sure she wouldn't give up. And I didn't care about letting her win the hidden competition between parents for their children's love, I didn't care if they loved her a bit more than me, just as long as she was happy. Because when she wasn't – I wasn't either. Even if I had to give up my dreams because of the children. You know, I always wanted to be a therapist. To study alternative medicine. Three years ago, during the World Cup, when we each wrote down our ... OK, we won't go into that now. What I wanted to say is that I didn't care about giving it up. I didn't care about working like a dog so there'd be money for nappies and wipes, then go home and work like a dog at being a parent. The main thing was that, at the end of the day, Ilana and I got into the same bed and talked. Even for just a few minutes. And her wisdom would shine a different light on everything that had happened to me that day. And now? Now I get into bed alone. And there's no point to anything. No point.

Amichai stopped talking. As if he suddenly sensed that if there was no point to anything, there was no point in talking either.

The millionaire looked at his watch. He was suntanned and small, smaller even than me, and he had an almost completely round face, the face of a man who smiled a lot. But he hadn't smiled even once since we came into the room.

Ofir looked at me for the OK, then turned on the presentation again and explained the structure of the NPO. And why we wanted to establish it.

During the explanation, the millionaire looked at his watch twice.

When we reached the question stage, which I was in charge of, he didn't have a single question.

Is there something that's important for you to know? I said, trying to pull him into a dialogue.

No, thank you, he said, and stood up.

*

Sorry I ruined everything, Amichai said after we left the hotel.

You didn't ruin anything, I hurried to reassure him.

You said what you felt, Ofir said.

Yes, but I didn't say it to the right person, Amichai said, his forehead wrinkled with pain. There are psychologists for monologues like that.

Who knows, I joked, perhaps he's a psychologist too.

No, Ofir said knowingly, he's too tanned to be a psychologist.

Amichai was silent. He didn't laugh. He stared for a while at the flock of birds flying from north to south in a formation that resembled a question mark, and then said, you're such good friends. I feel bad, you invested so much in that presentation.

Don't be stupid, I said. I didn't have anything better to do anyway.

My teacher in India always said that good energies never go to waste, Ofir said and put his hand on Amichai's shoulder. How about a walk along the seafront?

Great idea, I said. I'm in no hurry to go anywhere.

I'm in a hurry to get everywhere, Amichai said bitterly and looked at his watch, but still agreed to join us for a short stroll against the strong wind that made sails belly out to the bursting point, and drove the red flags into a frenzy, and swirled old advertising flyers around in the air, and whipped the waves into a foam, and leafed through the pages of a book that an old lady sitting on a bench was reading, and also the pages of the book that her Philippino caregiver was reading, and ripped into the sleeves of the good shirts we'd put on in honour of the meeting in the hotel, and penetrated our nostrils and mouths and ears, making us walk next to each other in silence at first, because anyway, whatever question we asked then, and whatever answer we gave would have been blowing in the wind. It wasn't till we were close to the Opera Tower that the whistling of the wind died down a bit, and walking became easier, less of a battle, and Amichai said, it's nice here, on the promenade, and Ofir, who hadn't been able to tolerate one nice word about Tel Aviv since he'd come back from India, said, it's just a shame that the road is so close, and that the whole strip of beach has been taken over by concrete and commercial interests, and it's a shame that it symbolises everything that's happening in this city that has no depth, and everything in it is so exposed, so cellular, so lacking in intimacy, which affects the weak, temporary way people connect to each other here, and look, even the four of us, so many years here, and we had so many opportunities to make new friends, but we're still stuck with each –

Let's sit near the fountain for a little while, Amichai suggested, and I prayed that Ofir would shut up, because Amichai's voice was shaking when he asked to rest, and I had a feeling that he was on the brink, but as we were crossing the road, Ofir pointed to the new branch of Abulafiya's Pitta Bread and said look at that, because of the Intifada people are even afraid to go to Jaffa, to the original bakery, and they opened a branch here so God forbid they don't have to look at Arabs in Jaffa, because Arabs are not cool, right?

We sat down on the edge of the fountain, but not even the sight of the flowing water could calm Ofir down.

He grabbed his nose with two fingers and said, phew, what a stink, why do they put so much chlorine in the water? Then he pointed to the square behind us and said, look at how many massage parlours there are here, how many betting shops, it's just like the Roman Empire in its last days. Then he pointed to the entrance to the shopping centre and said, what are those statues of people with an accordion? And why are they hanging on columns with their heads down? What was the artist trying to say, that the minute they saw that ugly shopping centre they wanted to commit suicide? Nothing like this could happen in Copenhagen. In Copenhagen, they would get the best artists for a project like this, they wouldn't just stick some cheap statue there.

But actually . . . you've never been to Copenhagen, I said, trying to stop Ofir's tirade, mainly out of concern for Amichai, whose face was getting darker with every word Ofir said, and his broad camel's back was showing signs of breaking any second, any half-second.

What difference does it make, Ofir said, refusing to shut up, it's enough to see pictures of Copenhagen to under-stand how a big city should be planned. Not like this city, which is patched together with –

Bye, Amichai said suddenly, and before we realised what was happening, he had already crossed the road to the beach.

We hurried after him and managed to see him take off his clothes and jump into the cold, stormy water in his underwear.

Are you happy now? I yelled at Ofir. Amichai has gone off into this freezing sea all because of your stupid rant.

What's so bad about a freezing sea? he replied in a quiet voice. You know that in Copenhagen, people go into icy water all winter? They say it's better than meditation!

I waved my hand in the air in exasperation and walked away from him. And he, in response, waved his hands in the air, then lowered them to his hips and began making l-o-ong, s-o-o-ft t'ai chi movements.

*

My father liked to go into the sea in winter too. A kind of madness that didn't fit with anything else in his work-oriented life. He always swam out to the deep water, to the smooth, quiet sea past the waves. I would wait for him on the beach till he came out. My mother wouldn't join him because 'Only masochists go swimming in the sea in this weather', and she was very surprised that I wanted to go with him. 'Why do you go with your dad, Yuvali? You never go into the water anyway', she would say and try to persuade me to stay at home with her and watch a documentary series about the royal family on Middle East TV. What she didn't understand was that I had a job to do there, on the beach. I tried to pretend, to keep busy doing all sorts of things, building sandcastles, exercising, but I was actually watching out for my father. I looked for his head, followed the way it appeared further and further from the beach each time, making sure over and over again that he hadn't drowned. Sometimes his head would vanish among the waves for too long, and I would stand with my ankles in the cold sand, worrying, trying to decide whether to go to the first-aid station to ask for help, picturing his body spilling onto the beach and everyone blaming me for not doing anything, because in fact, deep inside, I wanted him to die. In the end, he would come out with a wet smile, take his thick glasses and his towel from me and say: that water, it's so invigorating! Shame you don't come in with me, son.

*

Now, too, I followed Amichai's head for a few minutes, as it disappeared and reappeared, until it suddenly vanished altogether.

Bro, I said, touching Ofir's shoulder, I can't see Amichai.

Ofir continued his t'ai chi movements and said, you worry too much, man. Amichai Tanuri is stronger than all those waves put together.

And you're a bigger idiot than all the jellyfish put together, I thought. After all, you're the one who said that if anything happened to Amichai, we'd never forgive ourselves. So why the sudden change?

I stripped, determined to go into the water and save Amichai from drowning, but before I could, a city patrol jeep appeared on the beach and an authoritative voice boomed from it: 'Everyone out of the water. Everyone out of the water. The water is polluted due to a malfunction in the sewage system. I repeat: the water is polluted due to a malfunction in the sewage system. Everyone out of the water.'

A few seconds later, Amichai came out of the water. He ambled towards us, and when he was about a metre away, launched into a perfect imitation of Ofir, including the nasal tone and the folded hands: did you hear that jeep? Did you hear what he said? In Co-pen-ha-gen, that would never happen!

Ofir laughed out loud at the great imitation, and I thought to myself that this was the first time I'd seen him laugh at himself since he came back from India, and that if a person can laugh at himself, there's hope for him.

Then Amichai dried himself off with his T-shirt and put on his clothes, and we started back.

This time we were walking in the same direction as the wind, which propelled us north quickly, as if we were kites (when I was little, my father used to call me 'kite'. Every time I drifted off into my thoughts, he would pull a thin, invisible string and ground me with a job he thought up: tightening an already tight table leg; washing an already washed car, taking apart and putting together a perfectly fine wall clock).

No matter what, in the end, we're going to set up that NPO, Amichai said as we neared Ofir's car. I thought about it while I was swimming and I'm telling you – in the end, it's going to happen!

Ofir and I looked at each other and were silent.

Amichai trembled slightly as a sudden gust of wind slid across his skin, and he hugged himself.

And . . . if we don't manage to do it, I said quickly, we

can go back to watching football together, because . . . we've been neglecting that lately.

There's a championship league game on Wednesday, Ofir reminded us.

Who's playing? Amichai asked, his curiosity piqued.

Real against Bayern, Ofir replied.

Group qualifying stage?

Are you joking? It's the quarter final already.

*

On Wednesday, Ya'ara called to tell me that there were developments. The last millionaire, the suntanned one, said no, as expected. But Mr Goldman – our first meeting was with his representative – had suddenly decided to back us after all.

But what . . . what made him change his mind like that?

Turns out that he didn't feel well over the weekend and spent a whole night in hospital, and that . . . changed his perspective somewhat. But wait . . . it's too soon to celebrate. He's ready to fund you for a year of activity, she said, and then, if he sees that you're serious, he's ready to fund you for another two years. But he has two conditions . . . pretty annoying conditions, to tell you the truth.

So tell us.

He . . . he insists that the organisation bear his mother's name. That means . . . not Ilana's name.

What a bastard, Ofir blurted out.

We looked at Amichai. We knew how important it was for him to commemorate Ilana. Written on every slide were the words 'Our Right – The Ilana Abramowitz-Tanuri Non-Profit Organisation'.

Amichai nodded slowly, taking in the news, and then said confidently into the phone: I'll take care of it. Go on, Ya'ara, what's the second condition?

He wants matching.

Matching?

He doesn't want to be the only sponsor. He wants someone else involved. Someone with Israeli citizenship.

Why?

I didn't ask. I was afraid that if I asked, he'd withdraw the offer.

What a nightmare. What are we going to do? Where are we going to get fucking matching now?

*

A week later, Amichai received an envelope in the post with a large cheque in it. Very large.

With an accompanying note.

My Bro, Amichai,

I want you to know that I haven't been able to stop thinking about you since the shiva. *I really wanted to be with you in your hour of need, but life is a big, strong river and it carried the small, broken piece of wood that is Shahar Cohen far from all of you, and for the time being, I can't come back to Israel. But a little bird told me about the NPO you're trying to set up to help people that doctors aren't nice to and I think that's a great idea, so I'm attaching a small cheque for you in the hope that it will help you get organised. Don't make a big deal out of it. I happen to have some free cash I made last year and better to invest it in my friends than in clothes, right?*

Regards to all,
Shahar

How did Shahar Cohen hear about our NPO? To this day, we have no idea. A few weeks before that, someone we knew in high school who went to Berlin told us that he saw a panther in the city zoo whose face looked amazingly like Shahar's. That led us to the inevitable conclusion that after drifting around the world, Shahar Cohen had drifted into the body of a panther.

Ya'ara admitted that the idea of turning to Shahar Cohen had actually crossed her mind, and without telling us, she even called the Israeli embassy in Canberra, the last place we'd had signs of life from him. But the embassy told her that they had no documentation suggesting an Israeli citizen named Shahar Cohen, or Ricardo Luis, had been in Australia during the last ten years.

*

Three months later, we held an event at the Rokah House to launch Our Right. The media people there were more interested in Amichai's personal tragedy than in the organisation, but Ofir said that's how media people are and it doesn't matter: the main thing is that we get coverage.

A lot of people went up to the podium set up for the occasion and pledged to work as volunteers. Many of them were former members of the health system: people who had been fired or had retired or had been taken ill and found themselves suddenly on the other side of the fence, victims of the system they had once been part of.

Surprisingly, one of the people who went up to the podium was the director of a small hospital in the centre of the country that had recently been the focus of a series of investigations into the disgraceful treatment of patients by the hospital medical staff. The publicity had led to such a drastic drop in the number of people seeking treatment at the hospital that it was on the verge of financial collapse.

The director took Amichai aside, had a short conversation with him, put a fatherly-conspiratorial hand on his shoulder and arranged a meeting to check out the possibilities of working together.

At night, when the last of the guests had gone and only the three of us were left, we tried to persuade Amichai to go out and celebrate the success of the event. Not to celebrate, to have a drink. Not to have a drink, to sit somewhere. In short, whatever he liked.

He said he wasn't in the mood. The evening had reminded him of Ilana, and all those newspaper interviews had made him sad. They pretend to care about you, he said, and then, the minute they've sucked everything they can out of you, the minute the interview is over – they're not interested in you any more.

That's just the way it is, Ofir said. That's how newspaper people are.

And Amichai said that he was sick of hearing 'that's just the way it is'. And that now, he wanted to go home to his children.

*

So Ofir and I went out to celebrate alone.

We didn't actually know where to go. When Ofir had worked in advertising he had always updated us on the hot places, but now he'd gone far away to Michmoret and depended on me to guide him. And I was never big on going out. So we went to a bar we once used to frequent, and when we got there, it turned out that its name had been changed. And also the façade. For a minute, we considered leaving, but Ofir said it didn't matter, all we wanted to do anyway was talk. So we went inside. People were dancing in the aisles between the tables to the sound of pounding, ear-splitting music. Well, they weren't exactly dancing, because it was too crowded. It was more like they were rubbing up against each other. We squeezed into the last two empty stools at the bar and signalled to the barman to come over, but he didn't notice. We tried to talk to each other, but we couldn't hear anything. The hideous song that was playing when we walked in ended and a new, even more horrible one began, a cheap cover version of a beautiful ballad from the '80s. If there's something I despise, it's cover versions. They always make me miss the original. So I put my mouth up against Ofir's ear and asked if his flat feet weren't . . . hurting him by any chance.

He smiled with admiration. It was nice that I remembered his old excuse.

We escaped on to the street and walked without speaking till we reached a kiosk. We bought beers and sat down on a public bench that was badly in need of paint. Every once in a while, women walked passed and looked at Ofir.

Women always looked at Ofir.

We've already forgotten what it's like, haven't we? I said, pointing back to the place we'd just left.

Yes, he said, sipping from his can of beer. It was . . . too noisy . . . too frantic . . . I'm not used to that any more. And the people there . . . I felt a bit . . .

Yes . . . The generation that came after us is . . .

Nothing to write home about . . . nothing at all . . . Ofir said with a slight Polish accent.

They don't care about anything, those *cholerahs*, I said, adding a Yiddish curse.

All they care about is money.

And crazy dancing.

And wild parties.

Oy, today's youth.

They're not yesterday's youth.

Definitely not. So, Mr Zlotochinski, how's your health?

OK. We're going to the Dead Sea for the holidays.

For Rivkele's psoriasis?

No, you have it mixed up. Rivkele has rheumatism. The psoriasis is mine. All mine.

*

Ofir has always been the ideal partner for imaginologues (that's what he called our imaginary dialogues). In the army, we used to call each other when we were on night watch and really get into it: imaginologues between a worried mother and her DJ son, between the Chief of Staff and the Minister of Defence, between a Kit Kat and a Mars Bar.

In our last year in the army, when we were both a minute away from losing it completely, we took it one step further and wrote long letters between two characters we'd invented: Adva Auerbuch and Nurit Sadeh. I was Adva, a virgin from a kibbutz who was stationed at a base down on the Egyptian border where there were only guys. Ofir was the poetic Nurit, who grew up in a small town near Haifa and was stationed in General Headquarters in Tel Aviv, where she was exposed to all the less well-known aspects of the military big shots. She was desperately in love with her commander, Dan Rom, head of the Parade Branch, but he never even noticed her.

We wrote those letters for a whole year, devoting ourselves to the inner worlds of Adva and Nurit. Ofir's letters were especially brilliant. He was able to eradicate his own identity and turn himself completely into Nurit. She had this kind of language that was hers alone, with expressions like 'Threesomes are wearisome', or 'All the hearts are purple today', or 'The woman inside me is still a child'.

Later, when Ofir tried to get an ad agency job, he asked my permission to include parts of that correspondence in his work portfolio. I said yes, even though I thought it was a little weird.

*

You know who I was just thinking of? Ofir asked. We were still sitting on the bench.

Yes, I said, Nurit Sadeh.

How'd you know?

Because I was just thinking of Adva.

I wonder what finally happened to her.

Adva was killed in a terrorist attack. Not long ago.

A fitting end for her.

She and Shahar Cohen. Their pictures were printed next to each other in the papers.

And tell me, was she still a virgin when she . . .

Unfortunately, yes. They even mentioned it in the news-papers, in the caption under her picture: A quiet girl. She died a virgin.

And Nurit? What about Nurit Sadeh?

You're asking me? You should know.

I know, Freed. I always knew. I wanted to see if you picked up on it.

On what?

Her commander, Dan Rom, he was in love with her too. But afraid to show it because he could have been charged with sexual harassment.

Tragic.

But in the end, she left the army.

And he confessed to her that . . .

Yes. But then she didn't want him any more. Because what she actually loved was the endless yearning for him.

Because that way . . .

That way she could speak in that language of hers, which is a language of yearning, not of actually having.

So, in fact, the language was more important to her than love?

Exactly.

Very nice. You have the gift, Ofir. You should write. Really, why don't you? After all, one of your World Cup wishes was . . .

The World Cup was before Maria.

Ofir said those words with finality. As if the fact that the World Cup came before Maria explained everything, and there was no room, not even a crack, for doubt.

I didn't say anything, and took another swig of beer.

Besides, he said with a smile, it's all your fault. If you'd been killed in the army like you promised, I would have made an Oscar-winning film about the four of us and then I wouldn't have had to work in advertising at all, and everything would be different.

Before I could apologise and promise to try harder to die soon, an older woman with a green scarf around her neck came up to us. I thought she wanted to ask for money, but then she shook Ofir's hand excitedly and thanked him, saying that she felt a lot better this week. I'm glad to hear it, he said, lightly massaging her palm. See you on

Thursday? Thursday, Thursday, she repeated like an echo, and added, you're the last person I expected to see here.

I wouldn't expect to see myself here either, Ofir answered, and they both laughed heartily.

*

It's all ego, Ofir said. A long minute had passed since the woman had gone, and I wasn't sure what he was talking about. All the things I wished for then, at the World Cup, he explained. They were all ego. Why did I want to write a book? Not because I had something important to say, God forbid. I wanted to stand at a stall during Book Week and have thousands of people ask me to autograph their copy of my book. That's what was in my mind when I made that wish.

What's wrong with that?

It doesn't lead to happiness. Just frustration. Because the ego is never satisfied, it'll always demand more. And you live with the constant fear that one day, your inspiration will dry up. Or your audience will disappear. And I don't want to be like that, always on the edge of the abyss. I mean, I can live that way, but I don't want to.

So what *do* you want?

To live for someone else. To give. To be a father. To listen to my body. To heal. That woman who shook my hand before? Five years ago, she accidentally ran over her daughter in a car park. She backed up without noticing that the girl was standing there with her scooter. You know how much sadness there was in her back the first time I touched her? Whole lumps of sadness. In her shoulders. Between her shoulders. In her lower back. Do you see? What can you say to someone like that? Are there any words that can console her? Any words that can touch her? And writing . . . writing is just words . . . a collection of words . . . I might have believed in words once, but after all those years in advertising, with all the slogans I thought up . . . 'Bid your wrinkles farewell', 'Natural, triple-action schnitzels' – I realised that people use words mainly to lie. Either to themselves or to others.

I was silent. The more emphatically Ofir spoke, the more I suspected that he wasn't absolutely sure of himself.

It's not that I don't have moments when . . . he went on. But still, you know me, my flat feet still hurt me sometimes . . . and sometimes ideas for stories pop into my head . . . and all the work on the NPO, for instance, came just in time for me, because the treatments . . . they don't always . . . I don't always really manage to be there, not like Maria . . . and recently, Maria, ever since Ilana . . . she isn't like Maria . . . maybe that's why it was convenient for me, all those meetings about the NPO . . . away from home, I mean.

Of course.

But running away is the easiest thing to do. That's what my father did, that's what I've done all my life. Jump to the next thing. So this time I'm trying to stay and tell myself that there's no rush to get to anyone, to anything. Not that I have a choice. You know, because of the girl.

The girl?

It's enough that one father left her. And she relies on me, you know? No one has ever relied on me like that before. My father never did because you can't rely on a boy who was raised by his mother. And in the army, they didn't rely on me because I was always the youngest guy in the unit. And at the agency, the minute they did rely on me – I fell apart. And here I can't allow myself to fall apart. Because I can't disappoint her. And that's the most important thing to me. More important than anything else. More important than writing. Do you understand?

Of course.

An elderly couple walked past, their arms around each other, their shoulders touching.

It's nice that they walk together like that at their age, I said.

His lower back hurts him, Ofir decided, and hiccupped like a drunk.

What?

That man has back pains. Bad ones.

How do you know?

Look at the way he walks. It's not balanced. He walks crookedly to avoid the pain. And she's supporting him with her hand. That's why they're walking that way, close together.

You can actually see things like that? I said in surprise.

Yes, Ofir said and pointed to the guy working in the kiosk. For instance, he has a stiff neck because he's always raising his head to look up at the TV. It's hanging too high.

I looked at the guy. There really was something robotic in the way the lower part of his body moved. Wow, I thought. Ofir is truly *good* at this. He didn't say a word to those people, and yet he knows such intimate things about them. So really, what does he need words for?

But *you* can write, Ofir said suddenly.

Me? I said, startled.

Yes, you wrote some really good letters back then.

Me? Write? Are you joking?

Why not, you're the one . . .

No way, I interrupted him. You must be wasted to have ideas like that.

We got up from the bench and staggered towards the cars. We were light-headed, a little fuzzy, and perhaps that's why we reacted so slowly to what happened. A guy wearing light-coloured jeans and a long-sleeved white shirt was walking towards us. At the time, we didn't notice that he was wearing light-coloured jeans and a long-sleeved white shirt. Only later, when we tried to recreate it, did we remember that. And the cap he was wearing. And the fact that there was something foreign about his facial features. Something not from here.

A van stopped next to him when he was about twenty

or thirty metres from us. A huge van. Whale-like. Three men got out of it, grabbed the guy and forced him into the back seat. He didn't try to resist. It was weird. He didn't shout. Didn't kick. Didn't wave his fists around. But even so, one of the men hit him on the head with something that looked like the butt of a gun. The whole thing took a few seconds, no more than half a minute. Then the men got into the van and drove away. They didn't drive fast and the tyres didn't squeal on the turn. Just the opposite, they even stopped for a red light at the next junction. And then, when the light turned green – they drove off.

What . . . what was that? Did you see it too? Ofir asked.

Yes, I mean, I think . . . I don't know . . . maybe we should call the police?

Perhaps they *were* the police, Ofir said.

So where's the flashing light on the roof?

Maybe they're undercover, Ofir offered a logical explanation. But we still called the emergency police number. And waited a long time for them to answer. The jingle playing in the background kept repeating the words 'service' and 'for you'. Carmit, the desk sergeant, sounded like we woke her up. She wrote down my description of the events without sounding particularly interested. I tried to be as detailed as possible, but the more details I gave, the more I felt like I was losing her. You sound pretty indifferent, Carmit, I said angrily. This isn't something that happens every day. A person gets pushed into a car and abducted like that, in the middle of the city.

You'd be surprised, Carmit said. The immigration police are hunting down foreign workers at the moment.

Wait a minute, so you know about it? That's what this was?

I don't know, Carmit said. Maybe it was the Security Agency.

Security Agency?

People staying in the country illegally. Palestinians from

the territories hiding at their employers' places. They're being hunted down now too.

So it's the hunting season now, is it?

Excuse me?

Never mind. Will you give us an update on how this turns out?

We don't update citizens.

So what . . . how will we know what . . .

Read the papers. If there's anything unusual about what you saw, it'll be reported in the newspapers. In any case, the Israel Police thanks you for your alertness. And wishes you . . . a good, quiet night.

*

We walked towards our cars in silence. I think we were both slightly ashamed for having stood by and not lifted a finger. Even though there wasn't much we could have done.

When we reached the car park, Ofir said, what a way to end the evening.

And I said, yes. They don't let you celebrate in peace in this country.

And Ofir said, something's gone bad here these last two years. Or . . . or was it always like this and I'm only noticing it now because of Maria? Everything here's become so base. So brutal. And you people in this city, you think you can escape it. That you're some kind of cosmopolitans. But that's crap. It's worse here. Everyone in this city pretends to be liberal, but the truth is that smoking grass is the whole extent of their liberalism. God forbid they should be truly open to other people. Or care about the injustices going on right under their noses.

What does he want from this city? I thought. What sore point of his is it pressing on?

Remember what I'm telling you, Ofir went on, in the end it'll explode in your faces. And it'll come from the most unexpected direction.

Why 'your faces'? By what right did he exclude himself?

I wondered. Because he lives in Michmoret, or because Maria convinced him to throw away his mobile, or because he takes an afternoon nap every single day 'because that's what our bodies truly want'? – but that didn't seem like the right time to bring up the subject. So I didn't say anything.

And Ofir said, I have a request. If you can, don't tell Maria about the . . . about what just happened.

No problem, I said.

She's been a bit . . . since Ilana. And I don't want her to . . .

No problem.

*

Maria wasn't the only one I didn't tell about the kidnapping. I didn't tell myself either. An article I translated recently claims that the first two years of our lives are erased from our memory because the dramas that take place during infancy are too intense to bear. And I repressed the memory of that kidnapping as if it had never happened until the first session of the creative writing workshop I was taking. The tutor asked each of us to tell a true story and a false one about ourselves, and suddenly it rose to the surface like a lost navy submarine. I talked about how we were strolling down the street and the large van stopped and a man was swallowed up inside it, like Jonah in the whale, and we didn't do a thing, we didn't have time, or we couldn't, or we didn't want to. I told the story in great detail, as the instructor had asked, but still, the whole group, except for one timid girl, thought I was lying and that the true story was the one I'd made up about still using a youth pass to ride the buses even though I was thirty, and no one suspected me because of my baby face and height.

To tell the truth, I was insulted. Even though the purpose of the game was to trick the group, I felt like shit that no one believed the first story. Wait a minute, I asked, why doesn't the story about the kidnapping sound believable?

The way you told it, it sounded like a scene from a Hollywood movie, said a guy in glasses who looked like a Hollywood movie director himself.

It sounds more like something that would happen in America. Things like that happen in New York, not in Tel Aviv, a girl said.

You didn't flesh out your story with enough non-contingent details, the tutor said. That's why we found it hard to believe.

That group was pissing me off more from one minute to the next. They don't believe me even now. And what the hell are 'non-contingent details'?! It's so annoying when teachers use words no one understands. And how maddening it is that it has exactly the stupid effect they're aiming for. And what is this chair they gave me to sit on? It's not a chair, it's a stool. It's not a stool, it's a rug. Why do I deserve this? Why did I pay for the whole workshop in advance? This is the last time I come here.

Tell me, the timid girl asked, was there anything . . . I mean . . . was there anything about it in the papers?

Nothing, I admitted. I had rushed out to buy all the newspapers first thing in the morning. I read all the inside pages. There was no mention of it. Not one word. All week.

*

On the other hand, they devoted two or three inches to the event that launched 'Our Right – The Jennifer Goldman and Ilana Abramowitz-Tanuri Non-Profit Organisation for Human Rights in the Health System'. Accompanying every story was a close-up photo of Amichai, and the brief text contained mainly direct quotes from the press release we'd handed out at the event (Ofir had said that journalists don't like working too hard, so we should prepare a few quotable sentences for them beforehand).

The overall tone of the reports was quite favourable. One newspaper wrote that it was an 'interesting initiative'. Another maintained that establishing the NPO was 'a welcome idea'. A third took the trouble to print the NPO phone number at the end of the item. The next day, there were 5,421 voicemail messages on the answering machine Amichai had set up, and by the end of that week, almost 8,000 people had called. It turned out that Amichai's initiative had broken through a locked door, had got under the public's thick skin and sent an electric charge along an exposed nerve of Israeli society. And it turned out that among the callers were many professionals – lawyers, accountants, electricians – all of whom had personally experienced a violation of their rights and offered to volunteer their expertise for the NPO's use.

Within only three months – and without leaving his job at Telemed, because 'you don't leave a good job' and 'I have subscribers who depend on me' – Amichai, with the determination of a long-distance runner and the patience of a jigsaw-puzzle assembler, had succeeded in turning the NPO from an idea on paper to a living organisation.

The administrative backbone of the NPO consisted of four salaried employees, but most of the work was done by dozens of volunteers. Amichai himself divided his time between the day-to-day running of the organisation and meetings with senior officials in hospitals and in the Health Ministry to discuss the implementation of the pilot that would examine how the presence of mediators and interpreters from the Our Right NPO in a hospital accident and emergency department would help guard human rights in the institution.

Ofir and I followed the reports in the media about Amichai's activities with proud surprise. It's always weird to see someone you knew as a teenager becoming so successful in the grown-up world. You remember him choking on his first cigarette behind the basketball court – and now he was making hospital directors choke when he showed them the critical reports prepared by the NPO's undercover volunteers. You remember him shaking in his boots as he stood in front of the teacher's desk – and now he was banging on the Health Minister's desk.

But there was something else here that was less comfortable to admit.

We had always been a bit disdainful of Amichai, perhaps because he was the least verbal of the three of us (and perhaps that's why Ilana refused to get close to us? Perhaps she sensed that hidden current?). The three of us moulded Hebrew to serve our purposes. Ofir liked to be clever. Churchill liked to be precise. And I, perhaps because my parents never mastered Hebrew, insisted on knowing it inside and out. I read dictionaries in the bathroom as if they were novels. I turned on the radio every day at five to five to hear 'A moment of Hebrew'. And I enjoyed inventing Hebrew substitutes for foreign words that the Academy of the Hebrew Language still hadn't got around to working on.

I can't really say if that attraction to words was what connected me to Ofir and Churchill from the beginning, or if we became alike in that regard only after our friendship had deepened. But we were already doing quite a bit of verbal jousting at school, and after the army, when the three of us chose professions in which language played a major role, our tendency to verbalise everything grew stronger and caused some of the people who spent time with us to raise their eyebrows – a tight-lipped smoulder is the hallmark of the manly movie star, so what's all that talking?

Amichai, unlike us, always preferred doing to talking. And when he did speak, he spoke heavily and used outdated words like 'swell' or 'way-out', and when one of us entertained the others with a complex play on words, he was the last to understand. And he married someone who, at least outwardly, showed no great love for him. And there was that endless talk of his about studying shiatsu, which never came to anything. And those ridiculous attempts to eradicate the blotch on his neck. And his pathetic 'brilliant ideas' that we sometimes enjoyed, but more often made fun of.

And now, just like in the pavement shell game you see con artists running, the pea turns out to have been hiding under the most unexpected shell – in Amichai's project, a project that the great, omniscient Churchill had declared 'not serious', that, at first, I didn't think had a chance either. It was Amichai's project that was taking off. That had financial support. And influence.

*

About a year after the NPO was established, the first scheme was initiated in the same failing hospital whose director had spoken to Amichai at the launch event.

A week later, the pilot was almost stopped. An Our Right representative was hit by a patient's brother who thought that he and he alone was responsible for his brother's death. A group of interns in one of the departments all threatened to quit, claiming that their shifts were inhuman. And in another department, doctors refused to cooperate with Our Right representatives, arguing that they would be violating the patients' right to privacy if they did.

What have you done to me? the director shouted at Amichai. The situation has only deteriorated! But Amichai wasn't fazed. For several moments, he let the director's shouts crash over him like water on a wharf, and in the end, he said quietly: Micha, I don't have to explain to you that it takes time to absorb changes. Especially in large organisations. That's why I suggest that we judge on the basis of the long-term results.

How long? the director demanded to know.

At least three months, Amichai said.

After three months, an objective poll revealed that, along with the problems that it created, the presence of the Our Right representatives did indeed improve doctor–patient communication and significantly decreased the number of complaints.

In light of this, Amichai was invited to the Health Ministry to examine the possibility of expanding the scheme to additional hospitals, and he was asked to appear on several morning TV shows to explain the idea behind the NPO (he comes over really well on the small screen, Ofir said, because he projects something sincere. Notice that he never gets drawn into that carefree façade the presenters put on, but he still doesn't come across as patronising).

During his appearances, many women called the studios to ask for the phone number of the widower with the earth-coloured eyes.

Amichai politely rejected all those interested women.

But why? I asked when he told me about it.

It's too soon, he said. His heart was still mourning. In bed at night, he still reaches out to embrace Ilana. During the day, he still automatically calls her mobile to tell her about the little things that have happened to him. Every time he looks at the children, he sees her (Noam has her tiny freckles; Nimrod, her expression). Every time they play Aviv Geffen's song, 'Oh Ilana', on the radio, he turns it off. Every time he hears an ambulance, he remembers *that* ambulance. Every time he hears a car alarm, he remembers that ambulance. Every time he . . . hold on a minute. He doesn't want to talk about it. How did I drag him into talking about it? Talking about it only makes him feel terrible.

OK, I said. And left him alone.

But the women didn't. They kept calling him and sending letters and pictures and sad songs. And he kept dodging them. To the ones who sounded particularly desperate, he mentioned his best friend, a fantastic guy, very serious, from a British family. He's writing his philosophy thesis now.

I even went out with one of them. In principle, I thought it was dishonest, very dishonest, to exploit the NPO for personal gain, but –

Her name was Ya'ara.

And I really loved rolling the name around on my tongue when we spoke. Ya'-a-ra, I'd say slowly, lingering on every syllable, feeling as if I were sitting in a rocking chair that someone was tilting further and further back. So where do you live, Ya'-a-ra? And where are you from originally, Ya'-a-ra? And isn't it amazing that you like the Chamelons, Ya'-a-ra, and what do you think about skipping the first date, Ya'-a-ra, and starting with the second? What does that mean? It means that we ask all the usual questions now, on the phone. So on the second date, we can really talk. Great. So let's start. What do you do?

Coach.

I thought she meant she was a personal fitness coach, and was already picturing myself running my finger slowly along her calf muscle, but when we met, she explained that she was a mental coach. What they call a life coach. She meets privately with executives and helps them:

1. To define their vision.
2. To identify the obstacles blocking their way to fulfilling that vision.
3. To achieve significant breakthroughs.

That's it in a nutshell, she said, and cut her mushroom pie into small squares of exactly the same size.

I nodded. My inner oracle prophesised bad things, but nevertheless I told her almost personal things about myself, and at the end of the evening, I said I'd like to see her again. Her upper lip curled upward slightly, the sort of curl you feel like kissing. Her self-control, evident in every movement, made me want to know what happened when she lost control, and more than anything, I was thrilled by the idea that while I made passionate love to her, I could whisper Ya'-a-ra, Ya'-a-ra.

It didn't happen. Even though, at first, everything went according to plan. As I always do on the second date, at some point I mentioned that I was colour blind. So what colour is my dress? she asked, the way girls always do, and, as always, I hesitated in order to intensify the suspense, then said: red. And explained that it's not that I can't identify each colour separately, it's just hard for me to differentiate between them when they're next to each other. For example, if she were standing in the middle of a green field in her pretty dress, I might not see her. That's so weird, she said, as expected, and I was already preparing myself for the next stage, where I usually ask the girl sitting across from me something personal about herself, and she, influenced by my blind openness, tells me a lot more than she'd intended, and then, to justify herself in her own eyes, agrees to come up to my flat, or is silent and looks intently at my lips as if to say: let's kiss. But a tenth of a second before I bent to kiss Ya'ara II, she said there was something she wanted to tell me, had to tell me, and I straightened up and said, go for it.

You have no vision, she said. From everything you told me about yourself, you live your life blindly. Without mapping out your wishes and your opportunities.

So . . . so what do you suggest?

Create a vision for yourself, she said: I wouldn't mind if we did it together. I don't usually mix work with my private life, but in your case, I can make an exception.

Look, I said, moving to the far end of the sofa, I'm sure you're a great coach, and that your method has helped a great many people, but for me . . . it won't work . . .

Why not?

Just that word, vision, gives me a chill. Not of excitement. Of the flu.

That's a real shame, she said, placing a large cushion between us, because that's not something I can live with. In the long-term.

So maybe we can console each other in the meantime? I said, and put my hand on the cushion.

Console each other? For what?

For being alone. For the coldness of an untouched body. For the heat trapped in a cold, untouched body.

She shook her head and said, heat, cold, I don't do things like that any more. My vision is to find a serious life partner. And things that don't lead to that are a waste of my time. And by the way, she added when she'd already gone to the door, if you ask me, what's blocking you is your friends.

My friends?!

I've never met a person who talks so much about his friends, shows albums of their pictures to the women he's dating, and hangs framed photos of them in his flat instead of paintings. If I were your coach, I'd say you were a classic case of the parallel-train paradigm.

Parallel train?

When your train is standing in the station and a train on a parallel track starts to move, you think that your train is also moving. But it isn't really moving. It's just an optical illusion.

What exactly are you trying to tell me?

Nothing. Just that if I were your coach, I'd say that you might be living your friends' lives instead of your own.

But you're not, I said.

Not what?

Not my coach, I said and slammed the door in her face, trying as hard as I could, without success, to feel satisfaction for having had the last word, and the standard responses to her claim rang in my head, responses I could have made but didn't: let's say that I may not have a vision at the moment, but the whole NPO thing actually gave me the desire to do something with myself soon. Really soon. And as far as my friends are concerned, she's completely wrong. I talk about them a lot only because I love them, and to say that I'm living their lives instead of my own is a load of crap.

*

Towards the end of the year, the country's leading news-paper published the names of its nominees for Man of the Year. Among those listed in the category, 'Man of the Year in Society' was Amichai Tanuri. And this is how the judges explained his nomination (I cut that part of the article out of the paper and pinned it on my kitchen noticeboard): 'In a short period of time, Amichai Tanuri has succeeded in turning the discourse on human rights in the health system into a common subject of discussion among patients and doctors alike. The Our Right NPO, led by Mr Tanuri, is still in its infancy but has already borne fruit and influ-enced the daily lives of the citizens of this country. The story of Amichai Tanuri and Our Right is one of a private initiative that grew out of personal tragedy, but attracted many other people because of the human, universal idea it is based on. For that reason, in our view, Amichai Tanuri merits inclusion in our list of nominees for 'Man of the Year in Society'.

*

The nomination brought with it further media exposure. Amichai's face appeared occasionally on evening programmes (all of them, by the way, had to meet his terms: to tape the interview in the morning because he had to be home with his children by five at the latest).

The questions were always the same questions, and Amichai – the same Amichai. He always spoke heavily, and in the plural. He always scratched his upper chest, the part closest to his neck, while considering what to say. And he always trembled slightly when the interviewer interrupted him.

One of those times, an interviewer interrupted him because of a special report from the programme's law corre-spondent, Michaela Raz. A surprising turn of events in the case that has been rocking the country for several months, she said, her eyes almost popping out of their sockets. Yoav Alimi, the chief prosecutor and the person who has been heading up the case for a year and half, was forced to resign today due to what the district prosecutor's office was calling 'embarrassing personal circumstances'.

Could you shed a bit of light on those circumstances? the presenter in the studio asked.

Not yet, I'm sorry to say, Michaela Raz replied in a voice completely devoid of sorrow. The rumours are spreading like wildfire here and on the Internet, but have not yet been officially confirmed. We hope to get back to you shortly with Alimi's own response to the affair.

OK, Michaela, we'll wait patiently for your update, the presenter said, and again turned towards Amichai. Until we hear Mr Alimi's response, the presenter continued, we'll go back to Amichai Tanuri and Our Right. Mr Tanuri, don't you find something distasteful in the fact that half your funding comes from the United States? Isn't this ultimately what used to be called the 'looking-for-handouts culture'?

Amichai said nothing. For the first time in any of his media interviews, his vocal chords had dried up. Churchill resigned? he thought, stunned. Why?

10

Churchill is the focus. Even though he's standing on the side holding a relatively small placard, it's clear that he's the focus of the picture. It's hard to explain. It's something in his posture. And something in the way the heads of the others at the demonstration lean towards him for guidance or approval. Written in large letters on the placard he's holding are the words 'WE ARE ALL SHAHAR COHEN', my placard says 'NO SHAHAR COHEN – NO CLASSES', and the placard Amichai's holding says, 'SHAHAR STAYS OR WE GO'. Ofir thought up those slogans, of course. And Amichai's little sister printed them in her beautiful, round handwriting.

Two days earlier, Shahar Cohen had been expelled from school. There'd been a scuffle during break. Scuffle is too nice a word. It was a fist fight, and Shahar Cohen was involved. He'd also been involved in a copying incident during the Bible final exam. And in a graffiti incident in Arabic. And in the inflated-sex-doll-in-the-headmistress's-office incident. He hadn't initiated any of those pranks, but he had the rare talent of joining them at the worst possible moment, when the real initiators could put the blame on 'the one who came with the integration' and vanish from the scene. Sometimes it seemed as if Shahar Cohen derived a strange pleasure from always being blamed. As if, instead of fighting the prejudice against 'the one who came with the integration', he'd decided to submit to it. To validate it.

Churchill couldn't stand Shahar Cohen. There was some hidden grudge from the time they were kids growing up in the same neighbourhood. But more than he couldn't stand Shahar Cohen, he couldn't abide injustice. And the more he heard about that punching incident during break, the more he suspected that the school governors had taken the easy way out. It turned out that the fight had been started by the son of the president of the school alumni association. And it turned out that he had provoked Shahar Cohen, verbally and physically, for quite a while before Shahar finally punched him. It turned out that he had called Shahar Cohen's mother a whore, and Shahar a petty criminal. It turned out that his friends had bet secretly that he couldn't get the petty criminal hiding inside Shahar to come out.

Each one bet fifty shekels.

Those bastards are afraid that his father will cancel his donation for the computer lab, Churchill explained, so they're putting it all on Shahar. Blaming Shahar is the easiest thing to do, because who'll defend him?

We'll defend him! Churchill answered his own question, and dragged all of us to a non-violent demonstration at the school gate.

After standing there for an hour, screaming what was written on the placards to the tunes of football songs till we were hoarse, we moved on to the next stage of Churchill's plan of action and tied ourselves to the gate with iron chains. I don't have any pictures of that stage (there was no one to take them, we were all shackled), but the photo in the newspaper clipping I kept shows Churchill stretched out against the gate, and in the corner, there's a white arm that looks like Amichai's.

It didn't take long for the governors to back down. The article in the local newspaper clearly supported our position and printed additional testimonies by students who had been involved in the scuffle. The alumni association held an emergency meeting and decided to set up a committee to study the incident so that such episodes could be avoided in the future, a committee that has not convened to this day. Shahar Cohen was readmitted to school on probation, and thanked Churchill emotionally for all he'd done for him.

It wasn't for you, it was for the principle of the thing, Churchill said, and added, as cold as iron: don't think I've forgotten what happened, Shahar. Don't think we're going to be friends now.

*

None of us knew exactly what had happened. Every time we tried to ask Shahar about it, he cracked a joke. And every time we tried to ask Churchill, he said nothing.

Only years later, on the way back from Mitzpe Ramon, did Churchill tell me. In a quiet voice. Without looking at me even once during the entire drive.

*

Churchill's father was the handsomest man in Haifa. Even in his forties, Michel Alimi had a full head of carefully combed hair. And greying temples. Impressive. He had very tanned, muscular arms, especially the part you lean on the car window. And he had the smile of a man who knows that his smile is alluring.

He was a driving instructor, and his speciality was married women. From the Carmel. In the mid-eighties, the 'second-family-car' rage spread through the wealthiest section of the city, and dozens of women who didn't have a licence or whose licence had expired, flocked to take lessons with the best instructor in town.

Welcome to my kingdom, he would say at the first lesson and open the door gallantly. Waiting for them inside was a beautifully upholstered seat, air conditioning, and the light scent of aftershave, and in the glove compartment, a box of sweets awaited them: mint and caramel and lemon and the kind that, when you took a small bite, filled your mouth with a warm flow of chocolate.

Sometimes, a boy was also waiting for them in the back seat. The boy's face was broad and light-skinned, totally unlike the long, dark-skinned face of his father. This is Yoav, my son, Michel would explain to his new students, and they would smile at the boy through the mirror or turn around and shake his hand or turn around and stroke his cheek. Or ignore him completely.

With time, the boy learned that it was actually those women who ignored him – the ones who got into the car determined to show that they had come only to learn how to drive and not for anything else – who were the first to be caught in his father's net.

It always began with compliments. 'That colour suits you.' 'Your new hairstyle is very flattering.' 'Could you please not wear that perfume any more when you come for a lesson? It makes me lose my concentration.' Then came the touching. Brief, supposedly accidental touches on the elbow or palm. Then more lingering touches: 'May I? Let's do it together. Hand on the gearstick, foot on the clutch, and now change gear, gently, not with force, pretend you're holding something that's pleasant to the touch, OK?'

Later, just when the atmosphere in the car was beginning to warm up, came the planned outburst of anger: 'Not like that! What are you doing?! You want to kill us all?!' He would raise his voice and stop the car with a squeal as he slammed on the instructor's brake pedal. 'I'm explaining it to you but you're not listening. I'm sorry, but if you keep this up, you'll never pass the test,' he'd say, putting his tanned hand on his chest, and the woman would leap out of the car at the end of the lesson, upset, sometimes in tears.

A week later, he'd be waiting for her in front of the car with a bouquet of flowers. Or a box of chocolates. And apologise from the bottom of his heart for having shouted. And they would suddenly melt. Suddenly surrender. As if a cord of control had snapped. And by the end of the lesson, he was already allowing himself to run his fingers through her hair, or rest his hand on her thigh. And all that time, the boy watched them from the back seat, two conflicting voices inside him: one admired his father, wanted to be as handsome as his father, beloved like his father, and the other wanted to shout that something here wasn't right. But he didn't know exactly what that something was.

As the boy grew older, the second voice overcame the first, until one day, when a young woman with a very short skirt and blonde-streaked hair planted an unashamed kiss on his father's cheek before she got out of the car, he could no longer control himself and said: Dad, that woman has lice.

Lice? his father said, and turned to him, amused. Yes, she has lice in her hair! the boy insisted. Besides, our mother is much prettier. Our mother? His father's expression suddenly grew serious, as if only at that moment did he realise what might be going through the mind of the boy who was always sitting in the back seat. Our mother is a wonderful person, Yoavi, Michel Alimi said. I adore our mother. And all these . . . all these women you see here in the car, they're only good for one thing.

One thing? What thing? the seven-year-old boy asked.

Never mind, the father said and moved into the driver's seat. Then he looked at his son several times in the mirror, started the car and said loudly, remember what I'm telling you, boy, none of those women can hold a candle to your mother, do you hear? Not one!

*

Churchill's mother was also a well-known figure in Haifa. Dina Hayut-Alimi, head of the neighbourhood association. And the parents' association. The woman who inserted a firm hyphen in her surname long before that became fashionable among Tel Aviv-Jaffa women. The woman who raised six sons in the lowest neighbourhood in Haifa and taught them that lying is wrong and that you have to do what you think is right, not what people say, and most importantly – you mustn't be afraid of anyone. Don't be afraid to be smart. Don't be afraid to be first. Don't be afraid to succeed. Because if a person wants to succeed – he will. It doesn't matter where his grandfather came to Israel from. And it doesn't matter what neighbourhood he grew up in.

She didn't succeed to the same degree with all of her six children. Her rigid distinctions between good and bad actually caused some of them to grow up wild. But Churchill was his mother's pride from the moment he was born. You are God's gift to me, she would tell him in a whisper so that his siblings couldn't hear, and she paid for special courses they didn't get, bought him a bicycle two years before his bar mitzvah because 'I know I can trust him', and appointed him to arbitrate in arguments between the other children because it was clear that they would all accept his decisions.

When Churchill reached the age of twelve, his mother decided that he would attend the best school in the city, no matter what the courts said (determination of status in Haifa was ridiculously topographic: the higher you lived on the mountain, the higher your status was). According to municipal policy, it was impossible for children from the low neighbourhood in which Churchill lived to go to school on the Carmel, but Dina Hayut-Alimi checked it out and found that there was a quota of ten children that the good school had to accept from other neighbourhoods in the city, and she made sure that Churchill took the entrance examinations. And prepared him for them from morning till night, for three months.

Only two children passed the entrance exams to the school on the mountain: Churchill, and Shahar Cohen.

Several days after he received the letter that began, 'We are pleased to inform you', Churchill saw Shahar Cohen at Stella Maris, the place on the mountain slope from which, without paying, you could watch the matches being played in the Kiryat Eliezer stadium. I heard that we're going to go to the same school together, he said with a broad, proud smile.

Instead of answering, Shahar Cohen grabbed him by the shirt and slammed him up against the trunk of a pine tree.

Don't you talk to me, you bastard. If you don't tell your loser father to take his filthy hands off my mother, I'll kill you, I swear to God. I'll kill you on the first day of school, you hear me?

After the 'lice incident', Churchill's father no longer took his son along on his driving lessons, so Churchill had no idea that something was going on between his father and Shahar Cohen's mother. But he knew that Shahar Cohen's mother had given birth to him when she was sixteen, which made her the youngest mother in the neighbourhood. And he knew that Shahar Cohen's father was an officer in the army stationed on a base near Beersheba who came home only once every two weeks. And that a month before, he had been promoted to major and was given an army car, so he was able to leave the family car at home. For the use of his wife. Who didn't have a licence.

All those facts ran quickly through his mind when Shahar Cohen had him pressed up against the tree trunk, but none of them turned into speech. His hands spoke instead, trying to break him free of Shahar Cohen's grip, but Shahar Cohen, though shorter than he was, had the advantage of rage and didn't let him go. Locked in a clench, kicking each other, butting each other, they fell onto the ground.

The other children gathered in a circle around them, but none of them dared intervene.

Unlike the regular brawls, which were an inseparable part of their childhood (like the tune of the ice cream van in summer and the flooding sewers in winter), there was something different in this fight. It was hard to explain, but at certain moments, the spectators thought that Churchill and Shahar Cohen were actually hugging. At certain moments, they seemed to be consoling each other. But on the other hand, they kept trying to hurt each other, and after a few minutes of hard punching, their faces and hands and chests and thighs were covered in hot, sticky blood.

*

Churchill didn't go home that day, not even after nightfall. He waited for his father's car to turn into their street, then he stood in front of it in the middle of the road. His father stopped the car with a squeal of brakes and jumped out in a fright. They had a brief conversation, very brief, in the light of a flickering streetlamp. Michel Alimi combed his beautiful hair back for several seconds, tossing sideways glances, and spoke in a very quiet voice. Look, he said. I want you to understand, he said. I'm only a man, and . . .

So what if you're a man? Churchill interrupted him, silenced him, and quashed the rest of the arguments his father tried to make with exactly the same focused silence that, years later, he would use to quash the arguments made by opposing counsel.

The next day, Shahar Cohen's pretty mother moved to a different driving instructor. And so it happened that on the first day in his new school, Churchill was not murdered. On the contrary, he flourished.

Already on that first day, he managed to persuade Shoshana Roth, the scary maths teacher, to give less homework by showing her a detailed table of the homework given that day in all their subjects, plus a statistical calculation of the impossible amount of time, on the average, it would take each student to do justice to all of it. And at break, he went out to the football field and authoritatively settled the argument two teams were having about whether there had been a foul, and at the end of the day, he went up to Rona Raviv, the snob, whom no one had dared to approach since primary school, and simply spoke to her, without lowering his gaze, and even managed to make her laugh twice. And within a few weeks, had already formed a small group of admirers-friends around him who emulated the way he walked, dressed, laughed, smoked, and hung on his every word.

Shahar Cohen never belonged to that group of admirers, even though he always hovered around near them. The secret rancour between him and Churchill continued to simmer all those years without any of their friends knowing why. And it wasn't till that night, on our way home from our unsuccessful search for the vet, Ricardo Luis, in Mitzpe Ramon, with Ofir and Amichai asleep on the back seat and Radio Amman the only station we could get on the radio, that Churchill looked out into the vast darkness on our right and told me everything, and in the end, said, I want you to know, Freed, that no one in the world knows about this but you, and I kept quiet and felt lucky and important and special.

*

Fourteen years later, I got a first-hand report of the 'embarrassing personal circumstances' from the source.

Churchill knocked on my door a few nights after the story broke on TV.

He was dressed strangely. The bottom half – black trousers and polished shoes – was lawyerly. But above it was an old Maccabi Haifa T-shirt with Eyal Berkovic's number on it. A small Israeli paunch protruded from the T-shirt. I wondered whether he'd got fatter recently or I only just noticed it now.

Can I come in? he asked. Sorry about the late . . .

No worries, I said, inviting him in.

I made him a cup of strong instant coffee, carefully stirring in one and a half teaspoons of sugar the way he liked, and brought it to him in the living room.

Thanks, *Baba*, he said, and left the cup on the table.

That was a hell of trip, he said, pointing to the framed picture of our trip to the Sinai that was hanging on the wall.

I haven't seen that picture for years, he added when I kept silent.

You haven't been here in years, I said dryly.

Yes, he said, and looked down at his shoes. He usually sat with his legs spread wide, as if he were having sex with the air, but now his knees were pressed together.

I know, he said, that for the last two years, you and I haven't . . . I mean . . . we've grown distant . . . after what happened . . . rightly so, of course . . . He stopped and looked at me.

I nodded like a judge, giving him permission to continue along the same lines. For the time being.

But as far as I'm concerned . . . you've always remained my friend . . . and now, I'm in trouble . . . and I have no one to talk to, no one to ask for advice . . . Ya'ara, she won't any more . . . and Amichai, he has enough on his mind . . . and Ofir . . . he called and starting telling me how every mistake is a lesson, and maybe he's right, but those clichés of his drive me mad . . . and my parents . . . my father doesn't understand these kinds of things, and my mother . . . I'm ashamed to talk to her about it . . . you know, she started law school this year? She said that seeing me succeed gave her courage, you see? So how can I tell her what happened, disappoint her this way . . . ? But still, I need to talk to someone . . . someone who thinks clearly . . . because I can't do it alone any more . . .

Your coffee's getting cold, I interrupted him. I still didn't know what I wanted more: to help him or to throw him out.

Anyway, he said after a few quiet sips, you're the only one who can understand me in this thing. Because you're the only one who knows who Keren is.

233

Keren?

Keren from Cusco. You remember when you were sick and I took care of you? And that's exactly when I met a girl who . . .

The one with the secret?

Yes. The one I asked to wait till you recovered, but she left, saying that 'whatever is supposed to happen . . .'

Happens. And if you're supposed to meet – you'll meet. I remember. But how is she connected to the 'embarrassing personal circumstances'?

She *is* the 'embarrassing personal circumstance', Churchill said. And began to tell me.

Churchill had a special tone to his voice when he talked about his conquests. When he talked about women he'd been able to seduce, his voice would become slightly deeper, rougher, a bit like the voice-over in a Hollywood trailer, and his gestures were sweeping, illustrative, and he always went into the most intimate detail. Where he touched her. And how, at first, she wouldn't. Then suddenly she would. Wow, would she ever, she was dripping from every opening. And the sounds she made, oh God! And the smell of her breath. And the taste of her lips. And her lips down there. When we were teenagers, there was something very provocative about it, and I usually had a hard-on when he spoke that way, but later, when we were older, we grew tired of it and just found it embarrassing. And gross. But I still had a hard-on sometimes when he spoke that way.

Now, in any case, his tone was different. Hesitant. Hurt. And occasionally, he stopped and rubbed his head where his hairline was receding (I wondered whether it had receded a great deal more recently, or was I simply noticing it only now. And then a thought flitted through my mind: if he already looks so much older, do I as well?).

She came up to me after a court session, he explained. And, idiot that I am, I didn't ask myself what she was doing there. I was just glad to see her.

You recognised her?

Immediately. She looked exactly like she had then. Actually, not exactly like she had then, better. More womanly. She was wearing a long, wine-red dress slit up the side. In retrospect, I know that everything was planned, but at the time, I didn't suspect a thing. She said she'd just happened to be nearby and had come inside, and that sounded reasonable to me. She said I looked good in a lawyer's robe and then, when we were sitting and talking outside in the museum plaza, she said that a day didn't pass when she didn't think about me.

Since Cusco?

Yes. So I immediately said that I . . . I hadn't stopped thinking about her either since then.

I didn't know that.

I never told anyone. I thought it was pathetic to keep thinking about her all those years. Who was she anyway? Just a girl I spent two days with and . . .

Kept thinking about. What's pathetic about that?

I don't know. I thought that if I talked about it, if I said it out loud, it would just grow larger in my mind.

Or if you told anyone, I thought, your image would be tarnished.

Shall I tell you something else that no one else knows? Churchill went on. A few days before I got married, I went to Ashdod. I remembered Keren telling me she had family in Ashdod. So I went down there and drove in circles around the city. Looking for her. I drove slowly. For hours. Ashdod has grown into a large city over the last few years. It's divided into quarters. So I drove from one quarter to the other. I told myself that if I saw her, it would be a sign.

A sign of what?

I don't know. But it had become really urgent that I find her. Talk to her. Before I got married.

And you didn't find her.

No. Then she suddenly shows up with that slit up her

dress, still radiating the sense that she has a secret she's keeping to herself, and she tells me that not a day has passed that she hasn't regretted not waiting with us in Cusco, because there was a special magic between us. A one-time thing. And no matter how hard she tried to recreate that magic with other men, it was never the same.

Wow.

It was nothing, just clichés. But I didn't get it then. And she kept touching me as she spoke, light, fluttery touches. First, only on the back of my hand. Then on my knee. And in the end, there was one especially long one here, on the inside of my thigh.

So you slept with her.

More or less . . . Churchill said and stood up. Usually, at this point in his stories, came the detailed descriptions. But now he stood up, sighed an old man's sigh, went over to the window, pushed the curtain aside and stared down at the street.

Unbelievable, he said.

I thought he was talking about himself, about what happened, repenting. But then he said again, unbelievable. Come and see what's going on here.

I went over to the window. It was one in the morning, and on my little street, some ten young women wearing traditional yellow dresses were dancing their way among the cars. The procession was led by an older woman with long black hair who was banging on a large drum in an ever faster rhythm. In the centre of the group, dressed in white, were a woman and a man, a bride and groom, who looked amused and excited by the commotion. Every few steps, the young women stopped their dance for a moment to throw confetti on the couple, then went back to their dancing and singing.

It's a *hinna*, Churchill explained.

In the middle of the night? I asked.

That's what's so great about this city, he said. Anything

can happen. And what's even greater is that no one makes a big deal about it.

True. In Haifa, the neighbours would already be calling the police.

A parking warden turned into the street just as the *hinna* party reached the junction. In seconds, she was swallowed up in the sea of yellow dresses – female arms touched her, stroked her, pulled her into joining the dance. She resisted at first, tried to break out of the circle that formed around her, but then, suddenly, as if something inside her had surrendered, she abandoned herself to it – she let down her hair, unbuttoned the top button on her blouse and danced in front of the groom.

Look at that, what a scene, Churchill said.

The warden finally broke away from the group and went back to putting parking tickets on windscreens, but Churchill continued to hold the curtain away from the window.

Remember that trip on Independence Day? Remember that I made you swear to come here with me after the army?

Of course.

Do you think it would have been different if we'd stayed in Haifa?

What would have been different?

Everything . . . us. Do you think this city changed us?

Of course. I don't even remember how to drive a manual car up a hill any more.

And . . . apart from that?

I don't know. I'm not sure. Because meanwhile, time has passed, so how can you separate what . . .

Look, look at that woman with the drum. She must be the bride's mother. Shame Ofir can't see this now, it might make him feel like coming back to live here.

That's hard to believe, I said. I think he's already gone past the point of no return.

The joint of no return, Churchill said, repeating one of Ofir's quips from his copywriting days.

The colourful procession disappeared around the corner, but Churchill lingered at the window for another long moment, as if saddened that he would have to continue his story now. As if he would rather join that group of dancers, bang the drum loudly and forget everything.

Tell me, he suddenly asked, at my wedding, did I look as happy as those two on the street?

I didn't know what to say. At his wedding, my eyes were mostly on the bride.

No, he went on without waiting for an answer, even at my wedding, I was thinking about Keren. Thoughts of her went through my mind at least twice during the ceremony. That's why I drank so much, to stop those thoughts. And thoughts about our World Cup wishes – you remember those wishes we wrote? She was one of the two wishes I didn't read aloud. '*I want to meet Keren purely by chance after thoughts of her are gone from me*', that's what I wrote.

'I once loved a little girl in the Galilee,' I said, reciting the next line of Meir Ariel's song.

Churchill flashed me a warm look, the kind we used to exchange once, before the rift. A look that says, 'How great it is that there's someone in the world who understands my most personal associations.'

And you know what the best bit is? he went on, slightly heartened, she'd really been living in the Galilee all those years, in some small village above Carmiel.

Alone?

Sometimes alone, sometimes not. At least that's what she told me. Now I don't know any more what is the truth and what isn't. She said she wasn't ready to give up her freedom for any price, and in the same breath asked me to come and see her there. I told her I'd drop by sometime, and then she crossed one slit-exposed leg over the other and said, I meant now.

So you slept with her, I said impatiently.

Yes, but only to exorcise the dybbuk. I told myself, I'm cheating on Ya'ara, but it's actually for her own good.

Her own good? I shouted. I was beginning to feel that Churchill was misleading me again with his brilliant arguments.

I know it sounds bad, he said, but that's what I thought. That if I sleep with her, I'll find out the secret she's always been hinting at. And if I find out the secret, it won't drive me mad any more.

So, did you find it out? I asked, trying not to sound disparaging.

Yes, Churchill said sadly. After a few minutes of kissing in her house, she suddenly stops me and says: there's something I have to tell you. And you have to realise that at that point, I'm already on fire, burned at the edges, like those birthday cards I used to make for you guys once. But she moves my hand away and tells me that she thinks I should know that she wasn't in the court by accident.

So what was she doing there?

She's the defendant's daughter.

Wow.

The oldest daughter, from his first marriage. She's not really in contact with him. Just the opposite, she's angry with him. Even changed her name so it won't be the same as his. In fact, she's not sure whether she came to court to support him or to gloat.

Wait a minute, is that legal?

What?

For the prosecutor to get chummy with the defendant's daughter?

It's problematic ethically, but if he doesn't know she's the defendant's daughter, it's hard to fault him.

So that's why she . . .

Told me, right. So that later, when they hear the tape, it'll be clear that I knew.

The tape?

The tape, a hidden camera. They were very methodical.

But what . . . why did they invest so much effort? If it's not you, another prosecutor will be appointed, no?

They think that, from the beginning, I personally pushed that case. That I'm obsessed with getting a conviction, for personal advancement. They always claimed that.

And you didn't . . . at any point . . . with Keren . . . you never suspected?

Churchill sniggered sadly. Suspected? To suspect, you have to think. And at that point, I wasn't thinking at all. Ten years! Ten years, since Cusco, I'd been thinking about her, and there she was, right beside me. With that slit. Do you see? It was like trying to stop breathing.

Churchill stood up again and went to the window. His eyes sought some other dramatic event in the street, an event that would save him from having to finish the story.

The next day, he said, turning back to me, I went into the district attorney's office to confess. It turned out that she already knew. They'd sent her the tape during the night. Actually, she was fine. She said she appreciated that I'd come to her of my own volition. Said the fact that the family had made such a great effort to get me off the case proves how frightened they were of me. But she had no choice but to remove me from the case. She suggested we do it as quickly as possible, before it got out to the media, because it would be better if it came from her and not as a result of public pressure. She put a hand on my shoulder and said that I was still young, and it was important that I learn from that mistake . . . and that was that. Two hours later, they sent someone to take the cartons.

What cartons?

The boxes we keep all the legal material in. I'd been working on that case for a full year. I dreamed about it at night. And within two hours, poof, it was all over. The next morning, when I looked at the docket . . .

What docket?

You know, the screen that shows all our scheduled court appearances – when I opened it, I saw that they'd already replaced my name with that of one of the senior attorneys. Do you understand? he asked, his eyes pleading for a good word, a sympathetic look. I remembered something I'd seen carved into one of the walls in the court on the day I'd gone to see his appearance. 'My hope is in thy ordinances', it said in large letters. And now Churchill's hope was in mine. And I – I just looked at the living room wall.

I would have been proud to say that, at that moment, I was not gloating, as might have been expected, but that wouldn't be quite true. I *was* gloating. But I also felt pity. And anger. And surprise. And the faint, pleasant sense of superiority you feel when someone asks for your advice.

So what exactly are you undecided about? I finally asked.

Undecided?

You said you came to ask my advice, didn't you?

Ah . . . yes. It's just . . . she . . . the district attorney . . . she left it up to me to decide whether to leave the prosecutor's office or stay. On the one hand, she might be expecting me to leave. On the other, I don't really have anywhere to go. But on the third hand, people look at me with pity . . . pity and gloating. And it's driving me mad. Yesterday the gang I usually have lunch with didn't call me when they went out to eat. And today, I thought that even the car park attendant had heard about my disgrace. It took him half an hour to raise the barrier. Maybe I'm imagining things. Maybe I've become paranoid. What do you think? What do you think I should do?

I reminded Churchill of his 51:49 theory, which states that with every 50:50 indecision you consult a friend about, in your mind you tend to favour one side slightly, and when you ask him the question, you do it in a way that guarantees he'll back the side you're favouring anyway.

Just ask yourself which is the 51 side, I said.

Great idea, Churchill said. And after a brief silence, added unsmilingly, I have a new theory: every smart-arse theory you develop comes back at you like a boomerang.

More coffee? I offered after a few seconds. It was embarrassing to sit there feeling sorry for him.

Maybe tea, he said ('Tea is the hot babes' drink', he always said, making fun of Ofir).

Tell me, I shouted from the kitchen, what's the story with the Maccabi Haifa shirt?

Ya'ara threw me out of the house, he shouted back.

What?! I said, hurrying back into the living room. I wondered if he could hear the small rise of happiness in my voice.

She changed the lock and left me outside on the doormat with a bag of underpants and socks. And this Eyal Berkovic shirt.

She always did have a sense of humour.

So she did, Churchill said, lightly scratching the space between the wide shirt sleeve and his arm.

The truth is, he said, his eyes suddenly clouding, that's what hurts me the most. OK, I lost the case, but if I lose her . . . that's not . . . that's too much. She . . . she wouldn't let this one pass . . . Do you undertand?

I was silent. I wasn't sure I wanted to understand.

She's the first woman who wouldn't let me wriggle out of it, Churchill went on. She always used to say to me: you're a coward. You don't know what love is because you're a coward. But you can forget that. I won't let you be a coward with me.

Churchill stopped for a moment, and I pictured Ya'ara saying those words to him. Taking off her glasses. Pronouncing the word l-o-o-ve the way only she can. Brushing his hand with hers just as she spoke the words 'you can forget that'.

You know, he continued, no one has ever said things like that to me before. No one ever understood that I give only twenty per cent of what I'm capable of giving. But she does. And she said that to me so many times that I was starting to feel it seeping into me. That I had a chance to get over myself. But now . . . it's over. I ruined everything.

What's he expecting, I thought angrily, that I'll console him for losing Ya'ara? There's a limit, surely?

Churchill must also have remembered whom he was talking to, and didn't pursue the subject any further.

We were silent together for a while. I went into the kitchen and came back with a cup of boiling hot tea.

He drank it slowly, all of it.

So where have you been sleeping? I asked.

Yesterday, I wandered around the street all night . . . and today . . . I don't know, he answered, his eyes lingering on the sofa.

You're welcome to stay, I said. And immediately regretted it. How much pleasure it would have given me to refuse to take the hint, to let him suffer.

Thanks, *Baba*, he said.

I spread a sheet on the sofa for him. I fluffed a pillow. I brought him a blanket, even though it wasn't cold, because I remembered that when I stayed at his place during my first few months in the city, he always gave me a blanket and said, 'It'll give you a feeling of home.' I turned on the TV to the sports channel and told him how to use the remote to change channels and turn off the TV.

England against Greece? Why are they playing against each other? he asked, pointing to the screen.

World Cup qualifiers, I explained.

Already?

Of course, what's with you? The World Cup is in ten months.

Where?

Japan and Korea. They're hosting it together.

Seriously! I'm so out of touch with everything. Wait a minute, what about us? What about Israel?

The deciding game is against Austria next week. If we win, we go to the knockout stage.

And if we make it through the knockout stage?

We're in the World Cup.

*

Towards morning, I got up to pee, and on the way back to bed, I glanced into the living room. Churchill was sitting on the couch with his eyes closed, asleep. He had a finger jammed into his right ear and he was jiggling it rapidly up and down and deeper as he slept. I knew about that ritual from our trip, from the less pleasant parts of it. The weeks we didn't meet any new people who could confirm his greatness. But on the trip, it only lasted for a few seconds, the time needed to clean your ear, but this time, Churchill kept shoving his finger in deeper and deeper, as if he were in a trance, as if he wanted to clean out not only his ear, but also his soul. I thought that in another minute, he'd tear his eardrum, but in any case, it was obvious that he was hurting himself a lot. I remembered from our trip that just calling his name loudly would cause him to open his eyes and stop, but I wasn't sure it was right to invade that private ritual of his now. Perhaps it made him feel better? Perhaps he *wanted* to hurt himself?*

* I think that, in this description, Mr Freed is trying, with his customary nobility, to preserve my honour. I am sorry to say that the actual scene he saw that night was not one of mysterious ear-probing, but of simple, unrestrained weeping. I must emphasise that, as an adult, I have cried only twice: the first time was that night at Mr Freed's home when I first truly understood that I was about to lose the only woman, apart from my mother, who truly loved me. The second time was approximately a month ago, when Mr Freed's father called and told me what had happened.

To the best of my knowledge, Mr Freed borrowed the image of feverish ear-probing from a boy he tutored as part of the Student Association project to help underprivileged children when he was at university. Though Mr Freed remained in close contact with that boy for years after the official project ended, he gets no mention at all in the book.

I stood there until he finished torturing his other ear as well, made sure he went back to sleep and returned to my room.

On the days that followed, Churchill did not move from the sofa. He watched a great deal of football and said that there was no case waiting for him at the prosecutor's office anyway, and that watching football was the only thing he was capable of doing now (I once caught him watching reruns of the same edition of Sports News over and over again).

He occasionally called me over to watch a particularly horrendous referee's mistake (Churchill awaited those mistakes eagerly and enjoyed them no less, perhaps even more, than the goals). Sometimes he tried to get Ya'ara on the phone, without success. She didn't answer her home phone or her mobile when he called, and every time he called her at work, the secretary said she was in a meeting, and with every such failure, his cheeks contorted with pain that started in his ears. But he didn't talk about it.

Actually, we didn't talk about Ya'ara at all the week he stayed with me. Instead, as if seven years hadn't passed, we reverted to that lazy flow of conversation we'd had towards the end of the long trip we'd made together. After you travel around with someone for months on end, all the regular, strained channels of conversation get used up, and

---

But that boy is not the only one given no mention: many other details of Mr Freed's life are kept hidden from the reader – such as, for example, his daily telephone calls with his mother, the regular allowance he received from his father on the first of every month, and the fact that he wrote particularly acerbic talk-backs to Internet sites that posted remarks by army officers, and signed them 'Major Kierkegaard'.

As editor of this book, I should, as a rule, respect this choice to conceal material, even if it is occasionally beyond my understanding (why did Mr Freed decide to conceal his regular chess partner? After all, that emaciated old man's suicide by hanging was certainly one of the main reasons Mr Freed ended up in the situation he did later!). (Y.A.)

that's when conversations take on a certain naturalness. You speak sparingly. You can be comfortably silent. And occasionally, as if offhandedly, a conversation develops that has something new in it. That's how it was during that week he found refuge in my flat. We played a lot of chess (I always won) and looked at the photo albums from that trip we took together. I had the opportunity to recall some of his unbearable habits, like always leaving the shampoo bottle uncapped, or putting his cup on the table without a saucer even though he knew I hated it, or simply not knowing how to wash dishes and always leaving pieces of food stuck to the plates. On the other hand, I also had the opportunity to recall his natural generosity (the day after he came to my place, he did a huge supermarket shop, and every evening, he cooked us 'a meal fit for a pig'), and I was able to enjoy that appealing, sincere curiosity of his again. He was interested in hearing about the articles I was translating, so I told him that now I was doing one by an Oxford professor who had studied the platforms of the large political parties that had participated in the last elections in Western Europe and compared them to the policies of the governments actually formed after the elections. He came up with a fascinating finding: in a large number of cases, the winning party ultimately implemented, item after item, the ideology of the losing party. That sounded unlikely to Churchill, so I read him several surprising examples the professor had brought from Italy and Germany, and then we tried to decide whether that model applied here in Israel as well. We came to the conclusion that on the one hand, it did, because it was Menachem Begin who made peace with Egypt, but on the other, if it were true, that meant that Arik Sharon, winner of the last election, would implement the Labour Party platform, which advocated withdrawing from Gaza, and that was totally out of the question. Later, he quite enthusiastically helped me translate an article discussing the legal aspects of Shakespeare's works in general, and of *Hamlet* in particular. While he was surfing the Internet to check a concept he wasn't sure of and I went to brew us some herbal tea – because that was all he wanted to drink that week – I thought that, actually, apart from him, I had no other friend with whom I could have a meaningful dialogue about Shakespeare, and that it was refreshing not to be alone in making all the small, annoying choices a translator has to make.

*

We hardly left the house that week. Anyway, I was the sort of person who'd rather read the Israeli *Time Out* than actually go to any of the places or events it lists, and Churchill was simply afraid to go out.

He told me that the media had been pursuing him since the affair exploded into the headlines, and he was especially irritated by the correspondent on the leading TV channel. I tell her that I don't want to be interviewed any more, and she keeps calling me seven times a day, he complained, and asked me to look through the peephole before I opened the door to anyone, because 'that leech could come here too'.

What does she look like? I asked, and he sat me down in front of the news broadcast so that her image would be burned in my mind.

The news was bad. Murders followed by injuries followed by accidents followed by drug raids followed by beatings followed by stabbings followed by murders. I noticed something strange: the words coming out of the newsreader's mouth were dynamic, full of momentum, words like 'breakthrough', 'escalation', 'dramatic developments', but the reality being described by those words moved in closed circles. Stuck. And I also noticed that the journalists treated their interviewees with obvious resentment and disapproval. As if the violence dripping from every item they read with closed, official expressions on their faces had seeped into their bloodstream. They rudely interrupted the people sitting across from them and drummed their fingers on the desk and made a show of swallowing their saliva, and throughout the broadcast, I felt that, in another minute, they would no longer be able to keep up that damned pose required of all TV presenters, and all the anger and frustration that had been building up quietly inside them would erupt from their bodies like lava and demolish the studio.

The legal correspondent appeared at the end of the broadcast. Light brown hair, rapid speech. Glasses. She looked a bit like Ya'ara. That Michaela, she actually looks like a nice person, I said to Churchill. Watch out for her, that niceness of hers is a trap, Churchill warned, then reminded me: don't open the door to anyone, OK?

*

For the first few days, I did what he said. I didn't open the door before looking through the peephole.

The first person to knock on the door was Menashe from the second floor, who asked for my dues for the house committee.

Then there was a surprise visit from a Federal Express messenger holding a large package sent by Mr Shahar Cohen, Lubliana. We opened it cautiously and found a large cardboard box inside filled with five orange tubes. There was no logo or name on the tubes, and instead of instructions for use or information for the consumer, Churchill found a personal letter from Shahar in the box.

Hi Baba

How are you

I heard you've been having a pretty hard time lately and even though I know you never forgave me for what happened in the neighbourhood and also the last time we saw each other at Amichai's shiva you hardly spoke to me I'll always remember that demonstration you organised for me at school so I tried to think of a way I could help the guy who helped me and the first idea that popped into my mind was to send you that salve for heartache we've been working on for two years in our lab here and still haven't put on the market only for technical reasons that have to do with licences and documents and that's why there's no leaflet with consumer information but that's nothing because there's not much you have to know about that salve except that it's natural and made of essence of the dulcinea plant which is a sort of lotus that grows in Bled Lake in Slovenia and as far as instructions for use are concerned that's not complicated either you just have to spread the salve twice a day on the left side of your chest where you heart is and in two or three days you'll feel significantly less sadness and I know this not from experiments with mice but from my own personal experience because I've had my disappointments too but this is not about me it's about you and I really hope this will help you and in any case I want you to know that I think only good things about you and know that you'll come out of this a winner with or without salve

   Regards to all the guys
   Shahar
PS Sorry there's no punctuation in this letter it's just that I hardly ever write in Hebrew any more and forget where the marks are on the keyboard

A few hours after the orange salve arrived, Amichai and Ofir arrived. They dropped by for just a few minutes 'to see if Churchill's alive', and stayed to watch the Israeli team's last-chance game.

That was actually the first time all four of us had met to watch football since Ilana died and, for the first few minutes, there was a sense of cautiousness in the air. How are you, what's happening, everything's fine. As if we were four strangers or four people who had to carry out a mission together in order to pass a screening test and get hired for a top job, and not four best friends. I thought that part of the awkwardness came from the fact that, for the last year, Amichai had been a well-known, even admired, public figure and here he was, the man on TV, the man in the newspapers, sitting with us in the living room and we weren't sure how to treat him. Like one of the guys or one of the gods?

But then Churchill told everyone about the special package he'd received from Shahar Cohen, and they encouraged him to try that dulcinea because what did he have to lose? So he squeezed some salve into his hand and spread it carefully on the left side of his chest just as Shahar had explained, and in less than a minute, the whole area began to itch terribly.

What a bastard that Shahar is, he said, scratching his chest with his nails.

Not a bastard. A genius! Ofir said with a laugh, it'll itch you so much now that you won't be able to think about anything else.

What are you so happy about, *ya sharwal*?! Churchill screamed, threw the tube of salve at him and ran to the shower to cool the burning.

He came back, still scratching, and Ofir rolled a thick joint for all of us and explained that he was happy because they're pregnant, that is, his Maria's pregnant. And in honour of the event, he went to Jaffa, like he used to, to bring us all premium weed, something especially strong recently brought in from Lebanon. We all stood up and hugged him warmly, one after the other, and said *mazel tov*, Daddy, *mazel tov*. Then we passed the joint around slowly and Churchill laughed and said, if only the police would come in now and catch us red-handed, that would solve my dilemma about whether to stay in the prosecutor's office or not, and Amichai paled slightly and said, I don't know if the police is such a good idea, my adversaries in the health system would have a ball with that, not to mention the media, and that lit a fire under Ofir, who said, yes, I can just see the headlines: 'Our Right to Smoke? Founder of the Our Right NPO to Advance Human Rights in the Health System suspected of using drugs'.

'Tanuri defends himself: "There's smoke without fire"', Churchill suggested a subhead.

'Tanuri defends himself: "I thought it was the JOINT organisation"'.

'Tanuri defends himself: "My actions have been taken out of context"'.

'Tanuri defends himself: "I was just trying to support the Arabs of Jaffa"'.

'Tanuri defends himself: "It wasn't me. It was Shahar Cohen"'.

We continued writing virtual headlines about Amichai's brush with the law. The less funny they were, the more we laughed at them. I could feel the awkwardness fading, and we were connected once again by the fine strings of unforced closeness. And the Israeli team wasn't doing too badly either. The blue-and-whites were awarded a penalty kick and, amazingly enough, scored a goal to make it one-nil against Austria. Now they need to play an eleven-man defence till the end, Amichai said, and Churchill objected, are you kidding, now's the time to attack. And Ofir suggested, they should play defensively, then counter-attack!

As the game drew closer to the end, they stopped arguing about tactics and switched to planning our trip to the World Cup. Ilana's brother is working in Japan now, and we can probably crash at his place. Maria has a friend who has a flatmate who is the secretary of some FIFA big shot, Ofir said. Maybe she can pull a few strings and get tickets for us. Four tickets for the semis, the final, and all of Brazil's games, Churchill fantasised out loud.

Only I was quiet. My pessimism would not allow me to get carried away with them, much as I wanted to. And at the last minute, I was proven right (when a pessimist is right, he feels no joy. Just a tiny, bitter drop on the tongue. That's all).

Austria was awarded a free kick from outside the penalty box. The wall (of course) wasn't positioned right. The Israeli goalkeeper (of course) didn't see the ball in time. And the ball (of course) landed in the net.

How predictable, Churchill said.

It was in the air, Ofir said.

Maybe we can still score another goal, Amichai dared to hope.

But the referee blew his whistle to end the game and the analysts were already demanding the coach's resignation more emphatically every moment, and fragments of shattered dreams drifted in the air of my living room. Ofir quickly rolled another thick joint, because now that we were finally all together, it would be a shame to sink into gloom, but instead of making us happy the second joint had the opposite effect on us, and so intensified our disappointment at the team's failure that from drag to drag the disappointment grew into a deep, overall depression about our individual lives, how they were turning out, how different they were from what we had expected. Suddenly, everything seemed so pointless, almost hopeless, and at the same time, we all felt stomach-turning, heart-pounding anxiety and a desire to open the window and jump out and crash onto the sidewalk because even if it hurt, it would be better than what –

That stuff . . . Amichai mumbled, his pupils dilated, a bit strong, isn't it?

I'm sorry, Ofir said. I went to Jaffa, to my old dealer. But it turns out that he's back on the straight and narrow and counsels street gangs now. So they sent me to someone else, and that someone else told me this was good stuff . . . What do I know? I used to understand this kind of thing once. I'm sorry, I'm really sorry, guys. I just wanted to make us all feel good.

Don't worry, I told him.

But then, without any warning, he began to cry.

You couldn't have known, Amichai said, trying to calm him down, but he sobbed, you have no idea, you have no idea. And was silent. Then took another drag of the joint and said, you have no idea how worried I am about Maria. She spends all her time wandering around the territories, at those checkpoints. I try to explain to her that it's not right. That she's pregnant now. But she doesn't listen. She keeps going there . . . I don't know . . . Sometimes I think she doesn't even want this pregnancy. That if it was up to her, she'd rather join Ilana in heaven.

Amichai's face suddenly darkened when he heard Ilana's name. I'm not enjoying this, he said, and took a drag on the joint. I haven't enjoyed anything since Ilana . . . Once, everything used to give me pleasure. Every little thing. Having a shower. Dipping artichoke leaves in mayonnaise. Driving fast with the windows open. And today – I've become like my mother after my father was killed. I live to survive. To exist. Even that NPO – I don't enjoy it at all. And if I feel a moment of satisfaction, I immediately begin to feel guilty for being happy when Ilana's dead. And then . . . and then I'm not happy any more.

I listened to Amichai and Ofir and couldn't understand them at all. Just the opposite. They pissed me off. What were they complaining about? At least they had love. At least something important had happened in their lives. And me? The most important thing that had happened to me was Ya'ara. And Churchill had taken even that. And now he was asking me for refuge. And I was giving it to him.

We continued passing around the joint. It was clear now that it was poison, but we couldn't stop. Some senior official in the Football Association who was being interviewed explained that the fact that the team didn't make it to the World Cup couldn't be considered a failure, and even if it could, he wasn't responsible for it.

What a loser, Ofir hissed.

What a shit, Amichai spat out the words.

What a pathetic bunch we are, I thought and looked at the three people sitting in my living room. Suddenly I felt contempt for them. That Ofir, whose spirituality stops at the green line. He always talks about giving to the 'other', but when his wife goes to stand at the checkpoints, he makes her life a misery. And Amichai too, pretending not to enjoy the NPO. Of course he enjoys it. The NPO and the attention. He's like a note that's been folded for a long time and is spread open now for all to see. But he won't admit it. Not him. Because then he'd have to admit that it all began with Ilana's death. With the fact that he no longer had to expend all his energy on making her happy. And Churchill, why's he vomiting now? Why on the carpet? What is he, a little boy? Why do I always have to clean up his vomit? Fuck that. He can clean it up himself.

In the end, Ofir cleaned up Churchill's vomit. And carried him like a wounded soldier to the shower. And washed his face with cold water. And put him on the bed to recover. My bed.

It's all my fault, Ofir apologised later on his way to the door, and I said, forget it, it's Shahar Cohen's fault. But Ofir insisted and said that he'd go to Jaffa the next day and find out what exactly they'd sold him there. I'll let you know if it was something dangerous, he promised, and I thought, nice of him to take responsibility like that, and perhaps I'd been wrong to put him down, and Amichai also said he might drop round the next day to see how Churchill was and to bring him some clothes, because they're more or less the same size –

So the next evening, when Churchill was in the shower and there was a gentle knocking at the door, I was sure it was them. And I forgot Churchill's request to look through the peephole to see who was on the other side of the door before I opened it.

Ya'ara was standing in front of me. Ya'ara the First. The Ya'ara of my dreams.

He's in the shower, I said. You want to wait for him?

I didn't come to see him, she said and gave me an intense look over her glasses. Only then did I notice that she was wearing her blue cloche skirt, the one she knew I liked. The one I'd pictured her wearing dozens of times in the last three years when she came here just to tell me she'd chosen the wrong friend. And to ask if she could still change her mind.

I felt that thing begin to swell in my chest.

Wait a sec, I said with a dry throat, left Churchill a note saying that I'd gone out to play chess in the club, put on my coat and went out to her in the hallway.

Where should we go? she asked.

To Hagilboa Street, I said with uncharacteristic assurance.

Halfway down from the second floor to the first, the staircase light went out. I felt around in the dark to find the wall and press on it, when suddenly she was enveloped in my arms. And suddenly I felt her stomach pressing against mine. And suddenly I smelled her scent in my breath. And suddenly she buried her small, cold mouth in my neck and said: I made a mistake. I chose the wrong friend. Can I still change my mind?

From: 'Metamorphoses: Great Minds who Changed their Mind', an attempt at a philosophy thesis by Yuval Freed

...And then, suddenly – at the last minute, in the appendix! – David Hume had a change of heart. After trying for dozens of pages in the body of the text to prove that there is no such thing as a permanent 'I', after working hard to persuade his readers that there is nothing beyond the flow of consciousness to which that flow can be attributed, and that our mind resembles a republic in which a series of entirely different people and perceptions exist side by side – after all those coherent arguments, Hume recants.

I have no way of explaining it, he writes with obvious embarrassment in the appendix. All my logical thought indicates something different – and yet, I am unable to deny that we feel that our changing bundle of perceptions is based on something simple and personal. What is that constant thing? Hume asks himself. This is too hard for my understanding, he confesses sorrowfully. And in the next two paragraphs – the last in the book – he attempts to meticulously correct two minor errors that appear on pages 106 and 144 of the book: if I have erred all along the way, then at least let it be a glorious error.

11

I know it sounds unbelievable. Almost too pat. What are the chances that Ya'ara would speak exactly the same lines I'd given her in my fantasies. But that is what she said. Word for word. And as we began walking in the street together, I really did start to wonder if what was happening now was really happening or whether it was taking place in a sort of purgatory between reality and imagination that you reach if you hang on to a false wish for a long enough time. Like Churchill after he drank the San Pedro, I urgently needed a human sign, someone I could call twelve times a minute, and he would come and assure me again each time that it was all real, tangible. But I could find no such sign, so I continued walking beside Ya'ara, struck mute by the fatefulness of it all, till we reached Hagilboa Street.

We walked side by side along the brick-paved path that wound around the houses, inhaling the different air that street has, our gazes wandering to the soft balconies, the tranquil trees, the cars that only here looked as if they were anchored in a safe harbour, while in the rest of the city they looked like ships that had crashed onto pavement reefs.

Ya'ara had shown me Hagilboa Street when we first began going out, and we used to escape there from time to time when we felt life closing in on us. We'd sit next to an adjoining stone backgammon table and stone chess table, and instead of the game pieces moving around on them, leaves jumped from square to square at the whim of the wind, ignoring the rules of the game.

Now too, we sat down on opposite sides of the chess table and she reached out over the black and white squares, took my hands and said, I thought you'd be happy.

I am.

You don't look happy.

I'm absorbing it.

Good. So tell me when you're finished.

She leaned back and inhaled the scent of the canopy of honeysuckle. She took off her glasses, cleaned them with the edge of her shirt and put them back on. For a long minute, she made a show of watching an old man walking slowly down the street, but in the end, she couldn't carry it off.

I know what you're thinking.

What am I thinking?

That I want to get back at Yoav. That I'm angry with him for that Keren and I'm not thinking clearly, and that when I calm down, I'll change my mind again. But that's not true. It's just not true!

Her collar bone rose and fell with emotion as she spoke. I knew that lips brushing lightly across it excited her.

So what is the truth? I asked, already protesting less.

She reached over and took my hands again. Her touch was her touch.

Truthfully, it was never good with Yoav. It was interesting, it was annoying, but never good. I wasn't happy. And it wasn't only because of his infidelities . . . OK, they probably helped . . . but even without them . . . I never had a moment's peace with him. We argued all the time. Not about major issues, but about stupid little things. And that's . . . exhausting. Every argument like that injects more poison into your blood, until you . . .

She coughed lightly, as if the poison she was talking about was real and now it was burning her throat.

A phone rang in the ground floor flat of the building we were sitting near.

I don't want to cry any more, Ya'ara said. I cried too many times this last year. And I felt lonely too many times. And unwanted. I felt that our house was a prison too many times. And I lay beside him in bed and couldn't fall asleep too many times. And that's not how it should be. Love should be a good thing, right?

I nodded hesitantly. What did I know about love?

When I was with you, she went on, there was a kind of flow between us . . . a harmony. I remember our Saturdays together . . . When evening came, I didn't know where the time had gone. You remember those Saturdays?

(Her tanned, naked body on my bed. Her glasses open on the bedside table. A newspaper left on the bed, the edge of the page touching her foot. The ends of her unruly caramel-coloured hair curled on her cheek like a garnish. The smell of a freshly baked roll rising from her drowsy body. And I am lying beside her with my eyes wide open, thinking: you have to stop. You have to stop being afraid and wanting her to leave you.)

And the sex between us was so good, Ya'ara continued. I've never had such good sex with anyone.

So why did you leave, Ya'ara? If everything was so great, why did you leave? I asked in a hoarse voice and remembered that terrible conversation. She'd said she needed time to think. It's taken her three years to think?

The phone in the nearby flat rang. And rang.

Ya'ara stood up, walked around the table and sat down next to me.

Hug me, she said in the voice of a little girl with white sandals and pigtails.

I hugged her.

Tighter, she said, till it hurts.

I hugged tighter, but not so much that it hurt. I couldn't hurt her. Not her.

I'm fucked up, she said. Something basic is wrong with me. Her body trembled in my arms.

We're all fucked up just because we're human beings, I told her, just as I'd once told Ofir.

But I'm more so, she said. You don't understand . . . except for you, all the men I've been with have always treated me badly . . . There must be something in me that asks to be treated that way. That wants it.

I remembered all the times I was even slightly mean to her – I teased her, moved a sweet out of her reach, refused to tell her my World Cup wishes – and how much she loved it.

But I want to change, I want to break that pattern, she said, moving away from me slightly and giving me a serious, almost determined look. And I think I can! I'm sure I can!! she added, and for the second time in that conversation, she reminded me of Ofir – with him, when the exclamation marks began to appear at the end of his sentences, we knew he was unsure of himself.

Anyway, she said – as if she sensed my doubt – you've changed too.

Me? I said in surprise. (I still translate articles into English. Still eat an apple with a knife like my father. I'm still short. Still in love with you. Where's the change?)

She unbuttoned the top button of my shirt, threaded her hand inside and began to play with the hair on my chest. First of all, I see you've grown some hair.

A little.

A little is good. Besides, when I helped you all with the NPO and we talked on the phone, you were different from before.

Different?

Rougher. More together. Three years have passed, you know. Things have happened in your life.

(After all those conversations when I sounded so rough, I would go and take your sock out of the closet. And I dated a girl just because she had your name. And every time you sat next to me at those meetings with the guys, I felt as if my insides wanted to fly out of my body to you, and there are whole parts of the city I avoid because they remind me of you, and I've had enough. Keep. Stroking. My. Chest. You know how much I love it. Nothing happened during those three years. Except you. I got up in the morning and met people and bought fruit for the weekend and raw tahini and new shirts and the only thing I felt was longing for you. The only reason you thought I was rougher and more together during our conversations is that they were on the phone. And I could be calm, cool and collected because you weren't in the room with me and you had a ring on your finger, but now that you're touching me, I can't, keep doing it, keep doing it, everything's on fire, and this is the only way I can love you, the only way. Perhaps I could love another woman differently, but with you, it will always be boundless, with you I melt, and yes, I'm beginning to understand that you might never save up ninety-one thousand dollars, and I'm beginning to realise that you make all those incisive comments about other people to hide the fact that you're simply lazy and very much afraid of change, but now, as you unbutton another button on my shirt, all my good judgement and all my insights and all my caution melt into bubbling, liquid love, and that's exactly what you couldn't stand, that's exactly what sets off the fucked-up part of you and will keep setting it off till you get up and leave me again and take that clean smell that makes me want to lick you and now I'm licking the inside of your ear and you abandon your neck to my lips and I kiss it and bite it gently the way you like it the way you liked it and you seek my lips and now we're kissing and you taste of fake vanilla fake vanilla everything's fake but so lovely so lovely and in another few seconds another few seconds less a second there will be no more words so perhaps I should use my last ounce of strength to stop and try to stop to say enough keep on doing it enough my God it's too much perhaps –)

Stop.

Stop? Ya'ara said and moved away from me, surprised.

I want to tell you something. I have to tell you before . . .

So, come on, tell me, she said, moving away a little more, her neck flushed.

It's not . . . What you said before . . . I haven't changed . . . When it comes to you . . . I'm exactly the same.

So?

So maybe your expectations . . . are too high.

Maybe, Ya'ara said pensively.

And I immediately wanted to convince her of the opposite.

It could be that you're right, but let's leave that for later, she said and resumed stroking my chest. Now – she gave me that look over her glasses – my only expectation from you is another kiss like the last one. Is that expectation too high?

A Hollywood hero would have got up and left at that point, proving he was morally superior to the other characters in the movie and showing in no uncertain terms how much he had changed: from adolescence to maturity. From irresponsibility to responsibility. From being an idler living on the fringes of society to being a successful media tycoon.

But I'm too short to be a Hollywood hero anyway.

And I wanted to taste that vanilla on her lips again.

And after I tasted it one more time, I wanted to taste it again and again.

After we fooled around like that for half an hour beside the chessboard, I suggested that we go to my flat, and she reminded me that Churchill was there and took me to their place, which was three blocks from there, and on the way, we stopped twice and squeezed into the dark spaces between buildings to kiss, and I kissed her on the back of her neck just as I'd wanted to that day when we came back from

Ilana's shiva in Haifa, and she stood motionless and said that the waves of pleasure reached all the way to her big toe and she was probably going to be the first woman ever to come through her big toe.

*

Somehow, sex written in Hebrew always leaves the characters unsatisfied. As if something about our Jewishness will not allow us to let them enjoy it fully, or perhaps writers are afraid their descriptions will turn out pornographic, so they take it to the opposite extreme. And I might have done that too if it hadn't been a lie.

It's hard for me to go into detail. I'm not Churchill.

So I'll make do with saying that the body is a wonderful thing. And in one night, two bodies can express such a wide range of feelings: regret, apology, despair, hope, hurt, pride, loneliness, abysmal loneliness, deep understanding, gratitude, and simple, pure joy. And revenge. And love.

Perhaps I'll quote Ya'ara, who said later that now she knows for sure that I am the best she ever had. And if only all men were so intent on giving pleasure to the women with them.

And perhaps, having no choice, I'll add that words can deceive, thoughts can drive you insane, but the body – the body knows. The morning after that night, we both knew there would never be another one like it. That I could never hurt her as she needed to be hurt without faking it, and even though she might want to believe that she could, the truth was that she couldn't live more than a few hours with the unconditional love that I have to give. Because after a few hours, she begins to feel slightly annoyed. And tries to hide it. But with my sharp senses, I pick up that evasive look. And the shoulder growing colder. And that makes me insecure, makes me afraid that in another minute, I'll lose her. And then I become even more unconditional. Love even more. I'm not like that with any other woman. Only with her. And she simply cannot accept it. Not from me. Not for very long. And I can't live with insecurity for very long. That is our vicious circle. The circle that will always remain closed no matter how we spin it, trapping us inside until we have to break out of it. And escape.

*

The next morning, we devoured a huge meal, in silence.

I put on one of Churchill's shirts (at the time, in my flat, he was probably wearing one of mine) and Ya'ara didn't put on anything.

I forgot how you eat cornflakes, she said.

How?

Funny. Every spoonful you put in your mouth has barely one cornflake in it.

And I forgot how you eat cornflakes, I said.

How?

Funny. Every time you raise the spoon to your mouth, your right breast moves a little.

She raised the spoon to her mouth to check it out, and laughed. You're right, she said.

After a brief silence, she said, I think we could really be a great couple.

I agree.

We could have such a great relationship. A healthy one.

With a lot of intimacy, but space for each of us to grow individually.

And good sex.

Great sex, I said. And reached out under the table and began sliding my hand between her legs.

She abruptly squeezed her knees together hard on my hand.

Ow! Ouch!! You broke my fingers!!! I pulled my hand away and waved it in the air as if it had been burned.

Let me see, she said, leaning across the table and taking my hand between hers. She kissed my knuckles, one by one. January, March, May, July.

Actually, why not? she asked. The eyes she fixed on me

were innocent, but at the edge of her voice was a note of seriousness, as if she herself knew the answer but wanted my words to express her feelings.

Why not what? I asked, feigning innocence.

Come on, she said, dropping my hand impatiently.

Because if we were together, I said with a sigh, we'd have to be happy.

Happy? she said, backing away from the table dramatically. My God! Anything but that!

You see, I said.

And we both smiled a smile whose happiness stopped at our cheeks. And a drop of sadness dripped from it into the small delta between the two neck arteries.

I love you, she said, don't you know that? She moved her chair closer to the table. And again took my hand with a kind of solemnity.

Yes, I said.

How?

Your body told me, I admitted.

And last night . . . Yuval . . . I'll never forget it . . . It was . . . very special for me . . . I want you to know that, OK?

We kept eating our cornflakes, each in our own way, and then she spread some white cheese on black bread for me, and I told her that she was losing out if she didn't taste the avocado salad I'd made.

You're going back to your flat now? she asked.

Yes, I said. I have a translation to finish by tomorrow.

What's the article about? Ya'ara folded one naked leg over the other. I suddenly noticed that her legs were short.

The title is 'Back to the Future', I said. Actually, it's an abstract of a speech given a few years ago by the chairman of the Canadian Psychologists Association, Jeremiah Miller, at their annual conference. His thesis is that there's an underlying struggle in modern psychology between the American school, which has an eye to the future, and the

European school, which is focused on the past in a big way. When an American psychologist looks at a person, the first question he asks is: where does this person want to go? When the European psychologist looks at a person, his first question is: where has this person come from?

But they're interconnected, aren't they?

That's exactly what Miller says. That you have to find the synthesis. More accurately, that the Canadians have to find it.

Why the Canadians?

He claims that the United States is a relatively young country with a short past, and there are large parts of its history – for example, what happened to the Indians – that it's not interested in looking at. But he believes that the Europeans, on the other hand, cling to their glorious past and the days when they were the cultural centre of the Western world, and that's why they find it difficult to look ahead. It turns out then, that only Canadians, in whom both cultures are combined, are free enough to offer a true synthesis.

A bit pretentious, don't you think?

It sounds OK in English, somehow.

I don't know, Ya'ara said and put her finger in her mouth to lick off the remains of avocado salad.

What don't you know?

I'm with the Europeans. You can't escape the past. Look at that idiot friend of yours. He acts just like his father. Last year, he and Michel even started looking alike. The same receding hairline. The same swaying walk he swore he'd never adopt. He talked so much about being different from his father and, in the end, he's just following in his footsteps.

Determinism is the last refuge of . . .

The scoundrel. Ya'ara completed Churchill's famous remark. And Australia was settled by prisoners expelled from England, I know. And yet . . .

She was silent. And so was I. I crumbled black bread. I crumbled the crumbs of black bread.

How is he, she said. There was no question mark at the end of her sentence, as if she wanted it to sound as casual as possible.

Shattered, I said, telling the truth.

Good, she said, her tone indifferent. But you could tell from her eyes that she cared.

Then I offered to wash the dishes, and she said, just leave them. So I dressed in my original clothes and put on my shoes the way I had taken them off, without untying the laces and, meanwhile, she went to the bedroom and came back with a plastic bag full of shirts for him and said, how long can he wear that stupid Berkovic shirt?

I thanked her in his name and took the bag. We hugged for a long time, a concluding hug, and I felt something different begin to swell in my chest, and I kissed her on the cheek and left. I walked lightly, almost floated down the street, feeling at least five centimetres taller, feeling that everything around me was tiny in comparison, that my life was going to be different from now on in a way I still couldn't grasp. I didn't know whether I felt that way because it was over, I was finally free of the hope that had taken over my life since the last World Cup, the hope that one day, against all odds, the three Ya'ara-wishes I'd written down would come true, or that I felt that way because my body was simply happy about the night it had enjoyed with her body. Happiness that, by its very nature, would be brief.

As I walked happily, I thought about Major Kierkegaard, the melancholy Danish philosopher, and the night of his metamorphosis: on 19 April 1848, he spent a long, dramatic night falling in love with God again. The next morning, he wrote with intense emotion in his diary: 'My whole being is changed. My reserve and self-isolation is broken – I must speak . . . Dear God, shed your grace on me!'

But what happened after that morning? Did the joy of

inner clarity suffusing Kierkegaard last for more than a few hours? Did he formulate a coherent doctrine? Was he able to leave behind the melancholy nature he'd had since childhood? Reading his writings provides several answers to those questions, some of them contradictory.

Apparently, I summed up for myself, it will take a few days before I know what this euphoria means.

And so it was. A few days later, Ya'ara called and told me she was pregnant.

12

Ilana must still have been in the recovery room because she isn't in the picture. Amichai is in the middle of the frame with two identical plastic cradles, the hospital kind, in front him. He looks tired. Wrinkled. But a kind of new glow illuminates his face. We're all smiling at the camera, smiles both happy and awkward. We're twenty-five, if I'm not mistaken, still children ourselves, and overnight our friend has become a father, of twins no less. We can't even begin to take that in. You can see it in the picture. It's not just the bewildered smiles, it's also the way we're standing. Ofir's hands are shoved in the pockets of his jeans, Churchill's hands are folded on his chest as if they're protecting him from something, and my hands are on Amichai's shoulders, but it looks like he's the one who's supporting me. 'You're our advance party,' Churchill had written to him in all our names on the card attached to the bouquet of flowers. 'You can check it out, this business of kids, and if it seems good, we'll join you.' Later, going down in the lift, Ofir said it was because Amichai's father had died when he was little and he never had a normal family – that's why he's started his own family so young. And Churchill said, bullshit, he did it just to make Ilana happy, that's all. And I thought to myself that Amichai actually looked quite happy there, beside the cradles, and in some cultures a twenty-five-year-old man can already be the father of four children, and perhaps it was Amichai who was acting naturally for his age and we were the ones dragging our feet for no reason and squandering our days with meaningless love affairs.

*

It's not yours, Ya'ara hastened to reassure me.

How do you know . . . I mean . . . how can you be sure? (If it turns out to be mine, the thought flitted through my mind, then one of my three World Cup wishes – a child with Ya'ara – would be coming true.)

I calculated the days, Ya'ara said. It comes out exactly on the last time I slept with Yoav, three weeks ago.

OK . . . if that's the case . . . then congratulations, I said. I didn't know what else to say.

Yes, Ya'ara said.

We were silent. I tried to picture her compact body pregnant. I couldn't.

OK, let me talk to your idiot friend, she finally said. I called him and he took the cordless phone to the bathroom, and they spoke for three and a half hours – at some point, I couldn't hold it in any longer and went down to pee in the cats' yard – and in the morning, he collected his things, hugged me, told me I was a prince and went back to their flat.

*

Amichai and Ofir couldn't understand Ya'ara. How could she give him chance after chance after chance when it was clear he would never change? That question was directed at me, as if I were an expert on Ya'ara. We were sitting in the square in front of the Cinematheque, group after group of children passing us on their way to the nearby school, and I sniffed and said that all sorts of things hold couples together. And sometimes it's that ability they have to hurt each other where they're most vulnerable. And even that analysis, I added, should be taken with a grain of salt, because we have no idea what happens between them when they get home and remove their masks, because we're never there. Ofir said that in principle, I might be right, there were hidden energies flowing between him and Maria too, but when it came to Churchill, he thought that in another few weeks, or a few months at the most, we'd be hearing about another infidelity of his.

Churchill, on the other hand, claimed that knowing he was going to be a father calmed him down and put into perspective what was important and what wasn't. Personally, I thought he was spouting the clichés that football players speak in one-on-one interviews, and what had really put things in perspective for him was the blow he had taken when they'd removed him from the case. I thought that we'd called him Churchill so much and treated him like Churchill for so long that he'd forgotten he was originally Yoav. It had always been convenient for him to have friends a bit less successful, a bit less brilliant than he. And I also thought that, with our cooperation, he had nurtured the messianic belief that he was not an ordinary person. Not just another guy from Haifa. Not just another guy from Tel Aviv. Not just one of the six Alimi siblings. I thought that his success as a lawyer fed that belief until it grew to monstrous, voracious proportions that swallowed up his good qualities, one by one.

*

A day after he officially resigned from the prosecutor's office, Churchill received a call from Amichai, who offered him the job of running the legal arm of Our Right.

He choked up in response. But . . . how . . . I was a shit . . . When you formed the organisation . . . I didn't even come to . . . I didn't come to your meetings . . . So why, all of a sudden . . . How . . .

Listen, Amichai interrupted him. I'm not happy with the guy who's doing the job now and I think you can do it better. All the rest is irrelevant.

But I didn't even apologise . . . I didn't have the chance to say I'm sor . . .

Your retroactive apology is accepted, Amichai said. You start work Sunday morning, eight-thirty. And now I'm sending a volunteer to you with all the material you need to read. You should go over it.

Thank you . . . thank you so . . . much, Churchill stammered.

*

Do you believe it? Amichai said with a chuckle when he spoke to me on the phone half an hour later, Churchill stammered!

Churchill stammered, and finished work every day at six, and got home at six-thirty without stopping on the way at Sharona's, or Keren's or Hagit's. And he spent quiet evenings in front of the TV with Ya'ara, and catered to her every whim and put his hand on her stomach to feel if the baby was kicking yet, and complained that she never asked him to bring her ice cream or gherkins the way women do in films.

And she threw the application to the University of London she'd downloaded from the Internet into the bin and gave up once and for all her dream of studying theatre, because at the moment 'it's not practical anyway' and 'the working hours at her father's office were very convenient', and altogether, 'theatre is not exactly a profession that goes with motherhood, and there's no ignoring that'. Considering how easily she slipped into the role of the perfect mother, I thought scornfully, the world of the theatre has truly lost a great creator. I know what you're thinking, Yuval, she said on the phone, and before I could deny it, she begged me, please don't say it. I'm in the middle of trying to convince myself now, so don't hassle me with the truth, OK?

The further her pregnancy progressed, the less I spoke to Ya'ara and Churchill. They seemed to have withdrawn into their own private cocoon, where there was no room for old friends.*

And Amichai also withdrew further and further into himself. Maria's daughter had surprised the twins with the announcement that from now on she wanted Noam, only Noam, to be her friend, and so, in a single moment, she split the threesome apart. In response, Nimrod shattered all the pictures in the house (except for the one of his mother) and hurled a mini-disc player, including speakers, out of his bedroom window into the street. Professionals explained to Amichai that actually, through his anger at Maria's daughter, Nimrod was allowing himself to experience his mother's death for the first time. Amichai thought they were wrong, that they did not fully appreciate the autonomous power of children's love (he'd once had an Irit whom he loved in the second grade. For months, he'd

* While in all other places in the book, Mr Freed's descriptions, even if they are inaccurate, are based on a kernel of truth, here, in this short paragraph, he so distorts reality that even I, as editor and friend, find it difficult to accept. It was not we who withdrew into our own private cocoon during that period, but he himself. My spouse and I invited him to our home many times and he never bothered to respond to our invitations. I have no idea why Mr Freed chose to paint a picture in which his friends abandoned him. Perhaps in order to justify his own escape into writing a book and making us its protagonists without informing any of us. Perhaps for the pleasure latent in self-pity of this kind. And perhaps every narrator is always limited to his own point of view. After all, if each of us, his friends, had been asked to tell the story of the last four years, four different stories would certainly have emerged, and rightly so. Be that as it may, in this case, the bare facts do not fit with Mr Freed's claims. Not for a moment did my spouse and I stop taking an interest in what he was doing, in his mood and the condition of his asthma. Not for a moment did we stop being grateful to him for the large gifts he gave to us both, for the refuge and consolation and true friendship. Yet despite all of the above, Mr Freed did indeed feel that we had abandoned him, and I can only apologise to him for that (and owing to his present condition, he is unable to accept or reject my verbal apology, so I am offering it here, in writing). (Y.A.)

planned to ask her to be his girlfriend when they were at the end-of-year party, but she never showed up). Anyway, he delegated most of his authority to the managing director he'd appointed to work under him, cut his media appearances to a minimum, and tried to spend 'quantity time', as he put it, with his Nimrod.

He called his friends less often, and if I called him, he would usually promise to get back to me after the children were asleep. But he didn't.

Of all of them, Ofir and Maria were the only ones who tried to show an interest in what I was doing (or, more accurately, in what I wasn't doing), and once they even formally invited me to a family dinner.

My inner oracle prophesied doom. It claimed that this was not a good time for family dinners. But, as mentioned, I was educated to believe that, when invited, the polite thing is to accept, so I pulled myself together and drove to Michmoret.

On the way, I listened to naive Hebrew songs on the radio. A pleasant breeze came through the open window, and drivers passing me on the road looked to me like people, not just drivers. I said to myself that it was very kind of Ofir and Maria to invite me over. And that, all in all, I should be happy for both of them, now that they were pregnant.

But from the minute I walked into their wooden house, I couldn't stop feeling envy. Bitter, bubbling, maddening envy.

I envied their small, modest house. And the fact that they were a five-minute walk from the sea. And the breeze that carried a salty smell into the living room and gently rocked the hammock. I envied the fact that they'd had the courage to leave the city. And the courage to do what they love. I envied Ofir for having Maria who, even after three years of being together, still occasionally stroked the back of his neck for no special reason. I envied Maria for having her daughter, even though they actually argued throughout the entire meal.

First, the girl didn't want to sit with us. And then she didn't want to eat with a knife and fork. And then, while we were still eating, she insisted on sliding down the banister of the narrow staircase that wound down from the gallery to the living room. Get off there, you're doing something dangerous for no good reason, Maria said. Look who's talking, was the girl's cheeky reply. What is that supposed to mean?! Maria said, tensing up. Ask Ofi what it means, the girl hissed at her, and stayed on the banister. Maria looked over at Ofir. My trips to the checkpoints are my private business, she said, trying to contain her disappointment, I don't understand why you had to talk to her about it. Because I don't think it's your private business, Ofir replied, without raising his voice even slightly.

And she answered him. And spoke about Lana, saying that this was her way of missing her.

And he didn't answer her. And tried to touch her hand. But she moved it away, though not roughly.

They both got up to take the girl off the banister and bring her back to the table. And all that time, despite the angry, tense words of all three, you could sense how close they were. Intertwined. I've never had anything like that, I thought, and continued to eat my rice-and-lentils à la Copenhagen, and tell them about the articles I was translating, and about the latest, condensed news of Amichai and Churchill, but inside, the envy was blazing. Scorching. I envied the fruit salad that was served for dessert (a single guy would never make fruit salad for himself). I envied the fact that they didn't have cable (that's the way to live!). I envied the silence that filled the room after we stood up from the table and reclined on the cushions in the living room (a comfortable silence, as if they hadn't had a bitter argument a moment earlier). And I even envied the fact that they talked about the problems they were having with the clinic.

They said that since the second Intifada had begun, people were hesitant about spending money on luxuries, and alternative therapy – there was no denying it – was still considered a luxury in Israel.

And I thought, how much they care about that clinic of theirs. How much it means to them. And how I had nothing like that in my life. Nothing that really means anything to me.

Ofir said that, the way it looked now, if the number of clients continued to dwindle, he'd have to go back to working in advertising at least for a short time, because there were bills to pay. But that didn't scare him because a lot of water had flowed in the Ganges since his break-down, and this time he'd be coming from a totally different place.

And Maria took his hand in hers and added, this time, you won't be alone with it. This time you'll have me.

I looked at them and thought, it's love, stupid. It's her love that changed him. Not those spiritual clichés, not the flapping *sharwal* and not the swaying hammock. It's her. Maria. She calmed him down. Family-ised him. Hugged him so hard that he had no choice but to stop moving in her embrace. Caressed him so much that lately he even stops shrinking in alarm when a hand accidentally nears his face.

How about sleeping over tonight, Maria suggested and rubbed Ofir's stomach, as if he were the pregnant one.

Yes, Uncle Yuval! Yes! her daughter said happily. And we'll play Trivial Pursuit!!! (The girl was a world-champion player. Most grown-ups didn't dare to play with her because they were afraid they'd lose, but I had collected enough marginal information through my translations to give her a fight.)

I'd love to stay, sweetie, but I'm going out tonight, I lied.

A new girl? Ofir asked casually.

Yes, I lied again.

That's great, Maria said, happy for me. I think you deserve it. You deserve love. She said it warmly, and her eyes looked at me with warmth, but it made me cold. There was nothing patronising about the way she spoke, but I felt as if she were patronising me. That they both were being slightly, almost imperceptibly condescending. The natural way they rested in each other's arms. The murmuring of the sea coming through the window. The gentle, caressing breeze. The thick, intoxicating smell of incense that blended with the light scent wafting from the shelf of Himalaya brand shampoos and creams. Damn it, two years had passed since they'd come back from India, how did they still have so much left? And why did they keep it in the living room and not in the bathroom? What was it, furniture?

I couldn't stand it any more. I felt an intense need to see the city again. To hear the honking horns again. And the bulldozers. And the groaning buses. To sweat in the humid air. To stop at the shop for an ice lolly. To see people walking their dogs as if they were their spouses. Stroking them. Talking to them. To see people walk slowly, earnestly out of a cinema. To feel the tumult of the city overwhelm me, slowly silencing the tumult inside me.

Thanks for the invitation, the meal was great, I said, and stood up to leave. Maria and the girl gave me long hugs, and Ofir insisted on walking me to the car.

Hey, is everything OK with you? he asked on the way.

What . . . Yes . . . Why do you ask? I stammered.

Your body . . . he said, putting his hand on my back, between my shoulders.

What about my body? I asked, shaking him off.

Nothing, it's just that you seem . . . But if you say everything's OK, then . . .

Everything's fine, I said, putting an end to the conversation.

But nothing was fine. After the Havatzelet junction, at the spot where you first see the glittering lights of the metropolis, I pretended to be relieved. Look, I thought, trying to convince myself, you're going back to the city. Its pulsing life will recharge you.

But near Herzliya, the morose thoughts took over again. All your friends have finished the plaster stage with a sense of purpose, and you're the only one still wallowing around in doubt. An exciting new time in their lives is about to begin, and your train is still stuck in the station. Soon they'll be talking about nappies and nurseries, and what will you be talking about? A scientific article on parenthood that you translated?

And anyway, it's over. You have to admit the truth: the group's golden age has ended. For fourteen years, that quartet was the whole, entire world. Earth, fire, water and wind (and if you add Shahar Cohen, then we had ether too, the fifth, elusive, divine element that Aristotle talks about). But that's over. Friends come and go, and women remain. Anyway, Ya'ara might be right and the world has changed and there's no longer room for groups of Haifa guys like us. Perhaps everyone has become impatient and inattentive and horribly self-interested, and even the Chameleons announced this week that they're splitting up, and from now on, each member of the band 'will focus on personal projects he is interested in promoting', and exactly the same thing is happening to us, and if it hasn't happened yet, it will soon: each of them will be in his home with his love and his children and the personal-project-he-is-interested-in-promoting, and I'll be in my flat, without love, without children, without a project, and I'll end up as a kind of eternal Uncle Yuval you invite to parties out of politeness.

My flat looked small and ugly when I walked into it that night. All the little defects glared out at me: the old Formica cabinets in the kitchen. The yellow stain in the toilet.

The too-small windows. The broken shutters. Those lying photos of my friends hanging all over the walls. The photo from the Chameleons performance. The photo from Amichai's birthday. The photo from the Sinai. All lies. Because in reality, that Chameleons performance was terrible. They sang their old songs indifferently, and their new stuff was completely mind-numbing. And on Amichai's birthday, he and Ofir had a long argument about some stupid thing, and the whole atmosphere was ruined. And that trip to the Sinai? On the trip to the Sinai, you could sense that we were on the beginning of a downward path. I can't remember a single genuine conversation we had on that trip. Everything was already coated with a thin layer of estrangement. And that's been the direction ever since.

The photos drove me to the bedroom. Suddenly, it also looked small. Suffocating. Reeking of loneliness. I went over to the wardrobe and pushed aside two piles of folded shirts to reach it. I held it in my hands. A plain red sock with a yellow stripe around the top. There was nothing special about that sock except for the fact that it had been Ya'ara's, but that alone had been enough for me the last few years. Every time I felt that my life was empty and everything that happened to me was merely a hollow echo, I would go to the wardrobe, find it and once again be filled with hope that one day Ya'ara would come back to me and put on that sock, in this room, for me, the hope, no matter how unfounded, that had managed to keep me from falling into the black pit of total despair, for if there was even the smallest chance she might come back, then there was a reason to shave, a reason to go to sleep, a reason to get up in the morning, a reason to translate another article. And another article. And another article.

I touched the fine, feminine cloth. Crushed it between my fingers.

And felt nothing.

*

One night, on our big trip, Churchill and I got lost on a small Indian island in the middle of Lake Titicaca. We wanted to see the sunset from the highest hill on the island and ignored the rather basic principle that with the sunset comes darkness. On that island, whose name I've forgotten, there was no electricity and we didn't have a torch, and in the dark, our hosts' house looked like all the others. Blinded and a bit worried, we walked down the hill and began searching for the house in the darkness. We stumbled on hidden furrows, fell into covered pits. By mistake, we reached the lake shore. And went back. We knocked on doors, but no one answered. Slowly, we began to fear that we were imagining everything – that island, the group of travellers we'd come there with, our hosts – and perhaps we were really on a fake tourist island whose inhabitants left it every night.

And then – as we were about to give up hope and Churchill said in alarm, the dark is touching me, I swear, Bro, the dark is touching me right this minute – a clear, continuous sound split the darkness. The sound of a saxophone.

Our hosts didn't have a saxophone, so we actually had no reason to walk in the direction the music was coming from, but that's exactly what we did, because in the total darkness of that night, we had no other point of reference, and because everyone, of course, needs a saxophone to walk towards. Even if the playing is shaky. Even if it's occa-sionally off-key. A person walks towards the saxophone because he knows that otherwise he might surrender to the darkness.

(The saxophone player turned out to be a hugely tall Indian who was playing for three drunk friends from a student's music book written in Spanish. And at the end of the concert, he led us easily to our hosts' house.)

*

Ya'ara had been my saxophone over the years that had passed since the last World Cup. I had walked in her direction again and again, every time it grew dark. The hope that she would come back to me played inside all the time. Quietly, but constantly.

Now the playing was silenced.

And I was left in darkness.

*

It's hard to describe what happened to me over the next few weeks.

It was as if there was less of me every day.

It was as if the shutters covering the windows of the chambers of my heart had broken. And couldn't be opened.

It was as if I was burning up from the inside. But with a very cold flame, like the kind fireworks make.

It was more like smog than fog.

It was as if my bed were sleeping in me and not I in the bed.

It was like lead weights. Iron chains. A kibbutz at twelve noon. The dead letter office. Plastic flowers.

OK, enough of those similes – they're just another way of evading the truth. Of posturing. Faking. How comfortable to translate everything into lively, picturesque images when, in fact, it was as if only the image remained and the actual thing being described was gone.

I slept a great deal during those weeks. And when I wasn't sleeping, I wanted to sleep.

I couldn't translate anything. Simple sentences suddenly seemed impossible to decipher. Clients called to ask what was happening. I told them there'd be a slight delay. Very slight.

I said to myself that I'd been waiting for a fall like this for years, for years I'd been fighting gravity, and perhaps once I should simply let myself fall.

Clients called again a week later and asked what was happening.

I apologised. The translation wasn't ready yet.

Clients left.

Gila from the bank called, said we had to meet. I thought it might be amusing to call her and talk to her about real things, about the huge hole that had opened in my body, for example, or about futility. The futility of everything.

That was my last amusing thought.

Then I completely lost my sense of humour. I lost the crucial ability to look at my life objectively and laugh at it.

I was obsessed with the thought that everything happening to me now was delayed punishment for the sins I had committed in Nablus during the 1990 World Cup. A direct result of the old Arab woman's curse. Proof that you can never truly rub out the stains of the past, only blur them, and that sins are like a virus, waiting for the moment you're weak to attack and demand its pound of flesh.

I knew that it was all a bit weird, but I couldn't get those thoughts out of my mind. So I disconnected the phone and stopped shaving and spent hours staring at direct broadcasts of the Australian Open golf tournament. I set up a mini-golf course in my living room. Instead of a golf ball – a ping-pong ball. Instead of a club – a squeegee mop. Instead of a hole – a soup bowl. My sense of taste became blunted. Spaghetti had the same taste as rice. Oranges had the same taste as apples. And it took five teaspoons of sugar to sweeten my coffee.

I think I started to worry the minute I noticed that my sense of taste was impaired. The minute that the line between body and soul is crossed like that, I thought, I won't be able to stop it any more.

I told myself that I had to do something before my other senses began to betray me as well.

I called a psychologist that one of my clients had recommended, but as soon as I heard her voice, I hung up.

I knew exactly what would happen: whatever I said, she'd connect it to my relationship with my parents. And even if I protested, even if I claimed that she was forcing me to fit into her theories, she would hint that my protest was not actually directed against her, but against my parents. And besides, I still didn't have an answer to the question of whether people, myself included, are capable of changing. And if they are, how? And before you pay 350 shekels an hour, you should have answers to those questions, right?

So I called Hani. We hadn't spoken for more than a year, but it suddenly seemed to be the only thing left to do. I called the number I had, and a recorded message gave me her new number. And when I called the new number, a recorded message referred me to a third number. From one announcement to the next, my desire for her intensified. I remembered her honey hair. And the sneezing that shook her body right after she had an orgasm. And the time she danced in front of me, so happy, in the Coliseum. The only reason it didn't work out between us was the shadow that Ya'ara cast over everything. And now that I'd finally thrown that red sock with the yellow stripe into the rubbish bin, who knows, perhaps we had a chance.

How are you? her voice asked, and I thought that it was a good sign that she still recognised my number on her display.

I, . . . ah . . . so-so. And you?

Thank God, she said. My son was born last month.

Wow . . . a son? A boy? Congratulations.

Yes, it is a great joy to us. May parents are thrilled too. It's their first grandchild.

Your parents? Don't tell me you went back to Bnei Brak?

Of course I did. You can't live without family. Without roots. And this is where my family is. You know, I'm glad you called. I've . . . wanted to call you for a long time to thank you.

Thank me? For what?

It's just that . . . you were so awful to me . . . and after you there was someone else who treated me the same way, and . . . What happened to me with both of you made me

283

think that maybe all that secularism I wanted so much . . .
When I got close to it . . . it was empty. Sad.

Sad?

It's sad to always wonder if people are telling you the
truth. Sad to have a relationship when the possibility of
breaking up is hovering over it from the minute it begins.
How can you devote yourself to someone that way? With
Jacob . . .

Jacob?

My husband. From the first time we met, I knew he was
serious about me. And if he was, then I could love him
without being afraid. And I want you to know that he's
from Boston. He has an open mind. He isn't frightened by
questions the way my parents are. And he doesn't think
that a woman is a defective creature. You see, I did manage
to take something from the two years I spent in the secular
world. But it's hard to live without God. Without a way of
life. Do you understand?

It's like living without a saxophone.

What?

Never mind. Go on.

Look, sooner or later I would have discovered all of this,
but I think that you . . . brought me closer to redemption,
as we say in our world. So thank you and . . . come and
visit sometime. Really.

It sounds like you're all very busy.

In the middle of the week, yes. But at the weekends,
you're more than welcome. Spend the Sabbath with us.
Sing the Sabbath songs with us. Eat well. Rest. And maybe,
with the doing of the deeds, you will grow to love them.

What do you mean? You want to make me re . . .

No . . . Of course not . . . Don't be alarmed. I only meant
that you'd have the chance to cleanse your soul. It sounds
to me like you need it.

Yes, I thought, I need it. But not with the help of faith.
Jewish culture might be in my blood, and the Bible might

underlie every word I say in Hebrew, but faith, unfortunately, is not an option. God cannot save me when I'm at my lowest. Like Soren Kierkegaard, I'd like to wake up one morning and discover that during the night I had been filled with boundless, unconditional love for God. And perhaps I really could be filled with such love for God if I had grown up in the right home. But my parents planted in me a deep, secular suspicion of all things religious. And even if that suspicion was unjustified, I was no longer able to uproot it from inside me.

I'll come over sometime, I said.

Wonderful, Hani said. There was no emotion in that 'wonderful' of hers. There had been no emotion in her voice during our entire conversation. Listen, she said, ending the conversation, I have to feed Benjamin now, so . . .

Bye, I said in an effort to save my self-respect and have the last word.

*

That's just like you, I said to myself after hanging up the phone: have a whole relationship with a girl without including her in it, nurture the thought that one day, when you want her, she'll want you back. And never bother to find out what reality has to say about it. You got what's coming to you, I said, flogging myself. But not even the lashes of the whip managed to hurt me. Make me feel something. The darkness engulfed me in the days that followed. Every small action – going to the toilet, pouring a glass of water, turning off the TV – seemed like a huge boulder I had to roll up a mountain. Even though I was tempted, I didn't call my friends because I had the feeling that I had to climb out of that hole myself. Bullshit. That's my pride speaking in retrospect. I didn't call my friends because I didn't want them to see me like that. No, even that's cover for the truth. I didn't call my friends because, in a way that's hard to explain, I'm a solitary person. A solitary person who has a lot of friends. A solitary person who learned how to function in the world as if he were sociable, but when he's in pain, always withdraws to his original position. And perhaps that's also a lie. In any case, I knew that I had to do something to get myself out of the mess I was in, but I was too tired to do it, or to think of anything. Actually, that isn't accurate either. I'm putting a nice face on things again. Two extreme solutions did occur to me at the time, and I rejected them both out of hand. The first idea was to take mood-altering drugs. Clients had told me that there are great new drugs now that have no side effects, that that's what helped them finish their degree. But, considering my tendency to become addicted, I was afraid that the minute I started taking them, I wouldn't be able to stop. The second idea that occurred to me, and not for the first time, was to change my sexual orientation – to admit that the whole business with girls was too much for me and I always ended up lonely, so I would try homosexual relationships. After all, I've always got along with men. So perhaps that's a sign?

There was only one small problem with that idea: I'd never been attracted to men (except for one erection I had during a ping-pong game with Shahar Cohen, a single, random erection, that I am willing to admit only in parenthesis).

No, I thought, pulling myself together, you need a saxophone. Something you can move towards. But what, damn it?! What?

*

I tried to go back to that bloody, unfinished thesis of mine. Perhaps there, I'd find a melody of meaning. The last philosopher I'd begun writing about, and stopped in the middle, was Martin Heidegger. In 1927, Heidegger published part one of his book, *Being and Time*, but the second part of that book never appeared, and Heidegger's students claim that it was because of *die Kehre*, the change that occurred in his thinking. Beginning in the 1930s, he stopped analysing structures of acting, the structure of anxiety, perhaps under the influence of thinkers from the Far East he had been exposed to, and began to speak of contemplation, inner observation and openness to experience. Philosophy, he claimed, must return to the openness that characterised the pre-Socratic philosophers and wean itself of the desire to impose itself on things by force.

That was all well and good, but during the years he spoke about openness to experiences and how much he missed the simplicity of country life, Heidegger joined the Nazi Party. When he was the Nazi rector of the University of Freiburg, all democratic policies in the University were cancelled, three public book burnings were held and his former teacher, Edmund Husserl, was denied access to the library only because he was a Jew. In hearings held after the war, Heidegger denounced his actions during the Nazi period, but the French occupation government did not allow him to take a teaching position, claiming that his influence on students might be destructive.

*

I went over the dates again, perhaps I'd been mistaken. Perhaps not. All of Heidegger's texts that spoke about openness to experience and deplored 'efficiency for the sake of efficiency', which characterises modern society, actually were written when he was a Nazi (he remained a member of that too-efficient movement to the last day of the Second World War).

Tell me please, Mr Heidegger – I'd ask him if I could – exactly what experiences were you referring to when you wrote about experiences we should be open to? *Kristallnacht*?

Again, like the last time I tried to touch Heidegger, I had an overwhelming sense that I had to stop working on my thesis. If I couldn't understand the metamorphosis of one philosopher, how could I put together a thesis that would include the metamorphoses of all of them? Even worse: perhaps Heidegger's case proved that all my attempts to connect philosophers' lives with their views were fundamentally mistaken, and I had to separate their private lives and their philosophical thought into two parallel lines that never meet? Or, in other words, to throw that fucking thesis into the rubbish bin. And that whole academic language too. There's something depressing about it. Watery. Yes, the idea suddenly overcame me with devastating force, that thesis is killing me, everything is the fault of that thesis! All that research on people who changed keeps me from moving forward. Keeps me from breaking out of the corral, keeps me from finding a normal profession. Or love.

Out of despair, I deleted the file with my entire thesis from my computer.

Then I inserted the back-up disc and deleted it from there too.

I thought I'd feel enormously liberated. That the second I pressed the delete key, a wave of hope for a new beginning would wash over me.

For the first few seconds, I felt nothing. And right after that, I had a horrible anxiety attack.

(I should have known that would happen. That's how it always is with me: only when I just lose something, do I start to really miss it.)

What have I done?! What have I done?! I shouted and turned the place upside down trying to find another disc on which I once saved part of the text. Or maybe not. I wasn't sure. In the end, I found a dusty disc, but I didn't have the courage to insert it into the computer and find out that it didn't have the file with my thesis.

So I ran away. I went into the city to look for a saxophone, anything not to wither away at home, not to go crazy, but every place I went to was being frantically, feverishly renovated. The nearby avenue had been turned inside out. All the hidden ugliness, usually covered over with concrete and cement, was now exposed. I tried to make my way among the heavy sacks of sand, piles of bricks and the iron rods that were sticking up from the ground. Time sweated over me, the noise of drills deafened my thoughts, and I accidentally kicked a bucket of whitewash. A second later, I almost fell into one of the open pits that workers' heads were popping out of. Hey, zombie, watch where you're going, they shouted. I've hated the word zombie ever since the commander of Training Base One used it during the hearing to kick me out. But I didn't answer them. I avoided another pit and with a great deal of difficulty reached the corner shop. I bought iced coffee and sat down on a bench to drink it, but it tasted like orange juice. A couple walked past me with their arms around each other, and the girl suddenly gave me a searching, sideways glance. It's unbelievable, I thought. Even the couples in this city are always on the prowl. How can you find love that way? I went back to the shop and bought a tuna sandwich which, based on the picture on the menu, should have been tasty. But it had no taste at all. The deterioration of my sense of taste was freaking me out. There was something too symbolic about it. Someone stopped next to me with a squeal of brakes and asked: are you coming out of this parking space? And I thought he asked: are you going out of your mind? Someone with a drill stood next to me and started drilling, sending up a huge amount of dust. Huge amounts of dust were rising from everywhere I went that day in Tel Aviv. The dust entered my lungs with every step I took until I began to feel an attack coming on. The symptoms were familiar to me: a tingling in my nostrils, a growing itch between my chin and my throat.

I skulked back home and didn't have the guts to go out again over the next few weeks.

Mornings were the hardest. I lay in bed like a corpse, limp but not relaxed. Dulled but not hurting. My thoughts kept unravelling at the edges and I couldn't complete any of them. I was extinguished like a memorial candle whose wax is dripping, and yet everything was infused with the aura of a stage play. There was someone inside me watching the melodrama of it all from the wings.

Little things drove me crazy. Things were in the wrong places at home. One morning I moved a salt shaker five times, and in the end returned it to its original place in the kitchen. And another morning I took apart the shelf where the loudspeakers were and put it up near the door. Over and over again, I listened to a Chameleons CD that had come out two years ago (we didn't know then that it would be their last). A shitty album, I'd said to Churchill when I finished listening to it the first time, and buried it under a pile, determined never to listen to it again. And here I was now, unable to listen to anything but muted, morose drums and faint, whining guitars. Introverted music alien to itself, weary, monotonous melodies that never took off, even at the chorus, and the lyrics that I hadn't understood then, two years ago, now felt as if I'd written them myself –

Sleep without a sheet
Alone in my bed.
They're renovating the street
But I'll be gone
Before it's done

Or:

The countdown's over
And nothing took place
After zero comes the silence
After zero comes the silence
Of empty space

*

The Chameleons' tired melodies rocked me slowly, defeating me into a too-early, sweaty noontime nap that I woke from in a panic, my heart pounding rapidly as I tried to grab onto the tail of the nightmare that had attacked me while I slept. Once it was a car I was driving that suddenly had no brake pedal, only the accelerator, and once it was Ilana, who wanted, demanded, that I kiss her cracked, dead lips. Once it was the handcuffed boy from Nablus limping towards me, a club in his hand, and once it was Shahar Cohen who was shooting ping-pong balls at me through a gun, and when I couldn't catch them, he said contemptuously, 'How do you expect to save money like that, man?'

After years, the recurrent nightmare of my childhood returned: I'm a little boy sitting on the beach in Haifa with my mother and father, building sandcastles, when suddenly a huge wave the height of a four-story building comes rushing towards us. We get up and start running away from it, but the wave pursues us up Mount Carmel, engulfing buildings and cars and other people on the way, but not us, because we manage to race all the way to the Muchraka which, for some reason, was called Masada, and we stood there and watched the huge wave finally retreat into the sea like all the other waves.

The water-pursuing-me feeling was so palpable that every time I woke up from that dream, I needed a few seconds of open eyes to be convinced that it wasn't really happening. Every morning I would promise myself not to fall asleep in the afternoon so that I wouldn't have one of those nightmares, but every day I'd give in to the temptation to lie down on the sofa 'just for a minute' to listen to 'only three songs' from the Chameleons' CD.

A light breeze would come through the window in the afternoon, and that would get me off the sofa and energise me a bit. But that renewed energy had something even more frightening in it: the whole time I was comatose, I wasn't a danger to myself, but the minute I began to move around the room, there was always the chance that my legs would take me to the window. To the window ledge.

I had gone through a dark period like that when I came back from the long trip with Churchill. I couldn't fall asleep at night then either and used to snatch a few hours of nightmare-ridden afternoon sleep. Then too, things seemed to be in the wrong place and I thought that the parts of my body weren't working properly. But that had been a shorter period – about a week – and at no time did it go as far as the window ledge.

I was young then. After the trip. And still had hope that things would change. That I would change.

Eight years had passed, and there I was, an old man of thirty-one. I'd completed the plaster years Ilana had spoken about and the plaster hadn't set and I hadn't found a cause, and even my friends, who had once been the reason and the result and the ground and gravity – even they were already moving away from me, each towards his own star. I assumed they still loved me, cared about me, but their feelings seemed faint, like an alarm clock ringing in another house. And my parents – I'd spent ten years trying to get away from them, and I'd done it so well that now they were too far away to help me, and even if I tried, what could possibly happen? My father would tell me, again, how good I used to be in maths, and wonder, again, why, for heaven's sake, I hadn't continued in that direction, and my mother – she's a wonderful person, but ever since she left the printing house and signed up for an Arabic course because 'that is the space we live in', and for a singles group because 'why did she have to miss out on meeting inter-esting people just because she was married', and for a course for tour guides because 'someone has to show the world the beauties of Haifa' – ever since this late blooming had begun, her optimism, which had been quiet and pleasant, had turned into something quite stormy, and a few days ago, she left me a message that she's at a Ministry of Tourism course at Kibbutz Shefayim, and if I want, I can pop by in the evening, but I didn't call her back because I could picture us sitting together in the kibbutz dining hall that had been transformed into a restaurant, she with that happy moon face of hers and me with my limp paleness, and I try to explain to her what I'm going through, and she nods politely, supposedly listening, but at the first opportunity, she changes the subject and tells me that it's not at all certain that Harry is Charles's son, and that the hottest conspiracy theory in London now is that Diana wasn't killed in the accident, but was murdered by assassins from British intelligence.

*

And anyway, if I were living in the time of the Second Aliyah, or during the War of Attrition, when *Late Summer Blues* takes place, then I could join something that was nourished by a great, important cause, or alternatively, I could be like Aara'le from the movie and write slogans against the great cause. But now? There was no one and nothing to live for (and that's a lie too. I don't have Aara'le's daring, and even if I lived in an important period of time, I would probably find reasons to question its values, to observe the action from the sidelines and then complain that I had no purpose in life).

*

One of the times that I was a step away from giving up – I picked up a pen and wrote a list of the small things, not the big ones, that are still worth living for.

It took a long time, and while I was doing it, doubt was gnawing away at me – why bother with a list? Words and more words –

But in the end, the pen started moving:

Apricots – during the very short season (about two days) when they're not too hard and not too soft.
The CD of collected Chameleon songs that would come out after they split (specifically, the moment I open the wrapper at home, and take out the booklet with the lyrics and read them).

A visit to Sydney, Australia (I had never been, but people who
  had said it was fantastic).
The first days of summer at university (a female hand tucking
  a short skirt behind her knees).
To live outside the city and see if it helps my asthma.
The fact that I still haven't had the chance to do it with two
  sisters at the same time (or to do it in a respectable public
  place like, let's say, the Israel Museum).
The fact that perhaps once, when we're very old, there will be
  peace.
Ah, yes. Also the fact that the next World Cup is really close.

A small smile unwound in me when I added the World
Cup to the list. Somehow, of all the things I'd written, that
was the one to slip between my dry ribs and strum on the
string. Suddenly I thought it really would be a shame to
leave before the World Cup, to miss the great little dances
the African players do after scoring a goal, not to see the
bloody Germans go home in defeat after the semi-final,
and not to hear the English fans chanting for their team,
and the *batucada* in the Brazilian stands, and the analysts'
stupid predictions, and the reports on the suspension of
the civil war in Togo, or Ethiopia, or anywhere else but the
Middle East, for the month of the matches. And the yellow
cards, the red cards and the close-ups of the players' faces
when they get a red one, and the black-and-white archive
clips of England's crossbar goal in the '66 World Cup, and
Spiegler's goal in '70, and the hypnotic white ball moving
from foot to foot to foot, and the fans doing the Mexican
wave in the stadium stands, and our improvised wave in
Amichai's living room, and the slight nausea you feel after
you've watched three terrible football matches in one day,
and the elation pulsing inside you after you've seen a truly
great match, the kind that will go down in your own private
history, and the joy of knowing that for a month, you can
devote most of your time to something that has no other

purpose than to give you pleasure, and that wonderful internal contradiction in football between the enormous effort of the coaches to prepare the game and the natural randomness that suddenly bursts from the players' feet despite themselves, happily sabotaging all the predictions, and that moment when the hypnotic white ball lands in the bottom of the net and the scoring player breaks into a run, shaking off everyone who dashes over to hug him, and he has no idea where he's racing off to, what his final destination is, but he is simply so damn happy that he has to do something with his body, has to take off his shirt, skip past the billboards, climb onto the fence, hug the coach, get down on his knees in thanks –

*

True, I admitted to myself, everything is very bland now. And far from being happy. But perhaps I could drag myself through another few months, till the World Cup, and climb onto the window ledge only after the final match?

The question of how many months there were till the World Cup – exactly how many months would I have to carry on – suddenly bothered me a great deal.

For the first time in an age, I reconnected the phone and called Amichai.

Tell me, Bro, I asked in a rusty voice, when does the World Cup start?

Wait just a minute, he protested. What's happening with you? I left you loads of messages. There's going to be an absolutely final performance of the Chameleons and we thought we'd all go together. Where did you disappear to?

I'll tell you in a minute, I lied. Just tell me first when the World Cup is. It's important.

It usually starts in June and ends in July, doesn't it?

Another nine months, I calculated quickly. That's a lot, but not eternity. Perhaps it was still worth waiting.

You know, Amichai said, I still have the World Cup wishes we wrote.

What wishes?

The ones we wrote at the last World Cup, don't you remember? We each wrote on a slip of paper where we thought we'd be in another four years. Where we wanted to be.

And you kept them?

Yes, they're here. In a shoebox. I haven't touched them since then, but a while ago, I was taking some of Ilana's things out of the back of the wardrobe and saw that they were still there. Four nicely folded slips of paper. We'll unfold them during the final, right?

Sure, sure we'll unfold them. That should be really amazing.

Wow, so many things have happened since then, Amichai said, it's hard to believe that less than four years have passed.

I didn't say anything. Lots of things really had happened to him and the others, I thought, but to me?

It's a good thing we have the World Cup, I finally said. That way, time doesn't turn into a big lump and you can stop every four years and see what's changed.

You said the same thing then.

What?

That remark about time . . . that it's a big lump.

I said something like that?

Who else but you can philosophise that way?

*

As I recreate that fateful phone conversation with Amichai, it seems to me that the light bulb didn't flash right away. It took another few minutes for the current to reach the wires.

Meanwhile, Amichai talked about other things. And at some point, between his story about what Nimrod had done on a family trip to the Judean Desert – he'd climbed onto his lap and asked him, Daddy, where's your smile? – and the report on two female interns in the legal branch of the NPO who had complained to him the day before that Churchill was always hitting on them – it lit up.

Like a spectacle. Suddenly I saw it before my eyes: the Bahai Gardens.

I cut the conversation short despite Amichai's protests (but you haven't told me anything about yourself yet! You always do that! It's not right!), and after I'd put the phone down, I picked up a sheet of paper and wrote down our names.

Next to each friend's name, I wrote the wish he'd read out at the World Cup four years ago.

And I began to draw lines.

Churchill was ousted from the case before he'd been able to fulfil his wish 'to be involved in something that would bring about true social change', but on the other hand, he'd been granted my wish: to be with Ya'ara.

Amichai hadn't fulfilled his wish to open a clinic for alternative treatment, but he'd founded the Our Right NPO, thus fulfilling Churchill's wish to be involved in something that would bring about true social change.

Ofir didn't publish a book of short stories, neither in Hebrew nor in ancient Danish, but the natural knowledge, stronger than any piece of paper, the same knowledge that makes an olive tree seedling turn in an olive tree and not anything else, led him to fulfil Amichai's wish and open a clinic for alternative treatment.

I stopped for a moment and looked at the page.

Only one line remained to be drawn. Only one line separated the four of us from an amazing, almost Bahai-like symmetry in which none of us had fulfilled our own wish from the last World Cup, but each had fulfilled one wish to the right of his own, his friend's wish. For that last line to be drawn and the symmetry to be perfect, I had to fulfil Ofir's wish: to write a book.

I imagined the end of the 2002 World Cup, and Amichai taking the papers out of the shoebox, and each one of us taking his. Then Amichai unfolds his and reads his wishes and laughs in embarrassment. And after him, Churchill, who stammers a bit when he reads the wish about Keren. Right after that, to blunt the effect of his words, he urges Ofir, come on, Bro, your turn. And Ofir hands Maria their baby boy (girl?) so his hands will be free, unfolds it and reads, and the first glint of suspicion, of understanding, shines in Churchill's eyes, but it isn't until I read my three Ya'ara wishes that he begins to notice the shifts I see in front of me now, and for a few seconds, you can see the lines I've just drawn on the page being drawn in his mind's eye, until the full beauty of the entire Bahai garden fills his head, and he taps me on the shoulder and says, man, if you went and wrote a book, we'd have one hell of a situation here. And while he explains to Ofir and Amichai what he means, and what a waste it is that I'm the only who hasn't fulfilled my part in the symmetry, I bend over my briefcase in slow motion, and take out the book I've written secretly over the last nine months.

*

Desire flared in me at that moment: to create the focal point, the one without which there is no symmetry, to do my part, to complete the picture, to add the missing instrument so that our quartet could play the harmonic music that the guide in the Bahai garden had spoken of. Everything depends on me, I thought with awakening enthusiasm. If I don't do anything, it will all be pointless, like a messy room in a hostel, but if I dare to write the book that Ofir dreamed of, that would be so symmetrical, so beautiful, like an elegant philosophic proof, like an exact translation of a sentence from English into Hebrew. Like a neat room. The kind I love.

For a few moments, I felt that finally, I had a purpose. Finally something inside me really wanted.

(And perhaps to tell it in a different, more genuine way: for several moments, I saw an opportunity to grab onto something before I was shot down once and for all. Before I gave up. I wasn't sure it would really help. I wasn't sure

I hadn't already reached the point of no return. But for several moments, I thought that perhaps –)

*

But at the very end of those lovely moments stood my father, holding a bucket of cold water. Freezing water.

Write a book? Are you serious? He tilted the bucket over my head. Who are you to write a book?

From 'Metamorphoses: Great Minds who Changed their Mind', a shelved philosophy thesis by Yuval Freed

Only after the death of Plato, his spiritual father, did Aristotle leave the Academy in Athens and move to Asia Minor. And only there (with the confidence that distance brings?) did he dare for the first time to refute the theory of his teacher and master, the theory he had been raised on for twenty years, from the age of seventeen. Plato had erred all along, Aristotle claims. There is no point in talking about abstract ideas we do not have the ability to see or feel. All our attempts to discuss anything beyond our experience are destined to fail. Therefore, philosophy must limit itself to a study of the space accessible to our senses, which, in and of itself, is a broad subject that calls for much deliberation.

'So farewell to Platonic ideas, for they have no more meaning than singing la la la,' Aristotle writes. And that sentence is so coarse and resolute that it immediately raises the question: when did that extreme turnabout in his ideas occur? Had the doubt germinated in him during his studies at the Academy, and did he keep silent in order not to disrespect his spiritual father, or was it Plato's death and Aristotle's liberation from his great shadow that made the change in his thinking possible? Were there intermediate stages on the road to the great defection, or did Aristotle awaken one morning in his home in the port city of Assos, look at the actual fishing boats and tangible fishing nets and suddenly understand everything?

And another question, to which, of course, there was and never will be a single answer: what would have happened if Plato had lived longer?

Would Aristotle have stood up one evening in the presence of all the students and confronted his spiritual father face to face?

13

My father showed great respect for the writers who came to his printing house in the lower city.

There weren't many of them. Most tried their luck in the large Tel Aviv publishing houses, and when they were rejected, gave up on the dream. Only a few were persistent enough or desperate enough to self-publish their books and, except for one, none ever came back to my father to publish their second book. Anyway, they had only one story to tell – the story of their lives – and the indifference with which that story was received by readers weakened their resolve.

Not even anyone in my family read the book, they would complain to him, not even my children! And he would console them, placate them, put a hand on their shoulder and explain that books tend to make their way slowly, and he's even heard of some of our own writers, from Haifa, who received emotional letters from readers in distant lands – even Scandinavia! – many years after their books were published. Scandinavia? Really? the writers would say, their eyes shining, and my father would nod confidently and compliment them on the unique quality of their writing, surprising them with an exact quote from the book. (It was only when I worked for him before the army that I noticed the quotes were always taken from the first page.)

OK then, they would say with pleasure. A wise man has been found in Sodom! A true literary connoisseur! And my father would smile humbly and lead them gently towards the door and send them on their way with a pat on the back and an invitation to come back and visit, no need to call in advance, because now, after reading their wonderful book, he feels as close to them as if they were friends.

He would wait a few moments till the happy, mollified writer was out of earshot (I had a kind of hobby the summer I worked for him – counting to myself how many seconds passed from the minute the writer walked out the door of the printing house until my father said what he really thought of him), and then he would say with profound disdain, Good for nothing! Then, when he was already at his desk, he would say to my mother, spitting out the words, Every nobody thinks he can write a book. Every nobody! It wasn't like this in England. In England a writer was a writer. And here, every little piss artist thinks he's Bialik! (In grim situations, if the writer made him especially angry or asked, God forbid, to pay in instalments, he would end with, Every piss artist thinks he's Agnon.)

*

The only one of my father's writers who survived the crisis of the second book (and the third, and the fourth) was Yosef Miron-Mishberg. An old man with light-coloured, almost insane eyes who every autumn would burst into the printing house, a new manuscript under his arm.

Here he is, the great writer! my father would say as he went to greet him, his voice free of ridicule.

My father would introduce him excitedly to his employees, most of whom already knew Miron-Mishberg quite well, but they still stood up to show him respect, and he would walk among them as if he were Moshe Dayan in the Yad Eliyahu basketball stadium, shaking each one's hand. When the lengthy round of handshakes was over, he would close his eyes, take a deep breath through his nose and say: ah, the fragrance of printing presses. There is no fragrance more intoxicating in the entire universe!

Well then, perhaps you will put our small printing house into one of your books, my father would suggest again every year. Now that's an idea! An excellent idea! Miron-Mishberg would say enthusiastically again every year, and the two of them would sit down at my father's desk and drink whisky from small, glass coffee cups.

So, what is your book about this time? my father would ask.

To know that, you have to read it, Miron-Mishberg would scold.

Still, my father would explain, in order for us to design the cover . . . as soon as possible, of course . . . still, you should tell me what it's about. A love story? A thriller? Murder? An historical mystery?

There is only one thing worth writing about! Miron-Mishberg would say, raising his voice and slamming his fist on the desk, frightening the glasses.

Certainly, certainly, my father would say in apology . . . So I understand that . . . again . . .

Again and again and again! And I still haven't said anything!! Miron-Mishberg would shout, his light-coloured eyes threatening to burst out of their sockets.

Of course, I understand, my father would try to calm him down, and immediately shift the discussion to the technical aspects of the printing process and to the schedule, fully aware that the moment those practical matters were on the table, his interlocutor would begin to stare into space, his thoughts would wander, and his righteous indignation would fade.

Miron-Mishberg would sign his contracts distractedly. Unthinkingly. Even though my father would caution him over and over again to read everything, even the fine print. I trust you, Miron-Mishberg would tell him. You English, your word is your bond. You have self-respect. You didn't collaborate with the Nazi persecutors. What did Churchill say? Blood, sweat and tears! Tell me, will you, what are today's leaders compared to Churchill?

There is no comparison, my father would agree, hand him a copy of the contract and stand up to indicate to Miron-Mishberg that the meeting was over.

I apologise, but I must return home to write, Miron-Mishberg would say, as if he was the one who had decided to end the meeting. We have to complete as much as possible before the angel of death comes to snatch us away.

Good for you! my father would say, patting him twice on the back, the first time to encourage him and the second to push him forward, towards the door.

So, Miron-Mishberg would say as he shook my father's hand, we'll talk again in three weeks?

God willing, my father would conclude, pat his back one more time and watch to make sure he was going. Then he would go back to his desk and sit down. And get up. And sit down. And wait another minute –

And erupt into a stream of invective.

The loathing he felt for Yosef Miron-Mishberg behind his back was as profound as the reverence he showed him to his face.

That invective wasn't the usual 'good for nothing', 'nobody', and 'piss artist'. It was much more personal.

That poor wife of his, he would say to my mother as the employees of the printing house lowered their heads in embarrassment. Those poor children of his, to have such a father. They're starving and he – he's a writer! A writer? A hack! A graphomaniac! He got one good review in the local rag – even that was less than a hundred words – and ever since, he thinks he's God's gift. And he quit his job. Sent his wife with her back problems to work, and 'devoted himself' to writing. Writing my foot. He writes the same book every time. The name changes, but the book – exactly the same! And he isn't even ashamed!!!

Norman, dear, aren't you overreacting a bit? my mother would say, throwing a spanner into his blind rage.

Overreacting . . . overreacting . . . my father would mutter, circle his desk searching for an appropriate answer, and then he would pick up the pile of papers Miron-Mishberg had left and slam them onto her desk in despair. You know what, Marilyn, you print his book if you think I'm over-reacting.

*

For years, I attributed my father's dual attitude towards writers to the same duality that characterised my parents' attitude towards people in general. With them, words were always a cover to hide the truth. They were nice to all the neighbours on the stairs, then at home, I'd hear what they really thought of them. They were quite cordial to all the employees in the printing house – right up to the day they fired them.

They had three couples they called 'friends' (as Wittgenstein said, the same word, in the mouths of different people, can serve to describe a totally different essence) – and they saw them twice a year for conversations on politics and cars and lounge suites, on nothing painful or real, and there was an ever-growing list of unpleasant subjects they simply 'preferred' not to speak of, even between themselves. You know I prefer not to talk about that, my mother would say every time my father mentioned the rift between her and her sisters. I prefer not to talk about that now, my father would say every time my mother suggested making changes around the house. And so, gradually, they vetoed every subject of conversation except other people's lives, which they always analysed with haughty disapproval.

I understood, therefore, that behind the words my father spoke to writers was contempt, and that all his compliments had one purpose only – to get them to give him their money. It wasn't until that summer, after high school and right before the army, when I worked as a messenger in the printing house and saw it all close up, day after day (and perhaps it wasn't the closeness that enabled me to see, but my eyes, which had matured?) – it wasn't until then that I began to suspect that my father's attitude towards his writers was absolutely real, including the respect. And the contempt. And the condescension. And the avarice. And the generosity. And that all those contradictory passions could wrestle with each other within the same person.

*

That summer, for the first time in my life, a writer gave me a signed copy of his book.

I'd been sent to take Miron-Mishberg the first copies of his new book. He opened the brown package and ran his hand over the cover, flicked through the pages from the end to the beginning and gently separated two pages that were slightly stuck together, lowered his face to the book and inhaled the smell and said, to me or to himself, Every book has its own smell.

I said nothing. I thought about my father, who claimed that all of Miron-Mishberg's books were the same and I actually had no idea whether my father was right or not, because I didn't read them.

Miron-Mishberg fixed his pale, disturbing eyes on me and said, you have thinking eyes, boy. Do you know that? I looked down. Thoughts are always running through your mind, through your little head, he said, giving me a crooked smile. Is it true? Tell me, am I right or not? There was something frightening in his tone, so I didn't answer. And he burst into strangled laughter that quickly deteriorated into a paroxysm of phlegm-filled coughing. When the cough had subsided a bit, he picked up a copy of his book, opened it to the first page, wrote something in large, messy letters and handed it to me. I said, thank you, mumbled something about other deliveries I had to make and got out of there while I still could.

It was only two days later, in the light of my bed lamp, that I dared to open that book.

It said, 'To the boy with the thinking eyes, in friendship, Yosef Miron-Mishberg', and under it was his curlicued signature, which looked like the flames of a camp-fire.

That night, I tried to read his book – and gave up after twenty pages. It was very beautiful, but I didn't understand a word. I mean, I had a clear sense that the story had internal logic, it was just that I couldn't follow it.

I blamed myself, of course. He was a great writer, that was obvious. The problem was mine – a small body, a small mind. Handicapped.

*

That was the feeling I walked around with for years.

There is a lofty, noble, frightening world of writers.

And there's my world. The simple one. And a high fence separates the two. When I translate, I can climb that fence and peek into the other world, but in the end I always have to return to my world. Because I'm just a dull, ordiary person. And who am I to write anything?

*

For the first few weeks after deciding that I wanted to write a book and publish it before the World Cup, that was the voice that echoed inside my head: who are you to write anything? Who are you to write anything? Who are you to write anything?

I sat in front of the computer for a week, fingers frozen, refusing to move.

After a week, I decided that my problem was the computer. There's no inspiration in trying to write on the computer. So I switched to a notebook. And to the fountain pen I'd received as a gift from one of my old clients.

Two days later, I realised that there was also a problem with a pen. There was something pretentious about it that impeded movement. And the black ink – it was ominous.

I went to the shop and bought a simple Pilot. Blue.

That didn't help either. The page – remained white.

As white as the part of the body that's covered by a

bathing suit and doesn't get tanned. As white as paleness. As white as emptiness. White – white.

*

True, I had no idea what the hell I wanted to write about.

My first thought was to call Ofir and ask if he had an idea. After all, he was the one our literature teacher said had talent. He was the one who wrote all those songs for our graduation play. And even the ads he created for banks and biscuits always had some kind of spark. And writing a book – writing a book was originally his dream, not mine, so let him take some responsibility, that *sharwal*!

But I stopped myself: you're not writing for a Nobel Prize, you're writing to complete the amazing symmetry and surprise your friends at the World Cup final. How can you surprise them if you ask for their advice?

While I was staring at the notebook, I remembered that one of my clients had told me about a writing workshop he goes to. I called him and he gave me the phone number.

The slip of paper with the number on it rested in my pocket for four days. A clear and determined inner voice objected strongly to the idea: who needs a workshop? A workshop is a group, and except for my friends, I don't like groups. Besides, writing is one thing, but reading? Out loud? To other people? I simply won't be able to do it. And another thing, the tutor – I categorically do not like his books. Too many descriptions. And it all tries to be so symbolic. I definitely wouldn't want to write like him, definitely wouldn't want him to guide me in that direction, definitely not –

A small item in the sports section silenced that determined inner voice of mine.

'South Korean president personally supervises the logistical preparations for the World Cup and promises: we'll be ready on 31 May.'

31 May? That means that the final will be at the end of June! And that means that I have less than eight months

to write a book and publish it! And what am I doing? What do I always do! Nothing!!!

The first meeting of the writing workshop confirmed all my fears.

From the minute I walked into the host's flat, I had the feeling I'd already been there in the past, and that feeling only grew stronger as the meeting progressed. Besides, after so many weeks of being home alone, I'd forgotten how to behave with other people. When to smile. When not to. When to look them straight in the eye. When to look down. What the proper distance is between your bottom and the bottom of the person sitting next to you on the sofa. When it was my turn to introduce myself in the round of introductions at the beginning of the meeting, I was at a loss for words for too long, and in the end, I stammered that I was a translator . . . well, not really a translator . . . I mean, not books . . . more like student papers . . . I mean, not really papers . . . just articles . . . that they can use later to write papers, if they want . . . themselves . . .

The hostess's tangle-haired dog nibbled from one of the snack plates and everyone burst out laughing. It took me a minute to realise that they were laughing at the dog, not at me. But I felt that if they were laughing at me, they'd be right to do it. The round of introductions kept moving clockwise, and everyone – so I thought – had a more fascinating life than I did, wider writing experience than mine and happier clothing.

The only exception was a rather timid girl who had arrived late, from Jerusalem, and when she was asked to introduce herself, she said in a barely audible voice that it was a bit too soon for her to talk about herself. Perhaps later, if she felt comfortable.

The tutor let her be and told us a bit about the first workshop he'd participated in as a writer, twenty years earlier, and about how cruelly people had reacted to the first piece of writing he'd read to the group. In his group, he told us, there would be no cruelty. In his group, there would be honest but respectful criticism.

His tone was soft when he said that, and, all in all, he made a much warmer impression than the male characters in his books.

See? I said to myself, restraining the urge to get up and leave that I'd been feeling from the minute I'd sat down. Stop being so reserved. For once in your life, try to give yourself over to something.

I gave myself over to it for about half an hour, till it was my turn to tell my true story and my false story. When no one but the timid girl believed my story about the kidnapping I'd witnessed with Ofir, I withdrew into myself and was filled with the desire to see my friends. It would be enough for one of them to be here, I thought, and I'd feel a bit less odd. A bit more understandable.

After the instructor asked us to write one of our stories and everyone but me hustled to put pen to paper, I made my final decision: I would never come back to that workshop.

As I leaned back on the sofa with the relief that an admission of defeat brings, I suddenly remembered why that flat was so familiar to me. I'd sat here once, in this living room, on the last Independence Day before the army, when Churchill went into the bedroom with Atalya, the artist, and Ofir and Amichai, tired of their arguments, fell asleep beside me on the sofa.

Even that flat had changed since then, I thought. And I? Thirteen years had passed and I was in exactly the same place, sitting in the living room and waiting for everything to be over so I could go home.

At the end of the workshop, when the tutor handed out printed pages of homework, I took one out of politeness. I planned to throw it into the bin the minute I got home – it and the list of the participants' phone numbers. But the minute I got home, I was seized by a bitterness blacker, more despairing, more intense than any I'd felt before: I would never be able to write the book. I had nothing to write about. And if I found something, I had no idea how to write it. I doubled over in pain. At the next World Cup, I'd read my three Ya'ara-wishes and laugh at myself together with everyone else. In fact, it would be better to end it, to end the exhausting, humiliating thing called life before the next World Cup. That way, I'd save myself a lot of embarrassment.

Closer to the window ledge than ever before, I took the homework page out of my briefcase.

*

The first exercise was to describe a picture.

'Take out your photo albums', the tutor had written. 'Browse through them. Choose one picture you find interesting, that reminds you of something. Look at it for a while and describe, in writing, everything that you see. After you have described it, try to step out of the description into the story behind the picture.'

I looked up from the page and the large picture on the wall caught my eye: the four friends on a trip to the Sinai desert mountains. I looked at it for a several moments – and then, the pen heavy in my hand, I began to write.

*

The four of us are leaning on a stone fence, and on each other. We're all wearing blue Telemed visor caps that Amichai got for us. We're all smiling at the Bedouin snapping the picture, except Amichai, who at that point in the trip was already suffering from a serious case of missing Ilana and the twins, and every time we stopped to drink, he searched desperately for a spot that had mobile reception. That was the last trip we took as a foursome, and a week later, I met Ya'ara. I'm easy to spot in the picture: I'm the shortest one. I can't really say more than that (is anyone able to see himself? Truly see himself?). A girl I dated once claimed I had a baby face. Here, in any case, my face is distorted because of the sun, my eyes are very squinty and my skin roasted. I'm standing at the right edge of the frame, and standing next to me, a head taller, is Ofir. His large, light-brown curls make him look taller than he actually is. If you ironed them, he'd be half a head taller than me, that's all. It's funny how pictures deceive. He's smiling more broadly than any of us. A true advertising smile. But during the actual trip, he didn't smile at all, and kept complaining that he couldn't 'get into the Sinai spirit' and suggested we head for Ras-el-Satan because it was 'probably a lot more fun there'. To the left is Churchill, his hands clasped behind his neck. Clasping your hands behind your neck is a great, masculine pose. I've always admired it, and there was a brief time in the army when I managed to adopt it for myself. There's a large sweat stain in the middle of his shirt and the logo, 'STAND UP FOR YOUR RIGHTS'. Churchill sweats easily. When the four of us used to go dancing together at the Muse after the army, he'd turn into a dishrag after two songs, which never kept him from hitting on every girl who entered his radius. And succeeding. Amichai, standing next to Churchill in the picture, never hit on girls at the Muse. He always believed that girls didn't want him because of the birth-mark on his neck, which had the shape of the map of Israel. In the picture, you can see that it's more in his mind than in reality. He has a solid body, all his stability projects the message that you can lean on him, and he has earth-coloured eyes, eyes that many women could have loved. But he always loved only his Ilana. He'd loved Ilana the Weeper even before he met her, and he would continue to love her with the same quiet loyalty even when she was no longer alive, and the night after that picture was taken, I got up to pee and saw him in his sleeping bag, smiling as he shone his torch on a snapshot of her and the twins.

The story behind that picture is the story of our friendship. The four of us. It's not clear exactly how it began. It's not clear what keeps it strong to this day. And it's not clear whether it will continue to exist now that our lives have changed. I think friendship is a strange thing altogether. I've been translating English academic articles in the social sciences into Hebrew for

five years now, and still haven't come across an article that studies
the subject in depth. Yes, everything today has to be statistical
and empirical, and it really is difficult to quantify and calculate
distance and closeness and loyalty and betrayal and love and
longing. And perhaps it's not necessary.

*

I was fairly satisfied with what I'd written. Mainly with the
last paragraph. I decided I'd go to the second meeting of
the workshop to hand in the exercise and hear what the
tutor had to say.

He returned the exercise a week later. He'd written on
it in his long, narrow handwriting:

The description of the picture itself is rich and detailed, but
the paragraph that comes later, the one that's supposed to tell
'the story behind the picture', explains and analyses and does
everything but tell the story.

I think that this exercise could be the opening into a larger
story about the characters that appear in it, but you still need to
find the narrative path along which you wish to lead yourself
and your reader.

*

What does he want from me?

That was my first response when I read his comment.

Idiot, I thought a few hours later. How can he say that
the last paragraph isn't good?

The next morning, I reread what I'd handed in. Perhaps,
I thought. Perhaps there is something in what he says.

A week later, while shaving, I suddenly had the general
idea for a plot that would grow out of the earlier World
Cup wishes and end with the approaching World Cup.

With racing, burning fingers, I began to write the book.

*

The flow that swept me along as I wrote the first pages
bore no resemblance at all to what I felt when translating,
and, in fact, it bore no resemblance to any other state of
consciousness I'd known in the past (except perhaps for my

especially successful masturbation fantasies – the ones I invested so much in that my fingers could actually feel the nipples of the girl I was fantasising about).

But after the first explosion of enthusiasm, I realised that writing is not a leisurely sail down a river –

I discovered, for example, that apparently unimportant physical handicaps also handicapped me in writing. Since I was colour blind, for example, there were too few colours in my descriptions, as if I were afraid to mistakenly call red green and green red.

But on the other hand –

A few of my shitty traits actually worked to my benefit in writing: the obsessive memory that would not let me forget Ya'ara, even for a minute, over the last four years helped me when I had to recreate a situation. I remember everything that was said. Everything that was worn. Every song on the radio playing in the background. And if there is something I happen not to remember, I invent it. And how wonderful it is to invent. As a translator, you're bound to the original text by chains of fidelity, but here – here you can be unfaithful. Replace an uncle with a father. One friend with another. Invent entire conversations you've never heard. Lie. Take revenge on people through your words. But you can atone as well.

I also discovered that never losing sight of the great goal of finishing the book is both a blessing and a curse. It makes me sit down in front of the computer every morning, but there are days when nothing gets written and I have no choice but to go outside, sidestep the renovation pits and walk all the way to the northern wall of Yarkon Park where the paved path ends. And lie down there. And simply stare at the shifting clouds.

Though it's so easy to get confused between days like that and days when you're just being lazy. The dishes were always clean during the ten months I was writing. The laundry was very nicely folded. And my translating business revived.

Every now and then, I tried to escape into reading other people's books, but I soon discovered what a problem that could be. This, for example, is what I wrote after I finished reading *Lips* – a collection of erotic stories by foreign women writers. I couldn't fall asleep all night, and in the morning, the following scene wrote itself:

Ilana runs her fingers over Maria's lips, flutters over her upper lip and continues the imaginary line that stretches from the corner of her mouth to her cheek, to the large artery in her neck, to her collarbone. Slowly, like a fine brush, her finger moves under her shirt, raising it slightly, and climbs up to her shoulder.

Ilana presses her ear against Maria's breasts. Maria's heart has a three-beat rhythm: oh-my-love, oh-my love. Or perhaps: Oh-my-God. Oh-my-God.

For a moment, Ilana imagines them dancing a tango to that rhythm.

The word 'tango' also flickers in Maria for a moment. It's not clear where it's coming from.

Ilana presses her lips to the coffee stain, two fingers from Maria's navel.

Maria asks soundlessly: how many sugars?

They transform. On the first transformation, they're scorpions. Then tortoises. Then it's their souls that are transformed.

Maria feels no guilt.

Neither does Ilana. At least not while they're doing it.

Pain has collected in Ilana's back. Spots of pain. Maria presses gently on them and feels how each spot tells a story.

Ilana's thighs are poignant. A bit scratched, a bit wounded. Maria kisses them, then kisses them again, slightly higher up.

How strange. Maria kisses her thighs but she feels the pleasure on the back of her neck.

And suddenly she's embarrassed by her nakedness and wants to cover up with something.

There is no blanket, so Maria climbs on top of her and covers her with her large, blazing body.

*Where, in all that, was the point of no return? The point
when it was still possible to stop.*

*Before. Long before all that. The moment, three weeks earlier,
when Maria suggested that, if Ilana had back pain, she would
treat her. The moment her touch was soft. The moment they
went to the sea together and their hands touched accidentally,
under the water. The moment Maria pulled her onto the dance
floor, at the wedding. The moment she told her, with simple
frankness, about her winter depression. The moment she expressed
an interest in her articles. The moment she came into their apartment for the first time, with Ofir. The moment Ilana met
Amichai.*

*Their first time in the living room. On the sofa. Later, in
the bedroom. On the carpet. And after that, in the kitchen, when
Maria sat on a chair and Ilana sat on her, her hands wrapped
around her neck, her stomach pressed up against her, her glance
direct, evasive, frightened, bold.*

*Ilana moves on Maria's muscular leg, back and forth, back and
forth, until . . .*

*Maria looks at her, how beautiful she is when she's enjoying
herself. Her lips.*

Lana, Lana, Lana, she says her name silently.

Writing those lines was a joy, I won't deny it.

But more than that: suddenly, as I was writing, I began
to feel that the encounter was actually taking place, and
when I finished writing, I was absolutely positive that it
had happened and that Ilana had taken the secret with her
to the grave.

In any case, I couldn't go on writing like that. It was too
horny and too necrophiliac, and, even worse, the tips of
my fingers itched with a sense of falseness.

And that's what happened every time I tried to write
'like' someone. It didn't matter whether that someone was

a foreign woman writer of erotic fiction, or Garcia Marquez, or Tolkien. My fingers would freeze after a few sentences. I realised time after time that they would agree to tell the story about my friends in only one voice: the natural, primal voice that had written itself when I'd described the picture of us in the Sinai desert for that first exercise.

*

I barely spoke to my friends while I was writing. They were all caught up in their pregnancies, and I – in my literary pregnancy. The few times we spoke left me with a strange feeling. Not quite natural. And even worse was the fact that carrying on a real conversation with the imaginary characters I was writing about confused me so much that for several days after every conversation with my actual friends, I was unable to write.

So I tried to talk to them as little as possible. There were a lot of terrorist attacks during the months I was holed up in my apartment. People left their homes and never reached their destinations. Rivers of blood were spilled. Distant ambulance sirens wailed, then less distant, and then close by. But even when the shock waves actually shook the windows of my flat, I made do with the general knowledge that my friends were alive. I didn't feel the need to hear from them how they were supposed to have been on the bus that blew up, or how exactly a week earlier, they'd been sitting in the café that had been destroyed. And when Ofir called and left a message that Yoram Mendelsohn the genius had committed suicide and left a letter explaining that his suicide was an experiment aimed at strengthening his scientific theory on reincarnation, I didn't go to the funeral with them. And when Amichai called to ask what was happening with me and did I want them to buy me a ticket to the Chameleons' absolutely-definitely-final performance, I called him back when I knew he wouldn't be home. And left a message that, unfortunately, I wouldn't be able to join them.

But on the other hand –

Throughout all the months of writing, I felt as if my friends were with me. Totally with me. Like they had been once, in high school, before the jobs and the ambitions and the Ya'aras came and caused us to grow distant from one another. True, they had no choice: I was the writer. I pulled the transparent strings and moved them from place to place and decided how they'd look and what they'd feel and when they'd speak and when they'd only bite their lips. And I gave myself the best, the cleverest lines in compensation for the fact that, actually, when we saw each other, I was silent most of the time, thinking my bitter little thoughts, or my generous little thoughts, and now all those thoughts had thrown off their restraining shackles, had broken out of their prison and were dancing the freedom dance on the enormous, white expanse of the page.

My sense of taste gradually returned. Hummus tasted like hummus again. Tahini like tahini. And my wave-pursuing-me nightmares ceased completely. I dreamed instead about letters and commas and full stops flickering on the walls, and I didn't go near the window ledge any more because I knew that I had to live, had to stay alive another few months at least, to finish that book so that the matrix of World Cup wishes would be complete and beautiful and harmonious, like the Bahai Gardens.

And then, we'll see.

*

In early April, three months before the World Cup final, I finished writing.

Due to time pressure, I gave the first version to two readers only: my tutor and the timid girl from the workshop.

The tutor came back to me with two major comments.

The first depressed me, but I had to admit that he was right: no matter how hard I worked on my Hebrew, no matter how much I improved it in an effort to uproot what my parents had planted inside me, there would still be many passages where vestiges of English syntactical structures echoed. The tutor marked twenty-two such places and recommended that I go to a copy-editor who would uproot all the rest. After going over what he marked, I realised that I had no choice but to follow his recommendation.

On the other hand, I utterly rejected his second comment. He claimed that the narrator has many blind spots, and he was particularly bothered by the one related to the wider context in which the events take place. 'You write about changes in your characters, but almost completely ignore any dramatic changes occurring in the time and place you've chosen to write about. It can't be that none of that seeped into the friends' world!'

But that's the whole point with friends, I argued with him (not to his face; he himself had gone to the Sydney Writers' Festival). Friends are like a desert oasis where you can forget the desert . . . or like a raft in a stormy sea . . . or like . . .

Still – he interrupted me in my imagination – the 'harmony' your narrator is always trying to achieve, all that 'Bahai symmetry' – I ask myself, considering the disharmony in which he and we live, whether such an attempt isn't inevitably doomed to failure.

Doomed to failure? Now I was really pissed off. Why?! Because in his books, which I didn't like at all, every little personal moment always has to be symbolic of some great national issue? I don't write to symbolise something national. I write to fulfil Ofir's wish and complete the picture by the World Cup final. That's all. And don't nod at me now with that know-it-all, prophetic forgiveness, OK?

*

What bothered the timid girl most was the character of Ya'ara.

I don't understand what she has, she said. Why are your protagonists so crazy about her?

I didn't answer, as if admitting my guilt. Outside the workshop, the timid girl wasn't so timid. Perhaps she's one of those people who shrink into themselves in groups, I thought. In the workshop, her shoulders were always stooped, and now, in the café, they weren't. In the workshop, her gaze was always cast down, especially when the tutor asked who wanted to read, and now her eyes shone at me. In the workshop, she hardly said anything, and now she leaned towards me, gesturing expressively with her hands as she spoke.

There's something annoying about that Ya'ara, she said (her long fingers scratching the air). OK (her palms turned upwards in a 'there's-no-denying' gesture) she's beautiful (her hands drew cascading hair), so what? I personally felt (her hand moved to the top of her breasts) that your men deserved more.

Could be, I said, and thought: the fact that women don't like Ya'ara is nothing new. Ya'ara has a sexual aura that women simply can't feel, a way of making men feel very strong beside her, and then, all at once, she nails them with a remark that immediately sets their loins quivering. She's always two contradictory things. And there's something about her . . . there *was* something about her . . .

In any case, the timid girl said (and placed her hands firmly on the pile of pages), thank you for letting me read it. I mean, I'm glad I was the one you called.

She didn't smile when she said the word 'glad'. In general, there hadn't been a drop of affectation in her voice during the entire conversation. From under her hand gestures flowed a sort of inner quiet, as if she already knew something very basic about herself and needed no confirmation of it.

And what about you? I asked after a brief, awkward silence. What about your writing?

I'm always writing in this notebook (a hand takes a notebook out of her bag and places it on the table), but they're such personal things (two hands move in circles, as if around a crystal ball or as if throwing a pot on a wheel) that . . . I don't think anyone would be interested in them.

I'm interested. And . . . I'd be very happy to read them, I said, remembering the only piece she'd read in the workshop. It was a secular description of Yom Kippur eve in a Jerusalem synagogue, and there was something so lucid and unpretentious about her words that even the tutor had no criticism when she'd finished reading.

Read them? No, no (a small smile, a large gesture of dismissal), thank you. Of course not, I'm a conservative girl. I don't do things like that on the first date. Besides, sometimes there's power in keeping things to yourself, don't you think?

I liked the timid girl more every minute. There was something provocative in the contradiction between how withdrawn she was in the workshop and how open she was with me. She never tried to charm or impress me while we were talking, and that in itself was charming and impressive. So impressive that I can't remember a single detail about the café we were in. Not the menu. Not the waitress. Not what I ordered. Just her lovely shoulders and her hands constantly speaking to me.

When she finally grew silent and put her eloquent hands on the table, I wanted very much to stroke them, to stroke her forearm from her elbow to her wrist. Not since Ya'ara had spoken to me in the campus cafeteria four years earlier had I felt such an intense need to touch a girl. To know her. To resolve her contradictions.

But I stopped myself. I didn't pick up the lacy gauntlet she'd thrown down by calling a work meeting a 'first date', and I didn't ask her out on a second one.

Only two months were left till the World Cup final and I couldn't allow myself to get caught up in that maelstrom called love.

I promised myself that the day after the final, I'd call

her, and as we stood at the door of the café, I gave her a long kiss goodbye on the part of her cheek closest to her mouth.

Good luck with your manuscript, she said, tenting her hands.

Thank you, I said, and tented my hands too.

She walked away towards the car park, and I wanted to run after her, grab her by her shirt and promise she wouldn't lose me.

But at that moment, my desire to complete the wonderful symmetry – however suspicious it might sound – was stronger.

*

Two months seemed enough time to publish a book: to copy-edit, typeset, design a cover. But during the first talks I had with publishers, I discovered that their pace was slightly different from that of the Efroni Printing House.

Send the manuscript, you'll receive an answer within a year, the first publisher I contacted told me.

A negative answer within nine months, a positive one – up to two years, the second place told me.

What is the book about? a senior editor at the third publishers asked.

It's about a group of guys, friends who . . . I began to explain.

Men friends?! she interrupted me. Men aren't *in* these days, but send it, you never know.

Two weeks were left before the opening of the World Cup, and only a month and a half till the final.

With a heavy heart, I printed out the manuscript, put it into a transparent plastic bag and drove to Haifa.

14

I drove slowly, very slowly. I thought it would be quite stupid for me to die in an accident when I was so close to making Ofir's dream come true.

When you drive slowly, you notice the different shades of green in the fields between Netanya and Hadera, and the flocks of birds flying in rapid-shifting formations over the Maagan Michael fish ponds, and the new neighbourhood going up next to Neveh Yam, which has the water park with the the bluest slides in the country, and as you slide down the slope of your memories, other drives on this road – officially known as Road No. 2, but it's number one in your life – float to the surface. Like the time Churchill helped you move your things to the apartment in Tel Aviv, following you in his Beetle, and a little past Wingate he called your mobile and said he was thirsty, did you have anything in the car to drink, and you said there was mineral water, but you didn't feel like stopping now, so he drove up alongside the car, you passed him the bottle through the window, he took a few sips and returned it to you, driving the entire time. And there were those late Saturday night drives back from Haifa listening to the army radio station, your heart fluttering with the hope that a gorgeous girl soldier would be standing at the hitchhikers' stop and you would pull over for her and 'fall for her instantly', like the words of the Eran Tzur song. Then there was the driver who gave you a ride to Gelilot when you yourself were a soldier, and he kept nodding off, until he actually fell asleep near the Havazelet junction and you lunged to grab the wheel hard and saved both your lives, and he thanked you effusively and took your address so he could send you an invitation for a free meal in his restaurant in Ashdod, which he hasn't sent to this day. And there's that enormous chair, God's chair, on the cliff at Atlit. Once, driving past it, Ya'ara asked if you knew who had put it there and why, and you were embarrassed to admit that you didn't, and she suggested that on the way back you both climb up and check it out, and if it isn't a monument to the fallen or some other sad thing, you can have sex there, because unusual places turn her on, but on the way back, she fell asleep and her cheeks were so soft that you didn't have the heart to wake her. And now's the moment the road emerges from between the limestone hills and you can see the sea, not a narrow strip but the entire expanse of blue, the place where you always wanted to forget all your plans, all your important goals, and simply pull onto the hard shoulder, strip and run into the waves. Even on the way to Ilana's funeral, you recall, Ofir's glance occasionally moved to the left, and he said, look at the colour of the sea today, but you didn't pull up because Maria's jagged sobs were heart-breaking, and who goes to the beach on the way to a funeral anyway. Even now, you don't pull up, you keep driving straight, because you must, you simply must talk to your father, and he closes at five on the dot on Sundays because he thinks the printing presses are more likely to break down on Sundays after having rested on Saturday, so you actually have less than an hour. And if you're late, you'll lose a day's work. And every day counts, because the World Cup is getting closer.

*

When I went into the printing house, I looked around for my mother, out of habit.

For twenty-five years, she had worked alongside her husband, handling the pre-printing stage: photography, montage, plates. When business was good, there were four people working under her, but in recent years, the whole process had become computerised, making her and the four employees redundant. At first, my father tried to hold out against the change and delayed buying the modern equipment (perhaps he already knew in his heart what would happen?), but when long-time clients threatened to go elsewhere if he didn't update his operation, Efroni finally entered into the new, less romantic, era of printing, and one day, a little before six in the evening, closing time since forever, my mother got up from her chair and began filling a cardboard box she'd brought to work with all the optimistic little signs that had always stood on her desk.

AN APPLE A DAY KEEPS THE DOCTOR AWAY

SMILE – IT'S A CURVE THAT MAKES EVERY-
THING STRAIGHT

SMILE AND THE WORLD WILL SMILE BACK
AT YOU

IN GOD WE TRUST. ALL OTHERS PAY CASH

My father watched her in silence. When she took the design books and magazines from the shelf behind her and put them into the box too, he added a raised eyebrow to his silence. And when she began to remove the series of pictures of Princess Diana (with Harry, with William, with both sons together), he could no longer control himself and cleared his throat.

She turned to look at him. For a brief moment, their eyes met, then looked away in embarrassment.

That's it? he asked.

That's it, she replied. There was no aggression in her voice. Or anger. Only the sort of silent determination that makes it clear there is no room for argument. And just like that, with two words, twenty-five years of joint creativity, joint failures, joint successes came to an end. The thread of their work that bound my parents together was cut, the bond that forced them to speak to each other in the printing house even if they never exchanged a word at home, that forced them to stand up and face life together after my little sister wasn't born. That prevented them – even then – from taking more than a week's vacation, because 'it's much easier to lose a client you have than to find a new one'.

*

After she left the printing house, my mother tried to make all her dreams come true at the same time.

She reconnected with her university friends after long years of not being in touch, when each was busy with her own family. They met once a week for breakfast, which lasted till evening, signed up for a series of lectures on the New Wave in French cinema and went on a heritage tour to Morocco, though not one of them was of Moroccan descent. Encouraged by her new-old friends, my mother dyed her hair blonde and wore it in a new style, and she still had the most beautiful face I had ever seen. She smiled more, wept more. And she took a course for local guides given by the Tourist Ministry, despite my father's scepticism. He claimed that no tourist would want an old woman for a guide when he could have a young one.

But it turned out that most of the tourist groups that come to the city are made up of older people who actually feel more comfortable with a woman their own age who has perfect English and a sunny smile. And so, in less than a year, my mother became the star of local tourism. Every day, you could watch her striding along in her worn-green Teva sandals, trailed closely by an enthusiastic clutch of people wearing visored caps and carrying cameras. The route was always the same: from Yaffee Nof Street, through the Bahai Gardens, down to the German Colony and the port – and from there, a cable car ride back to Stella Maris. But my mother added a special stop to that regular route: 49 Haatzmaut Street. The official reason for the stop was that one of the Haganah's gun caches used to be nearby, offering her an opportunity to relate the sort of hair-raising battle stories tourists from peaceful countries like so much. The unofficial reason for the stop was that the ground floor of the adjoining building, 47 Haatzmaut Street, was home to the Efroni printing house. My mother would appear there almost every day, stand with her back to the place she'd worked in for twenty-five years, turn on the small microphone attached to her collar and begin to talk about the history of gun caches.

She knew quite well that the owner of the printing house could see her from where he was sitting, and to be sure that he could hear her as well, she would raise her voice to almost a shout. Sometimes, when she was in the mood, she would end the visit by drawing the attention of her listeners to the fact that in the building next to where the cache had been was one of the first printing houses in the city of Haifa and an important local monument that had no peers.

Think about it, dear, she said to him with a laugh during a family dinner, there are now hundreds of people in Japan who have a picture of Efroni in their photo albums!

My father failed to see the humour. He thought that her public promotion of the printing house was meant to ridicule and remind him, in a particularly cruel way, that she now earned more money than he. Every day, he would swear to himself all over again that the minute he saw the front end of the tourist bus approaching, he would get up and go to the back of the printing house, behind the presses, to a place where the street wasn't visible, and every day he remained rooted to his chair, watching her fragile back. And listening to her speak. How eloquent she was. And full of life. And knowledgeable. And how patient she was, and open to the group's questions.

The truth is, your mother is a terrific guide, he admitted to me one of those Fridays after she'd gone off to bed. But he was not able to say it to her.

And she, for her part, never came into the printing house to say hello after she left. Not once.

And he, for his part, put pretty young designers in her chair, hoping that one day, she would come inside, see them and eat her heart out. But none of those young women lasted more than a month. He would pay them a pittance and tyrannise them regularly with tirades and complain that their work ethic was poor and they had no soul, no real love for the profession, and in the end they would simply get up and leave – which amazed him time after time, because 'people used to know the value of a regular job'.

After four different designers had taken flight in a year, he 'reached the conclusion that he didn't really need a designer because he knew how to do the basic things himself, and what he didn't know, he could always outsource'.

That's what he told me when I asked why Mum's chair was empty.

After a brief silence, during which he eyed me and the bundle of papers under my arm, he wondered aloud if someone like me, who had done a degree in lying-on-the-grass, even knows what outsourcing is.

I tossed out the Hebrew term, which I knew well from dozens of translations, and ignored the disdain inherent in his question (you didn't drive all the way here to fight with him! I told myself).

To what do I owe this honour? he asked, browsing through some cheques lying on his desk. He always browsed through cheques when he was embarrassed, his large hands – the ones that had wrapped me in towels on that rainy day – sifting through them, straightening an errant crease.

I wanted to ask you something, I said and sat down.

I never thought otherwise, he said and signed a cheque.

After all, you wouldn't come here just to see how your father is, would you?

So how are you? I asked.

He looked up at me, a flicker of surprise in his eyes. Then immediately lowered his gaze to his desk again.

Business isn't good now, not good at all, he said (when asked about himself, my father always gave an answer about his business. And business was never good. I can't ever remember him being satisfied. Or happy. I once asked my mother about that, and she said, 'Your father has many abilities, but the ability to be happy is not one of them.').

These bloody terrorist attacks, he went on, people aren't in the mood to spend money. And this street is deteriorating all the time. I got here one morning last week and found a fat junkie in the doorway. Tell me, aren't junkies supposed to be thin? Three policemen could hardly move him!

So perhaps you should move up to the Carmel? I suggested the usual solution.

Perhaps I should, he gave the usual answer. Anyway, I have to find a buyer first. Rule number one, son, never buy with money you don't have! he said, waving his finger at me. Rebuked, I said nothing. He, meanwhile, signed another cheque. All the printing machines were still except the '72 Roland, which was plugging away. It was the first printing machine my father bought when he opened the business, and over the years, he refused to let anyone else get close to it. At the end of every day, he would oil it, clean it, wash it. And on several occasions, I even heard him talk to it.

Tell me, Dad, I said, trying to renew the conversation, how's that writer, Miron-Mishberg?

Why do you ask? My father raised suspicious eyebrows above his glasses.

No reason, I said. I just suddenly remembered him.

Went mad, the poor bastard. I called him a few weeks ago. He didn't come in with his book, like he did every year. So I wanted to see how he was. His wife answered.

Told me that he was institutionalised in Tirat HaCarmel. She committed him. I had no choice, she said. He bought an aquarium the size of a wardrobe and decided he was going to live inside it. For two months, he lay there in the living room, in the aquarium, ate his meals there, slept there. Wrote there. Watched TV from there. Can you imagine? In the end, she couldn't handle it any more and committed him.

Wow.

She says it's because of what happened to him in the concentration camp. That he never managed to get over it. I don't think so. I think that anyone who sits at home all day and does nothing but write, doesn't go out to work and doesn't see people, is bound to go mad in the end.

I nodded hesitantly and remembered what Ofir had said about the yawning abyss of fear lying in wait for every artist. I put my foot on the bundle of papers I'd put under the chair and squashed it down hard in the hope it would shrink. Shrink until it disappeared.

So what . . . what did you want to ask me? my father said, putting the cheques aside and starting to work on a stack of receipts.

The hero of an American TV series would probably have said, 'Never mind', creating the bitter-sweet effect of missed opportunity and stretching the plot out a bit more, another episode, even another season, if the ratings were high enough. But I – I had the World Cup on my mind.

I wrote a book, Dad, I said. And then I picked up the manuscript and put it on the desk.

And . . . You want me to print it for you? he asked without looking up from the receipts.

Yes . . . If it isn't too complicated.

It isn't too complicated, he said. His tone was suspiciously matter-of-fact.

I've spoken to the big publishers in Tel Aviv, I explained, and they just work terribly slowly.

And what's your hurry, if I may ask?

I have to publish the book within a month and a half from today. I simply have to.

O-k-a-a-a-a-y, my father stretched out the short word as much as he could. And took out his order book. How many pages do you have?

One hundred and ninety-two, at the moment.

One-and-a-half line spacing?

Yes.

You've already done the copy-editing?

No.

I'm surprised at you, son. Didn't you work here for an entire summer? You know I can't start working before you finish the copy-edit. Give it to that friend of yours, the one who married Ya'ara. He must have a lot of time now since they threw him out of the prosecutors' office.

They didn't throw him out, he left.

Whatever you say, just ask him. It'll save you money. How many copies of the book do you need?

Four.

You're joking! What do you mean, four copies? Don't you want your book to reach the shops?

Not exactly.

Then why . . . never mind. You know what, it's none of my business. But take into account that the smallest edition I can print for you is the 'poetry edition' of three hundred copies. And yours isn't a book of poetry, if I've understood correctly.

No, it isn't.

Actually, it doesn't matter. It's your book and . . . you can do what you like with the copies you don't need. For all I care, you can throw them into the rubbish bin.

OK.

How soon did you say you need it? A month and a half? That's a bit tight. Textbook season begins next week. It's going to be a madhouse here.

He wrote a few numbers in his notebook, humming to himself, then took out a calculator and resumed the calculations he had made in his notebook (he always did the numbers twice, to be on the safe side. And it was always the calculator that served as back-up to the more reliable by-hand reckoning).

The Roland continued working. I inhaled the thick, sweet smell of the print. When I was a child, I was ashamed of that smell that stuck to all my shirts, but now I realised that I missed it. I suddenly remembered our only family trip abroad, classical Europe in ten days. We walked along the streets of a large city – Munich? Vienna? – and he suddenly left us and began walking, then running, in the opposite direction. Later, it turned out that he thought he heard a printing press working, and he had to, simply had to, find where the click-clacking noise was coming from and see whether it was a Roland or a Heidelberg. Are you completely out of your mind? my mother had asked him when he came back. And he didn't answer her. The silence between them lasted until we reached the hotel.

Now he shifted his glance from the calculator to me. I'll do my best, he said, adding: it'll help if you get the copy-editing done this week.

That's great, thanks, I mumbled, finding it hard to understand his response. None of the cries of despair I had expected. No hair pulling. Strangely enough, he even seemed to be slightly pleased.

I also wanted to ask you for something, he said, leaning forward a little in his chair.

Here it comes, I thought, sighing silently in relief, here's the price tag. He pulled out a small orange Post-it and wrote a phone number on it. I want you to call Yanke'le Richter. You remember him? He sat next to us at Ya'ara's wedding. I want you to ask him where the best place is to retrain for a career in the hi-tech industry. And I'm asking you to enroll there.

I nodded in submission. My father is a businessman, and I had imagined that he'd ask for something like this in exchange for agreeing to print my book. I took the Post-it, hoping that because of the slowdown in the field, even if there were courses, they wouldn't begin for a long, long time.

Then I stood up.

He took the manuscript from me and weighed it in his hands. Well done, son, he said and suddenly patted me on the shoulder. Writing a book is not easy, not easy at all.

That was the first time he'd had anything good to say about me since I left home, and another sort of pride, not about business, shone in his eyes.

I'm thirty-two years old. I have spent the last ten years desperately trying to be different from him. I went all the way to Tel Aviv so that I wouldn't end up, God forbid, inheriting the printing house and becoming a replica of him, developing his suspiciousness, his asceticism, his open scorn for anything that yielded no monetary profit –

And yet, when he made that short, complimentary remark, I felt a rare flutter of satisfaction.

Writing a book is not easy, I repeated his words as I wound my way down towards the sea on Freud Street. It's not easy, but I did it. I moved. I came out of my corral and galloped forward for two months. Without running out of oxygen. True, it was for Ofir. And true, it was for the matrix of the World Cup notes. But if I did it once – that means I can do it again. I can escape from the chains of myself. From the mire of my pessimism. From my scepticism and restraint. I can make new wishes for the 2006 World Cup, and, this time, make them come true. I can change. Find myself. Find a purpose. I can love a woman other than Ya'ara. I can – now that the sea is opening before me in all its sparkle – I can even keep being my friends' friend in the future, not just freeze them in time in my writing. Yes, soon their lives are going to be very different from mine, but that doesn't mean my book is destined to be a requiem.

*

When you drive fast on Road No. 2, which is the number one road in my life, the landscape races past the window and you don't see the different shades of green or the fields on the way out of the city, you don't see the flocks of birds flying in swift-changing formations over the fish ponds of Maagan Michael or Jisar a-Zarka, the wretched, depressed village where, a few months ago, someone threw a concrete block from the bridge that crosses over this road, but you don't remember that block and, in fact, you don't remember anything about the past because your thoughts are liberated from it and race confidently towards what has not yet happened, to what will happen, and between Zichron Yaakov and Hadera, you forget the road completely, forget you're driving, because you suddenly think that, even though there will be only four copies of the book, you should still make a few changes and disguise a few things, change names and places and physical descriptions so people won't be needlessly hurt, and perhaps you should even add relevant passages from the philosophy thesis, save it from total annihilation. The imperious Ikea sign rises high not far from the South Netanya junction, but you don't see that either because at that exact moment, you suddenly realise that apart from the necessary disguising and additions and fact-checking, like for example, which teams played in the various World Cup finals, your book still needs an appropriate closing scene, and as you approach Herzliya, you amuse yourself with several possibilities for such a scene. One of them includes the timid girl, lying beside you on a towel on the beach at Gaash, and another takes place in the year 2022, in the stadium stands at the World Cup that Israel has finally managed to host, and all your friends drive there to watch the game together, but when you pass the Kfar Shmariyahu junction now, the only possible final scene, the truly appropriate one, crops up or blows in through the window with the wind. When you reach home, you turn on the computer and write:

*

During the summer holiday between junior and senior years in high school, I was supposed to pick up Churchill and drive down to South Beach with him. When I turned into his street, I saw from the distance that he wasn't alone. Standing with him in front of the building were two other guys from school whose faces I knew, but not their names. I turned the car around and drove away. I didn't feel like going to the beach in a big group. I wanted to go to the beach with Churchill, just the two of us, and I hated that he'd invited other people to come along without asking me. As if my being short made my opinion irrelevant. As if the fact that he was the great Churchill meant he could do whatever he wanted. So what if I was the only one who had a driving licence, I thought bitterly, that doesn't mean I have to be the driver for the entire class.

Two traffic lights later, I turned around and drove back to his street. It's not nice, I thought. He's sitting there outside, waiting for me. And only yesterday we ran all the way to the university and he kept slowing down so I could keep pace with him.

The two guys whose names I didn't know jumped into my back seat the minute I pulled up. The curly-haired one had too-long legs, and his knees were embedded in the back of my seat like spears.

Churchill sat down in the passenger's seat, pointed to them and said to me, that's Ofir and that's Amichai. Then he pointed at me and said, this is Yuval, the guy I told you about.

Hi, I said coldly without turning my head. And started to drive. A pine tree twig got stuck in my wipers and I couldn't get it out no matter how many times I turned them on.

So, ah . . . Yuval, the curly-headed one said, maybe you

can help us with a little argument we've been having. What do you think is the right way to say it: Haifaite or Haifian?

Haifaite.

I told you so! the curly-haired one exulted and stuck his knees deeper into my back.

So how do you explain that the announcers on the Saturday afternoon football broadcasts always say 'Haifian'? the other one grumbled.

Not all the announcers, curly-hair answered, only Zoher Bahalul. And he's an Arab.

But Zoher Bahalul speaks the best Hebrew on the programme.

Bullshit.

You know what, I have an idea! Maybe instead of going to the beach, we should drive to the Academy of the Hebrew Language and ask them.

What a brilliant idea, curly-hair ridiculed. The Academy of the Hebrew Language is in Jerusalem. You want to drive to Jerusalem now, Amichai?

No, but they must have a branch in Haifa. They have branches all over the country, don't they, Churchill?

Why didn't you st-o-o-op? Churchill suddenly cried.

What? Where? What happened? I said in alarm.

Didn't you see?! At the hitchhikers' stop!! Noya Green and that girlfriend of hers, what's her name, Eliana.

But, Churchill, I stammered, there's no room . . . there's no room in the car for them.

Yuval, Yuval, what is it with you? Churchill whacked the back of my neck. For girls like Noya and Eliana, there's always room! They could always have sat on me.

The passengers in the back seat burst out laughing, but their laughter was cut short by Churchill himself.

You two, he said, turning his body towards the back, you two have nothing to laugh about. It's all because of your stupid arguing. If it wasn't for you, Yuval would have seen Noya Green at the stop.

Curly-hair and the one next to him were silent. So was Churchill. Perhaps he was imagining what might have happened if Noya Green had joined us –

As I kept driving down to the sea, I thought, that twig, the minute we get to the beach, I'll pull it out from under the wipers, and I thought, if I step hard enough on the accelerator now, we'll fly into the air and land in the water, a soft landing, and I thought, two more hours, two and a half at the most, with these three clowns, then I'll go home and never have to see them again for the rest of my life.

Editor's Epilogue

On the way back from the shop which had printed the final version of the manuscript – which included the last scene and was apparently meant to be handed over for final copy-editing the next day – my beloved friend Yuval Freed drove into the car stopped in front of him at the traffic lights on the corner of Einstein and Brodetzki Streets. He didn't hit it hard: the damage to both cars was minor and included a broken headlight and slightly bent bumper. Nothing more.

What happened after that is shrouded in fog. To this day, there has been no clarification of the precise order of events that had such tragic results.

It appears that Mr Kfir Kliger, the driver of the car that was hit, got out of his vehicle and walked over to Mr Yuval Freed, opened the car door and pulled him out by the collar. They apparently had a short argument, accompanied by mutual shoving.

Witnesses for the prosecution reported that Mr Kliger was the attacker, and that Mr Freed was focused on trying to ward off the attack on him. Witnesses for the defence, on the other hand, claim that Mr Freed was equally responsible for the argument and the shoving.

From my years' long acquaintance with Mr Freed, with his characteristic restraint and mild manner, I tend to accept the first version, despite the fact that it cannot be denied that in this book Mr Freed himself claims that there was a little hooligan inside him, and 'perhaps in all men'.

Be that as it may, after several minutes of mutual provocation, Mr Kliger went and got an army club from his car and hit Mr Freed in the stomach with it several times. Then in the head.

Mr Freed fell unconscious onto the blazing tarmac and was taken to Ichilov Hospital by Mr Kliger himself.

A routine report from a volunteer worker for the Our Right NPO, who was in the hospital at the time, reached Mr Amichai Tanuri's beeper, and so, within half an hour, all of us – Amichai, Ofir, Maria, Ya'ara and myself – were standing in the corridor outside the intensive care unit.

The treatment Mr Freed received was irreproachable. As was the manner in which the team treated us during the long hours of waiting. Cynics would undoubtedly claim that Mr Tanuri's presence is what caused the hospital staff to treat us with so much care and sensitivity. However, in this case, I am unable to agree with them. As far as I could tell, the attending physician, Dr Eitan, is not the sort of person who needs special reasons to show sensitivity to his patients. He is a young man – almost our age – whose professional honesty and ability to infuse his surroundings with his humanistic spirit are remarkable and inspire me with hope that – perhaps – we have been blessed with a new generation of doctors.

After an eighteen-hour struggle, Dr Eitan came out of the operating room and told us and Mr Freed's parents that his life was no longer in danger, but there was no way of knowing when he would regain consciousness. The strong blow had caused a serious brain haemorrhage, he explained, and in such cases it can be difficult to predict when consciousness will return. It can take a week, it can take two years, and perhaps – and we must be prepared for this – it might never return at all.

The fact that your friend is relatively young works in

his favour, he said, put a warm hand on my shoulder and promised to personally monitor the course of treatment. Be with him, he said. I have no scientific proof, but I believe it's important.

We set up a schedule for shifts so that at any given moment, at least one of us would be sitting beside Yuval and talking to him.

*

Two weeks later, the indictment in the case of the State v. Kfir Kliger was issued. After reading the results of the psychiatric examination, Judge Yeshayhu Navi was forced to rule that Mr Kliger was not mentally competent to stand trial and should be sent forthwith to an appropriate institution. It turns out that Kliger was known to the mental health authorities as a victim of severe post-traumatic stress syndrome. He had served as a military policeman for two years during the first Intifada, and towards the end of his stint, as a result of an event that occurred during a search of the maternity hospital in Nablus carried out by his unit, had suffered shell shock. He was discharged due to the poor state of his mental health and began intensive treatment that combined psychiatric drugs and sessions with a psychologist. Documents submitted to the judge indicated that on the day of the event, Mr Kliger had slipped out of the closed ward of the psychiatric hospital, where he had been committed by his family out of fear that he might harm himself. When he came out of the hospital, a fellow soldier from his unit gave him his private vehicle, in which he had forgotten, purely by accident, his army club. Apparently, Mr Kliger's friend gave him the car so he could meet with a girl he'd been hiding his condition from. The date with the girl had been set for one-thirty in the afternoon, and at one twenty-five, as he was waiting at the traffic signal, Mr Freed's vehicle hit him from behind.

*

At the conclusion of the hearing, the judge read the following words:

'Legally speaking, the evidence before me leaves me no choice but to rule that the suspect cannot stand trial. Nevertheless, it should be stressed that this ruling in no way makes light of the specific act committed by the suspect, or of violence in general. A slow, subliminal change has taken place in our country over the last several years, and Mr Kliger's outburst is merely the tip of the iceberg informing us that the iceberg does in fact exist, or is the indication of a generation that has gone to the . . .'

While the judge's mouth was producing the bland legal jargon, my thoughts wandered to Yuval, who was lying in the hospital now, and this entire trial was of no use to him at all. I thought about his great desire to achieve the 'Bahai symmetry', and about the fact that ultimately there had been a point to what his creative writing tutor had said in the workshop, and perhaps the wish to achieve the symmetry and harmony of the Bahai Gardens here, in this place, is a bit like the Israeli team's wish to be in the World Cup: unfortunately, it always remains only a wish.

'It is not merely disturbed people who display this sort of contempt for others, but sin is crouching at the door . . .' the judge continued to intone his admonishments from the bench, and I remembered the absolutely final perform-ance of the Chameleons. After the group had given their always-sure-to-please encores, the audience demanded one final song. The musicians had a short argument (short and loud, in the best tradition of the band), and then we heard the first notes of 'Prophet'. Few people apart from Ofir recognised the poem, written by Yehuda Amichai, that was the last track on the group's CD of songs by poets.

I am the prophet of what was, I read the past
On the palm of the woman I love
I am the forecaster of winter rains that have fallen
I am the expert on the snows of yesteryear

I dredge up from the deep things that have been
I prophesise about yesterday and the day before

I am the prophet of what was
The prophet of what was

They sang the last line several more times, weaker each time, further away from the microphone each time, then walked off the stage. The audience was dumbstruck for a few seconds, then responded with quiet, scattered applause. What a weird song to end their last performance with, Amichai said when we'd gone out of the club into the night air. You don't understand anything, man! Ofir said, it was brilliant! 'The Prophet of What Was' is exactly . . . it. Exactly . . . them . . . Exactly their story!

*

I hope that when he opens his eyes, Yuval won't be angry about that Yehuda Amichai poem I felt should be quoted here, or about the other changes I made.

These last several weeks, from the moment I received the manuscript, I have worked day and night to complete the editing and proofreading so that the book would be ready for Yuval's target date: the World Cup final.

As I mentioned, reading the text was not at all easy for me. In many cases, I had to put the pages aside and let my overflowing emotion subside, and I had to stop myself from making too many changes (after some changes, does the text lose its original essence? I don't know. And that's why I was especially careful).

In his real, non-literary life, Yuval Freed was even more withdrawn and silent than he portrays himself in the book. Most of the remarks he attributes to himself in the book never came out of his mouth. Usually, it was only his pensive eyes that spoke. And sometimes, his actions: like that night he helped me survive after I drank the San Pedro. Or the way he helped Amichai set up the NPO.

And we got used to his quiet restraint, just as we got used to Ofir's exaggerations and Amichai's puzzles. That restraint was convenient for us. It was convenient that the group consisting of earth, wind and fire also included an element that burbles around the rocks like water, one that docsn't initiate any bizarre schemes and doesn't change its character every other day and doesn't demand absolute justice from everyone, but merely stays silent and smiles that wise smile of his (that smile, Ya'ara once told me, was what made girls fall in love with him).

I think that through all the years of our friendship, I never heard Yuval say more than three sentences at one time, and perhaps that's why this book, which is all one long monologue of his, surprised me so much. And embarrassed me. And infuriated me.

And made me feel close to him. Closer than ever.

Come back, I ask him when it's my shift (I speak to him out loud and I don't care if the other patients in the room hear). Come back, you're the best friend I've ever had. You taught me what being a friend means. And without you, I'm afraid I might forget. You know me from before I changed for the worse. And every time I'm with you, I feel I've become a slightly better person. You see through all my masks and hear in my words exactly what I manage, through them, to hide from the rest of the world. Come back, it's so sad here without you. Ya'ara is very sad too. I want you to know that. She's suffering from prenatal depression because of what happened to you. She loves you, do you even know that? And the fact that she loves you is a big problem now. Because she's so sad that she's almost stopped eating. And she needs to eat a lot, for our little girl. So come back, Bro. You have to come back. You're the glue. You were always the glue. There's one place in the book where you wonder what happened during those six months you boycotted us. What happened is that we hardly ever saw each other. And when we did, it was empty.

Cold. And that's the truth: without you, we're a random collection of people. With you, we're friends. Without you, the big city is all the bad things Ofir says about it. With you, it's home.

So come on, *Baba*, wake up. That's the only wish I have now.

If you wake up, we'll read our World Cup wishes.

If you wake up, this book won't be a requiem. Not for you and not for our friendship.

If you wake up, I promise not to shield myself with protective armour or poke fun at you with 'glittering legal arguments'. Look, I promised myself to write this epilogue with restrained formality, as befits a copy-editor and attorney. But I simply can't any more.

*

These last few nights, we've all stood around your bed in the rehabilitation hospital to watch the deciding rounds of the World Cup.

The timid girl from your workshop has joined us, and she sits on the side, silently, occasionally getting up to feed the two birds sitting on the ledge of the window near your bed.

They've been here since the first day they brought you. Sometimes they spread their wings and fly off to another place, but they always come back. Ofir claims that Ilana's soul has been reincarnated in one of them and Yoram Mendelsohn's in the other. Because they want to be at your side too.

Amichai says that Ofir is full of crap (so what else is new?).

Shahar Cohen is here from Slovenia, with his partner. He's selling properties in Eastern Europe to Israelis now, and between goals and misses, he tries to convince us to buy flats in Budapest and Prague because 'what happened to Yuval shows that our country is sick, and any reasonable person has to prepare an escape hatch for himself now, and if you all make the move together, it'll be easier for you'.

He's been trying to sell you a place too, by the way. And every few hours, he lowers the price in the hope that that's what'll wake you up.

Amichai claims that it would be most fitting for you to wake up when Brazil scores a goal, and insists that we practise shouting our 'Ye-e-e-s!' together.

I'm counting on the book. This book.

In another week, the day before the final, I'll drive to the Efroni printing house to pick up the first copy and drive right back here with it. I'll stand close to your bed, lean over you, and say into your ear, that's it, Bro, the four World Cup wishes have come true.

Then I'll open the copy and hold it in front of your nose. The thick, sweet smell, the smell of a new book, will open your nostrils, your eyes. Then your memory.

Who won the Cup? will probably be your first question, after you get your bearings.

The final is tomorrow, will be my answer. It's wide open.